To Aaron
my SECOND BROTHER

ONE Day
in the LIFE
of a FOOL

ONE Day in the LIFE of a FOOL

JEREMY M. GATES

iUniverse, Inc.
New York Lincoln Shanghai

One Day In The Life Of A Fool

Copyright © 2006 by Jeremy M. Gates

iUniverse books may be ordered through booksellers or by contacting:

iUniverse
2021 Pine Lake Road, Suite 100
Lincoln, NE 68512
www.iuniverse.com
1-800-Authors (1-800-288-4677)

This is a work of fiction. All of the characters, names, incidents, organizations and dialogue in this novel are either the products of the author's imagination or are used fictitiously.

ISBN-13: 978-0-595-39716-7 (pbk)
ISBN-13: 978-0-595-84124-0 (cloth)
ISBN-13: 978-0-595-84123-3 (ebk)
ISBN-10: 0-595-39716-6 (pbk)
ISBN-10: 0-595-84124-4 (cloth)
ISBN-10: 0-595-84123-6 (ebk)

Printed in the United States of America

To Heather and the girls for all their support!

"Never forget that life can only be nobly inspired and rightly lived if you take it bravely and gallantly, as a splendid adventure in which you are setting out into an unknown country, to meet many a joy, to find many a comrade, to win and lose many a battle."

Annie Besant

CHAPTER 1

The Beginning of Time

Isn't it funny how we can look back upon life and think about weeks, months, and years that have gone by? They often seem as if they were all lived in one day. Sometimes we make good choices, and sometimes we make bad choices. We often feel like fools when life throws us for a loop. No matter what happens to us time marches on, and if we are lucky we can learn and grow from our mistakes. "Someone once told me that time is a predator that stalked us all our lives. But I rather believe that time is a companion who goes with us on the journey that reminds us to cherish every moment because they'll never come again. What we leave behind is not as important as how we live it. After all, we're only human."—*Author Unknown*

It was a warm summer morning when I pulled out of the driveway of my parent's house with most of my belongings in the trunk and back seat of my 1980-something Mercury Topaz. This was the day I had been dreaming of for years, the day when I would leave home for good and make my way into the world, the first day of the rest of my life, for me it was the beginning of time. I pondered as I turned my car onto the freeway about what I might expect to find within the great and spacious edifice of higher education; a place where dreams could come true and my life could finally take on the meaning that I had hoped for through all of my high school days, and every day up to this one.

I had graduated from high school nearly two years before but had spent some time traveling, seeing the world, and trying to "*find*" myself. When I was in high school I was a rather smart kid with near perfect grades. The kind of person whom always shattered the grading curve by getting scores ten to twenty points higher than everyone else in the class. It seems hard to believe now, and it's almost embarrassing to admit, but I would actually lie about my grades to my fellow classmates in order to appear cool. I knew in my heart that I could be a perfect 4.0 student, but it was very unpopular to have perfect grades and even more difficult to have good grades and be accepted by your peers when one is floating in a sea of mediocrity in the public education system.

The truth was I loved to learn, I enjoyed science and literature, I loved reading classic novels like "*The Hunch Back of Notre Dame*" and "*The Invisible Man.*" I often felt that I would have fit in just fine with the artistic writers who had created those characters. I used to think of how wonderful it would be to sit in a crowded little cafe with great writers like Hemmingway and Edgar Allen Poe; I wanted to discuss the essence of their greatness and try to understand their brooding creative intelligence. I would often dream of living back in the day when I could have studied architecture under the great Frank Lloyd Wright. I would have loved to been part of the Taliesin movement, to be on the design team for the Guggenheim Museum. I wanted to take part in the great arts and crafts movement, to have a hand in Falling Water and work along side the eccentric, yet brilliant Frank Lloyd Wright. Not all of my friends fit the mediocre mold I had to protect myself against. In fact, some of my closest high school friends were actually smarter than I was, and I looked to them for support, they had a grasp of art, poetry, and English that I envied.

It was about 2:30 in the afternoon when I pulled into the parking lot of the University of Utah student-housing complex; this was to be my new home for the next two and a half years. I stepped into the crowded lobby and made my way through the sea of people who, not unlike me looked excited, apprehensive and a little bit confused, I found out later that some of these people were new students, but most were actually staying at the dorms while attending band camp, football camp, cheerleading camp, and a host of other camps. There were signs everywhere pointing the way to the various check-in desks, arranged in alphabetical order. After a moment or two of consideration I chose what appeared to be the shortest line falling within the boundaries of my last initials, I then began what was to be a long drawn out "check in" process. I was, despite the long line, excited and thrilled to finally be here, my holy grail in life, the place I had dreamt of for years, college.

This was however not my first time within the halls of higher education, I actually attended one quarter at a small business college in Salt Lake City. I had earned a scholarship through the efforts of one of my high school professors, but truth be told I was never really excited about this particular business college, however my professor was very adamant that I go and at least "give it a try," as he said repeatedly. He believed that I could be successful there, and since it was where he had gone to college, he believed it was the number one college in Utah. This kindhearted and well-meaning teacher went out of his way to secure the proper paperwork and the necessary signatures to get me into "*his*" college of choice. He all but wrote the acceptance letter for me when I received news that I had been granted the scholarship. I believe that he would have gone in my place had the opportunity arose. Out of respect for my professors' hard work I attended one quarter at this business college, however after that one long and tedious quarter I went on my personal sabbatical in search of my own inner peace. Upon returning home I promptly transferred to the University of Utah, and never looked back.

I was pondering the events of that rather unpleasant experience when I realized I had made it to the front of the room assignment line. I looked up and saw standing in front of me on the other side of the counter; a tall, nicely built young man, who spoke with a thick Australian accent, "G'day mate, "what's your name?" He asked.

"Jeremy…Jeremy Gates." He looked through his big book of names and thumbed through a number of pages.

"Here we are mate, Jeremy Gates Architecture right?"

"Yes," I said.

"Good to have you here mate, your room is on the third floor, here is your room key, your mailbox key, and your room mate is Jack Erickson, he is from California but it doesn't look like he's arrived yet. I think you will like your stay here at the University student housing, we have barbeques, dances, parties, and lots of fun social events every month."

I thanked him and promptly made my way to room 303. I slowly opened the door to the musty room. The student housing projects had been erected sometime in the 1940's or 1950's, and had the look and smell of an old army barracks from world war two. The walls were made of cinderblock and there were two small metal-framed beds on either side of the room, which could be stacked and made into bunk beds. There was a built in desk and closet on each side of the room and one large window on the far wall that separated the room in two.

"Very institutional," I thought to myself, the design was simple, cheap, and old; I was in a veritable heaven. It was exactly as I had pictured it in my mind.

After taking time to unpack my belongings and get situated, I figured that I had better give my mom a call and let her know that I had arrived safely. Even though I was only about forty minutes from home I knew she would want to know that I was all right. My mother had eight children of whom I was the third. I have six sisters and one brother. Growing up with almost all girls was both a challenge and a blessing to me. My mother cared for each of us in her own way. Since I was a boy I was expected to be more independent than my sisters. My mother didn't seem to worry about me the way she worried about some of the others. I talked to her on the phone for a few minutes, and she gave me the advice that she had given my two older sisters whom had already paved the way and been to college. My mother told me to be good, and to remember who I was. She told me to call if I needed any thing and to visit from time to time, but that it was ok to find my own way in life. I assured her that I was fine and was not in need of anything, so with that we ended our conversation.

The next phone call I made was to Amanda, a lovely girl whom I had been courting for the past few months. The story behind Amanda (or) Mandy as she preferred to be called was a rather interesting one. I had known Mandy for most of my high school days as a good friend. She had a boyfriend throughout high school whom was an acquaintance of mine but I must admit I was always a little bit jealous of. Shortly after graduation her boyfriend left the country and went over seas for a period of time. Mandy had gone to college in southern Utah, and even though we were miles apart Mandy and I had remained friends. We wrote each other regularly and called one another from time to time in order to find out gossip about other classmates and mutual friends of ours.

It was one evening shortly after Mandy graduated with her associates' degree and returned to Salt Lake City that we were routinely talking to one another on the phone. Mandy told me something that took me by surprise, she said, "Jeremy I have had feelings for you for quite some time now," she paused for a moment, I could tell there was a hint of apprehension in her voice,

"I have always admired your intellect," she continued.

"And have thought of you as someone with a bright future, someone who would be a good father and husband, and someone who would provide well for his family." Mandy was quite for a moment, but I gave no response.

"I think I have feelings for you," she said.

"I would like to get to know you better because let's face it, you are going away to school soon, and I hope to find a job that will be closer to my career goal. I would hope that I could find something close to home but it could be in another part of the country for all I know."

I remember making some sort of intelligent comment like, "ok," because I was confused as to where our conversation was going. Mandy finally got to the point,

"Jeremy I want to spend this summer dating you as boyfriend and girlfriend because honestly I think you might be "*the one.*" When she said that I finally figured out where she was going with our conversation and I was speechless.

"Oh, well, right." I said after stumbling over my own words for a few moments I told her that I would need to think about it. I had always found her attractive but had never suspected that she had any sort of romantic feelings for me. I did manage to ask her about her high school sweetheart who was currently out of the picture, but whom I knew would be returning in a matter of months. She told me not to worry about him, that there was no longer any feelings between the two of them. After the months of separation she had realized that by dating him exclusively through high school she had missed out on a lot of things and a lot of people, me being one of them. After pondering it for a few days, and really contemplating what my feelings were towards her, I called Mandy back and told her I felt good about the idea of dating for a while.

We spent the next few months getting to know each other better and enjoying one another's company. I would surprise her at work with roses and lunch; she would drive out to find me on the landscaping crew where I was working for the summer and would bring me dinner and give me words of encouragement. The job was hard, dirty, and didn't pay much, but I wanted to learn all I could about landscaping so that in the future it would help me to be a better architect. We would meet after a long day of work and go to the park, sit on the swings and talk about how our days had been. She always looked lovely in the moonlight as we talked late into the evening, and it didn't take long for me to fall in love with her.

As school loomed ever closer for me Mandy was both excited and apprehensive for me to go, I assured her that I would not be far away and that I would come visit her as often as I could. I tried many times to talk her into renting an apartment closer to the university, but Mandy lived in a very interesting situation.

She came from a broken home where her mother had abandoned her father leaving him to raise the children by himself. Mandy's father had a hard time with the rejection and couldn't handle the responsibility so he was gone a lot. Her loving grandparents decided that the best thing would be for them to adopt her and her brother for their welfare and well-being, making things better yet more difficult for Mandy. I always thought her grandparents were very noble for taking on such an astonishing task in what should have been their golden years. They were however, by the time I began to date Mandy, getting up in years and had become quite feeble. Mandy's grandmother had suffered a serious stroke, and had fought a lengthy battle with cancer, making it difficult for her to speak and consequently very hard to understand. I only remember meeting these extraordinary people whom had forfeited their latter years to raise Mandy and her brother once.

I had arrived at Mandy's house a few minutes before she arrived home from work. Her grandfather answered the door with a hardy handshake and a warm smile and invited me in. I had hardly sat down when her grandmother entered the room; shaking my hand she told me how happy they were to finally meet me. They explained how Mandy loved them, but was afraid that her friends would not understand their unique situation and would be unkind or make fun of her or her grandparents. I told them that I admired their strength and was sorry we had not been able to meet beforehand. At that moment I heard a car door slam and Mandy appeared in the doorway mortified that I had been let in to meet her grandparents. Mandy looked at me and then looked at them, and with tears filling her eyes, she asked me very calmly if I would escort her into the kitchen, I stood up and followed her rather timidly, not knowing or realizing what was wrong. Upon entering the kitchen Megan closed the door behind us, and took me by the hand and said,

"Why did you come over here when you knew I wasn't home?"

"I didn't know that you weren't home."

"Why didn't you call?"

"I'm sorry, I will be sure to call ahead from now on."

She thanked me and told me not to hate her or be mad now that I had met her grandparents. She then escorted me out the back door and told me she would call me later that evening. Mandy showed up at my front door later that evening her usual bubbly and kind self, but something was different something that I could not explain or put my finger on.

When Mandy answered the phone, I informed her that I had arrived and that I was all moved in and situated. She told me that she had a surprise for me and wanted to come see me later on that evening to take me to dinner. I told her that it would be great to go to dinner and that I would be happy to show her the new bachelor pad. I also had a big surprise for her, I had found myself a part time, work-study job on campus for a whole six dollars an hour, and I was elated to give her the news about her hard working college man.

During the previous week I had quit my landscaping apprenticeship from hell, and vowed that I would never be on that end of a landscaping project again. I had worked feverishly to find work and with a stroke of luck was able to find this job on campus.

We agreed on nine o'clock and as I hung up the phone, I looked at my watch and realized that evening had fallen but I had not yet seen or heard from my new roommate. I decided to make my way back to the main lobby to see what I could find out about his arrival.

The scene looked like France just days after the American occupation, there was fallout debris, and furniture in the streets, bewildered and confused looking people were digging through the rubble looking for signs of life and traces of any personal belongings. There was luggage everywhere in the main lobby, belonging to people who were off somewhere trying to find their rooms before moving their luggage through the maze of corridors, halls, and stairways. I made my way through this labyrinth of luggage, furniture, and lost souls to the front desk where I found my Australian friend still working behind the desk. He was still smiling but he had a look of overwhelming exhaustion about him, not unlike the occupying soldiers entering war torn France. I approached him, and this time I noticed a small name badge draped around his neck on a hand made coral necklace, "Steve," I said startling him to attention.

"Hello mate," he said.

"Did you find your room ok?"

"Yes," I replied.

"Not a problem, however I have not seen or heard from my roommate yet, has he signed in at the front desk?"

"Well mate, people have the rest of the week to sign in, so if you have not seen him yet he may not be coming in until later."

I thanked Steve for being so helpful and made my way to the atrium centered between two of the dorm halls and sat down on a bench to ponder what was about to be a long four-year ordeal. I had written to the school of architecture at the University of Utah several months before, and had met with the one of the department's counselors. We had gone over a very meticulous program that though difficult would have me done with my general education classes in just over a year.

The counselor had been instrumental in getting me enrolled into the freshman honors program to help expedite my freshman year, and get me into the architectural program as soon as possible. This meant however, that I would have to take 200 and 300 level classes and pass them with at least a B-in order for them to count towards the honors program. The way it worked was as follows; if I took for instance, English 210 and passed with the minimum B-requirement, I was to receive credit for all of the lower level classes as well as the 210 class and thus by passing one class I could top out of and be done with all general education requirements in the English category. This was also true of the math, science, social science, and writing requirements, in short I could accomplish in one year what would take the average student two or three years to achieve. I was very excited about this proposal and felt that it was worth my time and effort, even though it would prove to be quite difficult I believed that it was a good plan. So I enrolled in the honors program, and was about to embark on what would later prove to be the most difficult freshman year known to man.

"Jeremy what are you doing out there in the rain?" Mandy exclaimed. The sound of her voice pulled me back into reality.

"You are soaking wet, get in here and dry off."

I had not even realized that it was raining. I had lost myself in the contemplation of things to come. Mandy was standing in the doorway of the atrium wearing a very attractive, black dress. I was shocked, because I didn't even know she owned such a dress. As I came through the door I said, "Wow Mandy, I didn't know you had another boyfriend."

"What is that suppose to mean?" Asked Mandy.

"I've never seen you dressed like that, so it must be for your other boyfriend." I said. Mandy looked at me for a second and then threw her head back while putting her hands on her hips.

"His name is Ken and he is waiting outside in his limo to whisk me away to the Bahamas," Mandy looked at me and smiled.

"I don't have another boyfriend; just get out of the rain you look like a wet dog." We quickly made our way back to the main lobby.

"I want to give you your surprise at dinner so I will go pull the car around to the front while you change into something not so wet." I stared at her for a moment.

"Well, make it snappy, we have reservations for nine." She said, while snapping her fingers.

I met her down by the car a few minutes later feeling awkward and a bit out of place in my slightly large suit that was a hand-me-down from my brother-in-law, who happened to be a good foot taller and about 25 pounds heavier than I was. One thing about Mandy that I liked was that she had a much nicer car than I did because she believed that in order to be a successful working girl, one needed to have a car that told people they were serious. I on the other hand felt that a car was nothing more that a way to get from point A to point B and all it had to do was run. Although she was a very serous career woman, Mandy still had an old fashioned sentimental side. Lucky for me, she insisted on me driving whenever we went places together. This was something that I didn't argue with because I loved driving her car. Although I would pretend to have a nonchalant attitude about the whole thing, I think Mandy new how much I liked to drive her car. It wasn't everyday that I got to drive a brand new, off the show room floor Mercedes Benz.

As we made our way to the restaurant, Mandy asked me if I had met my new roommate yet. I explained that I hadn't seen or heard from him and he may not even be here for a few days. I quickly changed the subject to what was obviously a more important topic, "what's the surprise?" I asked, but before Mandy could answer I continued.

"Why are we going to a nice restaurant?"

"Be patient Jeremy and stop asking me questions, all will soon be revealed."

I felt like it was Christmas, and we were playing grown up all rolled up into one! Even though we were both in our early twenties I had not been to many fancy restaurants growing up, and I had defiantly not been to any restaurant dressed like we were that evening. As I stated earlier I came from a large family, so if we all got to go to Denny's as a family that was "*going out.*" Most of my fine dinning experiences had been at the distinguished and highly acclaimed bistro started by Colonel Sanders, or at the exquisite southwest café knows as Taco Bell. So for me to be going to a restaurant that didn't have the slogan "*finger licking good,*" behind its name or give away paper crowns, was something special.

As I nervously stared at the exquisite table setting in front of me, I found myself wondering what the three-pronged fork was for. Mandy looked at me with a loving smile.

"Don't worry dear just order what I order and follow my lead with your silverware." After getting situated Mandy looked up at me and shook her head.

"Take the napkin out of your shirt collar and put it in your lap and I will tell you what the surprise is," said Mandy.

I sheepishly removed the napkin from my collar, and as I began eating my salad with the wrong fork, I asked again.

"What's the surprise?"

With a look of excitement, and a sparkle in her eye, she began to tell me about a management job with a non-profit organization that performed social services for underprivileged women and single mothers. This was something that she had wanted to do ever since she got her associated degree in psychology. It would mean a lot more money than she was making as an assistant to one of the social workers where she was currently employed and it would not require any travel, like her current job did. Mandy had to travel to a number of the clinics in the valley and in some of the joining states to gather charts and other information on the people they were working with, and to deliver various items between the offices.

"The only thing that may be a bit of a problem," she stated.

"Is that the job is in Colorado."

"Colorado," I yelled at a level that was, I must admit a bit embarrassing for both of us.

"How the hell was this supposed to be a nice surprise for me?"

"Calm down, you're embarrassing me and quite frankly I thought you, of all people would be happy for me." She picked up her napkin and pointed to my glass.

"You have lettuce floating in your water." She said. I had accidentally projected most of the food out of my mouth and onto the table when I yelled "Colorado", but I was too upset at that moment to care.

"You haven't accepted the yet job have you?" I asked.

"Yes I have Mr. Man, and if you don't shut up and sit down I will walk out of this restaurant and leave you to pay the bill, Mr. Unemployed." I sat back down and looked at my plate while she continued.

"I didn't come here to be lectured about my decision, and I most certainly did not come here to be yelled at by you. I have taken this job to further my career." Mandy paused for a minute. I could tell that she was fighting back tears.

"I didn't take this job to destroy our relationship or to hurt you in any way." Mandy took her napkin and whipped the tears from her eyes.

"You known that this is something I want to do, and you have always understood or at least you made me feel like you understood that this was something very important to me."

I apologized and reassured her that I did understand how important her career was, and that I was sorry for acting so childish. The truth was I didn't want to lose her, after many years of friendship, and now after the few wonderful months we had spent together I didn't want to lose her. I felt like her leaving for Colorado would be the end of our relationship, she would find a rich psychologist or at least someone with more than a part time, campus job and he really would whisk her away to the Bahamas. After a few moments of silence Mandy smiled at me.

"So, what is your big surprise?" She inquired.

To be honest, after what we had just discussed the news of my pathetic campus job just really didn't feel like the triumphant news I had thought it would be. Looking up from my now unappetizing salad I mustered what excitement I could and told her of my new position with the General Stores department on the campus of the University of Utah.

"That's exciting news Jeremy, I'm proud of you for finding a new job in such a short amount of time!" She replied.

The rest of dinner and whatever conversations we may have had slipped from my memory, I was feeling shattered and hurt because after such a wonderful summer this could all be coming to an end. Mandy on the other hand seemed to think that there was nothing to worry about, she would come down for the weekends and I could go visit her in between quarters and she kept saying, "if we were really meant to be together, it would work out in the end."

I woke up around 3:30 a.m. the next morning to a bittersweet smell that I had only really been exposed to once or twice before in my life.

A few weeks after high school graduation, I was approached by one of my best friends, Jason. Jason had a dilemma and I was the answer to his problems. Jason, his brother Mark and I had become good friends almost instantly. I had moved a lot when I was growing up, and so had Jason and Mark because their parents had been divorced. Their mother wanted to get away from Wyoming and start a new life somewhere else. This made all three of us the "new kids" at about the same time and we found it easier to stick together. We found that we could fight the bullies off better as a team, and for some reason we just got along right off the bat.

I remember summers when I practically lived at their house. Maybe that was a bit much for their single mother trying to raise four rather unruly boys. But I grew to know their mom as a second mother and often looked to her for motherly advice, especially for those topics that one can't really talk to ones own mother about.

I remember that we were typical teen-age boys and that we did typical teenage things like making dry ice bombs in the back yard because we had heard about the awesome power that could be harnessed in a 2liter bottle with some dry ice and warm water. We didn't think it would work, and so after some careful planning and drinking a bottle of cola we decided that if any one could prove that it was nothing more than an urban myth it would be us, so we proceeded to the grocery store to buy dry ice. Back in those days a sixteen-year-old boy could buy two pounds of dry ice without being required to produce a letter from his parents and undergo an extensive background check. No one thought we were terrorists, or that we would make bombs, even though we did make a small one. And no one thought twice about selling it to us, especially after we explained that our mom had sent us to get it for some home made root beer. So here it was the dead of winter, and we had never made a dry ice bomb before, in fact as I stated we didn't even think it would work. I recall the conversation going something like this, "how much dry ice do you think we will need?"

"I don't know let's start with one pound and see what happens."

"Well if one pound will work why not give it the whole two pounds and see what happens."

So we did, we added as close to two pounds of dry ice as we could possibly stuff into that 2 liter bottle, added warm water, and rushed it outside in the snow bank we had built up to keep it from doing any damage. We ran back into the house and stared out into the cold back yard while holding our hands over our ears waiting for the explosion. After waiting for what felt like hours but could have only been a few minutes, we took our hands away from our ears and very proudly told our selves that we had successfully busted the myth of the dry ice bomb since it hadn't gone off.

As we began to make our way down to the basement, Jason's younger brother Rick, who had been watching our activities from his bedroom on the other side of the house inadvertently went outside, picked up the bomb and brought it into the house, to ask us what it was. As soon as the warmer temperature from the air inside the house hit the cold plastic 2 liter bottle it exploded in what was the loudest and most destructive display of terror I had ever experienced in my life. The noise was louder than anything I could have ever in my wildest dreams imagined, pictures fell off of the walls, the kitchen table vibrated violently, we could hear, above the violent ringing in our ears, car alarms going off outside, and dogs barking feverishly. After the horrific explosion we all looked back and there stood poor Rick in shock, holding the neck of the bottle in his hand, with plastic shrapnel in his chest, so of course Jason, Mark, and I did what any teenage boy in our situation would do; we ran out of the house, jumped in Jason's car and sped away. Later that evening, after Rick was released from the hospital we all felt bad, we felt really bad, for almost blowing him up. I remember some years later helping Jason and Mark paint the house and up in the corner of the kitchen above the cupboards we found pieces of the 2 liter bottle imbedded in the wall.

Needless to say Jason and I were good friends, and his dilemma was the classic, my girlfriend has a friend and my girlfriend won't go to this party unless her friend can go, so will you please take one for the team and be her date.

"No way, no how am I going to be the relief pitcher and get stuck being the third wheel while he and his girlfriend slipped of for some "alone" time at some party that I had no desire to attend." I said.

I didn't even like going to parties, because I don't drink, or smoke, or do any of the other things that young people are known for doing at these parties. Jason was very intelligent he had been accepted to Westminster College in Salt Lake City, and would be leaving soon so he wanted us to have one last fling. Of coarse Mark had refused to be this girls date, and had no desire to go to the party either, and I stood firmly with Mark in his, as well as my decision not to go. Looking back I do not know why I gave in, and I cannot remember if it was 20 or 30 dollars that Jason gave me, but I finally told him I would do it.

From the moment I rang the doorbell of the large home where my date for the evening lived, this girl treated me with total indifference, I was nothing more to her than a ticket into the party. My date was a rather attractive girl she was tall and slender, with bleached blond hair, she was wearing a nice dress when we got into the car, but as we pulled out of her neighborhood Brooke, Jason's girlfriend, looked back towards her friend,

"You're not wearing that thing to the party are you?" She asked.

"No, I just had to wear it to get out of the house," replied my date. Then to my astonishment she reached down and grabbed the bottom of her dress and pulled it up over her head revealing a tight white tank top, with a bright pink bra underneath that was practically glowing in the dark. She also had on a pair of very short shorts, and bright pink tennis shoes. She looked at me after performing her little magic act.

"You must be my date for the evening, let's get something straight right now, I don't like you and there is nothing between us now and no matter how much I drink, there still won't be."

With that lovely introduction I glared at Jason who I knew could see me in his rear view mirror, but he just pretended to not be looking. My date was from the east side, which was the more wealthy side of town, and we were just average good old boys from the west side. We never had much, and really never thought a whole lot of it. She wanted to go to this party because she had heard that parties on the west side of town were more fun than the stuffy parties she went to on the east side.

As we walked into the small west side bungalow where this party was raging, Jason and his girlfriend Brooke immediately disappeared amongst the throngs of people leaving me alone with the ice queen. I tried to make some pleasant small talk over the loud music but I don't think the dragon mistress could hear me over the noise because she just looked in my general direction giving me an occasional fake smile, and nodded here head whenever I said something.

"So, it looks like it could rain this weekend." She nodded her head.

"I really liked the band "The Smiths" it's too bad they broke up." She nodded her head.

"So did you just graduate from high school?" She nodded her head.

This one sided conversation went on for a while until out of nowhere she grabbed my hand and pulled me towards the stairs of this small and very crowded home. We pushed our way through the throngs of people, beer, and smoke making our way into a small corner of the basement living room. There were a number of people huddled into a tight group laughing and carrying on as if there was something humorous going on in the middle of their circle. Upon closing in on the group the ice queen tapped a rather grungy looking guy on the shoulder. When he finally turned around to see who was bothering him, the angry look on his face disappeared instantly when he recognized my date and the two of them began talking as if they were old friends. After a moment or two of small talk, the now smiling man hugged my so-called "date" and then handed her what I thought was a cigarette. She took a long drag from the small hand rolled object and held the smoke in her lungs for a painful looking amount of time. She then turned towards me and began blowing the bitter smelling smoke slowly into my face as if she were some black and white movie goddess, sexily blowing smoke into the face of Gary Cooper. Only I didn't see it as sexy at all.

"Do you want some of this baby?" She asked, pointing to both the weed in her hand and to herself at the same time.

"Well you can't have it," she said as she began to laugh.

With that revolting invitation I turned around and angrily made my way through the crowd, back up the stairs, and onto the back patio where Jason and his Brooke where sitting. I grabbed Jason by the arm, "Here is your money, the ice queen is down stairs getting high I am leaving, good night."

That was the last time I had been in a situation where I had known what that smell was, and now standing before me with the light of our small bedroom piercing my eyes like pepper spray, was my new room mate reeking of that same odor.

"*Hello,*" he yelled at the top of his lungs.

"*I am Jack Erickson, your new roommate.*"

The next few weeks were not so pleasant for me. Getting used to my pot head roommate, who come to find out was only going to school in Utah to get away from his rich parents who according to Jack, did not love him. They tried to buy his love in exchange for their continued absence. Jack was an only child of wealthy parents, who had been divorced for a couple of years, so they tried to "out perform" each other by purchasing lavish gifts for their son. Jack's parents were very upset when he left Stanford to go to some no account school, in Utah of all places. Jack had told me that he really had no intentions of staying at the University of Utah, because he figured after one quarter away from Stanford, and from his parents, they would pay him even more money to come back and live in the apartment they had furnished for him.

I guess I felt sort of bad for Jack, at least as bad as one can feel for a kid who never went to class, stayed out drinking all night, slept all day, never helped to keep the place clean, and who drove a Jaguar because. However I did have something he did not and that was a family who loved me and parents who cared for me, not with money but with genuine love.

My new job, the one I had has fought so courageously to obtain and the one that was to my big surprise for Mandy, was not as pleasant as I had hoped it would be. My first few weeks on the job consisted of filling campus supply orders. I would pull various items from the long rows of shelving in the warehouse to place the orders with. These orders could range from a small box of office supplies to cases of paper, and even the occasional bail of sawdust for the lab rats in the medical research building. I would then, after pulling the entire order take the filed boxes and position them into the delivery truck according to the day's route for the driver, who sat in the air-conditioned break room waiting for me to load his truck. I quickly realized that in order to survive at this job I would need to somehow become a delivery driver instead of a grunt order puller/truck loader. I remember sitting on the stairs outside of the warehouse, eating my lunch and thinking to myself,

"What on earth have I gotten myself into?" This was not what I had envisioned this job to be. It was hot in the warehouse, the hours, though accommodating with my new school schedule were long and tedious.

Along with the suffering I had to endure with the new job, I had begun my grueling freshman's honors courses and it was by far the most difficult and crippling set of classes I had ever encountered. I had an English Writing and Thesis Computation class, I had an Eastern Philosophy and Religion class, and the piece de resistance was my Advanced Economical Theories class. The whole honors thing had looked so good on paper. It seemed so enticing to be done with all of my general studies courses in one year. But it wasn't until this point that I had any real concept of what the honors program consisted of.

On top of all of this Mandy was getting ready to move to Colorado, and I must admit that I was less than thrilled with the idea. I felt as though I was going to have a melt down because of everything I was going through. I felt like Mandy was abandoning me to the ravenous wolves and pillaging pirates of higher education. She had already graduated from college and I needed her experience and support.

One evening about three or four weeks into my first quarter, I was sitting in my room trying to understand the difference between the Taoist views on the philosophical meaning of life. Which I believe is that all life forces are one, and one must do his or her best to help each other obtain a pure state of nirvana. Verses the Buddhist views, which I think, are based on the concept of ones actions being consequential to those around you. Thus by interacting with people in both good and bad ways you can actually alter another's life force to the point of damaging their chances of finding the higher level of reincarnation. So as I understood it, one is better off leaving his fellow man alone as to not hinder his growth. This was running through my head when the phone rang. It was Mandy calling me from the front lobby.

"Hello Mr. President, can a lonely girl come up and see you?" She asked in a playful tone.

I was thrilled to see her. Not only because the Taoists and Buddhist philosophers were raging a timeless and deadly battle in my head, but also because aside from a few messages we had left each other on our answering machines, I had not seen or heard from Mandy since the night we had gone to dinner. This was before the day when everyone had cell phones and e-mail. So if you could not get a hold of someone on the regular phone, you actually had to leave a message on a tape-recorded answering machine.

When I opened the door to my room Mandy was standing there with a cute puppy dog look on her face.

"What are you working on?" She asked. When I began to tell her of Buddha and the oriental beliefs of reincarnation she put her finger on my lips.

"It was a courtesy question, I am not your professor and to be honest I didn't come all the way up here to discuss the topic of reincarnation with you."

"What did you want to see me for?" I asked.

"Well you are still my boyfriend aren't you?" She asked, as she put her hands on her hips.

"And even though you don't know how to act at a nice restaurant I still love you." Mandy put her arms around me and squeezed tightly.

"I also assume that you still love me," she paused for a moment.

"Don't you?" She asked.

"Oh" I stated, somewhat taken back by the question.

"Of course I do don't be silly."

"Good, then let's go." She pulled something out of her back pocket.

"I have two tickets for the Utah Arts festival and tonight is the international Jazz review, I have no intentions of missing it or going alone and my other boyfriend "Ken," you remember him, the one with the limo, and the beach front property in the Bahamas, well he was busy this evening so you will have to do."

Mandy and I really liked jazz music a lot. We listened to all the classics together; Billie Holliday, Miles Davis, John Coletrain, and we liked the new up and coming jazz artist as well like Harry Connick Jr. and pretty much anyone who played the Newport Beach Jazz Festival. We also really enjoyed going to the local jazz clubs and listening to people we had never heard of.

It was a nice evening that had cooled off an otherwise hot summer day. Upon arriving at the festival we began to wander around looking at the local artists booths, and enjoying the electrifying atmosphere. After about an hour or wandering we were pleasantly surprised to find my sister Tiffany and her husband Daryl at the festival.

Tiffany was the oldest of my eight siblings and the funny thing was, growing up we didn't really get along very well. However after we got older, and especially after Tiffany went away to college we developed a bond that made us very close for a season in our lives. I had gone to concerts with Tiffany and Daryl, we went bungee jumping when it was all the rage, and I had spent weekends with them at their place in Provo. When I graduated from high school I spent the weekend after my graduation party with Daryl making home made rockets that would not launch, and roaming around the cities of Orem and Provo, just having fun and hanging out. I had really grown to love Tiffany and Daryl and had been consulting with Tiffany on what I should do with regards to my situation with Mandy.

Tiffany was studying psychology and Daryl was studying sports medicine at Brigham Young University. Tiffany always had advice for anyone who would listen, and even though, at times it was not really appreciated or wanted, I usually listened very closely to what she had to say. Tiffany being a career-minded girl herself told me that I needed to give Mandy whatever space and support that she may need in order to find herself, to be herself, and to discover what it was she needed and wanted out of life. If I wanted to impress her, and if I wanted to keep her, I needed to be a support to her and not be a demanding boyfriend. She also told me that I should do something with Mandy that was fun, something that did not have to do with school, work, or money, and that it should be a get away from all of the things causing stress in our relationship. So I had made arrangements for the four of us to go to Jackson Hole, Wyoming over the quarter break.

I had been waiting for the right time, and since we were enjoying the concert as well as each other's company, I felt this would be as good a time as any.

"I have made arrangements for us to go to Jackson Hole at the end of this quarter," I told her. "I thought it would be a nice get away, a relaxing weekend away from school and work."

"I would love to go." Mandy said.

So it was settled that in a month and half we would all go to Jackson Hole for a nice weekend get away. We sat chatting with Tiffany and Daryl for quite some time that evening, until we all realized how late it was getting. Daryl announced that he and Tiffany needed to get home, so Mandy and I walked Tiffany and Daryl to their car.

"It was nice to see you again Mandy," said Tiffany with a smile.

"And Jeremy," she said as she closed the car door,

"I hope your classes get a little easier for you," and with that they drove away.

Mandy and I made our way back up to the University and as we pulled into the dorm parking lot Mandy said something to me that took me by surprise.

"Jeremy, I have done quite a bit of thinking lately and I have decided to stay here in Salt Lake with you. I also think I want to get a place closer to the University. And I think I am going to tell my boss that I will stay working with him as long as he is willing to pay me a bit more money, and change my responsibilities so that I won't have to travel so much. When I told you that I felt you were the one, I was not kidding and I have realized the past few weeks that by my leaving, it must appear to you that I am not serious about us. I want you to know that I am." I did not know what to say, so like an idiot I said something to the effect of,

"Well honey what ever you think is best, is ok with me." After those embarrassing words came out of my mouth it was rather silent for a few moments.

"Thank you, it really means a lot to me that you are willing to stay here, and give up the job in Colorado. I have had so much fun with you the past few months and I really don't want you to move out of state. I know you are sacrificing a lot to be with me, but I hope I am worth it to you, and I know you won't regret it."

Work was beginning to pick up for me after enduring the first few weeks. The driver, who had sat in the air-conditioned break room waiting for me to load his truck, was a member of the University of Utah band, and his summer practice times had been changed, forcing him to quit his job. His leaving left an opening for a new driver. It was with a bit of apprehension that I went to John my supervisor, and asked him if I could apply for the driving position that had just opened up. John told me that in order to drive the truck, which was if I remember correctly, was a 25-foot box truck, similar to the biggest moving van a person could drive without a CDL license. I would have to be trained and pass the driving test given by Dan, and if I passed, Dan would be my new supervisor.

Dan was a large foul mouthed, ex-army ranger who smoked at least three packs of unfiltered "Marlboro Reds," during an eight-hour workday. Over the next two years I would come to respect Dan as a heavily decorated Vietnam War Veteran and come to know him as one of the best work friends I would ever know in my life. However at that period in time, a near heart stopping fear of the man had taken a grip on me and would not let go. I told John that I would like the chance to be trained and take the driving test. I knew that the drivers made 25 cents more an hour than the grunt warehouse workers did, so this was something that I felt I needed to do in order to improve my financial situation. I remember standing in front of the warehouse in what felt like 110-degree weather while Dan barked out instruction after instruction about the truck. He told me of the importance of checking the fluids, and the air pressure in the tires. He demanded respect of his vehicles so that they in turn would respect you.

"Treat them like a woman, put them to bed happy at night, and wake them up with love in the morning, never hit them, never yell at them, and most important make sure they stay properly lubed."

I had no idea what the hell he was talking about because the truck parked in front of me, was the oldest piece of junk I had ever seen in my life. The original vinyl seats were badly torn and had been covered up with seat covers, which were also torn. The smell left behind from the remains of a hundred fast food lunch stops was overpowering, and the floorboards had such big rust holes in them that you could see the pavement below you. The front head lights where permanently on at all times because one of the previous drivers had hit something, or someone, and destroyed the headlight housing along with the wiring. The headlights where now held on to the truck with some wire, and a few screws. The headlights had been hot wired to the ignition some how, so when you started the truck the lights came on automatically. The automatic lift on the back of the truck had hit so many dock doors that the paint had given way to rust. The once flat surface on the lift was now severely deformed, and consequently the lift would not quite close all of the way nor would it go all of the way to the ground. The back end on the passenger side looked like it had been used for target practice with all of the holes in it caused by the loaders pushing cargo to far into the truck and puncturing the sidewalls with the forks on the fork lift. At one time you could tell this GMC was white, but the campus repair shop, or "chop shop" as it was referred to by the other departments, had made so many patches for this hunk of junk that the only white paint left was the drivers side door and the top of the cab. Everything else was covered in gray primmer, or had been salvaged from some other old truck that was undoubtedly being used for parts.

"This son is to be your delivery transport, and you must treat her with the love and respect that she deserves, do you understand me boy?" yelled Dan while walking around me in circles.

"That truck over there," he said while pointing to the brand new truck parked on the other side of the dock, with all new lifts, lights, and matching paint.

"Is mine, and if you work hard maybe some day you can be my assistant driver, but for now you will drive this fine piece of American Automotive Engineering," he said while pointing to the old truck.

"You got that boy?" He barked.

"Yes sir," I yelled out.

"Whatever you say sir."

"Good, now get your scrawny butt up into that drivers seat and let's go for a ride."

"What?" I thought to my self.

"Me drive this thing, now." Where was the training, where was the chance for me to watch him drive it so that I could see how it was done? I had never driven anything with more than five gears and this moving death trap had eight.

"Is there a problem boy?" Barked Dan.

"Or have you forgotten how to drive a stick shift?"

"No problem," I retorted as I put the mammoth machine into first gear and lunged forward with a jerk that threw Dan's coffee all over the inside of the truck cabin.

"Give it some gas, this isn't no sports car, and by the way since you're new at this I will overlook my spilled coffee this once, but hear me now and hear me good, you spill my coffee again and you will be pushing this truck from delivery stop to delivery stop with your own bare hands, got it," he barked.

"And one more thing," he said with a growl.

"You owe me a cup of coffee boy."

I had not been so scared of anyone since I had been in the fourth grade and got into a fight at school with the class bully and was sent to the principal's office. This was that same kind of fear; I think I may have wet my pants just a little bit not two minutes later when I felt the truck jerk for a second time. It was lucky for me that Dan was searching for his lighter and was not paying attention.

The windows in this late seventies "fine piece of American automotive engineering," as Dan put it, did not roll down. The doors had been hit so many times by people throwing them open too close to other cars, or buildings, that they were caved-in to the point where the windows would only go down about two inches. As Dan sat next to me chain smoking one Marlboro after another I felt myself getting sicker and sicker. Not only could I feel my virgin lungs burning from the smoke that was now filling them to capacity, but I could also swear my arteries were filling up with a cottage cheeses like consistency of tar.

"Do you mind if I turn the air on?" I finally asked between coughing fits.

"No not at all, but don't you think if it worked I would have already turned it on dumb ass, it's 110 degrees in here."

So there I sat, in the cab of a vehicle not fit to be on the road, with the windows rolled up, and no fresh air. With a chain smoker yelling an unbridled barrage of swear words at me, some of which I had never heard before and silently questioned if they were insults or if he knew a foreign language.

I don't know why, maybe it was the heat, or perhaps Dan had more than just tobacco in his cigarette but somewhere between the stars I was seeing, and the tunnel vision I kept dancing around in, the thought hit me like a ton of bricks. I was doing the right thing by taking honors classes. I needed to get done with school as fast as I could, because this was not what I wanted to do for the rest of my life, or for any longer than I absolutely had too.

I felt like I was about to cry or throw up, or perhaps both, but because of the fear I had of being killed by this lunatic sitting next to me, and having my body found in some dumpster behind one of the abandoned buildings near the V.A. Hospital. I kept my emotions and my lunch deep inside and got through the days deliveries relatively safely.

When I went into work the next day you can imagine my surprise when John called me into his office. Dan was sitting in a chair on the opposite side of the room with his cigarette hanging out of one end of his mouth and a smile on the other.

"Good job," John said as he looked over at Dan and then back at me.

"Dan said, you were one of the best delivery drivers he has ever trained and so we would like to offer you the new position, as driver, under Dan's watchful eye of course."

It was with mixed emotions that I accepted the position, and the raise, and from that day forward I was no longer a warehouse grunt but I was a driver.

"Here are the keys to the truck, and here is your route for the day," said John.

"It is your responsibility to see that the truck is taken care of, and kept as clean as it was when you took it over." Explained John.

"You may do what you like to make the cab yours. Put up a picture or two maybe a hula girl dash boards bobble if you like, but when you quit or Dan fires you, make sure you get all of it out." That was my pep talk and training session from John all rolled up into one. After he was finished talking to me John looked at Dan.

"He's all yours; do with him as you please." He said.

It felt more like a prisoner exchange than a new job position, and what did he mean by keep it as clean as it is now? You could light the inside of that truck on fire and no one would know the difference. But it was mine now and I knew that I would have to make a few alterations before I started driving it full time.

I got home that evening to find Mr. Erickson, my roommate, passed out in a pool of his own vomit just outside of our room. His keys were in the door and I could tell he had made an attempt to open it before he went down for the count because the door was slightly ajar. I decided then and there that I needed to do something about my boarding situation, and my current roommate.

I made my way to the front desk where to my dismay I found Rhonda, sitting behind the desk looking disgruntled and frumpy. She was a most unpleasant woman not more than two or three years my elder. Rhonda and her husband, whom oddly enough no one had ever seen, were the resident babysitters or dorm attendants as the nameplate on the her office door stated. The job description for Rhonda and her estranged husband, as far as I could tell, was to keep the other attendants such as Steve, in line and keep things under control in the dorms. They were to make sure all of the rules were followed, and they coordinated all of the monthly dorm parties, and social events.

There were three or four separate dorm buildings on campus, each at a different price range, some for medical students only, some for married couples, and the rest were for us "regulars." Once a month it was up to one of the dorms, each taking turns, to sponsor a group "friendship" activity. Ranging from dances, to live bands, to the popular beach parties, and movie nights. It was all an attempt to bring the dorm community closer together, and make the student housing experience unforgettable, or at least that's what the big poster in the main lobby said.

These social events were the only times Rhonda came out of her living quarters. Aside from the rare occasion when one of the desk attendants called in sick or just didn't show up, which meant instant termination for the poor attendant we never saw Rhonda.

Unfortunately for me this just so happened to be one of those infrequent times when the queen herself was behind the desk allowing us humble peasants the privilege of beholding her glory, and greatness. I waited for Rhonda to put down her *Vanity Fair* magazine and acknowledge me.

"Excuse me," I finally mumbled. "I would like to file a formal complaint against my room mate." Rhonda looked up briefly.

"My roommate is at this very moment passed out in a pool of his own vomit in front of our room, and I would really like to transfer to another room, with a different room mate."

By this time those of us whom were there for the summer quarter had gotten to know each other pretty well. Steve, the Australian guy who worked behind the front desk and I were getting to be good friends. We would talk in the evenings while we studied in the lobby, and we had figured out that we had a lot in common. Steve had told me a few weeks earlier that he could work things out to get us transferred to a different room on the much-coveted ground floor and we could be roommates. I did not realize that Steve had not actually talked to Rhonda about this arrangement yet, and so I inadvertently made the mistake of asking her majesty if they had worked out the arrangement to get me away from my roommate, and move in with Steve.

Rhonda looked at me for three or four very awkward seconds.

"What do I look like your mother? If you have a problem with your room mate then take it outside and deal with it like a man." She said with an ugly grimace on her face.

"As far as you changing rooms, this isn't the Ritz Carlton, or the Hilton, and I am not your wet nurse, or your fairy god-mother here to make all of your problems go away. If you want to change rooms or roommates you can fill out a request form and I will review it." She said as she picked her magazine back up.

"Changes are only allowed at the quarter break, and all changes must be approved by me!" Was her final statement.

There really wasn't much I could say at that moment, so I decided that a silent retreat would be the best way to handle this humiliating defeat. After all General Ulysses S. Grant had lost nearly every battle he had with General Robert E. Lee but in the end he won the war.

I had left a message on Mandy's answering machine before I left work asking her if she would be willing to come and help me clean out my newly appointed work truck. She had left me a message while I was fighting with Attila the Hun telling me that she would be glad to help, as long as it was not too gross, and as long as she did not have to get dirty. After making my way back up to my room and scraping my disgusting roommate off of the floor, I grabbed one of his towels and tossed it onto the lovely gift he had left behind in the hallway. I then picked up the phone and called Mandy back asking her to meet me over by the warehouse, where the trucks were parked so that we could get it cleaned out.

I hung up the phone and made my way back to the warehouse so that I could get started on the truck. I was just beginning to scrape what I thought was a hamburger or perhaps a grilled cheese sandwich from off the back side of the big bench seat when I heard a blood curdling shriek coming from behind my left shoulder. The scream startled me, causing me to jump up and hit my head on the under side of the armrest on drivers side door. The armrest was nothing more than a rusty piece of metal screwed to the badly damaged drivers' side door, and the upholstery had either rotted off or had been torn off perhaps a decade ago or longer. I tried to see through all of the stars whirling around the inside of the truck while holding the back of my throbbing head. As soon as the world stopped spinning I thought I felt the sensation of something cold and wet running down the back of my legs. I turned around and saw Mandy standing behind me wearing a thick pair of yellow rubber kitchen gloves. She was holding a wire brush in one hand, and the bucket of soapy water that had been in her other hand was now lying on the ground beside me. All of the water that had spilled out of the bucket when Mandy dropped it was now running down the back of my legs, and pooling up inside of my shoes. Mandy was screaming in a high-pitched shrill voice, "*Is that a dead rat?*" While doing what appeared to be a cross between an Irish step dance, and jumping jacks.

"No" I told her calmly "it's not a dead rat, it's the remains of someone's lunch from a long time ago." Mandy stood back a little and took her sunglasses off her eyes and placed them on her head, she then began to walk slowly around my fine piece of American automotive engineering and looking me right in the eyes she said,

"Oh honey I don't want you driving this thing, it looks like it will either fall apart or blow up when you start it." I laughed out loud.

"No, it's not going to blow up," I said.

I could not in good conscience say that it would not fall apart, but I did not believe I was in any immediate danger of an explosion.

"What is that smell?" Asked Mandy, as she fanned the air away from her nose.

"It smells like death frozen over in here, and there is such a thick layer of smoke scum on the inside of these windows that you can't even see out, except for that small spot in the middle."

That small spot was where decades of coffee drinkers had placed their coffee; I guess the steam and heat had stopped the smoke film from building up in that one small spot in the middle of the front windshield.

"Don't worry," I stated,

"It will clean up just fine all I need is a razor blade and some vinegar, besides, since I don't smoke it won't get like this again as long as I am driving it."

Against every fiber in her being Mandy climbed into the cab of that long neglected truck and helped me scrape, chisel, clean, and pull all of the garbage and sick, out of the front of the cab. Mandy had brought a few different air fresheners with the idea that I could choose which one I wanted to use, but instead of one she placed all five of them in the truck, each one in a strategic place, like under the seat, in the glove box, on the rear view mirror, and over the stick shift. Just as we were finishing up Mandy got out of the truck.

"Oh, I almost forgot, I have something to give you."

She took out a picture of herself that had been taken by one of the street vendors the evening of the Arts Festival. I had actually forgotten that the picture was even taken, but upon seeing the photo it brought back memories of that pleasant evening.

"Now we will always be together were ever you go." She said.

Mandy bent one corner of the picture and shoved the bent piece into one of the many cracks on the dashboard in such a way that the picture was visible when I drove.

"Thank you," I said.

"That was very thoughtful, and it's a very good picture of you, I will have to be careful who I let into the truck now because they will defiantly try to steal that picture."

After finishing the truck we decided to go for a walk around campus as we had done many times before, and we found ourselves in front of the water fountain due south of the University of Utah's Marriott library. I remember taking off my wet shoes and soggy socks, and holding Mandy's hand as we both stood in the cool water of the fountain right next to the sign that read,

"No standing or playing in the fountain."

I remember looking up at the setting sun and thinking to myself, "what a wonderful day."

How could life have been more perfect than it was at that moment, I was standing there with a beautiful girl, in a lovely fountain, on the campus of what was now beginning to feel like my home, I had a good job, and I was fulfilling my dream of going to school, there was an absolutely breathtaking sunset that evening, turning the sky brilliant shades of red, pink, and yellow. It was one of those rare moments in life where one feels like everything is so right with the world and nothing can go wrong, but then life steps in and that feeling seems to fade so fast.

After watching the sun dip slowly down behind the Wasatch Mountains, we made our way back up the hill to Mandy's car and as I was opening her door for her a letter fell out onto the pavement. I picked up the envelope and handed it to her, and as Mandy took the letter from me I noticed it was from, her high school sweetheart, trying not to let myself look as concerned as I instantly felt I asked what the letter was, and how long has she had it. Mandy quickly put the letter in her purse.

"It's nothing, just a letter from an old friend," she said.

"You know how I used to write you when I was going to school in southern Utah, and you used to write to me, well it is just like that, it is nothing more than a "hi" how are things going letter."

With that Mandy gave me a quick kiss on the cheek and told me not to worry, she would call me tomorrow, and good luck with the new job. I stood there and watched her drive away knowing that there was a lot I needed to worry about now, and that it was not just a "how are you doing" letter from an old friend. I had know for a while now that he would be coming back home sooner or later, and as I had feared it looked like it was going to be sooner than latter.

I made my way back to the dorms and as I entered the main lobby I heard someone playing the piano, which in and of itself was no big deal, there were people playing the piano almost all of the time. But this was different. It was not like anything I had heard being played on this piano before. Usually I heard people playing show tunes, or chop six, or they would just be messing around and banging on the piano. However this was different, this was the sound of someone who really knew what they were doing. This was not an amateur, messing around or someone playing show tunes, this was the sound of someone truly gifted, playing something personal and from the heart. I did not see who was behind the piano because as usual there were a lot of people in the lobby, but I did think to myself "wow" that was some very pretty music.

As I found myself nearing mid terms and I began to spend more and more of my off time, I would say free time, but I would not consider the time I spent away from work and the class room to be free. Steve who was also in the freshman honors course, and like me was majoring in architecture, made the statement one evening that we needed to get away for a little while and do something fun, like go camping.

I had always enjoyed camping, I was an Eagle Scout, and I had done a lot of hiking and camping with Jason and Mark when I was in high school. After discussing some options for our little get away Steve finally said,

"We need to get out of here and do something with what is left of our summer and our sanity." He then looked at me, and then at Tom; one of our new found foreign exchange friends from Poland,

"What do you say mates, shall we have a go of it?"

I just so happened to still have all of my camping gear in the trunk of my car, mainly because I had not bothered to bring it up to my room, but partially because I had hoped to do a little camping in the hills behind the university. The University of Utah sits high up on the east bench of the Salt Lake valley, and at the time there was nothing behind the school except mountains, and brush. Steve was so excited to get going that he started to gather his things together on the spot, and within twenty minutes we were headed up into the hills behind the University. I remember thinking to myself,

"I hope Steve realizes what camping in these mountains can be like, it may be a warm and wonderful evening, but the rain and cold can set in very quickly and it could very easily take a person off guard if they weren't careful."

The three of us made our way up to the top of the nearest peak, which was about thirty minutes away from the furthest parking lot on the back part of campus, when we found ourselves on a relatively flat part of the crest, Steve turned to Tom and I,

"Well mates this looks like a good spot to tucker down for the evening."

We all turned and looked into the night sky and saw what looked like millions of stars, we then gazed down into the Salt Lake valley and from our vantage point we could see the entire valley lit up from all of the city lights below. I remember it being quiet and very still; it was the kind of evening where the temperature had finally dipped after a long hot day making it a perfect 75 degrees or so. We were about to find out that it was the calm before the storm. We built a small fire, and ate what meager items we had grabbed during our rush to get out of the dorms. I think we had some left over pizza, a couple of hot pockets, and some skittles. After dinner I decided to put up my little two-man tent as Tom and Steve watched with an air of disbelief. I can even recall Steve yelling over to me a couple of times,

"What are you doing? Are you some sort of Sheila or something, what do you need a tent for? Real mean sleep under the stars in their under-shorts."

"Well, we will see how much of a real man you are sleeping in your "under-shorts" in these mountains, you are from Australia where it may be ok to do that, but here it gets a little cool in the evenings." I said while completing my task.

Having set my tent up I sat down and we began to discuss life, school, and what we wanted to do with ourselves when we grew up. After a few minutes of small talk Steve and I turned our attention to Tom. Tom was a rather soft-spoken, blonde kid, with deep blue eyes, who spoke descent English, but who mixed his words and their meanings up a bit from time to time. We asked him why he had come to Utah of all places, and he explained that he had an aunt and uncle who had moved to the United States in the last sixties to find a better life. They opened a small restaurant in down town Salt Lake and had done all right for themselves in America. Tom said, because of the success his aunt and uncle had enjoyed, his parents felt that it would be best if he were to come to America, study business, and find work. Not only to help support the family back home, but also to improve his life in the process. He planned on applying for citizenship as soon as he met the requirements and he also wanted to find "nice American girl, who cook, clean, and have babies for him."

Tom seemed like a good guy, and his awkward ways made him loveable, kind of like a lost puppy. With the midnight hour quickly approaching we decided it was time to get some sleep if we were to make it to class on time the next morning. Steve stripped down to his boxers while Tom got under his blankets, and I slipped comfortably into my tent and sleeping bag. As I lay there breathing the crisp mountain air, I began to think about the letter I had seen in Mandy's car just a few evenings ago. I wondered what this new development would bring; I wondered how was I supposed to take all of this? I knew very well what their history together had been like, and how long they had been together, even though Mandy had stated that there was nothing to worry about, I had done nothing but worry since that evening. Quite frankly I was very worried that he would come back and take her to dinner or something. Then Mandy would tell me, "it's nothing," but next thing you know all of the old feelings between them would return, and I would be out of the picture, and all of the time we had spent together finding out if we were meant to be together would be for naught.

I suppose I had been stewing about this for what felt like hours, but what must have only been a half an hour or so when I noticed the sound of small but evenly spaced rain drops falling on my tent. A big smile came over my face as I though of Steve lying out there on a blanket in his underwear being a *"real man,"* while I was lying in my sleeping bag, in my tent warm and dry, and that is when the thunder began to roll in.

The thunder started out quite, in the far distance, and then slowly began to get louder and more frequent as it got closer and closer to where we were camping. I must have been dosing off at this time because when a huge flash of lighting light up my entire tent like the fourth of July it startled me and woke me up. There was a tremendous crash of thunder directly following the light show and I sat up in time to hear Steve scream like a little girl, and rip open my tent.

"Please let me in your tent for just a few minutes." I laughed at the site of Steve soaking wet, and shivering in his boxer shorts, looking like a wet cat.

"You better get Tom in here too before he drowns out there, besides I don't want him waking up in the morning and seeing the two of us coming out of my tent together with you in your wet underwear, it would give him the wrong idea about us, and I am not about to cook, clean, or give babies for you."

Steve did not even have to turn around, Tom had been listening to our entire conversation and he dove into the tent beating Steve and as he landed next to me Tom turned to Steve,

"I will not be giving you baby either, so put your pants back on." He said.

It was a cozy night with the three of us crammed tightly into my so called two man tent, made for two men whom could not have been more than ninety pounds a piece or any taller than five feet, but the truth was I was happy to have new friends and I was grateful to be doing something that got my mind off of schoolwork even if it was only for one evening.

"Which of the Ming dynasties was the following religious artifact taken from?" This was one of the first questions on my Eastern Philosophy and Religion mid term. I had studied so long, and so hard for this and all of my other midterms that I was having a total mind block. Buddha and thesis terminology, along with early American railroad economics, and the Rockefellers with their financial empire were swimming around my head in a colorful array of interpretive dance. I was struggling to remember which dynasty this particular artifact that was plastered across the screen in a larger than life slide show might be, when the next photo flashed onto the screen. I had scarcely pulled the answer out of my throbbing head to this question when again the next photo was brought up. It was a large terracotta soldier, one of thousands, each made in the likeness of a real live soldier in the emperors' army, complete with armor, weapons, and horses for the cavalry.

"Taken from the tomb of what emperor, from what dynasty, and where this tomb was located?" Boomed the voice from the front of the room.

My professor was asking the questions, which were coming at a feverous pace in order to get every one into the time slot available. She was standing in the front of the auditorium behind a large podium with a microphone in her hand while her "student teachers" were running the projector and policing the class like watch dogs looking for cheaters. It felt as if we were being treated like Columbian drug lords trying to smuggle thousands of pounds of illegal drugs in our pants through the JFK airport.

My professor was a very remarkable woman, who had somehow fallen in love with eastern culture. She had been all over China, Japan, Korea, and the Indies. Most of the pictures in the slide show, and the actual artifacts that she would show the class every Monday, Wednesday, and Friday, were taken and or collected by her during one of her hundreds of visits to the East. She was probably in her mid fifties, had never been married, due to the fact that she had a female "life partner," who came into the class from time to time to watch her teach, and help with some of the artifact presentations.

My professor often told the class that she believed she was the reincarnation of a Chinese manservant to one of the emperors of China in the late 2nd century B.C. Of course when this person is the one giving you the grade that could make or break your chances of continuing in the honors program you don't laugh, you don't make jokes, and if anything you pretend to be interested in what your professor is saying. One might even go as far as to state that they had often thought that perhaps they too may be the reincarnation of a man servant to the emperor of China. Not that I would personally sink that low. Because believe me if someone were to make a mistake like that, one could be thought of and labeled as a "brown-noser," and if that were to happen it would be likely that some of the other students in your class would not want to join, or allow you to join their after hours study group which was essential in passing these midterms and final exams. Should this grave error be made, one must quickly make a mends with his fellow honors students by purchasing three large pizzas from Pizza Hut and gluing thousands of tiny pictures of oriental artifacts to hundreds of 3 x 5 study cards in order to be accepted back into the study group. Not that I would know what that was like but I knew it could happen, and had seen it myself. I finished the grueling two-hour slide show-test and thought to myself, "I am not honors material, and if I got an "F" on this test it would be a better score than I am expecting at the moment," how was I ever going to pass a class like that, and if this class was to be a mere introduction of things to come I was going to have to drop out of the honors course for sure.

In comparison, the rest of my mid terms for that first quarter of my college career seemed to have gone relatively smooth. My finals would prove to be much more challenging, but for the time being I recall feeling very relived when I completed my last midterm a day or two later.

It was about this time that Steve and I decided, after having turned the paperwork into Rhonda for the requested room change and having received no answer or even an acknowledgement from her that we needed to take matters into our own hands. Steve, who worked at the front desk and who was the one who actually made, and typed up the room assignments to mail out to the new students, decided he would help the paperwork along and assure us that things would go our way.

He started out by contacting my roommate through official university channels of course, to get his written permission to have me, his current roommate transferred to another room, and for him to be assigned a new room-mate. Of course the way it really went down was more like this; late one evening after returning from one of his notorious drinking escapades Steve and I went into my room and explained to Jack what we were doing and had him sign the paperwork. He had no problems with what we were asking him to do; the only problem we had was getting him to sign the paperwork between his vomiting fits and passing out. Next we had to contact the student that was to be Steve's new roommate for the fall, so Steve just wrote him a new letter in place of the original room assignment and set him up with my current room-mate.

I really did feel bad for whoever was to be Jacks new roommate. I thought it was cruel and unusual punishment to assign this new and unsuspecting person to my current vomiting companion, but at the same time I felt like I had done my time, and served my tour of duty with honor and now it was someone else's turn to spend a little quality time in Jack-Ville. Steve's roommate for the sum-mer had not shown up due to any number of reasons, none of which we really cared about, and so for the most part I was living with Steve anyway. Upon returning home to the dorms one evening after school and work I found a note on my door telling me I needed to see Steve as soon as possible. I went to the other end of the hall where I found Steve busily and excitedly packing his stuff up in what appeared to be the garbage can from the laundry room. So I said; "Steve if you don't want your stuff I will take it but please don't throw it all away."

"No mate, I'm not throwing my stuff away I'm moving, and I suggest you get your stuff together too."

"Where are we going?" I asked in a state of confusion.

"There is a room on the first floor that has been vacant all summer and I confirmed today with the guys that were suppose to be living there that they won't be coming this summer, so I changed all of our paperwork to get us into the room now instead of waiting until fall."

"What if we get caught by her royal nastiness?" I asked.

"We won't get caught, she never comes into the boys' wing and you can bet she never looks at the room assignment book, besides even if she does I have taken care of everything, so don't worry."

To be honest I was a bit concerned, not so much about moving into the vacant room, as I was about Rhonda finding out and kicking us out of the dorms leaving us with no place to live. I went back to my room and found Jack sleeping on the floor with a beer can in one hand, and a piece of three day old pizza, that must have come from underneath his bed in the other hand. I told him I was moving out so he could have the place to himself now. I told him not to worry about me because I was going to be fine, and that there was no need to get up. I explained to Jack that I could manage moving my stuff out on my own, but of course I was just talking to myself because he was unconscious, as usual. When I went to unplug my answering machine I noticed the small red light on top of the recorder was flashing, signifying that someone had left us a message. I pushed play on the small machine, and a gruff mans voice that I did not recognize began to speak. After listening for a minute or two I realized the message was for Jack. The message was from his father and it said something to this effect; "Hi Jack, this is your dad; I have been working things out with Stanford for you to come back for the fall quarter."

The message went on to say something about a new car, and a raise in allowance if Jack would just come back home from that god-forsaken school in Utah. I woke Jack up from his drunken stupor and played the message for him again so that he could hear it this time, when the message came to the end Jack stood up, grabbed a hand full of clothes and his stereo and as he made his way towards the door he told me,

"So long, it's been fun, we'll keep in touch."

And then he stumbled out to his car and I never saw or heard from him again. Jack left most of his belongings behind, like all of his dishes, most of his clothes, toiletries, school supplies, etc., so Steve and I, being poor college students and not too proud to take a hand-out from time to time, rummaged through and pillaged whatever Jack had left behind, taking anything of worth, edible, or clean. We where not sure if Jack would send for, or come back for some of his things so we gave him the benefit of the doubt by waiting for two or three days to report his room abandonment. When we made the formal report the school took all of his belongings that had not already been claimed by Steve and myself, or any of the other bandits in the dorms, and gave them to the Salvation Army.

After having moved down to our new and very coveted first floor room, Steve and I decided that we needed to do something to spruce the place up and somehow add a little more space to the tight quarters. Jack had left a small refrigerator that I claimed for myself. Steve also had a little locker size refrigerator of his own. So between the two refrigerators, a large second hand television that Steve had bought for a few dollars off of a senior who had moved out at the end of the previous spring quarter, and the rest of our stuff we did not have much room. Steve and I, being rather mechanically inclined, began working on some ideas and drawings for a new room layout. We both came up with a number of solutions to our problem ranging from stacking our beds back up into bunk beds, to getting rid of the beds all together and sleeping in our sleeping bags. However it was actually our good friend Tom who inadvertently gave us the idea that we went with.

One evening shortly after Steve and I had changed rooms, we were sitting in the lobby watching TV with Tom while discussing our dilemma. Tom was listening to our conversation and after observing us argue about what the best solution would be for about a half an hour he finally said, "Why don't you just sleep on ceiling and that will solve problem."

He then started laughing about the idea of Steve and I sleeping on the ceiling, but Steve and I looked at each other and thought, wait a minute, Tom may have something. We both ran to the room and started measuring and drawing up our ideas. After about an hour or two of deep contemplation Steve and I had come up with a type of scaffolding that could be attached to walls with long masonry screws, and there would be (8) 6x 6 studs, about four feet high, one for each post of the bed. We would put our beds on either side of the room and set them on top of these wooden posts, and then we would place the scaffolding with a series of cross braces between the posts, and connect it to the wall for stability. We also figured out a way in which we could have shelves running between the two beds, at the foot of the bed, by bracing a few pieces of shelving material to the ceiling, and to the wooden scaffolding. This would leave the floor of the room virtually empty and would allow us to put whatever we wanted on the floor under the beds, there was about five feet between the beds, and each bed was about three feet wide, so there was plenty of room to get around.

The following morning we headed out into the world to gather all of the materials that we would need to accomplish our task. It is funny to think about the whole thing now, we never bothered to ask permission, because first of all we were not even suppose to be in the room, technically it was assigned to someone else, and second we were not suppose to be roommates, and finely there was no way anyone would give us permission to do what we were about to do. The first place we went was to the back side of the warehouse where I worked, we gathered up all of the old and broken pallets that were salvageable and then we took them back behind the dorms to take them apart to get the usable wood separated from the junk. After separating and salvaging what we could from the old pallets, Steve and I went to the hardware store to buy some screws, nails and a few pieces of particleboard to use for shelving material, and then we went back to our dorm room to begin construction. We chiseled out the tops of the 6 x 6 studs so that the steel legs of the bed frames would fit nicely into the wood post, we then built the cross bracing and attached it to the wall for stability, and finally we constructed the shelves at the foot of our beds and braced them to the ceiling and to our intricate scaffolding system.

The metal frame beds which came standard in every bedroom were actually designed to be used as bunk beds and could be staked if the occupants so desired, so consequently the beds had a higher post on them than what a regular bed would have, giving them an ideal amount of head room to sit under.

Upon completion of our architectural masterpiece, we decided that we still needed to do a bit more work in order to make the room perfect, so we went down to the Salvation Army and bought an old couch, and arranged for it to be delivered later that afternoon. We also bought a small children's blow up swimming pool at the supermarket to cool our feet off with in our hot, non air-conditioned room. Each dorm room was equipped with a swamp cooler, but the air had to travel down from the top of the roof, three floors above us, so by the time it got to our room on the first floor it was nothing more than a faint breeze. We had the deliveryman bring the couch into our room through the window, one of the endless benefits of being on the ground floor, and we placed it under the window, centered between and underneath our suspended beds.

When I thought we where finally finished with our remodeling project I sat down in the couch with an exhausted sigh and looked over towards Steve who was rummaging through and old paper sack. Steve looked at me after a few moments of digging into the bag and said,

"We are not done yet, we need just one more thing."

He then pulled out a long string of plastic jalapeno pepper lights, that he informed me he bought for a dollar at the Salvation Army earlier that day, and he proceeded to string them around the ceiling, around our bed frames, through the shelves and down to the outlet by our desks. He then plugged in the bright red lights and turned out the large overhead fluorescent lights and exclaimed, "There we have it mate, now we are finished."

I could have sworn I mentioned the move, and our great structural achievement to Mandy, but a few days after we completed our little remodeling project I called Mandy to see if she wanted to go out for ice cream. I did not get two words out when she interrupted me wanting to know where I had been, and why my phone had been disconnected; I calmly explained the events of the past few days and asked her why she had forgotten about it so soon.

"You did not tell me you were moving," was Mandy's reply.

"And when I came up to your room to surprise you yesterday, guess who got the surprise?" She paused for a moment, but I could tell that this was not the kind of question that I should answer,

"I did," she said, in a frustrated tone.

"After knocking on your door for five minutes I went back to the front desk and asked the guy to let me into your room, because I was worried about you, and when he opened the door there was nothing behind it except an empty room and some old pizza boxes on the floor. I figured you must have failed your mid-terms and they sent you home," she said in a teasing tone.

"Ha, ha, ha, very funny" I declared, however her comment did remind me, that in the course of all the excitement from the past few days I had forgotten to check my grades. Back in my college days, in order find out what your grades were, you would have to physically walk to wherever your class was located and search through the sometimes-long list of names posted on the door by the professor, once you found your name, there would be a row of scores based on things like homework, and quizzes, and next to all of your scores would be your final grade. Now days, I think that some the human rites folks would go absolutely ballistic if a professor were to post his or her grades on the door for all to see, but that is how it was done when I went to college.

Holding my breath I said to Mandy in a nervous tone, "will you please look for me, I can't do it." We stood out in front of the door to my Eastern Philosophy and Religion class, and with a sigh Mandy said,

"What do you mean you can't look at the grade sheet? You got an "A," so I don't know what you are so worried about."

I let the air slowly out of my lungs and opened one eye,

"*What*" I shouted, "*I got an A.*"

"Quite," Mandy whispered.

"People are starting to stare."

"Sorry," I whispered back.

I looked at the list of names on the door and quickly found mine. I then looked next to it and sure enough there was an "A" placed right next to my name in the midterm category. This had to be a misprint, there had to be an explanation, because surely I had not gotten an "A" on what was up to that point in my life the most difficult exam I had ever taken. Maybe my professor really thought I was a reincarnated manservant from the Emperor of China, or maybe she had been drinking when she graded my test. What ever the reason, reincarnation or inebriation there it was in black and white an "A" right in front of me.

"See all that worrying for nothing, I knew you could do it, you are after all the smartest guy I have ever dated," said Mandy as she nudged me playfully.

Her comment made me blush, she was always telling me how smart I was and even though I believed I was not a dummy, I did not think I was as intelligent as she had made me out to be. I was afraid on a subconscious level that Mandy had placed me on some sort of pedestal and that if I did not meet or exceed her expectations she may think less of me. We wandered around to all of my other classrooms that afternoon and all of the other doors had "A's" on them, I had not really been worried about any of my other classes but it was nice to see the good grades, and know that my studying and hard work had paid off.

"We need to celebrate," I announced to Mandy, Steve and Tom who were all watching TV in our dorm room.

"What for mate?" Asked Steve with a disappointed tone.

"I got a B-on that stupid Eastern philo-whatever class, and that isn't a reason to celebrate."

Tom sat there smiling at all of us like he usually did "I got all "A's" and am not so stupid like Steve, so we celebrate" stated Tom.

"Hey mate do you want all those pretty teeth to stay in your head?" grumbled Steve.

"O yes I need them to eat," replied Tom.

"Then you had better shut your…" that is when Mandy stepped into the conversation,

"Ok boys that's enough, Steve why don't you be the bigger man, and Tom that was not a very nice thing to say, why don't you two apologize and be nice to each other."

All of my friends liked Mandy, and were more than happy to have her around; they would fall all over themselves like dumb apes whenever she asked for anything. Although I was glad to see that the guys had accepted Mandy into our little group, I will admit that it made me a bit jealous from time to time, because of how quickly they had accepted her, and how much they were willing to do for her.

We all jumped into Steve's 1972 Cadillac super destroyer, aircraft carrier, forged out of three tons of America's finest steel, complete with a powder blue interior and electric everything! Only the electric windows did not work and rust had taken its toll on the floorboards and fenders, turning them from powder blue to orange rust. I am sure that in its day this car was quite the vehicle but it was also quite the oil refinery on wheels. Steve's parents had given him three or four hundred dollars to purchase a car with when he arrived in the United States, he was able to pick up this car for about half of the expected price and so Steve pocketed the remaining amount and used it for other items. Steve was quite proud of his bargaining abilities and he was even prouder of the car he had purchased at such a good deal, even though there were BMW's and Mercedes parked in the student housing parking lot he was not at all embarrassed to park the H.M.S. Titanic in the two stalls next to any other car.

With Steve and Tom in the front seat and Mandy and I in the back seat we set off for a place to "celebrate" our victories and Steve's defeats from the first half of the first quarter of our college careers.

"Where should we go?"

"Somewhere cheap."

"Somewhere nice."

"Somewhere still open because it is 11:30 p.m."

So we set off in Steve's large and spacious vehicle into the nightlife of Salt Lake City to find a place to celebrate.

"How about a dance club?" inquired Steve?

"No," replied Tom.

"Last time we went to dance club they think I was young school boy and would not let me in, because I did not know I need verification papers to get in," Tom said while shaking his finger at Steve.

"In Poland if you want dance you just go in, and dance. At last dance club you guys went in front of me and when police man did not let me in you left me in parking lot for three hours."

We all had felt really bad about that little incidence; none of us intended to leave Tom in the parking lot that night. In fact we truthfully did not know he was stopped at the door and none of us knew that Tom had not been let in. We all just figured that he had gotten in and was flying solo, doing the lonely foreign exchange student routine. It did not help that Tom looked like he was still in high school with his blonde hair, blue eyes and inability to grow facial hair, even though he was 22 or 23 he really did look like he was still 16. After about the first hour without seeing Tom, Mandy and I thought he was missing but when we asked Steve, he told us that he had personally seen Tom just a few minutes earlier going into the little boys' room. It wasn't until they were closing the club for the evening that we discovered Tom was not with us. After trying to explain to the man at the front desk that we still had a friend inside we were escorted out by security, and that was when we found Tom laying on the hood of the car soaking wet, curled up into the fetal position shivering and trying to keep warm. We had all enjoyed watching the lovely summer rain from inside the club, but obviously Tom had not found the rain shower to be quite as magical as we did.

"What's up Tom, you look a bit wet there mate, did you spill your drink or something?" Asked Steve with a chuckle.

I could tell by the look in Tom's eyes that we just needed to get him home and keep him away from Steve for the rest of the evening. I do believe that was the only time I have ever seen Tom without a smile on his face, in fact that is the only time I have ever seen anyone resembled a rabid dog, foaming at the mouth and ready to shred its unsuspecting prey from limb to limb.

"Tom you know we all feel really bad about what happened," said Mandy in a sympathetic tone.

"But we have all apologized multiple times for that, and maybe it's time to just let it go."

After driving around for about an hour and a half we finally decided that Eat a' Burger at the bottom of 4th south would be as good as any place to celebrate. We all piled into a small crowded booth and began ordering our meals when Steve told us he had an announcement to make.

"My sister is coming from Australia to visit for a week or two and she will be arriving at the end of the month, I told her she could stay with us in our dorm room," said Steve as he looked across the table at me.

"Is that going to be ok with you Jeremy?"

"Sure," I replied.

"We have lots of room and our big new couch should be very comfortable, or if that won't work she could sleep in a sleeping bag on the floor, or she can have my bed and I will sleep on the couch or maybe," a sudden and very swift kick to my right leg and the icy look of death stopped me mid sentence and suggested to me in not so many words that perhaps this was not a good idea.

"Steve," interrupted Mandy.

"Your sister is more than welcome to stay with my cousin and her roommates who just so happen to have an apartment a few block south of campus," said Mandy as I sat listening to the conversation with tears of pain filling up my eyes.

"Their place is within 10 minutes walking distance from your dorm, and I would be happy to give my cousin a call in the morning to find out if it will be ok with her, but I am sure it won't be any problem," exclaimed Mandy.

"Besides I am sure she does not want to sleep in the *boys* dorm on your stinky old urine stained, second hand Salvation Army couch."

"It's not urine I spill my ice tea last night," exclaimed Tom.

"No, your right Tom dear, I am just making a point that *no* girl will *ever* be sleeping in a dorm room with those two boys," she said while pointing at Steve.

"Or on their couch, or on their floor, or anywhere for that matter" she gave Steve and I a quick glance.

"Is that clear boys?"

"Yes, crystal clear."

"Good," exclaimed Mandy.

"So what is your sisters name?"

"Her name is Misty and actually she is my twin sister." Began Steve.

"She has been attending university in Australia but is thinking of transferring here to the University of Utah. My mum told her she should come out here for a week or two to get to know the area and talk with some of the counselors here to see if this is what she really wants to do. She has been studying nursing back home and I have been writing her letters telling her about the Universities medical program and she wants to look into it a bit further."

"Well that is very exciting Steve," exclaimed Mandy.

"I think that she will have a good time while she is here, and the less time she spends in your disgusting dorm room, the better her opinion of the University of Utah will be," said Mandy.

"Hold on a minute," I interrupted.

"You make it sound like Steve and I are total pigs and I think that is a bit harsh on your part!"

"Jeremy would you like to talk about the ant infestation that *you* told me not more that a week and a half ago!"

Mandy was right of coarse; Steve and I did have a bit of work to be done in the cleanliness area. A few weeks prior to that evening, just as midterms were going into their feverish height, I had gone to take a shower. When I finished, I walked back into the hallway that lead to my room and as I started walking I noticed a steady trail of ants coming out of one of the air intake grills at the bottom of the wall. I stopped walking because I noticed that the trail of ants following the base boards down the hall to someone's room. I remember thinking to myself,

"That is gross, who would let their room get so bad that ants would infest it."

As I continued walking towards my room I noticed that the trail of ants took a sharp turn at my door. The trail then went under the threshold, and disappeared into our room. I put the key into the door of my room and upon turning the handle and pushing the door open I saw the trail of ants making their way across our floor and up the leg of Steve's desk.

Steve and I had been so busy with studying, school, and work, that neither one of us had done any cleaning, or any dishes for about a week. Consequently there were dirty dishes, pots, pans, pizza boxes, fast food wrappers, half empty cups, and cooking utensils stacked up onto Steve's desk as well as my desk and chair, in fact we had run out of room on the desks, and chairs, a so a few items had been stashed in the corner between the couch and the refrigerators. Both Steve and I had fully intended on taking a few hours out of the next available Saturday to clean the room really well, but we had just not gotten that far. I continued following the trail of ants with my eyes up the leg of Steve's desk and watched as they disappeared into the abyss of dirty dishes. I must add that Steve and I had not accomplished such an amazing disaster by ourselves, we did in fact have Tom, and at least two or three other people eat with us almost every evening, and most mornings. We had every bit of silverware, and every piece of kitchenware that we owned piled up in heaps on our desks, as wall as the takeout containers, and fast food remains from about a weeks worth of meals.

I slowly started removing items from the pile. Dishes, bowls with cereal that had turned into cement, plates with forks permanently plastered to the edge on which it had been resting, pizza boxes with a single piece of mildew infested pizza left dried into the bottom, and pans with the last remains of chicken noodle soup crusted to the bottom. Upon reaching what I could only guess was the halfway point of disgusting yuck, I thought to myself,

"*Wow,* we are pigs," and then when I lifted one of the last pizza boxes nothing could prepare me for what I was about to encounter. There must have been hundreds of thousands of ants swarming in, on, and round, what I could only guess was someone's fish fillet sandwich that they had only taken two or three bites of and then added to our leaning tower of nasty. As the days went by we continued adding to the pile and inadvertently we must have entombing the sandwich deep within the belly of the beast. I could not even see the plate that the offensive fish was resting on because it was completely covered in a swarm of black, circling ants moving in unison as if they were one disgusting mass. Upon seeing this horrific infestation I began to dry heave, I could feel the candy bar and coke that I had eaten earlier that day trying to come up and escape to freedom, but I choked them back down as I ran into the laundry room and grabbed the big metal garbage can.

There I stood with my towel still stuck to my wet body, because I had not really dried myself off all that well. Throwing *every* dish, bowl, spoon, fork, knife, and plate we had into the trash. I ran to the kitchen and retrieved the broom from the broom closet and with one swoop I pushed everything from Steve's desk into the trash can, dirty dishes, alarm clock, books, pencils, pens and all. I figured if he saw what I was battling he would not begrudge me the loss of his alarm clock, and a book or two, after all ants were known to carry malaria weren't they?

With my door wide open I can only imagine what passerby's must have been thinking, but quite frankly at that moment in time I was fighting for my life and did not care what others were thinking. I heaved the now extremely over loaded garbage can out of my room, down the hall and out the back door, I then pulled it over to the big dumpster and with one huge deep breath I picked the entire garbage can up and heaved it into the dumpster. I stood there for a moment breathless and panting, while thinking to myself, what a brave warrior I had been to fight off the swarm of ants and save our room from impending doom, and it was at that point when I heard a car driving by and honking its horn. A moment later, another car full of girls this time, went by honking, while the ladies inside were whistling and hollering sexual obscenities in my general direction. I then realized that I was standing outside of the dorms in my towel, dripping wet. The knot I had tied in my towel was getting quite loose and consequently part of my backside was exposed to the traffic going by.

I had told Mandy about the ants but I had chosen to omit the part about the towel and the honking cars, consequently since Steve and I had lost all of our eating and cooking utensils, we had to go to the dollar store and buy all new plates, silverware, pots and pans, but we did vow that very day to never allow our room to get that nasty again.

"Ok you got me there," I said in a sheepish tone.

"We may not have the best track record in the cleanliness department, but we have gotten better after that little incident, and I will have you know that we have been washing our dishes after each meal, and we throw away all of our food related garbage before we go to bed each night."

"Well that is nice dear," said Mandy.

"But I would still not let any girl sleep in the same room with the two of you, even if your room was spotless all the time, she can stay with my cousin and I will make sure that she is taken care of." After a moment of contemplation Mandy looked at Steve.

"If you want your sister to have a nice time while she visits, and possibly consider going to school here, we don't want your room to be her only memory of the United States and this school when she goes home, so leave everything to me and we will make it a nice stay for her."

Deep down I know that Steve wanted Mandy to find a place for his sister to stay and that is precisely why he brought the subject up in front of her. Steve did not want to make his sister stay in the boys' dormitory while she was here, but he did not have the courage to ask Mandy if she would help him find a place for his sister to stay. Steve knew how boys in a boys dorm tended to act around a pretty girl, the whole concept of a boys dorm lends itself to being a den of iniquity, not that myself, or Tom, or any of our friends would do or say anything to embarrass Steve or his sister he just wanted to protect her from the rest of the wolves. Part of the football team lived at the other end of our building on the same floor as us, and even though we all got along really well he did not want to parade his sister in front of that group of guys, and for good reason. While the conversation was taking place our food had arrived and we were almost finished eating when I looked closely at the last bite of my hamburger and noticed that the patty inside was quite raw in the middle, in fact so much so that I cold still see ice on it. I took my last bite and showed it to Mandy.

"Does this look a little uh, raw to you?"

"Yes it looks a lot raw to me, you did not eat the whole thing raw like that did you honey?"

"Ohm, well, yes, as a matter of fact I did eat all of my burger like this, except for this last bite," I said rather timidly.

"I got caught up in the conversation and I didn't even look at my burger until now."

"Oh sweetie you are going to be sick," she said while giving me a disgusted look.

"And if you aren't I think I am just from looking at that thing," Mandy stated while making a sour face.

"That doesn't help me" I retorted, and that was about the time that Steve and Tom began to laugh out loud.

"Don't laugh Steve," I said.

"It will be you I am vomiting next to all night if I get food poisoning," as soon as I said that Steve stopped laughing and Tom began laughing even harder.

We all made our way back to the dorms and as soon as Mandy left for home the first wave of sickness hit me, I stood doubled over the small garbage can next to my desk unleashing a barrage of sight, sound, and smell that must have woken any one sleeping on even the third floor.

"Dude you have got to control that" Steve stated,

"Or you are going to have the whole flat blowing chunks before the night is over, I can feel myself getting a little flush right now."

"It's not like I am doing it to annoy you Steve, I can't help or control it" and with that I began round two of the technicolor yawns. This went on all night and into the early morning hours, to this day I still couldn't eat food from Eat a Burger if I tried.

It was about two weeks after my Eat a Burger experience, as I was getting ready to do my morning deliveries at work, when Dan came to me and said, "You have been doing a great job, and so I want to add the bulk deliveries to your route."

The bulk deliveries were actually something that I had been dreading because bulk meant just what it sounded like, the hospital would order two or three pallets of paper at a time and you could usually back up to the dock and unload the pallets onto the dock without much of a problem, but then you had to down stack the entire pallet, about 25-30 cases of paper per pallet, and deliver them with a hand truck to the different departments in the hospital. If you had some help this was not a horrible task, but because we were short handed you rarely had two people to go on these bulk deliveries. Up to this point I had been delivering large items like sawdust to the research center for the lab animals, however delivering a pallet of packaged sawdust was no problem because the wooded pallet that the bags sat on was heavier that all of the sawdust put together. I had also been delivering some pieces of office furniture like, chairs, and filing cabinets, which where challenging but with a hand truck not that difficult, bulk however was a different story all together and it was not what I wanted to do. I had assisted the last bulk driver a number of times with paper, so I knew most of the routes however I was not at all happy about it full time.

"What happened to Solis?" I asked Dan in a frustrated tone. Solis was the large Polynesian guy who had been our bulk delivery driver for the past few months.

"He got some sort of a research grant, and so he quit this morning to go breed rats, or some other crap like that," said Dan as he handed me the paperwork for the bulk deliveries.

"So you are our new bulk driver."

"O" lucky me," I thought to myself as I watched the warehouse workers loading my truck with pallet after pallet of paper. I sat in the cab of my truck staring at the picture of Mandy thinking to myself, "Some day when I am an architect I won't have to put up with these lame jobs, people will respect me for who I am, and I will get paid for what is in my head and not for what I can do physically."

Bang, bang, bang the dock worker smacked the side of my truck, indicating that it was all loaded, the lift was closed, and the door was securely shut, and I could now drive off. I made my way slowly across campus into the medical center and made my first delivery without incidence, however upon inspecting my second stop I noticed that it was in the research park down from the main hospital so I got on the C.B. and called for Dan.

"Hey Dan did you know that I have a delivery for some building in the research park?"

"Yeah so what's the problem?"

"Well, there is no loading dock in the research park is there?" I asked.

"No, so what's the problem?" retorted Dan.

"How am I supposed to unload a pallet of paper when there is no dock to unload it on?"

"You go around to the back side of the building and you pull the pallet onto the lift gate with the pallet jack, then you lower the lift and pull the pallet off onto the side walk, are you following me Mr. honors student?" Asked Dan in a rather degrading tone,

"Yes" I responded.

"Good, then after you have the pallet on the ground you will have to down stack the boxes of paper onto your hand truck and deliver each load one at a time, it's a bitch but that's the only way to do it in the research park."

"Great" I thought to myself that isn't what I wanted to hear. I backed the truck into position and slowly lowered the lift as close to the ground as it would go; I then jumped onto the lift and raised it back up. I climbed into the back of the delivery van and lifted up the heavy pallet of paper with the pallet jack, I carefully pulled the load onto the lift, being cautious not to let it roll too close to the edge, it was a tight fit getting the pallet and the pallet jack onto the lift but with some careful maneuvering I managed to get it situated just right. As I slowly began to lower the lift, I noticed for the first time that I had parked on a bit of a slope causing the passenger side of the truck to be just a little bit lower than the driver's side. As I continued to lower the lift slowly, it reached the half way mark when I felt the pallet starting to teeter towards the passenger side of the lift. That was when I made a huge mistake, instead of just continuing to lower the lift gate slowly, and allowing the rocking pallet of paper to correct itself, I panicked and stopped the lift gate instantly, and to my horror the entire pallet of paper with the pallet jack still attached to the bottom of the load, went spilling sideways over the edge of the lift falling to the ground and exploding with a horrendous crash.

It was like Christmas with huge flakes of snow falling all around me, except instead of snow it was paper. The top layer of paper had hit the ground with such force that the boxes and the reams of paper inside them exploded and now paper was flying everywhere, in the parking lot and on the lawn adjacent to where I was standing. I just stood on the back of the lift gate absolutely dumbfounded and confused as to what had just transpired in front of me. I stood there while the paper slowly floated back to earth, just staring at the enormous mess that had been created in mere seconds and I was absolutely frozen with disbelief. Then from the adjacent buildings I could hear the faint sound of laughter getting louder and louder, it took me a moment to regain my composer but as I began to look around there were people in the buildings surrounding me who had been looking out the window to see what all the commotion had been. Some of the people who were watching out their windows must have seen me standing there with a dumbfounded look on my face, and now they were watching the snow storm of paper engulfing my truck, the parking lot, and the lawn around me, they were pointing, laughing and grabbing other co-workers to show them what had happened. It was at that moment, just as I was thinking to myself, "this day couldn't possibly get any worse," when the automatic sprinklers turned on and all of the paper began to get wet. I remember just standing there thinking to myself, "why hadn't I fallen off the back of the truck with the paper and died," at that moment in time I was so embarrassed that I really wished I were dead, because then at least people would not be laughing at me, and I would not have to call Dan to tell him what happened. After regaining my composer I walked up to the front cab and picked up the C.B.,

"Dan we have a bit of a situation."

CHAPTER 2

Second Thoughts

Later that same evening, after my paper disaster, I was making my way back to the dorms, and as I walked across the parking lot I found myself felling quite disgruntled because I had missed my afternoon classes. I was frustrated because it had taken me somewhere in the neighborhood of three hours to clean up the mess and then deliver a new pallet of paper to the research park. I was also feeling a bit humiliated because of the embarrassment I had endured while explaining to Dan why I was bringing back a truck full of wet, mutilated paper and why I needed to pull another pallet of paper out of stock to finish my deliveries. Needles to say I had experienced better days! I pushed the door to my room open and there on the couch sat a tall, slender, beautiful red headed girl reading a magazine. I stood there for a moment looking around to see if I had walked into the wrong room, but everything from the beds on wooden scaffolding to the jalapeno lights was all looking familiar to me. I was about to say something to the girl sitting on my couch when Steve came up behind me and slapped me on the back, scaring the hell out of me, and as he grabbed my shoulder he shouted, "Here he is Misty, this is Jeremy my room mate."

I had totally forgotten that Steve's sister was coming into town, after we had eaten our victory dinner I spent the rest of that evening and part of the next day getting rid of my victory dinner, I had forgotten all about the conversations that had taken place at the restaurant that evening. Misty stood up and in a very flirtatious way walked across the room, threw her arms around me and said, "Oh Steve you didn't tell me he was so cute."

She gave me a kiss on the cheek.

"Hello I am Misty, Steve's sister." I stood there fumbling for words.

"Ah, I, uh, well, I, ah yes well that is me, I am Steve's mate room, I mean roommate, yes I am he, I mean I am Jeremy, Steve's room mate, mate, person." She gave me an even more flirtatious smile.

"Steve has told me all about you, and I think it's great that you guys are such good mates." She said. Misty then made her way back to the couch, picked up her magazine and continued looking at it. I turned and looked at Steve.

"Steve could I have a word with you, in private?" I asked. I grabbed his arm and briskly pulled him into the hall letting the door close behind us, I paused for a moment before speaking to Steve as I opened the door back up and smiled at Misty,

"We will only be a minute!" I closed the door and turned back towards Steve.

"Steve what are you doing to me? You didn't tell me your sister looked like that! You said she was sort of mousy."

"She's my sister," replied Steve.

"What did you want me to tell you? Steve paused for a moment.

"She is mousy, didn't you see her?"

"Ah, yes Steve, I saw her and if you think that is mousy you need to lower your standards a bit because your sister isn't mousy." I said.

"And what are you trying to do to me anyway? What do you think Mandy is going to think when she sees your sister here in our room? First she is going to kill you for letting your sister into our room, and then she is going to kill me for being in our room with your sister, Steve your sister is hot!"

"Hey that is my sister you're talking about there, don't talk like that, or I'll have to punch your face," grumbled Steve.

"Ok we have to think about this, what are we going to do? We have to get her out of here somehow and over to Mandy's cousins place."

"I don't know where her cousin lives, do you?" Asked Steve.

"Mandy has not told us where her cousin lives yet, unless she told you and not me," said Steve.

"Besides she is "*my*" sister, I think it will be ok if she is here for a while." Steve paused to think for a moment.

"I have an idea why don't you go get changed into something a little less…stinky and blue collar," said Steve as he held his nose.

"You look like hell and smell like…wet dog or something. We will grab Tom and go get a bite to eat just the four of us, and it will give you guys a chance to get to know Misty better."

Steve finished talking and immediate went back into the room, closing the door behind himself and leaving me standing in the hall trying to put the pieces of this horrible yet unexpectedly pleasant day back together. I did, but at the same time I did not want to get to know Misty better, those first few seconds I had already spent with her left quite the impression on me, although it was not the kind of impression I wanted to have while Mandy was around.

I found myself sitting across from Misty at a small booth in one of the local restaurant/dives that Steve, Tom and I frequented quite often, feeling very uncomfortable with the way she was smiling at me. I was feeling uncomfortable because Misty was so attractive and I actually caught myself staring into her deep brown eyes. As soon as I realized that I was staring at Misty I tried to shake it off by looking at something else, however, when I looked back towards her I found that she was staring right back at me making it even more uncomfortable. If I was not instantly attracted to her, or if Misty was not such a strikingly beautiful girl I probably would not have thought much about this uncomfortable situation.

There I sat however watching Misty drink her soda slowly from her straw while her dark red lipstick left a slight ring on the tip. For some reason watching Misty drink so seductively left me feeling like a little boy standing in front of the candy counter at the local convenience store. Tom had declined our dinner offer claiming that he had some sort of project due in one of his art classes. Tom explained to us that he had not understood what his art professor was asking for, so instead of a collage made out of things he was interested in, he had cut up twigs and leaves and glued them to construction paper, creating some sort of creepy modern art, collage, thing, and his professor was giving him until the morning to re-do the assignment or take an "F" on the project, for not following instructions.

Steve had excused himself to go to the restroom and so it was just Misty and myself sitting at the table carrying on a very uncomfortable conversation about me, and what I was studying, and where I was from, and what kinds of food I liked. I kept trying to change the subject to other things like Mandy, my girlfriend, but Misty would just change the subject back to me as quickly as I could changed it to some other topic. It was just about the time that Misty started eating her fries slowly and looking deeply into my eyes in such a way that it was making me feel quite warm and a little bit uncomfortable, that I started to feel myself slipping and I was once again getting lost in her eyes. I was beginning to feel that connection that exists between two people when they both come to the realization that they like each other, when I looked across the room and saw Mandy walking towards our table. My heart drooped right into the pit of my stomach and I sprang up from my seat and yelled across the room,

"Mandy, hi, this is Misty, Steve's twin sister, we are eating dinner here, but not together, Steve is in the bathroom doing bathroom stuff and he will be right back out here to join us, here for dinner."

"Sit down and shut up," said Mandy, as she motioned for me to sit back down.

"Misty and I have already met, and in fact I picked her up from the airport earlier this afternoon. We went to lunch and then we went shopping, it was a fun girls day out don't you think?"

"Oh yes it was a lot of fun and I really love your car," said Misty.

"I like having control over things with that kind of power, it is quite exhila-rating."

"You let her drive your car?" I asked.

"Of course I did, Misty is a wonderful driver, and we had a great time, didn't we Misty," said Mandy as she winked at Misty.

"Oh yes it was a very nice introduction to America if you ask me" stated Misty.

I sat back in my seat not quite sure what to make of this strange and rather unexpected turn of events. Not only was Mandy not upset about Misty and me eating dinner together, but also she did not seem to be the least bit threatened by Misty and the fact that she was a very attractive girl. To my surprise Mandy was treating Misty like she was a long lost friend whom she was finally getting together with after having been separated for some time. I sat there in a state of stupor trying to make sense of things when Steve came walking back and sat down.

"Oh Mandy I'm glad you made it, I was not sure if you got my message."

As Steve continued talking to Mandy about how he was unsure if he had called the right number or not, it dawned on me that I did not know how Mandy knew we were all going out to eat, and it did seem to be a bit more than just coincidence that she should walk in just as we were being served.

"I almost didn't make it, I had a bit of trouble talking my boss into letting me go early, but after I explained the situation to him he told me to go ahead and have a good time with my friends, besides you don't think I would leave

Jeremy here alone with such a cute girl," everyone at the table, but me, began to laugh.

"What was that suppose to mean?" I thought to myself.

"I can be trusted around other girls."

The truth was I had been caught, even though Mandy did not know how I was feeling inside, I knew what I was feeling, so when Mandy made that seemingly innocent comment I instantly became defensive, because, it is after all human nature to get defensive when we get caught doing things we didn't think others knew about.

That evening, after dinner Mandy took Misty over to her cousins' apartment while Steve and I made our way back to the dorms. When we entered the main lobby I could hear the piano being played once again just as I had heard it a few weeks previous.

"Who is playing the piano?" I asked Steve

"Dun-no," replied Steve.

"It might be a visitor, there are people coming and going all the time for summer band camps, and concerts."

"No I heard her playing the piano a few weeks ago, she isn't a visitor." I said.

"Well," said Steve.

"I will ask around if you are really interested."

"No," I replied, "It's no big deal, I was just curious."

"She is good," added Steve.

The next week proved to be rather interesting because as much as I wanted to spend time with Steve and more especially Misty, I really did try to avoid them because of the insane and instant attraction I had felt towards Misty. I did not want anyone, especially Misty, thinking there was anything between us. I had managed all week long to keep things quick and polite while still keeping my distance, Tom on the other hand wanted to spend every moment with the two of them, it got to be almost comical watching him follow Misty around offering to get her water, or a snack, or pretty much anything she wanted. It wasn't until the next to last day before Misty was suppose to fly back to Australia that I had an interesting encounter with her.

I had finished up at work, gone to all of my classes, and I even spent an extra hour and half at the library thinking this would give everyone time to get home for the day and begin their evening activities, so when I arrived back at my room around 8:00 p.m. I was quite surprised to see the lights coming out from around the cracks in my door. I put my key in the door, turned the knob and began to open the door when I noticed a note taped to the front of the door and it said something to this extent:

"Jeremy I will be in my art class until later tonight, and then some of the guys from my class and I are going out for a while, I will be back later this evening. P.S. if I am not back by 8:30 will you please take Misty back to the apartment, she is spending the day with Mandy and I was planning on taking her to dinner but my plans have changed. P.P.S. will you take her to dinner if she has not eaten, you are a real pal, and I will pay you back for what ever you spend on dinner," signed Steve.

I felt my stomach doing summersaults as I pushed the door open, I remember thinking to myself, "please don't be here, please don't be,"

"Good evening Jeremy." there was Misty sitting on the couch watching TV,

"I thought you would never get here, I am starving."

"O crap," I thought to myself.

"Misty how long have you been here?" I asked.

"Well Mandy and I had a nice lunch and then she took me to Crossroads Mall, where we watched a movie, and then went shopping, I told her I was having dinner with Steve and so she dropped me off here, but it looks like Steve won't be joining me for dinner so it will just be the two of us."

She smiled at me and turned her head slightly to the side while she stood twisting her long red hair with two of her fingers. Up until the time I met Misty, I had never had an instant attraction to anyone before, in fact aside from Misty there has only ever been one other person whom I have been instantly attracted to. Most of the relationships I have had in my life were with friends, or people that I had known for a while through other acquaintances, but I am getting ahead of myself. Misty stood there looking very attractive in a long red dress that accentuated her red hair and amplified her curved features very well, in contrast, there I stood in a dirty t-shirt and old pair of jeans, unshaven, un-showered, looking and feeling like a mess.

"Why don't you change into something a little nicer and I will wait in the lobby for you," said Misty, as she headed towards the door.

"I honestly thought I would be going to dinner with my brother, but you will be a pleasant replacement for Steve." She gave me a small kiss on the cheek and slipped quietly out of the room.

"Don't keep me waiting; we have reservations for 9:00." I could hear her say as she disappeared down the hall.

Panic began to take over as I stood there dumbfounded, and in shock, what was I going to do, I could not spend an evening alone with Misty, I had a huge crush on her and would undoubtedly make a total jack ass out of myself. I also had a girlfriend whom I loved and did not want to risk ruining our relationship over one small dinner with another girl who I had just met, and was going back to Australia in two days.

"I will call Tom, and ask him to take her," I thought to myself as I picked up the phone and dialed Tom's room.

"Come on, come on, pick up, PICK UP DAMN IT," I yelled into the phone as it rang for the fifth time and Tom's answering machine began to start talking. I soon realized that there was nothing I could do, so I started to change into something nicer and as I did I thought to myself,

"I will make this as short as I can, we will go to dinner and then I will tell Misty that I have an early class tomorrow and that I need to get back early. No one would need to know about this dinner date."

I paused for a moment and then said to myself,

"Wait, this was not even a date, I am just helping a buddy out be taking his sister to dinner, and after all she had to eat right."

And then I made one of those statements that would go down in history as a huge mistake like, "Great day for a car ride," by JFK, or one of my all time favorites

"How many Indians could there possibly be?" by general Custard. I said to myself,

"What could go wrong this is only a quick dinner and then we come right back home?"

After making a quick attempt to make myself as presentable as possible I made my way into the lobby where Misty was standing and chatting with another girl in the hall, "so now I am going to dinner with his hot room mate."

I heard Misty say to the girl she was talking to as I came up behind her. I cleared my throat a bit louder than was necessary so that Misty knew I was standing behind her.

"Are you ready to go?" I asked.

"Of coarse," Misty replied as she threw her arms around my shoulders and nibbled on my ear ever so slightly.

"I have been ready for two weeks," she exclaimed happily.

If I was standing in pot being boiled alive I don't think my face could have been any redder than it was at that moment, I was embarrassed, thrilled, mortified, and turned on all at the same time.

"You have some lipstick on your neck just above the collar love, let me help you get it off," said Misty as she pulled a white silk handkerchief out of her hand bag, licked the tip of it and leaned over to wipe the lipstick off of my neck. The lipstick was on my neck because she had put it there with a small kiss when she leaned over to help me with my seat belt just a few moments before.

"Love, you feel awfully warm, are you feeling alright?" Asked Misty.

"I'm fine," I said as my voiced cracked, I quickly cleared my throat, and tried talking to her again.

"I'm fine, why do you ask?"

"No reason, you have just turned the car off and on three times now and we are still sitting in the parking lot."

"Well I just wanted to make sure that the starter was working correctly, I have been having problems with it, and I don't even know where we are going." I felt like such and idiot, but I could hardly talk or pull two thoughts into one rational sentence I was so nervous.

"Well love we are going to the Roof Restaurant, have you heard of it?" She asked.

"Yes," I replied.

"Do you know where it is?"

"Yes," I blurted out.

"I know of it, and I know where it is."

The Roof Restaurant was one of the most expensive restaurants in Salt Lake, it was a very high-end restaurant and buffet where there were items like crab, and shrimp, not the little kind that you get at most restaurants but the big jumbo crab, and the shrimp tails are to die for, they had ribs, and steaks, and every kind of exotic meat you could think of, they had quail eggs, and fruit from around the world. I had never been there myself with the $25.00 a person price tag it was well out of my league. $25.00 a person may not seem like much today, but in those days when I was only making about $5.75 an hour that was a lot of money. I recall thinking to myself on the way to the restaurant,

"I will have to write a bad check to pay for dinner because I don't have $50.00 to my name," and then it dawned on me, I didn't have my checkbook with me.

I was deep in thought, contemplating going to jail for running out on a dinner check when Misty pulled me back into reality. "Sweet heart you look very nice this evening, and I must say that your girl Mandy is a very lucky lady."

"Thank you," I replied.

"She is a great girl, my girlfriend, Mandy, who is in fact my *girlfriend,* and we are dating and that makes her in fact my girlfriend." It was overkill but I wanted to make my point.

"You know I have a boyfriend back in Australia, his name is Jim, and he is a great guy." I could feel myself relaxing as though a huge weight had been lifted off my shoulders.

"Oh I did know you had a boyfriend, why didn't you say something sooner?" I asked.

"Because we broke up the other night over the phone, it seems he does not trust me here in America, he thinks I am going out with other guys and even though I told him to trust me he said he couldn't. I feel that a guy who doesn't trust me is not who I want to be with, so I told him we were finished."

All the weight that had been lifted off my shoulders only moments before felt as though it had not only been thrown back on, but it had also been doubled. I felt like Hercules holding the entire world by myself. "Well I am sorry to hear that," I said.

"Oh don't be," said Misty.

"Things have not been that great between us for quite some time, and this was just the excuse I needed to break up with him."

She then put her hand on my knee and looked at me with her deep brown eyes and a big smile on her face.

"How are things between you and Mandy?" She asked.

I don't remember much about the conversation after that point, however we soon found ourselves standing in the lobby of the Roof Restaurant waiting to be seated. Misty had her arm wrapped firmly around my arm, she had a death grip on my hand and she was resting her head slightly on my shoulder, I had been so uncomfortable up to this point, but the longer we stood in the lobby waiting to be seated the more I found myself getting comfortable and letting my guard down. Just as I was beginning to enjoy having Misty hold me so tightly, "*flash*" the hostess standing by the front desk of the restaurant had taken our picture. "You two are such a cute couple, I love to take pictures of young newly weds, you two have a sweet magic between you, the way she is holding on to you just makes my heart melt."

"*We are not married*," I yelled, just loud enough that everyone around us stopped talking and turned to stare at the idiot who had just shouted something.

"Not yet," said Misty in a playful tone, she then pinched my hand hard enough to say,

"Shut-up before you embarrass both of us," and then she gave the hostess a small wink, and the hostess winked back.

"Oh I see, well it just takes some men longer than others to ask the question, just be patient honey and he will come around."

I felt like I was in an episode of the twilight zone, I was thinking to myself, "what the hell had just happened to me?" I was standing there with the deer in the headlights look when the hostess smiled at us and said, "I have the perfect table for the two of you, if will you just follow me, I will show you to your seats."

We made our way past all of people in tuxedos and three piece suits, I then came to a realization that I had not shaved in a few days, and my suit was a bit wrinkled from being shoved into my closet for the last month, and when I sat down I noticed that my dress socks did not even match. Once we were seated I began to look around and I took notice of where we were in the room, it was right in the middle of everyone, but also next to the huge wall height windows.

"Let me open the curtains so that you two can enjoy the view," said the hostess.

We were sitting right next one of the windows that over looked the entire Salt Lake City skyline. Since it was nighttime the full moon seemed to fill the entire window with its glowing soft light, and it really was quite a site to see as it took my breath away for just a moment.

"Now isn't that just romantic," said the hostess as she lit the candle on our table and looked over to the piano on the stage while motioning for the pianist to start playing something soft and romantic.

It was at that moment that I looked across the table at Misty and something inside me stirred, she looked absolutely beautiful with her scarlet red hair all curled up to shoulder length, the moon light was hitting her face and reflecting a small sparkle in her deep brown eyes, I could feel my will power slowly sinking into my stomach.

"You look very neat, *nice*, you look very nice, and lovely this evening Misty," I was stumbling over my words again, how was I suppose to get through this evening when every time I opened my mouth I sounded like a total idiot.

"Thank you Jeremy, you are looking very, neat yourself, I really like the unshaven look, it makes you look older, and more sophisticated." I found myself lost in her eyes, and I was staring at her like a puppy begging for table scraps.

"Excuse me but may I take your order sir?" Asked the waiter for the third time.

"Oh yes I will have whatever she is having," I said in an embarrassed tone.

"Sir, the lady has not ordered yet," but may I suggest the buffet, it is our main attraction, however if you would like to order something off of our menu, I would be happy to bring it to you."

"The buffet is fine," I stated, and so he motioned for us to go and prepared our plates.

I was standing next to the shrimp platter filling my plate to capacity, because if I was going to prison for not paying the bill I might as well be going to the slammer with a full stomach, when I happened to look over at the people coming in and out of the main entrance and I saw none other than Jason my old high school friend. I tried to escape his glance but it was too late we had locked eyes, "Jeremy" Jason shouted from across the room.

"How have you been, you disappeared after that party and hey I am sorry about your date she did turn out to be quite the pot smoking hippie didn't she?"

"Ah, yea she was," it was all I could come up with to say in response to Jason's comment.

"So I heard you and Mandy have been dating for a while now, how is she doing?" Asked Jason.

"She is fine, doing just fine," I responded, and of course at that very moment Misty walked by.

"Jeremy, aren't you going to introduce me to your friend?" I was absolutely mortified, what was I going to say?

"Ah Jason this is Misty, my roommates sister, I agreed to take her to dinner for my roommate, as a favor, and as you can see she is drop dead gorgeous, but there is nothing going on between us." No.

"She is just a friend whom I am taking out as a favor to someone."

"A favor," Jason said as he laughed out loud.

"What a good friend you are, did this cost your room mate twenty bucks or are you doing this one for free?"

I could not believe I was having this conversation with Jason, could his timing have been any worse, I looked over at Misty as she looked back towards Jason and I with an amused look on her face.

"I am just kidding Jeremy," Jason retorted.

"You will have to excuse Jeremy but he and I go way back and if he isn't going to finish the introductions I will, this is my fiancé Brooke." Jason held her hand and engagement ring up for both of us to see

"And Brooke this must be Jeremy's roommate's sister, and if Jeremy is only taking her to dinner as a favor to his roommate he is a bigger idiot than I thought!"

With that Misty smiled at all of us and said to Brooke,

"Why don't you guys join us for dinner?"

"Oh we were just on our way out, but you have Jeremy call us, we will get together and go out on a double date some time." Misty then excused herself and headed back to our table.

"Jeremy she is beautiful, what are you thinking?" Asked Jason.

"Well Jason, Mandy and I."

"Mandy nothing," interrupted Jason,

"What's with the "I'm taking her out for my roommate," crap, when did you dump Mandy and where did you find her, her accent it something else."

"I am telling you the truth," I replied as I tired to explain the situation to Jason.

"She is my roommates' sister and she is visiting from Australia for a couple of weeks, Steve was supposed to take her to dinner tonight but he couldn't make it." I looked at Jason and could tell he was about to say something else so I tried to change the subject.

"So when did you and Brooke get engaged?" Jason looked at me for a second.

"Like three weeks ago but look, don't change the subject I want to know details." To my relief Brooke interrupted us and took Jason by the arm.

"You two boys can chat about this later, I am ready to go." She said.

"Jason we have tickets to the symphony and I don't want to be late." Jason's mom had played with the Salt Lake Symphony when we were younger so I knew how much Jason hated going to the symphony, and armed with this knowledge I took advantage of the situation.

"Yes Jason you don't want to be late for the symphony or your mom will kill you." I smiled because I knew the conversation was over now.

"By the way say hello to your mom for me," I gave them a little wave of my hand, and then turned and made my way to our table.

"They seem like a cute couple," said Misty.

"Oh yes they are old friends of mine."

"Too bad they were on their way out," said Misty.

"They seem like they would have been good company." On one hand I would have liked to talk to Jason a bit, I had not seen him in for a while, and I was excited to hear that he and Brooke were engaged but on the other hand this was not the right time to be running into old friends, especially ones that knew Mandy.

"Yes they are a fun couple," I said as I started shoveling food into my mouth so that I would not have to talk about them any longer. What was going on this evening? Every time I started to feel a little bit comfortable something or some-one had to put me right back on edge. I was only trying to help Steve and I was doing my best not to give any mixed messages to Misty, she was very lovely, but she was not my girlfriend, and things were going so well with Mandy that I absolutely did not want to mess anything up with her. As we started eating I could feel myself beginning to relax a bit, the view out the window was spec-tacular and the soft sound of the piano playing in the background was very soothing, I was almost comfortable when Misty looked at me with those big brown eyes of hers.

"Jeremy why have you been avoiding me the last two weeks, I have been try-ing to get to know you better but it feels like you are trying to avoid me, please tell me why," she paused for a moment,

"Am I not attractive to you?" I almost choked on the piece of shrimp in my mouth,

"No I think you are very attractive," I said as I took a drink to stop choking,

"In fact I think you are so attractive that I feel intimidated to be around you."

"You are just saying that," said Misty.

"I know you have a girlfriend but sometimes people get comfortable in a relationship and are afraid to look at what's around them, you know, shop the market a bit. What if Mandy isn't the one for you? What if there is someone else out there but you are too afraid to look outside of your comfort zone? True love could be looking you right in the face and you wouldn't even know it because you were too busy trying to avoid it. Look Jeremy I only have two more days here in America and then I am going back home to make the biggest decision of my life, am I coming back to Utah to go to school or am I staying in Australia for what will probably be the rest of my life! If I stay here I want to know that it is for the right reasons, and I want to make sure that I am making the right choice, do you follow what I am trying to saying to you?"

Now I felt really torn, I had never in my life had a girl throw herself at me, and I had never seen a girl get to the point so quickly before, as I have stated before, all of my relationships had been with girls I had known for a while, and our relationships slowly evolved from friendship to dating. I found myself sit-ting there wondering if Misty was right, was I hiding behind my comfort zone?

Was there someone out there sitting right in front of me symbolically, or literally whom I was meant to be with? I had all of these questions swimming around my head when Misty took a hold of my hand and said, "Jeremy I am not the kind of girl who comes on to guys like this, really I am not but I have never had an instant attraction to a guy before, you are my first. I am leaving in two days and that means I have to force a years worth of courting into one night, I really think I love you." Misty leaned over the table slowly, put her hands on my cheeks, and kissed me very tenderly.

"Please think about it before you tell me, or Mandy, or Steve or anyone else anything about this." I don't know how long I sat there looking dumbfounded and with a complete and utter loss for words, but after what must have felt like a life time to me and to Misty I looked back up at her.

"Let's get out of here shall we?" I then motioned for the waiter to bring us the check and that was when the reality of having no money once again took hold of me.

"Misty you may want to head towards the car while I pay for our meal."

"Non sense my parents sent me with money to take Steve out to a nice restaurant in their behalf, and he stood me up so it is his loss." She then took the check and slipped the money into the billfold.

"Are you ready to go?" She asked, as she once again took my hand.

"*Yes*," I blurted out; thankful that I would not have to go to jail that evening, because there was no way I could have paid that bill.

We made our way back to the car the same way we had made our way into the restaurant, with Misty's arm wrapped tightly around mine with a death grip on my hands. I was feeling so mixed up inside, I can't imagine displaying the kind of fortitude she had just shown by telling me the things she had told me back in the restaurant. It also left me feeling a certain amount of doubt about my relationship with Mandy; it also left me doubting myself as to whether I was doing anything right. Was I hiding behind my inadequacies? I was dating Mandy because she wanted to see if I was the one, did I owe her any loyalty? Was I obligated to keep the relationship going? Did I even love her? With all of this swimming around in my head Misty and I made our way back to the dorms.

"Please don't drop me off yet, let's go for a walk or something," said Misty as we pulled into the parking lot. I agreed and we got out of the car and began to make our way towards the center of campus.

"I can't imagine what you must be thinking right now?" exclaimed Misty.

"Here is this crazy Aussie, whom you have only just met, clinging onto your arm and confessing her undying love for you. You must think that I am a total loon!"

"No not at all" I responded.

"I think it must have been very difficult for you to say what you did, and I admire your convictions."

We made our way to the large fountain in front of the library, and sat down on its majestic stone ledge, while enjoying the summer air, and the sound of the water crashing down from the falls.

"If you tell me you don't love me, I will understand and don't worry I have not said a word to Steve about my feelings for you. It would be nice to have you in the family, you could finish school here and I will move out to finish my schooling here, then we could both go back to Australia when we have graduated, you would love Australia there is so much to do and see."

I was so consumed by the sound of Misty's voice and so confused as to what had taken place that evening that I had failed to notice the rain clouds forming above us. It was not until the lightening began lighting up the night sky and the thunder came crashing down around us that I even noticed the stormy weather. It began to rain very hard as we ran back to the dorm rooms, hand in hand, and when we made it safely back to my room I was quit surprised to find that Steve had not returned from his evening's escapades. I got a towel of my closet for Misty, and while she stood in the middle of the room trying to dry her soaked hair I found an old pair of Steve's sweats in his closet and put them on the couch for Misty to change into. I found myself some dry clothes and went into the large community bathroom to change. I made my way back to the room after getting out of my wet clothes to find Misty sitting on the couch waiting for me.

"I should really get you back to the apartment," I said to Misty.

"Why? It's only 10:30 and I am not ready to go yet, come and sit over here and let's finish our conversation." I went reluctantly and sat by Misty, the evening was such a blur to me, had it really happened, or was I just dreaming? This whole thing was just too much to take in; I was sitting there alone with my roommate's sister wanting to be there but not wanting to be there at the same time. My head was spinning a hundred miles an hour, and I was feeling unsure as to what I should do. Here I had the perfect opportunity to be with someone who loved me, but someone that I barely knew. She was willing to come to America and leave her life behind to be with me, but at the same time I was already feeling guilty for what had happened that evening, I did love Mandy and I could not betray our relationship like this.

"Misty you are a very beautiful girl" I started to say.

"But my heart belongs to someone else, and I just don't feel like I am ready to give up what I have with her." Misty looked up at me and with a timid smile.

"I understand, I suppose she is really lucky to have a guy like you, it was silly of me to think that I could change your mind in such a short time." Misty looked away from me.

"Please don't push me out of your life before you have even had a chance to get to know me, I am going home soon but if you say the word I will come back to visit you again."

When Misty had finished talking she leaned over very, very close to me and slowly put her arms around me, she then closed her eyes she gave me a kiss that made me feel weak in the knees, I could feel her small frame begin to shake, I was not sure if it was because she was cold, or if it was because she was crying. I could feel what I thought was a teardrop, or perhaps it was a water droplet that had fallen from Misty's wet hair, running down her face and slowly transition to my mine, it then ran down my chin and fall softly into my lap.

I took Misty back to the apartment where she had been staying but instead of going home I drove around the city for two or three hours thinking about all that had taken place that evening. When I returned to the dorm I found Steve and a few of his art class buddies playing cards in the lobby.

"Did you take Misty to dinner for me mate, and did you get her back to the apartment in good time?" Asked Steve,

"Yes," I said not even stopping to say hi as I walked toward the room.

"You are a good friend, and I owe you big time," said Steve with a smile. I walked into the room and saw the flashing red light on the answering machine, so I made my way over to it and pushed the "play messages" button.

"Jeremy, hi, this is Mandy, I was just calling to see how your evening at the library went, it must be some test you are studying for, it is 11:00 p.m. and I have not heard from you yet, give me a call when you get back, I love you, Bye."

I felt horrible as I stood there listening to the message over and over again; "I love you" was ringing in my ears, as I made my way up to my bed. I lay there for quite some time milling what had happened over and over in my mind.

I must have fallen asleep, but I did not remember going to asleep, I did not even remember Steve coming in and going to bed, but he must have because he was lying in his bed snoring away. I rolled over, climbed out of bed and that was when I noticed Misty's red dress that she had been wearing just hours before, still sitting on my desk where she had laid it out to dry, I walked over to the dress and while picking it up, I noticed that it was still damp. As I stood there trying to fully wake up, the damp dress in my hands confirmed that the previous night had not been a dream, and it had really taken place as I was remembering it, I was still so confused and not sure what I was feeling when the telephone started to ring. I quickly ran over and picked it up half hoping it was Misty but wanting it to be Mandy, "Good morning sunshine, I have missed you so much," it was Mandy's voice at the other end of the phone.

"Why didn't you call last night when you got home?" She inquired.

"I got home really late," I started to explain in a groggy voice.

"Me and some of the guys went out after I got back from studying and by the time I made it home it was like one in the morning." I was lying and I felt bad for doing it but I could not tell Mandy what had taken place the previous evening.

"Well I suppose that's alright but I was a bit worried about you," said Mandy,

"You know I think Misty has a thing for you and even though I like her a lot it had me just a bit worried last night. Misty and Steve were suppose to go to dinner last night, but when I tried to call you around ten o'clock, I was very surprised when Steve answered the phone. He said that he had not seen you all evening, but that he had just gotten back from a study group so you may have come and gone without him knowing, when I asked Steve how his dinner date went with Misty, he told me that you had taken her for him."

"Damn," I thought to myself, she knew more than I thought she had.

"Oh, well yes, I took her to dinner with Jason and Brooke; you remember them from High school right? Well funny thing they are engaged and so we went to celebrate."

"What was I doing?" I thought to myself, lying isn't going to help; I am just digging myself into a bigger hole.

"I remember Jason alright," said Mandy with a concerned tone.

"I don't want to be one of those girlfriends who is always telling their boyfriend what to do, but I don't really like you hanging out with Jason, Brooke is alright, but Jason has friends who do drugs and I don't really like you associating with them, but I am glad you had a good time." Said Mandy as she changed her tone from concern to happy.

"I would like to go to dinner with you tonight, since Misty has been in town I have felt like we have not seen much of each other, and I really miss you, so how does seven sound?" She asked.

"Sounds great," I replied

"Good then I will pick you up at seven."

I hung up the phone and turned around to see Steve standing behind me in his boxer shorts, looking at me in a state of bewilderment, "Isn't that my sisters dress you are holding in your hands?" Asked Steve.

"Yes.'

"Why does it look all wet?" Asked Steve.

I then began to explain "most" of the details from the pervious night, strategically leaving out the fine points that would have gotten me a black eye from Steve.

"Well," said Steve, as he began rummaging around the room for some clean clothes.

"What are you going to do? He asked.

"It sounds like you have a real dilemma on your hands, I mean on one hand I really like Mandy, and think you too make a nice couple, but on the other hand I don't want my sisters feelings to get hurt, if you know what I mean."

"Yes Steve, I know what you mean," I retorted.

"But on the other hand you would make an awesome brother in law," Steve said as he began to laugh.

"You would love Australia, there is so much,"

"To see and do, yes, I have heard that before, from your sister," I said, interrupting Steve in mid sentence.

"This is serious Steve, what am I going to do? You know how much Mandy means to me, and your sister is, well she is something else."

"Yes I know," he paused for a moment and then pointed to me while smiling.

"Brother," said Steve.

"That is not funny, I am trying to be serious here Steve, I have a real dilemma on my hands."

"Well why don't you start by putting my sister's dress down, because that is starting to creep me out, and then let's go get some breakfast while we talk about this whole thing, brother."

"*Stop it*," I yelled,

"That is so *not funny*."

Steve and I went to breakfast to talk about my "situation," and after talking to Steve I felt a little bit better about things. Steve was very understanding about the situation, he informed me that I was not the first person whom Misty had confessed her undying love too, however I was the first guy that she had confessed it to so early in a relationship. I told Steve that I felt like Mandy and I had such a good thing going right now that I could not give it up, at least not right now, it was very possible that Mandy was the one and I just had to see this thing through. Steve said that he would talk to Misty and smooth the whole thing out, and in the mean time he would keep quiet around Mandy and not tell her anything about this.

That evening just before seven o'clock, I looked out the window and saw Mandy's sitting in her car waiting for me in front of the building; I turned out the lights and headed out towards her car. "Good evening," I said as I got into her car.

"How was your day?"

"Fine," said Mandy.

"I thought we could go to the Olive Garden tonight, I have not been there in a while and it sounds good."

She went on telling me about her day, but I was still so wrapped up in what had taken place the night before that most of the conversation was just washing right over the top of my head, until Mandy said,

"I am taking Misty to the airport tomorrow and I was wondering if you wanted to go with us?" That was not a good idea by any means, in fact I was a bit apprehensive about letting Mandy take Misty to the airport at all, but if I was to say anything it might arouse her suspicions.

"I have to begin my study group for finals tomorrow, and so I am afraid I won't be able to make it," I said rather matter-of-factly.

"Really," said Mandy.

"Well that's too bad because Misty is such a cute girl, and I really think she likes you."

"Wouldn't that bother you to know if she did like me?" I asked.

"I mean wouldn't that make you jealous?"

"No, not really," replied Mandy,

"I love you and I trust you completely, I think our relationship is strong enough that you can be around a pretty girl without going crazy, and doing something stupid."

At that point I was not sure if I should feel guilty for what had taken place the night before or if I should feel good that she trusted me so much.

"So, what if a pretty girl was to make a pass at me?" I asked, trying to see what her reaction would be.

"Would you still trust me?"

"Of coarse I would," she said, as she looked at me and smiled.

"I know I can trust you, because if our relationship was not built on trust, then it wouldn't be worth having."

I could not tell if she knew something, or was genuinely so trusting, but I still found myself feeling guilty for enjoying parts of the previous evening. As we sat down at our table in the restaurant, I looked over at Mandy, who was busy searching through her day planner for an appointment she thought she had forgotten, and I realized that I had not made a wrong choice; Mandy and I were meant to be! I reached across the table and took Mandy's hand, "Mandy," I started to say as she looked away from her day planner and up towards me,

"I love you."

"I know you do." She said. I squeezed her hand just a bit tighter and said, "No Mandy, I mean I really love you." Mandy looked me in the eyes.

"Are you feeling ok?" She asked.

"Yes I am feeling fine," I replied.

"I just want you to know that I think things are going really well between us, and I am very happy that we decided to start dating. There is something to be said for couples that start out as friends long before they begin to date. They have time to get to know each other, and I am very glad that I have gotten to know you. This summer has been really wonderful and I think," I paused, because neither one of us had said anything like what I was about to say.

"I think you are the one, and I think that we were meant to be." Mandy looked at me and I could see tears starting to fill up in her eyes.

"Jeremy, please don't say that." I sat back feeling a little bit surprised by her response, but she continued to say.

"It is very flattering to hear you say that, but I still need more time." Mandy wiped the tears from her eyes.

"I really like you too, and this summer has been one of the best summers of my life, but I am not ready to make such a powerful statement, and such a big commitment, not yet." She said.

I was a bit confused because this was definitely not the response I was thinking I would get. I actually thought Mandy would agree with me, so now I was very confused because of the mixed message I was receiving. We finished our dinner without saying much, and it was not until we had gotten back into the car, and were heading to the dorms that I dared say anything, "Is everything ok?" I asked.

"Yes everything is fine," said Mandy, as she put her hand on my leg.

"Don't worry about what I said, it doesn't mean that I don't love you, it just means that I am enjoying this stage of our relationship and I don't want to rush anything."

"Ok," I exclaimed in a confused tone. I could sense that something was wrong, but I could not put my finger on it. She was obviously not going to tell me, so I just let the whole thing go.

Misty returned to Australia the next day and things quickly went back to normal. I found myself once again engulfed in schoolwork. I had struggled so much with my midterms that I felt I had to study extra hard for my final exams. It was back to ancient China, railroad tycoons, and the economy of the United States during the great depression. Steve, as well as many of my other fellow Honor students, had already spent countless hours, and countless evenings studying for the final exams that loomed over our heads like German warplanes. I did not have a moment to call my own, with work and school eating up so much of my day, and my study group eating up my evenings.

It wasn't until late Saturday evening that I realized I had not talked to Mandy in almost a week. I decided to call her up in-between one of my study groups in an attempt to get caught up with her, and to see how things were going. Our trip to Jackson Hole, Wyoming was quickly approaching and I wanted to finalize the details with Mandy before the time came to leave.

"I have a final exam on Tuesday and one on Thursday of this week, and my last exam will be on the following Wednesday," I said as we tried to organize our schedules.

"We will be leaving on the Friday after my last final, so we need to get together some time before then to discuss our trip." I said.

"My schedule is pretty full," replied Mandy.

"So why don't you just get things figured out with Tiffany and Daryl, and then give me a call next week to let me know what we are doing." Mandy sounded a million miles away as we spoke.

"Are you ok?" I asked.

"You don't sound like your usual self this evening." Mandy did not answer.

"I know, I have been super busy the last couple of weeks, but I am almost done with my final exams and then I promise we will spend some quality time together." Mandy sighed.

"It isn't you, it's just that some things have come up that have kept me a bit preoccupied lately."

"Well is there something you want to talk about?" I asked in a concerned tone.

"Because if there is something you want to talk about, I will ditch my next study group," I said.

"You are more important to me than a bunch of college nerds any day."

"No, no, don't skip your study group." Said Mandy.

"I will be fine, I just have a few things I am trying to work through right now. I think some alone time will be better for me any way," said Mandy, in an odd sort of melancholy tone.

"Ok," I replied.

"But you call me if you need anything."

We ended our phone conversation and it left me wondering what was going on. Why was she acting so strange? It was not like her to give me the cold shoulder. I thought the whole Misty thing had blown over, I was sure she could not be upset about that. Besides we had that entire conversation about "trust," and I thought she made it clear that everything was good between us. I went back to my study group and figured that Mandy's problems must be work related. Perhaps her boss was not following through on the promises he had made to her about the raise, and cutting back on her travel time. At any rate, I was so involved with my studies that I soon forgot all about the strange conversation, and I continued preparing for my finals.

Although I was apprehensive about taking my final exams, I felt that since I had done such a thorough job studying, and because I had done well on my midterms, I had gained some self-confidence. So I went into each of my final exams feeling relatively confident that I would do a good job.

The next week flew by, and before I knew it my first quarter of college was over. The night before our trip to Jackson I was finishing up some last minute travel plans over the phone with Tiffany, when Steve came into the room to tell me that Mandy was outside in the lobby, and she needed to see me. I finished up my conversation with Tiffany and promptly headed out to the lobby, as I got closer to where Mandy was standing, I thought I could see her wiping tears away from her eyes, "What's wrong sweetheart?" I asked.

"Nothing," said Mandy as she took a tissue from her purse and whipped her red eyes.

"How were your final exams?" Inquired Mandy.

"Well I think they went really good, but I won't know for at least a week or two what my final scores were," I said.

"I am sure you did great honey," replied Mandy. She then threw her arms around me and kissed me like I was going away to war, and would never be returning.

"Wow!" I exclaimed.

"What was that for?"

"Nothing," replied Mandy.

"I am just proud of you, and tonight is going to be all about you," she then took my arm and started walking with me back towards my room.

"Go and get changed," she said.

"I want to take you somewhere special for dinner tonight."

It was only when she mentioned going somewhere special for dinner that I noticed she was wearing the same black dress that she had worn the first night I moved into the dorms, and she caught me daydreaming in the rain. I ran upstairs and changed into my Sunday best, and then ran back down to meet Mandy in the lobby. "You drive, sweetie, I know how much you like the car," said Mandy, as she tossed me her keys.

"Where are we going my dear?" I asked in a James Bond kind of voice.

"To The Roof Restaurant," said Mandy with a big smile on her face.

"I know you have never been there before, and I wanted to surprise you with something nice for doing so well on your finals," I slumped back in the drivers' seat and did not say a word.

"That is somewhere you have always wanted to go isn't it?" Asked Mandy?

"*Yes*," I blurted out.

"Most defiantly, it is somewhere I have always wanted to eat," I began to fumble with my words,

"There with the two of us together, both me and you, together, as a couple, just me and you." Mandy looked at me like I was from mars.

"You've never been there, right?" Asked Mandy.

"No," I blurted out again,

"I have never been there, this will be a real treat," I exclaimed, trying not to sound or look any more suspicious then I already did. We got out of the car and made our way up the elevator to the waiting room of the restaurant. Mandy announced our reservation to the host, and he told us our table would be ready in about ten minutes. Mandy excused herself to the ladies room, and as I was standing there with my hands in my pocket, waiting for Mandy to return, I happened to glance at the glass display case just behind the front desk. As I casually scanned the ornate display case, I noticed a group of photos in the middle, and just above the photos were the words, "Love is in the air at The Roof Top Restaurant. I looked closer at the photos in the center, and to my horror I spotted the picture of Misty and myself. It was the photo that had been taken by the hostess the night we had come to dinner. I had completely forgotten about the photo, and as I quickly walked closer to the front desk to ask the Host if he would take my picture out of the display case, Mandy returned. She took my hand and asked, "is our table ready yet?"

I stood frozen in a temporary state of panic, trying not to look suspicious, but as Mandy turned to look towards the Host, and consequently the glass display case, I grabbed her by the arm and whirled her back around towards me, kissing her for as long as I could without seeming to anxious. "*Flash*," we turned around just in time to see the host taking a picture of us.

"I will have to add this one to the display case," he said. And that is when Mandy once again stared looking towards the case. I grabbed her once again, whirling her back around, kissing her once more for as long as I could.

"Sorry folks, only one picture per couple," said the host, as he watched us kissing for the second time.

"*Is our table ready?*" I blurted out to the host, trying desperately to keep Mandy from looking at the display case.

"Yes sir just follow me," was his reply.

"Thank the lord," I thought to myself as we entered the dining area; she had not seen the picture! We made our way to the table and then fixed our plates from the buffet. I had just started eating when Mandy gently took my hand.

"Jeremy the last six months have been absolutely wonderful, and I just wanted to thank you for everything you have done for me. You have been so kind, and such a gentleman, I will never regret the time we have spent together." I was felling a bit odd because of the way Mandy was talking to me.

"I have grown so much, and I have come to love you even more than I could have imagined." She said. She leaned over, took my hand, and gave me a very gentle, yet passionate kiss.

"We have our whole lives to continue getting to know each other, but thank you for the vote of confidence," was my reply. I continued eating my shrimp, but after a few minutes I looked up and noticed that Mandy had not eaten anything, I also noticed tears rolling down her cheeks.

"I know something is wrong," I said as I reached across the table and whipped one of the tears away from her cheek.

"What is it?" I asked.

"It is nothing sweet heart."

"You didn't see anything alarming in the front display case out there in the lobby did you?" I asked.

"The front lobby?" She asked while giving me a look of confusion.

"What are you talking about?"

"*Nothing*," I replied.

"Nothing at all, this is about you and what I need to do to help you feel better."

"There is nothing wrong," said Mandy.

"I am just happy to be here with you tonight." Mandy gave me a reassuring look, and then said,

"Let's get out of here, and go somewhere where we can be alone for a while."

We left the restaurant and made our way to the waterfall in the center of campus, by the library.

"I am not sure what it is about this waterfall," I said while Mandy rested her head on my shoulder.

"But it sure has a way of effecting people doesn't it!" I stated.

"It is very calming," exclaimed Mandy.

We sat with the moon in full view on that slightly chilly night, Mandy had her arms wrapped tightly around mine, and we were both holding hands. For just a brief moment in time, everything was so right with the world.

"I love you Jeremy," said Mandy as she looked up and gave me a very sad kiss.

I could tell something was wrong, but Mandy was not going to tell me what it was, so our evening ended with me standing in front of the dorms waving to Mandy as she pulled away. If I had known then what I know now, I would not have let that evening go by with such an air of indifference.

It was a brisk, yet pleasant morning, I could sense the last few days of summer were upon us, and with that crisp hint of fall lingering in the air I loaded my things into the trunk of my car. I was excited to finally be taking our trip to Jackson Hole, Wyoming. I drove to my parent's house, where Daryl and Tiffany were anxiously awaiting my arrival. After loading Daryl and Tiffany's things into the trunk of my car, and before going on to pick up Mandy, we headed for the closest gas station to get fuel, road trip munchies, and beverages. As we pulled up to Mandy's house, mouths full of donuts and soda pop, I jumped out of the car to meet Mandy, who was sitting on the front steps of her house waiting for us.

"Good morning dear, last night was a nice surprise, thank you very much for a nice dinner." I said with a smile.

I grabbed her stuff and crammed it tightly into the trunk, and then opened the door for her to let her into the front passenger seat. All of our informal greetings were made, and then we were off, heading for Jackson Hole, Wyoming, and a much needed break!

The plan was, to drive for three hours the first day and get to my grandparent's house in Pocatello, Idaho. We would spend the rest of the day with my grandparents, who were very excited to see us, and to meet Mandy. We would stay the night at their home and the next morning drive for three more hours to Jackson Hole, Wyoming for the day, and then drive back to my grandparent's home later that evening. We would get up the third day and drive back home to Salt Lake, having saved money by staying with my grandparents, and kept our sanity by not spending more than three hours in the car at a given time. Daryl and I had been carrying on a conversation about BYU and the University of Utah's football season and how we would get tickets to the games for each other. If I went to the BYU football games with Daryl, he would go to the U of U football games with me. BYU and The University of Utah were actually rival teams, so for me to be related to the enemy was kind of like having a family member fighting for the union army during the civil war, when the rest of the family members where all confederates. It wasn't popular and if your fellow soldiers found out you could be killed for treason, but it was a chance we were both willing to take. Tiffany had been making small talk with Mandy for a while when it dawned on me that Mandy had not said hardly a word to me as of yet. After completing our season game plans, I turned to Mandy.

"How are you doing this morning?" I asked.

"You have seemed to be a bit down lately, and I have been worried about you for the last week or so." Mandy did not look up at me she only shrugged her shoulders and mumbled,

"I am fine, I just have a few things on my mind that is all." I had been thinking to myself,

"This is a bit odd for Mandy to be acting this way," but she had been acting strange for the last few weeks, and since she would not tell me what was wrong, I continued asking her questions. I asked her about her job, trying to find out if anything was bothering her, but with each question came the same shrug and one word answer, "fine."

Have you ever been in a situation where you could feel the ugly darkness of extreme un-comfort slowly descending upon you like a cold winter breeze? It sort of hits you in the face, your ears start to sting, and then your nose, and pretty soon you can feel the cold going down your entire body. Well that was the sensation that started to take over my body. Thoughts of "Holy Crap," I am about to spend the next three days with my sister, her husband, and my grandparents, and there is something obviously wrong here. I had noticed that there was something wrong with Mandy for the past few weeks, but for some reason it wasn't until that moment that it hit me. I realized there was something wrong with our relationship, it wasn't Mandy's job, it wasn't her family, it was me.

I could feel Daryl and Tiffany staring at the back of my head from the rear seat where they were sitting. I quickly became aware of the fact that they had stopped talking, and they had heard my very awkward, one-sided conversation with Mandy. I slowly looked into my rear view mirror, and to my dismay I could see the same look on both Tiffany and Daryl's faces, the look of "wow," what is wrong with these two? They had better figure it out soon or this is going to be a very uncomfortable weekend for all of us.

Not sure what to do I panicked and turned the radio on to a volume that was just a little bit above comfortable. I was thinking maybe the awkwardness of being in a car with four people and having the radio on just loud enough that you had to raise your voice to be heard, would throw everyone off. I could at least pretend that Mandy could not hear me very well, and perhaps Tiffany and Daryl would think that the loud music was why Mandy was not really talking to me.

Plymouth is a small town, of about five people, all of which work at the only gas station-grocery store, post office in town, and it also happens to be the half way point between Salt Lake and Pocatello, so over the years it had become the obvious place, and to be honest the only place to pull off for gas and a quick stretch of the legs. I had many fond memories of traveling through Plymouth, as a younger boy I would spend the summers with my grandparents, and this was the place where we would meet them. It is funny how places like Plymouth never change; to this day Plymouth is the same little stop that I remembered it being as a young teenager. In fact I could swear that the post cards and travel mugs are literally the same ones they had all those years ago.

About a mile away from the exit, I made the announcement to my passengers that I was going to pull over for gas so if anyone needed to stretch their legs, this was the time to do it. As we pulled into the station, Daryl stated that he would help me get gas. The girls made their way into the station as Daryl turned to me and said, "Jeremy what is going on? You can cut the tension in that car with a knife."

"Don't you think I know that?" Was my reply.

"I have no idea what is going on, she has not said anything to me and the more questions I ask the more upset she seams to be. She has kind of been like this for the last few weeks, but it seams to be getting worse with every passing moment."

I told him about the phone call a few weeks ago where she seemed so distant, and I told him about dinner the night before and how she held me, like she would never be seeing me again.

"It is going to be a really long weekend if she keeps this up," Daryl stated.

"Once again I think I am aware of that." I said.

Daryl walked into the station leaving me to revel in my state of disbelief and bewilderment. What was I going to do? What had I done? Why was she mad at me? I wanted to talk to her and find out what was going on, but she would not open up to me at all. I stood there trying in vain, scanning my memory for something, anything that I could think of what I had done to merit this silent treatment. I felt as though I had been sentenced to 10 years hard labor, even though I was an innocent man.

I was in this daze of confusion when I noticed the gas flowing out of the now full gas tank and onto the ground. I replaced the nozzle and made my way into the small station to pay for the gas. Then, like a child on the first day of school, I reluctantly made my way back to the car to finish the next hour and a half of my sentence.

We arriving in Idaho, the birth place of such famous people as Joe Albertson (the grocery store king) and such land mark sites as Hell's Canyon, which by the way is the deepest river gorge in America, deeper that the grand canyon. As far as I was concerned, those disappointing land mark sites and my grandma's house were the only reasons on earth to ever go to Idaho. I was thinking to myself as we pulled into my grandparent's driveway,

"No one wants this uncomfortable situation to be introduced to his or her grandparents. The very word grandma means love, and cookies, and happiness." I could only hope that the silent treatment would end once we went into the house, and to my astonishment it did, sort of. Mandy was very warm and pleasant with my grandparents, introducing her self and talking very nicely with them. I was beside myself with disbelief, what was going on? Although she did not say hardly a word to me the rest of that afternoon or evening she was very cordial with my grandparents, she offered to help with the dishes, and was very kind.

Later that evening, after my grandparents had gone in to the living room to chat with Tiffany and Daryl, I took Mandy by the hand and led her out to the front porch. We sat down in the lawn chairs that my grandfather always had out on the porch, and as I took Mandy's hand into mine, I looked her in the eyes and asked, "What on earth is going on?" Mandy looked at me with a sad and confused face.

"I don't want to talk about it right now."

"Mandy please tell me what is going on, you have been acting strange for the last few weeks, and I know I am slow at picking up on other peoples feelings, but I love you and I know something is wrong." I pulled her close and kissed her warmly.

"Please just talk to me Mandy, what is wrong?" She put her hands gently on my face.

"I am tired Jeremy, I would like to go to bed now." She gave me a kiss on the cheek, and then she stood up and quickly went back into the house, leaving me all alone to ponder the meaning behind her abrupt exit.

I was stunned, what on earth was going on? What was she doing? What was she thinking? I sat there all alone, in the cool summer night air, thinking back upon our relationship, all of the things we had done together began to play in mind like a move on the big silver screen. I recalled how Mandy had been the one to approach me about the possibilities of dating and to get to know each other better. Mandy was also the one who wanted to spend the summer getting to know each other better to see if we were "meant to be." And then it hit me like a freight train, Mandy wanted to get to know me for the summer because her old boyfriend was coming back from over seas some time in the late summer or early fall, and it was now the end of the summer. I felt like a gambler who had placed a very large bet on a hoarse race, and although the horse had been in the lead for most of the race, without warning he got too close to the rail and stumbled, falling down just inches from the finish line. I felt myself getting pale and cold, I could feel my dinner doing jumping jacks in my stomach, I had been so involved with school, and work, and my own selfishness, that I had just assumed things were fine between Mandy and myself.

The truth was, I had been neglecting our relationship, and I had completely forgotten about this other guy, not seeing him as a threat, I paid no attention to the signs on the wall. I had thought, and truly believed, that Mandy had made up her mind, and I was the one, I just thought she needed more time and didn't want to rush things. We had grown so close in such a short amount of time, I thought we were meant for each other, but it looked like he was coming home soon, and now she was having serious doubts about our relationship and us. I felt that panic that comes over a person who has just realized that their relationship was about to end. I had spent the whole day up to this point, thinking Mandy was just worried about her job, or her grandparents, and that she did not want to worry me with her problems. Now, as the whole picture was painfully unfolding in front of me I could feel a deep pain in my soul, I felt an unexplainable darkness come over me, that feeling of being very, very alone, a feeling that can not be put into words but can only be experienced.

I must have sat out on the porch for a very long time, because when I finally made my way back into the house everyone had gone to bed, and all of the lights were out. I made my way to the couch, where my grandmother had laid out some blankets, and a pillow for me; I slumped down onto the cushions, staring aimlessly at the ceiling.

At some point in the night I must have finally fallen asleep, because when I opened my eyes there stood Daryl and Tiffany dressed and ready to continue on our journey. I remember dragging myself up and going into the bathroom to try to pull myself together enough to finish this trip. My fun weekend get-away, which I had been looking forward to for months now, began to feel more like a trip to death row than a vacation. We all climbed into my car and began the long, three-hour road trip to Jackson Hole. We found ourselves observing the same arrangement as the day before, Tiffany and Daryl in the back seat talking and laughing, with Mandy and I sitting in the front seat, not talking, and not laughing.

The day was pretty much a blur to me, other than the tram ride, which was the biggest and longest tram in the western united states, where we sat, not talking once more. I made one last futile attempt to get Mandy to talk to me while we rode the never-ending tram, she had not said anything about her old boyfriend up to this point, but I knew that his impending arrival was the problem. Sadly, I got nothing more out of Mandy than,

"Please, Jeremy I don't want to talk right now."

The trip back to my grandparents that evening and the trip to Salt Lake the following day felt so bleak and surreal. It was as if I were experiencing a bad dream, and at any moment I would wake up and laugh at the whole thing, only I could not wake up, because it was not a dream, I felt as though my life had been shattered into a million pieces.

When we arrived in front of Mandy's house, I opened the car door for her and then got her things out of the trunk. We slowly walked up to Mandy's front door, and as we turned to say good bye to each other, I looked Mandy in the eyes and said, "I'm no t sure what is wrong, but I am sorry I was not able to help you feel better, I think I understand what this is about, so if you want to call me we can go on as if this whole thing never happened," I paused for a moment.

"If you don't want to call me I will know why."

I leaned over, and pulled Mandy close, giving her what would be the last kiss we would ever exchange; it was a very difficult, and depressing moment for both of us. I got back into the car, and as we drove off I looked in my rear view mirror, somehow knowing it would be last time I would ever see my darling Mandy.

To this day, I have not heard from Mandy, no phones call, no letters, nothing. I sometimes wondered if she married her old boyfriend, or perhaps I had been wrong all along, and it had nothing to do with him. In my mind, I want to believe that Mandy left the country to work as an undercover agent for the FBI, or perhaps there was some other tragically romantic reason why she left me, but in my heart I always knew that was not the case, we were just not meant to be.

CHAPTER 3

The Great Depression

The next few days and weeks were a mesh of depression and self loathing, I did not want to go work, but I did, I did not go anywhere with Steve or Tom, and I spent most of my time wandering around campus alone, and feeling sorry for myself. I was left wondering why I had not taken Mistys' advice, and searched my soul a little bit deeper. If I had known then what I knew now, I would have asked Misty to stay and I would have told Mandy that we were through, but in life we take chances, and we make choices based on the experiences that fate throws in front of us. The truth was, I had fallen very much in love with Mandy, and I believed that she had fallen in love with me. I really had thought that at some point in time Mandy and I would get married, that was why I did not want to jeopardize anything by having Misty or anyone else get to close to me.

It was about a week before the new fall quarter was scheduled to begin, so all of the new and returning students began flocking to the dorms. Since I had started school during the summer, I really had not comprehended how packed the dorms became during the school year; it was quite impressive to see the miles of lines everywhere you went. At every turn there were people checking into their new rooms, buying books, and registering for classes, it was almost inconceivable to see so many people on campus. It was early one evening when I arrived back at the dorm to find a note taped to the door of my room, and it said something to this effect; "The she demon has found out about the room switch, she is boiling mad, don't go into the main lobby because she is looking for us."

I tore the note off the door and immediately made my way down to the main lobby. The way I was feeling those days I did not care if she threw me out of the dorms entirely; I was so depressed that I was beyond caring.

"I'll be right with you" was Rhonda's response as she looked across the main desk at me.

"Ok," I said.

She pointed towards the large door that lead into the back office, and motioned for me to come inside. I slowly walked over to the heavy wooden door, turned the knob and walked into the office. Rhonda was already sitting behind the rickety old desk, which had been awkwardly shoved into her cramped office. The office smelt like a combination of old mothballs and bad potpourri. Rhonda had kitten posters hanging on the walls, with a kitten calendar hanging slightly to one side on the wall above her head.

"I believe you know why we are having this little chat," said Rhonda, as she leaned forward in her chair,

"I don't think I need to explain to an intelligent person like you, that what happened here was wrong."

"Yes Rhonda and no Rhonda," was my response.

"Well," said Rhonda in an arrogant tone,

"We have rules here you know, and rules are made to keep everything and everyone in line, without rules there would be......blah, blah, blah."

I was looking right into her eyes, and I could see her mouth moving but I did not hear a word she was saying. I felt like Charlie Brown sitting in a class where the teachers all make that wa, wa, wa sound but you can't understand anything they're saying. My mind started to wonder, I started thinking about my new classes and what I needed at the grocery store when Rhonda said, "So I had no choice but to fire Steve, I have already talked to him and he told me you had nothing to do with this." I sat up at this point and started listening.

"He confessed to making all of the changes, forging those phony letters and telling the students who were suppose to be in the room that it was being remodeled." Rhonda rolled her eyes.

"I just wish that Steve hadn't involved you in this mess." Rhonda sat back in her chair, folder her arms.

"I am sorry you had to get mixed up in this, but don't worry Steve has been dealt with." I sat there for a moment contemplating my next move! Steve really had worked this entire scheme out, but I was a willing participant in this deception. From the sounds of it, Steve had already taken the fall, but I could not let him take it alone, and I could not let him lose his job. So after a moment of contemplation I said,

"Rhonda, I knew about the whole thing, and I helped Steve with all of it so please don't fire him."

"Well that is nice of you to want to protect Steve, but the matter is closed, you may return to your room." She said as she stood up and opened the door for me.

I walked back to my room feeling bad about the whole thing, but unfortunately I was still feeling so depressed about losing Mandy that I didn't really think about it any further.

The beginning of a new quarter is like an old vaudeville show, some of the old acts that had been there for a long time had to move on, some of the acts got better, while some acts were replaced all together, and of coarse there were always entirely new acts that took to the stage. This was one of the analogies Steve had used to describe each new quarter, and in a way I guess he was right.

"We have got to get your mind off this whole Mandy thing," said Steve.

"Tonight, there is suppose to be a barbeque and volleyball tournament out behind the dorms and we are going." He said.

"Whether you like it or not mate."

I did not want to go but around 5:30 p.m. Steve and Tom showed up to drag me out of my room.

"Get this man a big beautiful hamburger," yelled Steve at the top of his lungs, as we walked out into the crisp fall air. It was quite a sight to behold; hundreds of new students filled the lawn with the sounds of laughter, and the smell of hamburger patties and hot dogs being cooked on the huge barbeques filled the air. Having moved in to the dorms during the summer, when most of the students were gone, I only saw glimpses of what the dorms capacity really was, and now, seeing it filled to the brim gave me a new outlook on dorm life.

"Think fast mate," said Steve as he threw a Frisbee towards me, I quickly moved out of the way, but it hit Tom right in the side of the head, causing him to drop his drink and burger down the front of his shirt and onto the lawn.

"*What the hell man?*" yelled Tom in his broken English accent.

"You made me drop food."

Despite my aching heart and bad mood, I could not help cracking a smile and my smile quickly turned into a laugh. Steve, who noticed that I had started laughing, yelled over to me, "That's the spirit mate let's all laugh at Tom."

I found a place to sit and eat my dinner, and as I ate I watched Steve socializing with the lady's, something that he did very well. Being tall, well built, and having his Aussie accent, all the girls loved Steve, which made it even harder to be around him feeling the way I did. He introduced me to absolutely every girl that walked by, tall ones, skinny ones, not so skinny ones, blondes, brunettes, you name it he told them all that I was Jeremy and that I had just gone through a bad breakup.

"Steve this isn't really helping, I am not looking for another relationship, and I really just want to be left alone." I finally told him.

I stood up and made my way back up to the room. Steve did not give up on his poor friend though, despite my explaining to him that I was fine, he set me up on date after date after nightmarish date trying, in his own way to make me feel better. Tom on the other hand tried a different approach to help get my mind off of things; Risk, the board game! During the summer months we had played once or twice and I really enjoy playing Risk with Tom and Dave, so to help me get my mind off of things we began playing more and more, each game lasting for two, sometimes three hours or longer. I remember spending my evenings sitting in the room with up to six of us playing Risk until two in the morning; Tom liked it because it was something he was good at, I liked it because it ate up huge amounts of time, and Steve liked it because he could always get a couple of girls to come and play with us.

My other great diversion came in the form of a tall skinny kid, who was assigned to be Tom's new roommate for the year. I don't know if I ever found out what his real name was, but everyone called him Slim. He had dark brown hair and a very prominent Italian nose; he stood about 6 foot five and could not have weighed more than 130 pounds. Slim was a very outgoing and out-spoken guy who was going to school to get his business degree, so that he could to be a professional chef, and open his own restaurant in New York. I will never forget the day I met him for the first time, Slim took one look at me and said; "hey I know you, you are the guy in the glass case at work, looking all surprised with your fiancé hanging onto your arm."

"What!" I exclaimed.

"I work at the Roof Restaurant as a junior chef," replied Slim.

"I see your picture in our display case every day, you are standing there with the cute red headed girl, whom I assumed was your fiancé or girlfriend, or something like that."

"Oh that was not my girlfriend that was Steve's sister Misty, she was visiting from Australia last summer and I was taking her to dinner for Steve," I paused for a moment.

"By the way can you get that picture back for me, I would kind of like to keep it."

"Well," exclaimed Slim,

"I will see what I can do."

The thing I remember most about Slim was that he would try out his culinary creations on us, and let me tell you it was a very welcome change from the pre-processed frozen dinners, and chicken noodle soup that we had become accustom too over the summer months.

Despite my constant protesting, Steve continued his quest to find me a suitable girl. Unfortunately, most of the girls whom Steve tried to set me up with turned out to be less than desirable. There was one young woman however, who in time would prove to be the only girl to ever join our all boy club, and this remarkable person was a cute little blonde girl by the name of Robyn. Robyn was in the University of Utah's ballet program, and her name fit her too a tee, Robyn was small, thin as a toothpick, had long blonde hair, and as far as any of us know only ate once a week. Robyn was one of the girls whom Steve had set me up with on a blind date, I had protested at first, but after persistently nagging me I finally gave in and agreed to meet her. It was a weekday, shortly after I had returned home from work that I meet Robyn for the first time in front of the student union building. I remember thinking how polite she was, as we stood outside making our introductions, and after saying hello, we went inside to go bowling.

"So Steve tells me that your girlfriend just died of leukemia, I am very sorry," said Robyn.

"What?" I exclaimed, in a confused tone.

"My girlfriend didn't die of leukemia; she dumped me for her high school sweetheart."

"Oh," exclaimed Robyn.

"Steve told you that to make you feel sorry enough for me and that you would want to go out," I paused for a moment.

"I am sorry he lied to you, but in his own twisted way he thought he was helping me."

"Don't worry about it," said Robyn.

"I would have gone out with you anyway; I have been so involved with ballet since I was about six, that I have not really had much of a life.

"Don't get me wrong," she said.

"I love ballet, but my mom has pushed me so hard, and for so long, that I feel like a slave to it sometimes. I have really been looking forward to going away to college partially to get away from my mom, but also to get a life of my own."

"So, Robyn, where are you from?" I asked.

"I am from southern Utah," she said.

"You are a long way from home."

"Well," explained Robyn,

"I am going to school here for two reasons, first of all I have a full scholarship through the ballet department, and second, it is over 300 miles away from my mother."

"I see," I said.

"So you won't be going home for the weekends, and from the sounds of it you won't be having family visitors either."

"Not if I can help it," said Robyn.

"Listen Jeremy," said Robyn as we were making our way back to the dorms.

"I really don't have many friends yet, I have only been here for a few days, and I don't know my way around Salt Lake at all." Robyn paused for a moment,

"I have had a nice time with you and so I am wondering if you wouldn't mind some time showing me around Salt Lake, I would pay for gas if you want to drive or we can take my car if you like, I would even pay for dinner."

"That sounds fair enough," I replied.

"Tomorrow is my first day of class," I said as I took a mental look at my schedule,

"But this Friday night we can go and do something if you like!"

"Ok," said Robyn.

"This Friday it is, how about 5:00 or so?" She asked.

"That will be fine," I answered.

"Well," said Robyn,

"Thank you for a nice evening of bowling and I will see you on Friday."

As I left the front entrance of the girls' wing, I made my way back to the main lobby to check my mailbox, as I pulled out my mail I could hear the piano being played by the girl whom I had heard playing it so well just a few months ago. I decided to make my way over to the piano, and see who was playing such beautiful music, when I got about half way, I got a good look at her, and I recognized her from some of the dorm's summer activities, and to my dismay, I also noticed Steve talking to her as she played the piano.

"Oh here's the guy I was telling you about," said Steve as he gave me the thumbs up sign and walked away quickly.

"I am sorry to hear that your girlfriend died in a horrible car accident," said the girl behind the piano.

"My girlfriend didn't die in a car," I stopped mid sentence, thinking to myself, "there is no use explaining my personal life to everyone I meet, especially when most of them probably don't care anyway."

"Never mind about that," I said.

"I have heard you playing the piano out here before, and I think you have got to be the best pianist I have ever heard. Of coarse I don't really know any pianists, and so I guess coming from me that may not mean much, but I really do think you are good."

"Thank you," she said with a warm smile.

"My name is Megan, and I think I have noticed you a time or two."

Megan looked over towards Steve.

"Is Steve your roommate? She inquired.

"I really like his accent."

"Yes he's my roommate," I responded,

"And all the girls love his accent."

"You are lucky to have a roommate who looks out for you like Steve does," said Megan, as she looked back towards me.

"Lucky isn't exactly the word I would use, but yes I am glad he looks out for me." I looked across the room, and saw Steve talking to another girl while pointing in my direction, and waving. I pretended not to see him as I turned back to Megan.

"So what are you studying?" I asked.

"Well," replied Megan,

"I have a music scholarship and I am studying music composition, I have produced one record, and I am working on a second one."

"What kind of record?" I asked.

"It is a compellation of classical music and a few songs I wrote myself."

"Wow," I exclaimed,

"That is very impressive."

"Well it was nice to meet you," said Megan as she closed the piano lid and stood up.

"I've got to get going, my boyfriend is probably outside waiting for me." Megan got up and headed towards the door but just before she left she turned around and said, "It was nice to meet you, sorry about the car accident and your girlfriend, I hope the group therapy helps."

"Group therapy," I said to myself, I have really got to have a talk to Steve about not helping me anymore, or else I will be in group therapy, on death row, because I will kill him.

"This class is an advanced collegiate writing course, and it is intended to separate those of you who want to be serious writers from those of you who think the newsstand tabloids and Sunday funnies are real writing."

The Professor stopped and looked out into the class like a hawk looking for prey.

"Oh," he said in a malicious tone,

"One more thing, those of you "honors" students out there," he paused, scouring the audience for any movement.

"You may think this class is nothing more than a free ride, but I am going to make you work just as hard, if not harder than the rest of the class," he then slammed his fist on the desk.

"Just because you think you're gifted won't get you any special treatment in this class." That was the point when Steve turned to me and said,

"Ok mate, this is the end of the line for me, I am not honors material," he leaned in closer to explain,

"I had a teacher in high school who wrote some sort of letter to someone here at the University, telling them I was a genius and that I should be in the honors program." Steve shook his head and continued explaining,

"The only reason I got good grades, mate, was because I was the only one in my class who showed up every day, and I was also the only one who turned in any homework, at all."

"Don't be ridicules Steve," I said.

"You got good grades last quarter," I said in an attempt to make him feel better.

"I don't think "B-minuses" is good grade," piped in Tom.

"Shut up Tom," said Steve and I at the same time.

"Is there a problem up there in the cheap seats, boys?" Asked the professor.

"No sir my friend Steve is not as smart as rest of class, but we work with him, it be ok," said Tom.

"Well won't that be nice for your friend Steve," the professor put down his chalk for a moment.

"If it's ok with the three of you, I would like to continue teaching this class."

"Oh sure, it be fine with me, go ahead, continue," said Tom. Steve and I slid back in our seats, trying to look like we didn't know Tom, however, when Tom raised his hand and began to make another remark, Steve punched him in the arm.

"*Ouch*," yelled Tom, as he rubbed his arm.

"Shut the hell up Tom, you're not helping here." Said Steve.

After class we made our way to the student union building for a quick bite to eat.

"I'm serious guys," said Steve as we sat down,

"I don't think I can handle this class."

"But you got through all of your classes last quarter, and even though they weren't easy you did it," I said.

"Yes," replied Steve rather sheepishly,

"But I sat by Tom and got most of the answers off of his paper."

"But Tom got straight "A's" and you got B-minuses," I said.

"Yeah I know I couldn't read all of his answers so I made some stuff up, besides I can't copy his essays in this class, each person is given a different topic," said Steve.

"Look I have to get to work, but don't worry about it Tom and I will help you get through this one just like we did last quarter, seriously," I said.

"Don't worry about it." I said as I stood up to leave.

"Oh one last thing Steve, that girl Robyn, she seems really nice."

"Who is Robyn?" Asked Steve.

"The girl you set me up with last week, the one I went bowling with." Steve just stared at me with this blank look.

"The ballerina girl," I said in frustration. Same blank look.

"The girl you convinced that I was a wreck because Mandy *died from leukemia*." I shouted.

"Oh, right the little ballerina girl," replied Steve.

"Well can I pick them or what," stated Steve proudly.

"Yeah," I said in a derogative tone,

"Like the girl you set me up with two weeks ago who had her stuffed cat in her dorm room because, 'Mr. Sunshine' reminded her of better days." I looked at Steve who was now looking away as if I were not even there.

"Steve, her last two roommates moved out because she only believes in bathing once a week." I leaned over and got right in Steve's face.

"She told me that bathing removes all of the basic oils in her skin."

"Well," said Steve,

"She seemed lonely, like you, and I thought the two of you could be lonely together."

"No thanks Steve, and by the way *no more dates*." I yelled as I started to walk away.

"What about Rebecca?" Steve yelled across the room as I made my way towards the door.

"You were about to say something about Rebecca." I turned back towards him,

"She was nice, and I am taking her out again on Friday." I then yelled,

"Her name is *Robyn*." I walked out the door, leaving Steve and Tom to finish their lunch.

I sat in the doorway of the warehouse at work watching the new-boys load my truck, when Dan came up to me and said, "Mind if I stand by you and smoke?" Not that he was really asking me if I cared or not, but it was Dan's way of saying you look like you have something on your mind, do you want to talk about it. I relayed the events of the last few weeks to him, I told him about my trip to Jackson Hole and the loss of Mandy, after I finished speaking, Dan looked at me,

"I am really sorry to hear that," and he pulled the cigarette out of his mouth.

"I mean it; I'm not just saying that. I lost my wife of ten years and my three kids to the bottle, I just couldn't stop drinking, and now I am alone and unhappy most of the time."

This was a bit more information than I needed to know, but I was glad that Dan thought enough of me to share a portion of his personal life with me, to be honest I had just figured he lived in the warehouse all the time, because I could not imagine him outside of work.

"You can't let those sorts of things get you down, go to the bar and get real drunk," said Dan in a serious tone.

"When you wake up the next morning in the gutter, you will forget all about your troubles." Dan continued.

"If she left you, then she is the one who is stupid, some day when you are the next Frank Lloyd Wright she will be sorry for ever leaving you." I was quite impressed with Dan, not so much that he was trying to cheer me up, but for knowing who Frank Lloyd Wright was.

"Well thanks again Dan," I said.

"Other than the getting drunk and waking up in the gutter part, I will try to just forget about her and let the whole thing go."

"That's the spirit," said Dan.

"Now get out there and get your deliveries done, because that truck ain't gunna drive itself."

I climbed into the cab and turned the key to the ignition, the truck made its usual horrendous rumble, and as I sat waiting for it to warm up I looked up at the glaring sun. The afternoon glare was nearly blinding me, so I pulled down the sun visor to help stop the burning in my eyes, as I did however; I caught a glimpse of something small fluttering to the ground and landing between my feet. I picked up the small object and realized that it was the picture of Mandy that she had put in my truck at the beginning of the summer. I took the rather tattered and sun bleached photo in my hands and looked at it for some time. I ran my fingers over the photo and kissed it gently. I then pushed in the cigarette lighter and waited for it to pop out, indicating that it was hot and ready. I rolled up the picture and pushed it deep into the glowing embers of the lighter. It smoldered for a few moments and then burst into a small flame. I held it as long as I could but when the flames got to close to my fingers I dropped it on the floor and let it burn and smolder until there was nothing left but a small pile of black ash. I then put the truck into gear and pulled away from the dock to make my daily deliveries.

When I returned to the dock a few hours later, after having finished my deliveries, Dan was waiting for me on the dock, which was odd, because when Dan finished his deliveries he would usually sit in his office and smoke until it was time to go home. I seldom saw Dan this close to quitting time.

"Jeremy I have been thinking about you all afternoon, and I know when I get down, sometimes I just need someone to talk to, so turn in your keys and come with me."

I could only imagine what Dan had in mind, for a pick me up. I did not drink, and I was positive that my form of evening entertainment and his was on two completely different levels, but out of curiosity or perhaps an instinctive fear of telling Dan no, I turned in my keys and followed him to his light blue Chevy Blazer. We made our way to a little coffee shop just off the main campus; we both got out of his truck and went inside. We sat down at a table next to the window.

"Ok buddy I am here for you," Dan said. He then leaned over the table so that he was right in front of my face,

"You know when I first got back from Viet Nam, my doctor told me that I might have some problems adjusting to the civilian world, and he told me that the best thing I could do was find myself one of those support groups, kind of like the AA group I had been in before Nam, but one for veterans who had gone through some trauma during the war. I had a part of my leg shot off, and I spent six months being tortured every day in a Vietnamese P.O.W. camp, so I guess you could say I saw some disturbing things while I was there." He leaned back in his chair a bit,

"The army doctors thought it might affect my ability to function in the civilian world." He said.

I could not keep my eyes off of Dan; I was scared out of my mind to say the least. Looking back on it now, I knew that in his own slightly odd way, Dan was trying to help, and the fact that he was at least trying really meant a lot to me, but I was not sure what to say after that.

"I am sorry you got part of your leg blown off, and I am sorry you were tortured every day for six months, but my girlfriend left me and that is obviously worse?" No, I could not say anything like that, and so there we sat looking at each other for a few very awkward moments.

"I am sorry about the leg and the torture thing Dan, I think you function very well in public, and in fact I would not have known about your leg if you had not told me." I said in a very weak and quite voice.

"Well I'm not telling you for sympathy," barked Dan,

"I'm telling you this as an example, sometimes you need to talk about your problems and feelings in order to get past, whatever it is that's bothering you," said Dan.

I did not know how to explain to Dan that talking to any one about my feelings, especially him, was about the last thing on my mind, and after his story, all I wanted to do was go home.

"Well Dan, I appreciate your willingness to listen," I said nervously.

"You are a true friend indeed, but I think I am getting over this thing, I'm sure in no time at all I will have forgotten about old what's her name," I was so nervous that I had actually forgotten her name.

"See I am getting over her already."

"Well don't fight your feelings, if you need to talk I am here for you buddy," said Dan.

"Thanks again," I said as I got up and quickly headed for the door.

"You need a ride somewhere?" Asked Dan.

"No, I can walk; it's only just down the street." It was I bit farther than I cared to travel by foot, but under the circumstances I preferred to walk.

By the time I had trudged up the hill and made my way back to the dorms, it was about six or six thirty, as I walked into the main lobby I found Robyn sitting in one of the overstuffed chairs, hair tied back in a pink ribbon, wearing her University of Utah Ballet Company jacket, makeup on, purse in hand, and ready to go.

"Oh crap," I thought to myself, I had forgotten all about Robyn, between my little chat with Dan, my new classes starting, and work, I had completely forgotten that it was Friday, and we were suppose to be going out.

"Jeremy, there you are" shouted Robyn as I made my way over to where she was sitting.

"I thought you had forgotten about me."

"No, no, heavens no," I replied.

"I just got off work, it ran later than usual, I guess you could say."

"Well if it isn't going to work for this evening we can go another time," said Robyn.

"No come with me and I will get ready and we will go." I grabbed Robyn by the hand and we made our way into the boy's wing, down the hall, and into my room.

"Steve, you already know Robyn, Robyn this is Tom and where is Slim?" I asked.

"He is working tonight," replied Steve.

"Ok," I said as I rummaged around the room.

"I need to put on a clean shirt and then we are off." I was feeling a bit unorganized as I continued looking for something clean to put on.

"If you to think you can be nice to Robyn and not scare her off, I will run into the restroom and change." I finally found a clean shirt, and ran into the restroom to change. I quickly ran back to the room and taking Robyn by the hand we said goodbye to the Twiddle Dee, and Twiddle Dumb and were on our way.

"I was beginning to think you were not going to show up," said Robyn, as we made our way down the hall and out the door.

"I am very sorry about that, I was detained at work, but I would not have left you sitting out in the lobby all evening without saying something to you." I opened the big glass doors and we walked out into the parking lot.

"Where would you like to go first?" I asked.

"Well," said Robyn, as she thought about where she needed to go.

"I need to find the closest grocery store, and if you don't mind I would like to run in and get a few things." Robyn continued thinking as we made our way out to my car.

"I would also like to find the closest gas station, and if you would just show me some good places to eat, I think that will do for tonight," exclaimed Robyn.

"Ok," I said.

"Let's get going." As we made our way, we talked for a while about school, and our roommates, and then Robyn asked me,

"So what really happened to your girlfriend?" I sat there contemplating how much information I really wanted to disclose, because I was trying to get over the whole thing, and then Robyn, sensing my hesitation, said,

"You don't have to talk about it if you don't want to, I know we just barely met each other, and that is a bit of a personal question."

"No," I said.

"I don't mind, I guess we just weren't meant to be, Mandy, my ex-girlfriend, had a boyfriend all through high school, he left after high school for a while, and while he was gone Mandy and I dated. I guess when he got back she decided that she still loved him, and so that was that."

"Well I am very sorry to hear that," said Robyn in a sympathetic tone.

"I hope you can get over the whole thing soon, it must be hard to lose someone you love, I have never had a boyfriend so I wouldn't know."

"What!" I said in a surprised tone.

"You have never had a boyfriend," I looked over at Robyn.

"Excuse me for sounding forward, but you are a very attractive girl, did you go to an all girl school or something?"

"No," said Robyn, as she looked down at the floor.

"I was not allowed to date in high school, my mother said that dating would interfere with my ballet, so she would not allow it."

"So didn't you go to any dances or anything?" I asked.

"Well," said Robyn,

"I guess it sounds sort of sad I guess, but I was the prom queen without a date."

"*No way*," I exclaimed,

"I'm very sorry about that." I could tell that this was a sore subject, so in an attempt to not sound so uncaring I said.

"I bet you upset a lot of guys by telling them no when they asked you out."

"Well, actually they knew I was not allowed to date, and since I went to a private creative arts school, most of the guys were more interested in their art, or their music to really be interested in dating."

"Wow that just blows me away," I said.

"I mean, it's cool that you are so devoted to ballet, but you have to have some fun sometimes." Then it dawned on me; I was Robyn's first date.

"Robyn was our bowling excursion last week the first date you have ever been on?" I asked.

"Well," replied Robyn,

"I am kind of embarrassed to say it but, yes."

"*No way,*" I said, loud enough that the people in the grocery store around us turned and stared. I could tell, by the look in her face, that Robyn was a bit embarrassed by my outburst, I on the other hand, was used to having people stare at me in public, because I was always inadvertently doing stupid things. Thinking fast, not wanting Robyn to feel uncomfortable, I grabbed the box of cereal out of her hand and speaking loud enough for those around us to hear.

"That's two dollars more than it was last time we were here," and with that the gawking people went back to their shopping.

"I'm sorry," I said apologetically.

"That was a bit loud, I will be more careful from now on."

I followed Robyn down the next isle, as she continued adding things to the shopping cart. "I can't believe that I was your first date," I said, as we neared the checkout stand.

"I mean it was a lousy first date."

"No, don't say that," said Robyn.

"You have been going thorough a rough spell, it's ok, besides I had a good time, even if it was just bowling."

"Tell you what," I said.

"Let me make it up to you tomorrow night, we will go on a real date, and I will get dressed up and you can get dressed up, and I will take you to dinner, or a show, or something like that, what do you say?"

"That sounds nice," said Robyn, as we put her groceries in the back seat, and climbed back into my car.

"Thank you for being so nice to me," exclaimed Robyn.

"I would like to take you to dinner this evening for being such a kind escort," said Robyn as we pulled out of the grocery store parking lot.

"So where should we go?"

"Any where but Eat-a-Burger," I exclaimed.

"I had a bad experience there a few months ago." We made our way to my favorite "cheap" place to eat, Taco Bell! We ordered our food, and e sat down, to eat.

"I know we have just met, but would you be willing to go to my next ballet performance as my guest." Robyn paused for a moment to see what sort of a reaction I had to her question, but before I could answer she continued.

"I would really appreciate it, we are allowed to invite a few guests, and I know most of the other girls will be inviting their parents and their boyfriend, and I would be grateful if you would come as my," she hesitated for a moment,

"Guest," she finally said.

"I would love to go with you as your escort, and if it will make things any easier for you, you can tell people I am your boyfriend."

"Will you let me tell my mom you are my boyfriend?" She asked, as her eyes light up.

"Because my mom will absolutely freak out, and it would mean more to me than you would ever know?"

There was a strange excitement in her voice as she asked me to be her pretend boyfriend, and I found it odd but intriguing at the same time.

"Ok" I said,

"But if it gets ugly with your parents I want you to set them straight right there."

"No problem," said Robyn as she threw her arms around me and gave me a hug, she clapped her hands in excitement.

"Jeremy, you are the best."

We finished our dinner and then made our way around the city, I showed Robyn where a few gas stations, and restaurants were, and then we made our way back to the dorms. I was helping Robyn carry her groceries in, and as we were walking back towards her dorm room.

"By the way, when is this opening performance thing anyway?"

"Next Friday, but don't worry, I will pay for your tuxedo." Robyn opened her bedroom door, and took the grocery bags out of my hands. She then went into her dorm room, and as the door closed behind her she yelled,

"*Thank you.*"

"Well, ok then, have a nice night and I will see you tomorrow," I said to the door that had already closed in my face.

The following afternoon, I was sitting on the couch in my room, watching TV and reading one of my textbooks from my Problems in Human Values class, when there was a knock at the door.

"Steve did you forget your keys again," I yelled towards our closed door. Steve had walked out to take a shower only moment before, and all the bedroom doors locked automatically when they closed. Steve was always forgetting to take his key with him, and after nearly every shower, he would stand, dripping wet in the hall banging on the door, begging for me to let him in. I had even gotten back from work in the evening a number of times to find Steve playing card games with Tom in the common area wearing only his towel, waiting for me to get back, so that I could let him in. This time, however there was not the usual,

"Just open the damn door, I am in my towel" reply, instead there was another knock. I jumped up, ran to the door, and upon opening it, I found Robyn standing in the doorway smiling at me.

"Am I interrupting something?" Robyn asked.

"No, not at all come on in," I replied.

"I heard you talking to someone," said Robyn as she looked around the empty room,

"So, I thought you might be busy."

"No I was talking to Steve," I said. I could see her looking inquisitively round the empty room, but after seeing no one else, Robyn looked back at me with a rather confused look on her face.

"Oh," I replied.

"Steve's not here at the moment, I just thought that you were," I could see the look on Robyn's face becoming even more confused.

"Never mind," I said.

"Why don't you have a seat," I motioned for her to sit on the couch as I turned off the TV.

"What can I do for you?" I asked.

"Well, first off I wanted to see what time you wanted to go to dinner this evening, and second, I wanted to see when you would be available for your tuxedo fitting?"

"About the tuxedo thing," I began to say.

"Don't worry," interrupted Robyn,

"I will pay for the whole thing," she patted my leg in assurance.

"I will also give you the money to pay for dinner after the performance." Robyn paused for a moment.

"My dad will insist on paying for dinner, but you will have to have the money out, like you were planning on paying, otherwise he will think you are cheap, and I don't want them to think I have a cheap boyfriend." Robyn stood up.

"One more thing, if they ask, tell them that you own the tuxedo, ok." This entire thing was quickly spiraling out of control, and the ballet was still a week away.

"Well," I started to say,

"I am not sure about,"

"You will be fine," interrupted Robyn.

"And we can use tonight as a practice run ok."

"A practice run for what?" I was thinking to myself. I was about to tell Robyn that this whole thing was beginning to feel a bit awkward, when there was a loud bang, bang, bang, on the door.

"Spare me the key speech Jeremy, and open the door," said Steve.

"I am standing here dripping wet, in my towel, and *yes*, I forgot my keys *again*."

"That must be Steve," said Robyn.

"Yes," I replied.

"If you will excuse me for a moment I will make it go away." I opened the door just a crack,

"You can't come in here like that Steve."

"Why not, it's my room too," said Steve in an angry tone.

"Because," I exclaimed.

"Robyn is in here and you don't have any clothes on."

"Who is Robyn?" inquired Steve.

"The ballerina," I said as quietly as I could, because I new Robyn could hear our conversation. Steve gave me a blank look.

"The girl I took bowling," Blank look.

"*Leukemia, Steve,*" I yelled.

"The girl you told the leukemia story to.

"Oh yah," said Steve, as the lights came on in his head.

"Well good for you," he said while winking at me.

"I'll go see if Tom is in, and give you guys some time."

"No need Steve," said Robyn as she reached over and opened the door.

"I was just leaving," Robyn turned and looked at me.

"I will see you at three for the fitting, and seven for dinner Jeremy," she then started walking down the hall towards the exit.

"Hey Steve," said Robyn, as she turned back toward us.

"Nice towel." She said, and then whistled. Steve and I walked back into our room, and while he was getting dressed, Steve asked, "fitting for what?"

"Never mind," I said as I went back to my studying. At three o clock I met Robyn in the lobby, and we headed out to the tuxedo shop.

"This is a bit fancy isn't it?" I asked, as I stood in front of the full-length mirror, looking at myself in disbelief. I was dressed in one of the nicest tuxedos that I had ever seen.

"Not for the opening gala it isn't," said Robyn as she motioned for me to turn around,

"Besides, you look very hot in that tuxedo," she said with a grin on her face.

"My parents are going to die!" Robyn had been saying that a lot lately, and frankly I was getting a bit worried.

"About your parents," I started to say through the changing room door.

"I am beginning to think, that perhaps,"

"Oh don't worry about my parents, you will be fine," said Robyn before I could finish my sentence,

"Look," said Robyn.

"I need to go shopping for a few things, so go get out of that tuxedo."

As I finished changing, I was thinking to myself, "Robyn is not as timid as I had originally thought, in fact she was quite demanding, cute but demanding."

Next, I found myself in some sort of boutique, looking at accessories and sampling perfume. When I had agreed to go shopping with Robyn, I was thinking that it would be a simple trip to one or two stores, but it was turning into a major event. We found ourselves in the mall, and after buying shoes; we went to store, after store looking for dresses. In each store, I sat near the changing area while Robyn tried on dress after dress asking me which ones looked good, which ones made her look older, and which ones made her look fat. It was almost seven o'clock when I finally asked Robyn if we were still going to go out on our date that evening.

"Oh, well I thought we could get some take out and go back to my room while we worked on our story," said Robyn.

"Our story?" I asked in a confused tone. I had no idea what story Robyn was referring to.

"Well," said Robyn, as she put her hands on her hips,

"If we are going to tell my parents we are dating, they will want to know how we met."

"Robyn," I said.

"Why don't we just be ourselves, and let the evening take care of itself."

"Don't be ridiculous," replied Robyn.

"My parents would never buy it."

"Why are you so bent on making your parents think you have a boyfriend?" I asked Robyn through the changing room door.

"Especially having one so soon after starting college." Robyn was quiet for a moment, and then I could hear her starting to cry.

"I am sorry," I said as she opened the door and handed me a pile of dresses.

"I didn't mean to push you into this, and now you think I am some sort of crazy lunatic," said Robyn as she continued sobbing. I was actually quite amazed to see someone break into tears that easily.

"No," I said as I put my arms round her.

"I don't think you are a lunatic, I just think you're trying to hard, and you don't really have to." I looked down at the mascara stain, and watched as it continued growing on my shirt.

"I think you just need to relax and have a little fun. You don't have to plan out every minute of your life."

"But what about my mother?"

"Isn't your mother the reason why you're going to school 300 miles away from home," I interrupted.

"Yes I suppose you are right," she replied.

"Ok then, here is what we are going to do," I said as I handed the pile of dresses to the store clerk standing next to me.

"I am going to drop you off at your place, and you are going to go change into something comfortable, I will run over to my place and also change into something comfortable. Then, we are going to go get some dinner, maybe go to a movie, but we will be spontaneous, we won't plan it out, we will see how the evening evolves, ok". Robyn nodded her head as we left the mall for home.

We pulled into the dorm parking lot, and I helped Robyn back to her room with all of the boxes, and bags of items she had purchased.

"I will meet you back in the main lobby in 15 minutes," I said.

"Ok," said Robyn.

"15 minutes." As I walked into my room Steve and Tom were watching TV and laughing about something.

"How has your day with Robyn been?" Asked Steve.

"I don't really know," I said as I started changing my clothes.

"Kind of strange I guess, Robyn is really nice, but she is high maintenance."

"Are you guys going to dinner?" Asked Tom.

"Yeah," I responded in an inquisitive tone.

"Why?"

"Can we come too?" piped in Steve.

"We are really bored."

"I don't know guys I think I need to be alone with Robyn for a little while, to help her loosen up a bit, but why don't you guys meet us that little coffee shop on 4th south in about two hours."

"Ok, we will be there," said Steve and Tom.

I made my way back out to the main lobby and found Robyn standing by the main doors waiting for me.

"I am ready to have fun and be spontaneous," she said.

"Good," I answered back, "let's go."

We jumped back into my car, and headed to the other end of campus where "The Pie" Pizzeria was located. In those days, The Pie had live music on the weekends, it was always crowded, and it was the "happening" place to be. The restaurant was located in the basement of a 24 hr. pharmacy, it was an old, all brick building, and besides the good food, and electric atmosphere, The Pie had a unique feature, you were encouraged to write on the walls. Every square inch of the restaurants interior brick walls were covered with phone numbers, people's names, and football scores, various sayings, and beatnik poetry. It had a really cool and exhilarating atmosphere, so I figured it was as good a place as any to help Robyn relax and experience a little college nightlife. Steve, Tom, and I had been there quite a few times, we really enjoyed the atmosphere, and the pizza was pretty good too.

"What kind of pizza would you like?" I yelled in Robyn's ear as the band began playing their first set of the evening.

"I have never really been allowed to eat pizza," said Robyn in a slightly embarrassed tone.

"My mom says it to fattening, so whatever you want is fine with me," yelled Robyn back at me. I turned to the guy behind the counter and held up two fingers, which was a small pepperoni pizza.

"What do you like to drink?" I yelled back at Robyn, who was beginning to get sucked into the crowd. To keep Robyn from getting pulled into the main dining area by the crowd, I did something that Mandy and I had done many times when we were in a crowd, I grabbed Robyn's arm, pulled her quite close to my side, and put her hand in my back pocket.

"Don't let go," I yelled.

I meant nothing by putting Robyn's hand in my back pocket, and to be honest it was an innocent reaction on my behalf, as I stated earlier, Mandy and I had done it many times when we were in a tight crowd. Under the present circumstance, it was the only way I could keep Robyn close to me, and not lose her in the crowd. When I turned back again a few moments later to ask Robyn another question, I saw the look on her face, and realized that she must have been mortified by what I had done, she looked like she was going to pass out or start crying, or both.

"Two cokes," I yelled back to the guy behind the counter, I figured Robyn would just have to be happy with whatever drink I got her, because she was staring at me and wouldn't answer my question about what beverage she wanted.

The man behind the counter handed me our drinks, and a small plastic number to put on our table, I gave him a wad of cash and told him to keep the change.

"Follow me," I yelled back towards Robyn, but as I started to walk I felt a tug on my back pocket, I looked back toward her and noticed that Robyn was still frozen in place. Unfortunately I couldn't do anything about it, because I had a drink in each hand, and a plastic number stuck between my teeth, so I just started walking, hoping that Robyn would hold on, and follow me, to my surprise she did. Robyn and I slowly made our way through the maze of tables, and crowds of people, to a small, empty table in the corner of the room, and sat down. By then, the band had gone into a slower, and slightly quieter song, and for the first time since we entered the restaurant I could talk to Robyn without yelling.

"I am sorry about putting your hand in my back pocket," I said.

"I really did not mean to offend you." Robyn was blushing quite heavily at that point, and looked down at the table.

"It's ok, it just took me by surprise, I've never had my hands in a boys pocket before."

"Sorry," I said again.

"It was one of those instinct things, and it won't happen again." We sat there for a moment with an odd and uncomfortable silence between us, so to break the tension; I grabbed one of the markers off the table,

"Here, write something on the wall,"

"*What*?" asked Robyn.

"Look around," I said.

"The wall is covered in writing, you won't be vandalizing anything." Robyn just looked at me like I was crazy.

"Ok," I said.

"I'll write on the wall." I took the small lid off the marker and wrote,

"*Robyn was here.*"

"Why did you do that?" Robyn asked.

"I don't know, just because."

"Here you write something," I said as I pushed the marker into her hand, she just sat there staring at the marker and then at me, writing on the wall in public was obviously going against every fiber in her being.

"Don't worry," I said with a smile on my face.

"You don't have to write anything."

I reached out and took the marker from Robyn, but as I went to put the cap on, she grabbed it back from me and wrote, in the smallest letters I have ever seen.

"*Jeremy was here too.*"

"There you go," I said while laughing out loud,

"Way to be spontaneous and wild." The girl carrying our pizza soon arrived, and we started eating.

"Robyn," I said, in between bites,

"You have got to loosen up, or you'll have an ulcer by the time you're 23."

"I have an ulcer," said Robyn,

"I've had it since I was 15."

"*Crap,*" I thought to myself as I tired back tracking around what I had just said.

"I am sorry, I was only joking," I replied. Robyn looked at me and began to snicker.

"Me too," and a big smile flashed across her face as we both started laughing. After we had eaten our fill of pizza, I grabbed Robyn by the arm,

"Come on, let's dance a bit."

"No," said Robyn as she began to pull away.

"I don't dance," I gave her an odd look.

"Not like this," she said.

"Come on," I said persistently,

"You will be fine, there are so many people crammed in here that you don't really dance, you just sort of move to the beat."

I pulled Robyn up out of her seat, quite easily, because she weighed next to nothing. I took her arms and placed them upon my shoulders, and as I put my arms tightly around her waist, I pulled her very close to me, so that I would not lose her in the mob of people dancing and pulsating to the music.

"*Relax,*" I yelled, loosen up and enjoy yourself for a few minutes, tomorrow you can go back to being stuffy." We danced for about 20 minutes, and then when the smoke and congestion got to be too much for even me, I leaned in to Robyn and yelled,

"*Let's go.*"

I turned towards the front door, and as I started making my way through the crowed, I felt Robyn put one hand in my back pocket, and wrap her other arm around my chest,

"*Ok*" she yelled back.

"*Let's go.*"

I held Robyn's hand as I led her out to the car, and as I opened her door to let her in, I found myself thinking how glad I was that Robyn and I had met, for the past few days I had been so wrapped up in Robyn's life that I had not had time to think about Mandy at all. We arrived at the coffee shop to find Steve, Slim, and Tom sitting at a booth, discussing something I knew I didn't want Robyn to hear, because of the way they were all laughing, As Robyn and I approached the table I cleared my throat loud enough to get their attention and say, "time to change the subject."

"Robyn," I said while pointing at Slim,

"This is Slim; he was out the other day so you two didn't meet." They exchanged greetings, as we slid into the booth next to him.

"So," said Steve inquisitively.

"What have you guys been up to?"

"We had pizza," exclaimed Robyn, I looked at Steve as I proudly announced,

"Robyn wrote on the wall, ate pizza, drank Coke, and danced at The Pie, all firsts for Robyn."

"Well," said Slim,

"We have been sitting here discussing what we wanted to do this evening,"

"We go to medical library on campus and find pictures in medical journals, of wounds." Tom said, as everyone at the table fell silent, you could have heard a pin drop, and after a very painfully long silence.

"You are one creepy man Tom, and that is *not* what we are doing tonight." Steve said.

"Do I know you?" Asked Slim, as he stared at Tom.

"Yeah," I said finally breaking the second awkward round of silence.

"I think Robyn and I are going to stay here, order a hot chocolate, and do a little talking." I looked around the table.

"After I take Robyn home, I am going to bed, because I've had a long day in front of me tomorrow."

"Suit yourself," said Steve. He, Slim, and Tom left some money on the table, said "goodbye", and headed out the door.

"You have some really," Robyn paused for a moment, searching for the right words.

"Nice friends Jeremy."

"Yeah, well they are not always that weird," I replied.

"I think it is just past their bed times and they have gone a bit loony." Our hot chocolates arrived, and we sat looking at each other.

"Robyn, why don't we just take next Friday night as it comes and try to relax, I am sure you're parents will be fine." I said. However I could sense a bit of reluctance in Robyn's face.

"Don't worry about me I can handle myself and I can handle your parent, you'll see."

"Jeremy," said Robyn as she looked away from me,

"You don't know my parents." Once again, I found myself making one of those statements that I would later regret,

"Robyn how bad can your parents really be?" I asked.

I had arranged to get off work a bit early the Friday of Robyn's recital, so that I would have time to pick up my tuxedo, buy some flowers for Robyn and be ready to meet her at the ballet in time. When I got back from running all of my errands I showered, shaved, and got into my tuxedo.

"Where are you going dressed up like a penguin?" Asked Steve.

"I'm going to Robyn's ballet performance tonight," I said as I put on some cologne,.

"Remember, I told you about it a few days ago."

"Oh yeah that's right," said Steve.

"By the way did I tell you I got a new job," he said. I had actually forgotten that Rhonda had fired Steve, so I tried to act surprised.

"No, you didn't, where are you working?"

"I am a shuttle driver for the Marriott hotel downtown," said Steve rather proudly.

"I will be shuttling the stars around Salt Lake City when they come to visit." I could not think of any stars who had come to Salt Lake, but because I did not want to burst his bubble.

"Good for you Steve, I know you would find something soon, way to go."

"You know Jeremy," said Steve with a mischievous smile.

"You've been spending a lot of time with Robyn lately." He stood up and pointed his finger at me.

"Me and the guys are beginning to wonder if Robyn has replaced a certain girl, whom we won't mention."

"I don't know Steve," I replied.

"Robyn is really nice, and she's cute, but I just don't feel those connections, that spark, you know."

"Don't worry mate," said Steve reassuringly.

"Just give it time, things will get better."

"I just don't think there are any sparks between us," I continued explaining.

"We've had a good time together, but she is just not," I paused for a moment.

"Mandy," said Steve.

"I'm sorry mate, but Robyn, will never be Mandy, and no other girl for that matter, will ever be Mandy."

"No, that's not it," I said. Steve rolled his eyes.

"Honestly, Steve, that's not it at all, I have had fun the last few weeks, and Robyn has really helped me to move on, but I just can't explain it, there just aren't any fireworks."

"Well don't lead her on mate," said Steve as he sat back down.

"Don't make her think there is something between the two of you, and then just drop her like a rock."

"I won't," I said reassuringly.

"Besides, tonight isn't about us, it is about her needing to prove something to her mother, and I just agreed to help her out."

"Well just don't go hurting any one alright," said Steve.

"Don't worry," I replied.

"I won't, trust me this is not what it may appear to be, we are only friends and I am only doing her this one favor." I happened to notice the clock radio by Steve's bed and it said 7:15 p.m. I gasped,

"*Oh good hell!*" I said.

"Is it really fifteen minutes past seven?"

"Yep," replied Steve.

"Doesn't it start at seven?" He asked.

"*Yes,*" I yelled.

"And I promised Robyn I would be there early to meet her parents." I grabbed the flowers off my desk, and started off at a dead run towards the ballet recital. I ran, panting like a dog into the main lobby and came screeching to a halt at the ticket booth.

"I have a reserved seat," I told the elderly woman behind the ticket counter between huge gasps of air. I gave her my name, and she slowly started thumbing through the box of reserved tickets. After a few awkward minutes I yelled out,

"I am sorry Ms., but I am in a real hurry here," the elderly ticket lady looked up at me through her bifocals.

"I am sorry young man, but you are the one who's late, not I, and yelling at me will not help me find your tickets any sooner." After saying that, she went back to thumbing through the tickets,

"Here you are," she finally said pulling my ticket out of the box.

"Enjoy the show." I grabbed the ticket out of her hand and hastily made my way into the dark and very crowded Ballet West auditorium. I stumbled towards my seat noticing that the ballet was already in full swing, with the music blaring and two-two's flying, I was tripping over peoples feet and hand bags while apologizing left and right,

"Sorry, excuse me, sorry about your foot, sorry about that, whoops, sorry," at one point I even fell into someone's lap. I finally made my way to what appeared to be the only empty seat in the whole auditorium, it was right in the center of the row, and only three or four rows back from the stage.

I sat down and was catching my breath as I noticed a very regal looking woman sitting beside me, and next to her sat a tall man with a bad set of hair plugs. I had neglected to ask Robyn what her parents looked like, and so I could only imagine that these were her folks. I sat trying to catch my breath for a few minutes, and as I did, I looked up and happened to notice Robyn dancing on stage. She was wearing a tight, shimmering red dress, with black tights and black ballet shoes. From where I was sitting she looked very attractive. I figured this was as good a time as any to attempt a conversation with her mother,

"You must be very proud of your daughter," I said trying to break the ice.

"She is looking very lovely this evening, and I think she is doing a great job." Of course being the first ballet I had ever been to in my life, I had no idea if she was doing a good job, for that matter I did not even know what was going on! It all looked like a bunch of random dancing, with people spinning, and a bunch of overly feminine guys in tights jumping around with each other, and occasionally they would spin around with a girl in their arms.

"We are very proud of her," said the woman sitting next to me, after a few moments of silence.

"And so happy that she is fulfilling her dream to be a ballerina." I was thankful that she had finally responded to me, and I continued the conversation.

"When did you guys get into town?"

"We came in last night, and we are staying in a hotel down town."

"Oh," I exclaimed.

"She did not tell me that you were coming early," I leaned in closer, "We should have done something last night."

"Well," she replied,

"Karl had some business to attend to so we would not have been able to make it any way," she sat there for a moment looking at me rather oddly.

"I am sorry; I don't think we've met."

"Oh I am sorry," I stated.

"I am Jeremy, your daughter's boyfriend." She stared at me for a moment.

"Well, I must say, this is a surprise I didn't know our little girl had a boyfriend, this is wonderful news!" She nudged Karl, and whispered something in his ear, and then he leaned over.

"Nice to meet you young man." He gave me a hearty handshake, and a big welcomed smile.

"So, what are you studying here at the University of Utah?" Asked Karl.

"Architecture," I said and then with an even bigger grin, Karl shook my hand again.

"Good for you son, I am very excited to hear that our little girl has chosen someone with class."

I sat back in my chair and thought to myself, "wow" this is going much better than I had expected, what was Robyn so worried about these people were great. When the first half of the ballet ended and they announced a brief intermission, Karl asked me if I would like a drink or a snack from the concessions stand?

"I would love something, thank you."

While we waited for Karl to return Robyn's mom and I had a pleasant conversation about the University, and how her and Karl had both gone to school here, she went on to tell me that the school of business was where they met and that they were married soon after graduation. Karl returned with a drink and some candy bars.

"How much do I owe you?" I inquired.

"Nothing my boy," said Karl with a smile.

"It is on me!"

The lights soon went down again, as I sat happily sipping my soda, and enjoying my sugar daddies, the second half of the ballet came and went rather pleasantly. As soon as the closing curtain fell we all stood up and made our way into the lobby, Robyn's mom, dad, and I arm in arm standing there with big smiles on our faces waiting for the performers to change and make there way out to the front lobby.

"Jeremy, Jeremy," I heard from across the crowded lobby, I glanced over and saw Robyn looking rather concerned, she motioned for me to come over, so I told her parents that I would be right back.

"You did a wonderful job," I said as I handed her the flowers and gave her a small kiss on the cheek.

"Thank you, but where have you been?" Asked Robyn with a concerned look on her face.

"I waited for you before the performance, my parents wanted to meet you but you never showed up."

"Oh, don't worry about it," I said with a smile on my face.

"I sat next to your parents during the performance and we had a great conversation, I think things are good, and you don't have anything to worry about."

"How could you have sat next to my parents?" Asked Robyn with a confused look on her face.

"They were in the balcony," she said as she pointed upwards.

"When I tried to get you a ticket next to them, I was told the balcony was full, so I had to get you a seat in a different section." I was feeling a bit confused at that point.

"I left a message with Steve to tell you that you would be sitting alone," said Robyn as she shook her head.

"Didn't he tell you?" I stood there thinking for a minute.

"Steve didn't give me any messages, and by the way aren't those your parents over there?" I asked as I pointed towards Karl and his wife, whom I had sat next to for the entire performance.

"No," said Robyn.

"I have no idea who those people are, my parents are over there," and she pointed towards the front door where her parents stood waving at us, I sheepishly waved back, and as the realization of what had just happened sunk in, I became very embarrassed.

"Ok, let's get out of here quickly," I said while grabbing Robyn by the arm and dashing for the front door.

"Please," I said as we made our way towards the door.

"Don't look back." We met up with Robin's real parents, and made our way out the door. When we were safely outside in the parking lot Robyn said,

"Mom, Dad this is my boyfriend Jeremy," she then turned to me.

"Jeremy, this is my mom and dad." We all shook hands and then her father said,

"I am glad you could finally make it son, we were afraid you would be standing our daughter up for the evening," after hearing that comment, I began to wish that Karl was Robyn's dad.

"We have reservations for the Roof Restaurant at 10:00 so we need to get going," said Robyn's mother. As soon as she said where we were going for dinner, I could feel the color going right out of my face,

"They would see the picture in the display case, that damn picture would yet again be my undoing," I thought to myself.

We all walked over to her parent's brand new, jet-black Cadillac, and got inside. The inside of this car had the most immaculate interior I had ever seen in my life! It had a dark gray, full leather interior, the seats were overstuffed and felt like lazy boy recliners, the seats were also heated and everything was fully automatic.

"What's wrong?" Robyn whispered in my ear.

"Nothing," I whispered back.

"Is this car for real?"

"Yes," she said with a puzzled look on her face.

"What is that suppose to mean?"

"Nothing," I said.

"I just had no idea your parents drove a car like this."

"You never asked," whispered Robyn.

"You always drive, so you have never seen my car either." I sat up as my mind began to race, she had always offered to let me drive her car, but I thought nothing of it and we had been driving around in my rusty piece of garbage for two weeks now.

"What kind of car do you have?" I asked in a low whisper.

"I have a little red Mitsubishi convertible that my parents bought me when I graduated from high school." Robyn whispered back.

"What are you too whispering about back there?" Asked Robyn's mom.

"Jeremy was just commenting on how nice dad's new car is, and how when he graduates from the *Architecture* department and begins his own practice he wants a car just like this one, right Jeremy?" Robyn asked as she nudged me in the ribs.

"Oh, absolutely," I said.

"This car is amazing."

"It should be for the $52,000 I paid for it," said her father. I almost choked on my tongue like I was having a seizure, this car cost just short of what my parents paid for their house. Robyn's mom interrupted.

"You boys can talk about your little cars later!"

"Jeremy," she said while turning back in her seat to look at me,

"Honey, we are very happy to meet you, and we are glad that our little Robyn has found someone in her life, you do understand however that she will not be eligible for marriage until after she finished college and is accepted into the New York Metropolitan Ballet Company."

"*If*," said Robyn in a frustrated tone.

"If, I make it that far, and "IF," I decide to go any further with ballet after college we will see, besides there are lots of girls who get married and still have a successful ballet career," said Robyn.

"Yes dear, but when they decide to have little ones, that ruin their career and their bodies for life," Robyn's mother looked right at me.

"Do you want children Jeremy?" She asked.

"Well I, um, think that children are good," I was floundering badly, having been caught completely off guard by her mother's question.

"Mom we are not here to discuss that tonight, can we please just have a nice dinner and talk about something, *anything* else?"

"I was only asking a harmless question," stated her mother. The remainder of the trip was rather quite as we made our way to the restaurant. I felt really bad for Robyn at this point, I never had money growing up, at least not like she apparently did, but I got along with my parents and they were always supportive of what ever I wanted to do or be when I grew up. They never told me what I had to be or what I had to study in school, and for that I was always grateful.

We walked into the main lobby of the restaurant as I thought to myself,

"I have gone from never eating here before, to not only eating here a number of times, but now I have grown to hate it with a passion." I came to the conclusion that no good had ever come to me by eating at this restaurant, and from the looks of it tonight was not going to be any different.

"Well, would you look over there," Robyn's father said while looking directly at the glass display case, and with an air of arrogance he said,

"The young man in that picture looks just like you, Jeremy."

"Yes sir," I said trying not to look nervous.

"That is me, sir and that is my roommate's sister who was visiting from Australia. I was just trying to show her what an amazing cuisine this fine restaurant had." I figured at this point I had no other grounds to combat Robyn's parents with than my limited, yet somewhat impressive collection of five-dollar words. We had been studying these so called, "big" words in my writing composition class, so I figured I would probably never use them again in my life, and I was sure that I would forget them after the class was over, so I might as well get my tuitions worth out of them tonight.

"I don't mean to be supercilious, but I would assume that a business man as successful as you would appreciate the need for good hosting qualities when one was entertaining an important international figure who was showing a positive interest in such a highly esteemed institute of higher learning and education as the University of Utah." I had actually surprised myself by pulling off that articulate sentence, but with the way Robyn and her parents were staring at me like I was some kind of idiot, I assumed that I must have messed some of the words up.

"Well," said Robyn's father,

"I went to Harvard." And with that being said, we all turned and went into the restaurant. I could tell I was not going to win a war of words either, so it was time to resort to desperate measures, I would just have to be myself and hope for the best. We sat down and her father ordered off the menu for all of us, no buffet this evening, and then it began, the dreaded conversation about how Robyn was their baby and they loved her, and how they only wanted what was best for her, and how she had become accustom to a certain life style that I had better be able to provide for her, and so on and so forth. After about an hour of this barrage of comments and questions, Robyn leaned over and whispered in my ear,

"You have no idea how grateful I am to you for taking this abuse on my behalf," I looked over towards her, and could tell that she was fighting back the tears.

"I'm very sorry that my parents are this way and if you have had enough, I won't blame you, we can tell them the truth now." I leaned over and whispered back to her,

"I am fine, please forgive me for what I am about to do."

"What?" She asked.

"What are you going to do?" I grabbed Robyn by the hand and whispered back to her,

"Hold on this could get ugly." I then looked at her parents and did something I never in a million years thought I had the courage to do,

"I apologize for sounding forward, but I would just like to say, Robyn is a very beautiful girl and she loves the two of you very much. She wants nothing more than to please you, and she desperately wants your approval. Robyn is a very smart girl and she is completely capable of making her own decisions, if she wants to pursue ballet I am sure she will be the best ballerina in New York or Paris or wherever she decides to go, but if she decides tomorrow to dropt out completely and do something else with her life, I am sure she will do it with just as much passion and grace! You are lucky to have such a beautiful and talented daughter, and I am sure she will make a wonderful mother someday. It was very nice to meet the two of you and I hope you have a safe trip home, now if you will please excuse the two of us we are going to celebrate Robyn's wonderful opening performance with people that appreciate us." I then grabbed Robyn's hand and to her astonishment, and that of her parents, I stood up and passionately kissed Robyn right in front of them,

"I love your daughter and she loves me, and if you two don't watch yourselves we will run to Vegas and elope without telling, or inviting you, good evening." I then held Robyn tightly at my side as we made a mad dash out the door, down the hall, to the elevator and out into the street. As we exited the building and found ourselves standing in the cold evening air, I looked at Robyn and she looked at me and we both burst into laughter at the same time.

"I can't believe you did that," said Robyn.

"I can't believe I did that either," I replied.

"I thought your dad was going to reach over the table and strangle me."

"Did you see the look in my mom's eyes when you kissed me, I thought she was going to die," squealed Robyn with excitement. We made our way to a small café down the street and took a seat next to the window.

"Excuse me while I go call Steve and ask him to pick us up," I said as I stood up to find a payphone. I found a phone in the corner of the cafe and called Steve, explaining the whole thing to him over the phone.

"I said try not to hurt anyone's feelings tonight," was Steve's response to the situation.

"I'll be there in twenty minutes," he said and hung up the phone.

As I sat back down across from Robyn, she had tears in her eyes and I instantly felt bad for what I had done, I didn't mean to hurt Robyn, I guess I just figured, what do I have to lose, after all we were not really boyfriend and girlfriend.

"I am sorry," I said as I pulled some napkins out of the holder on the table.

"I will go back and apologize to your parents right now."

"It's not them," said Robyn.

"I have never had anyone stand up for me like that, and I am just grateful for you and what you did."

"Well, I would do it for any of my pretend girlfriends," I said in a light-hearted tone, and began to laugh. I quickly noticed that Robyn was not laughing, and in fact she had a hurt look on her face.

"Right," she said.

"Pretend girlfriend, I know, we were just pretending, and you did a great job, that was a very convincing kiss, my parents are freaking out right now I just know it, will you excuse me for a minute."

Robyn got up and ran into the girl's room. I sat there quite puzzled for a few minutes then I felt a heavy hand on my shoulder.

"Ready to go?" Asked Steve as I jumped.

"*Crap Steve*, you scared the hell out of me, I thought you were Robyn's dad coming in here to kill me."

"Where is Robyn?" Asked Steve.

"She is in the girl's room, and will be out in a minute," I responded.

Robyn came back out to where Steve and I were waiting, and although you could tell she had been crying she had a smile on her face,

"Ok boys let's go," she said as we headed for home. We pulled into the dorm parking lot and got out of Steve's car, Robyn put her hands gently on my face,

"Thank you for everything," she then kissed me gently on the cheek, turned around and disappeared into the dark cold night.

I stood there like a fool watching her walk away, but I did nothing, I was dazed and confused, I had only known her for a couple of weeks, and we had only gone out a few times. I knew that I had told Steve there were no fireworks, but as I stood there trying to decide what to do, I realized that perhaps there was something there, maybe it was not all pretend, and I took off after her. I ran into the main lobby, picked up the courtesy phone, and called her room, no answer, she either wasn't there, or if she was she had chosen not to answer. I ran out to the parking lot and looked for a red convertible but could not find one. Had she left already? Where could she have gone? After a desperate but fruitless search I found myself walking alone on the campus sidewalk thinking to myself,

"What am I doing? This is just a rebound affair for me, and I shouldn't pursue it any farther." I made my mind up then and there that we could only be friends because I was not in a position to handle another romantic entanglement. I have since wonder what would have happened had I been able to find Robyn that night. The next day, I went to her room and knocked on the door, Robyn's roommate opened the door.

"Is Robyn there?" I asked just as Robyn was walking out.

"I am going to breakfast with my parents, they want to talk about last night," she said.

"Do you want me to go with you?" I inquired.

"No, I think I am going to be ok now, but thanks again, you are a good friend, and I believe things will change for the better with my parents." She said as she walked past me and out the door, once again I did not try to stop her; I only stood there watching her as she disappeared down the hall.

CHAPTER 4

Friends

Things were different between Robyn and myself after the evening we spent with her parents, I mean we were still friends, in fact she became more and more a part of our little group after that night; going places with us, hanging out in our dorm room, and in time she actually became "one of the guys" but every so often she would give me a glance or walk by and touch my arm in such a way that kept me wondering if it was all pretend, or if there was something more between us then I thought. It was probably two or three weeks after my exciting night on the town with Robyn, that I found myself sitting in one of the lawn chairs on the dorms balcony, half asleep, and daydreaming with one of my books on my lap, when I heard a girls voice behind me,

"Are you studying or sleeping," it startled me, and as I jumped up my book fell out of my lap onto the ground.

"Oh I am sorry I didn't mean to startle you," said the voice from behind, and as she bent over to pick up my book, I noticed that it was Megan.

"Oh, yeah I was studying, but I guess I sort of lost it there, I was somewhere between here and never, never land."

"Oh," she said with a smile.

"If I am bothering you I can go somewhere else."

"No, no I am done studying for now," I said as I motioned for her to sit in the empty chair next to me.

"I hope your group therapy is going well," Megan said sympathetically.

"My what?" I asked.

"The therapy," she said.

"Steve told me you were in group therapy because your girlfriend died so tragically."

"Oh that, no the whole thing was a misunderstanding," I said as I shook my head.

"Steve was just joking around; you can't take anything he says seriously."

"Oh, well ok then," Megan said.

"I'm glad things are fine."

"So how is your boyfriend?" I asked, in an attempt to change the awkward conversation.

"We broke up a few weeks ago, things just weren't working out, he was just too into himself, and some other girl named Monica, or Monique, or something like that, anyway we just decided it was best to move on."

"I am sorry to hear that," I said in a sympathetic tone. It was just about the time when I was going to ask Megan if she wanted to go to dinner that Slim came wandering out,

"Hey Megan," he said loudly, startling both of us.

"You'll want to stay away from that slime ball, he's nothing but trouble." I turned to see Slim standing over us eating an apple, with a grin on his face.

"Oh well I suppose that's good to know Slim, thanks for the warning," and with that Megan stood up and walked towards the door.

"See you later boys," she said and waved as she walked back into the lobby.

"How do you know her Slim?" I asked.

"We had some classes together last year, that's all really," said Slim as he sat in the chair Megan was sitting in only moments before.

"I thought you were a new student," I said.

"Me?" Slim replied.

"No, I was here last year, I just took the summer off," Slim walked over to the trashcan and threw his apple core away as he continued talking to me.

"Megan was here last year too." I suppose I had just assumed that Megan had started this summer, because after all, my arriving at the U was the beginning of time.

"She is nice enough I guess," said Slim.

"She can make the piano sound like angels from heaven."

"Yeah, I have heard her playing in the main lobby a few times, she is good," I added.

"Hey, I have something for you," said Slim as he reached in his back pocket and pulled out a picture.

"Here you are," said Slim.

"The picture you asked for, I had to sneak it out last night after all the staff had gone home, she really is a lovely girl." I looked at the picture for a moment then I looked up as Slim,

"This harmless little picture has caused me a lot of grief you know," I sat looking at it for a minute or two,

"Thanks Slim, I owe you one."

"Good," said Slim.

"I know just how you can re-pay me." I hand only said "I owe you one," to Slim as one of those guy-to-guy courtesies. I really didn't mean anything by it, but on the other hand, Slim did get the picture for me.

"What do you need me to do?" I asked apprehensively.

"I need someone to try my food, and tell me what it needs, I know you frequent the Roof Restaurant so I'm sure you are a coinsure of good cooking. The Roof is where I'm a junior chef," explained Slim.

"And as you may or may not know, I'm training to be a chef, so I need to come up with some new dishes, and I need to practice my serving and cooking skills. "What do you say?" Asked Slim.

"Will you help me out?"

"*Hell yah*," I said perhaps a little bit too excitedly. I was a starving student and anyone who wanted to cook for me was more than welcome too.

"Great," said Slim with a smile.

"Meet me here tomorrow at six p.m. and bring a date if you like." He handed me a piece of paper with an address on it for an apartment complex somewhere in the downtown Salt Lake area.

The next day Steve, Robyn, Tom and I found ourselves driving around down town Salt Lake City looking for the address Slim had given me the day before,

"That has got to be it," Robyn said while pointing to the high-rise apartment complex on our right.

"No way, those are some big apartments," replied Steve.

"That has to be it," I said.

"We have circled the block like five times that has to be it." We found ourselves standing in the doorway of one of the most exclusive and expensive apartment complexes in the downtown area. Steve, Tom, and I shoved Robyn up to the intercom.

"Ask for Slim," we pushed the call button and moved back.

"Is Slim there?" Robyn asked with a rather timid voice.

"Come on up guys," Slims voiced echoed from the speaker box.

"Take the loft elevator to the top floor," there was a buzz as the door unlocked, and we all walked into the building. We made our way into the lobby, down the hall to the loft elevator,

"What is Slim doing in a place like this?" Asked Steve. The elevator opened and we found ourselves standing in front of a big metal door.

"I guess we knock?" I said just as the door swung open.

"Come on in guys," said Slim with a smile on his face, and mixing bowl in his arms. Slim looked at me, and then he looked at Steve, who was standing next to me,

"What, you call this ugly guy your date?" He took Robyn's hand and escorted her into the apartment.

"Robyn is defiantly my date, you can have Mr. Ugly."

"Ha, ha, ha," I said and as we walked into the apartment.

"What are you doing here mate, did you break in or something?" Steve yelled out.

"This is my dads place," said Slim, as he shut the door behind us.

"He is gone for the weekend on some business trip, and he said I could use his kitchen."

"Why would you want to live in the stinking dorms if you had access to a place like this?" Asked Steve, as he wandered around looking at the lavishly furnished apartment.

"Well," said Slim.

"I am tired of living off my parents, I want to be my own person, and I want to make it on my own." We all followed Slim into the kitchen and, wow, what a kitchen it was! Stainless steel fridge, huge gas range in the middle of the cultured marble island, double ovens in the wall, and all the cabinetry was done in a nice dark wood finish.

"Ok guys here we go," said Slim as he put on his Roof Top Restaurant chefs hat and coat.

"Please be seated at the bar and watch as I prepare your food like the professional that I am." We all sat down, as Slim turned on some nice music and then he made his announcement.

"Lady and gentlemen for this evening's meal we will be having a nice tossed salad, a lovely cheese soup, followed by rib cutlets, artichoke hearts, with steamed asparagus, and for dessert Crème Brule."

We all watched in amazement as Slim prepared everything right in front of us, except for the rib cutlets, which had been cooking since before we arrived. Slim was very professional with his presentation and he arranged the food on each plate as if it were a work of art, we all sat chatting, and watching as Slim wowed us with his culinary skills. There was only one scary moment, when Slim lit up the Crème Brule, and Tom bumped the lit torch by accident, causing the corner of Slims sleeve to start on fire. Other than the explicit words Slim used to inform Tom that he was not happy with his carelessness, the meal was perfect.

"Mate, you can cook for us any day of the week," Steve said as Robyn, Tom and I sat agreeing with him completely.

"Thank you very much," said Slim as he finished his first of what would prove to be many cooking masterpiece for us.

"Don't forget to tip your waiters and waitresses, I will be here all week, thank you and good night," Slim said while taking a bow.

It was a few weeks after our pleasant dining experience, when I found myself in the library late one evening trying to find information on one of my writing assignments. I had been given the topic of "The Turner Thesis" to write my research paper on by my professor. The Tuner Thesis was a series of essays written by a member of congress by the name of Turner in the late 1800's. Turner was assigned by the other members of congress to go "west," and report to the rest of the United States Government on the conditions and life styles of the western frontier. Turner did not make it much further than a hotel room in Chicago, and he based his writings on rumors and hearsay using the information he gathered from gold diggers, and gunslingers to write his reports. Turner then sent this false information back to Washington, where it was believed to be an accurate account of the western frontier. Because of the falsehoods behind these accounts, it is believed that the impressions of the west, which our society has assumed to be true for over a hundred years, were nothing short of a lie. Turner created the illusion of the white cowboy and the savage Indian, when in fact the Indians were very intelligent people and there were as many Asian, and Colored cowboys as there were "traditional" white cowboys. The "John Wayne" stereotype was what I had entitled my paper, and I was searching through books and old records to find out as much as I could about the subject.

Though it was not that long ago that I attended college, the Internet as we know it today did not exist, and all of my research had to be done in a library with actual books. I was pouring over some old books, or rather sleeping and drooling over some old books when I could sense that someone had sat down beside me.

"You will get more out of that book if you read it," said a voice that I did not recognize at first. I sat up and could instantly feel the dampness on my cheek resulting from drool, as I rubbed my cheek I looked down at the book which had been my pillow, and noticed that the print on the page I had been sleeping on was smudged.

"You have some ink on your face," the voice said, as I rubbed my eyes and began pulling myself together, I focused in the direction of the voice, and realized who was sitting next to me.

"Megan, what are you doing here so late?" I inquired.

"I work here," she responded in a playful tone.

"And we are getting ready to close, so you will have to go home now."

"Oh, what time is it?" I asked with a raspy voice.

"It is almost midnight," Megan said.

"Time for good little boys to be home in bed."

"Well that would be why I am still here," I responded, with a cheesy grin.

"What time do you get off work?" I asked.

"As soon as we can get everyone out of here," she said while looking at her watch.

"So in about fifteen minutes, why?" She asked.

"Oh no reason," I said as I began to gather my things together.

"I just thought you could walk me home and keep me safe from whatever or whoever might be out on a dark cold night like this," I said jokingly.

"Very funny," said Megan.

"Are you checking that book out tonight or are you just going to have a one-night stand with it?"

"Well," I said as I held the book close to my face while caressing it.

"I'm a gentleman, so I will be taking it home with me this evening."

"Alright," replied Megan while looking at me like I was an idiot.

"Give it to me and I will check it out for you, and then you can go away."

Megan walked over to the counter and checked out my book, she then handed it back to me,

"Good night," she said. I took the book and put it in my backpack then headed outside.

"You can walk me home if you promise not to take advantage of me," I said to Megan as she came walking out of the large, glass library doors.

"What are you still doing here?" Asked Megan with a flirtatious grin on her face.

"I thought I told you to go away."

"Well, I just wanted to see if librarians really had a home, because I believed from the time I was a kid that they just lived in the library."

"Ha, ha, ha," said Megan.

"If you are going to insist on walking me home then be a dear and at least offer to carry my book bag." I took her bag and held it in my arms as we made our way back up to big hill to the dorms.

"So, Slim tells me that I should avoid you because you are trouble, why would he say something like that?" Asked Megan.

"Because it's true, I guess," I said with a grin.

"I am just a troublemaker, and a menace to society."

"Well, then I better make sure to carry my pepper spray when you are around, just to keep you in line," said Megan playfully. When we arrived at the main lobby of the dorms I asked Megan if I could walk her to her room,

"No," she said.

"Why not?" I asked.

"I am carrying your book bag, and don't you want me to help you up to your room with it?"

"If I let every guy who carried my bags up to my room, my roommate would think I was someone who I am not, so thank you for the pleasant conversation, and for carrying my bags but I think I can manage from here."

She grabbed her book bag out of my arms, and said a final good night as she disappeared behind the door leading to the girl's wing. When I made it up to my room, Steve, Robyn, Tom and Slim were all sitting on the couch watching a movie; however I did not know they were watching movies so when I walked into the room I turned the light on.

"*Turn off the light,*" the four of them yelled in unison.

"Sorry guys," I exclaimed.

"What are you watching?"

"An old Hitchcock movie, now shut up," said Steve. I made my way towards the couch and took of my shirt as I stepped cautiously on the couch, trying not to step on anyone or disturb there movie night any more then I already had, then I put one foot on the back of the couch and hoisted myself into bed.

"Can I sit up there on the edge of your bed?" Asked Robyn.

"Slim made chili tonight, and Tom's stomach is starting to make some noises that I don't trust." I didn't even have time to answer. I felt the bed shaking as Robyn made her way up to my bed. She was wearing a pair of flannel pajama bottoms that I instantly recognized and a white t-shirt that also looked quite familiar.

"Aren't those mine?" I asked while yanking on the pull string that she had wrapped around herself nearly twice in order to get them to fit.

"I said she could wear them," Steve responded.

"After all you two are practically engaged aren't you?"

"Only in pretend land Steve, only in pretend land," I yelled back.

"I will change out of them if you want me to Jeremy," Robyn said with a look of surprise on her face, the truth was she made them look much better then I ever could.

"No, no it's fine," I chuckled.

"I don't mind I just hope for your sake that Steve got them out of my clean clothes pile, and not off the floor."

"They're clean," said Steve.

"Now shut up, the birds are going to attack this lady, I love this part."

I rolled over in my bed facing the other direction and when I did, Robyn moved back and was leaning up against me while she sat crossed legged watching the movie. I quickly found myself dosing off to sleep, and I vaguely remember having dreams about walking Megan home from the library while being chased by fake looking black birds on strings.

I was startled awake some time later by the feeling of something ice cold being pressed up to the back of my legs, and for a moment I panicked, sitting straight up in bed while hitting my head on the shelf above my pillow, I frantically looked around and as I came to my senses I noticed that the TV was on but there was nothing but static coming from the screen. Tom was not there but Steve and Slim were lying on opposite sides of the couch, arms wrapped around each other's feet with Slim snoring away and Steve drooling. I then looked over and saw Robyn curled up into a little ball sleeping soundly next to me; it had been her cold feet that were rubbing up against my legs. She did not have any covers on and she looked like she had been shivering for some time. I very carefully and quietly slid out of my bed and gently put my covers over Robyn's shivering little frame. I then went over to Steve's bed and figured if he would rather sleep with Slim far be it from me to break up the dynamic duo, I turned off the TV and climbed carefully into his bed.

When I came too the next morning, Steve and Slim were no longer there and as I opened my eyes I looked across the room to see Robyn still sleeping soundly, right where I had left her a few hours earlier. I quietly got up and put my shirt back on and then wrote a small note for Robyn, which read,

"Sleep as long as you like, stay as long as you like, our smelly little room is your smelly little room, Love Jeremy and Steve." I put the note next to her and quietly made my way to class.

The following evening, after school and work, I sat by the library fountain to finish some reading. Steve came by and asked, "What's up, mate?"

"Just trying to get the last of the information I need for my essay," I said and I closed my book. I willed myself to ask Steve what I'd been wondering all afternoon. Finally, I said as casually as I could pretend,

"What do you know about Megan?"

"Not much," Steve said.

"Other than she plays the piano."

"I know that," I interrupted,

"But what else?"

"I don't know," he said.

"Why? Do you like her?"

"Just curious."

"I'll ask around and see what I can find out," Steve said, and he winked at me.

"In the meantime, Slim is making dinner at his dad's place this weekend, sort of an end of the midterm celebration. Why don't you invite Megan?"

I gulped, but before I could respond Steve looked at his watch and said, "Talk to you later, mate," and he headed for the dorms.

I sat thinking about Steve's suggestion to invite Megan to dinner, and the more I thought about it the more I thought,

"She won't want to go with me," I had all but talked myself out of asking her, when I looked up and to my surprise Megan was standing right in front of me.

"I saw Steve a few minutes ago and he said you needed to talk to me."

"That sneaky little bastard," I thought to myself,

"I am going to get him one of these days."

"Yes, I did want to talk to you about something," I wasn't sure how to ask her, so I just gave it my best shot,

"You know Slim, right?" I asked.

"Yes, I know Slim," Megan replied.

"Well, he sort of cooks dinner for some of us on the weekends, and he is doing an end of the midterm dinner thing for us, so I was just wondering if you would like to go with me and some of my friends this weekend."

"Sure," she said, just like that, and quite frankly it took me by surprise.

"Really?" I asked in a surprised tone.

"Really," she replied.

"You look kind of cute and I suppose after brushing you off a few days ago, I really should give you at least one more chance," she said while smiling at me.

"I'm joking with you, it sounds like fun, and I would love to go."

"Ok great," I said.

"I will pick you up at 6:30 Saturday evening then."

"Alright," said Megan.

"I'll see you then."

It was hard to believe that midterms were once again upon us, the time when we all became insane with stress from the late nights of studying and preparing for our tests. This midterm was proving to be just as hard if not harder than the one before. We had our essays for our advanced writing class to prepare and Steve was a wreck.

"This damn paper is due in forty eight hours and I have only written seven of the thirty pages I need," exclaimed Steve late Wednesday evening.

"I am going to fail, and that will be the end of that."

"Steve, you're not going to fail," I said.

"What's your topic?" I asked.

"The history of steel manufacturing and its long term effect on Chicago's economy."

"Ok you might fail," I said jokingly.

"*See,* I told you I would," exclaimed Steve.

"You're not going to fail, I was just joking," I said while standing up.

"Grab your jacket and let's go."

"Where are we going?" Asked Steve.

"To the library, where the books are," I responded.

"So we can get some more information for your essay. I had to practically drag Steve to the library kicking and screaming the whole way, but I knew that if I didn't help him he would just allow his essay to fail.

"I am not going to find anything here," said Steve.

"Steve, it's a library, where do you usually find your information for essays?"

"I usually get it from the encyclopedia, but this time there was not enough information to get all the pages I need."

"*The encyclopedia!*" I yelled.

"You are in college for crying out loud, not Junior High School, and you are in an honors course."

"I know," said Steve, in a frustrated tone.

"That is what I keep telling you, I am not smart like you and Tom."

"It's not about being smart," I said.

"It's about knowing were and how to find the answers. Now you go sit down," I said while pushing Steve into an empty desk.

"I will start bringing you books, all you need to do is look through them and begin writing whatever information pertains to your topic, ok."

I went to the front desk and inquired as to where I could find some books about our subject, and within in a few minutes I returned with a hand full of books to where Steve had been sitting.

"*Steve*, I started yelling out,

"Where are you? How do expect to write this paper if you don't sit down and write it?" I soon found my friend standing next to the drinking fountain talking to a girl,

"I am sorry," I said to the girl standing in front of Steve.

"But my friend can't stay and chat, he has a paper to write and you're distracting him."

"Hey," said Steve in protest.

"What are you doing?"

"I'm helping you pass this class, now come on I found some books for you."

We marched back to Steve's table and I sat watching over him like a chicken watched over her baby chicks. Around 11:30 p.m. we had found almost all the information we needed, so I told Steve to keep writing while I went to see if I could find one more book.

As I stood searching in the same section where I had found all the books previously, I happened to look down one of the long isles next to me and notice Megan putting books back on the shelves. I found myself intently watching Megan work, and for the first time, I realized how attractive she really was, with her long brunet hair done up in curls, her deep brown eyes and the way she held her lower lip in her teeth while she concentrated. I was beginning to feel an attraction towards her. I reached down to grab a book from the shelf in front of me, and thought to myself,

"I think I will just casually walk over to where Megan is working and say hi," however, when I stood back up from retrieving my book I noticed that she was gone. I looked down the isles next to the one I had seen her in, and just as I turned to head back towards Steve, Megan jumped out from behind the isle.

"Who let you in here?" Seeing Megan appear out of thin air scared me so bad that I dropped my book on the floor, and did one of those yelling things where you make a funny noise but no real sound comes out. Megan began to laugh out loud; she had to place her hands over her mouth in an attempt to keep the sound from carrying to where the other students were studying. Meanwhile I tried to regain my composure by putting one arm on the shelf next to me.

"I knew you were there all along." Megan began to laugh even harder.

"No you didn't, I scared you to death," she said, as she continued to laugh.

"I'm sorry," she said while whipping the tears from her eyes.

"That was just one of the funniest things I have ever seen, the way you did that little dance."

"I didn't do a dance," I exclaimed.

"I really am sorry," Megan said.

"Let me pick up your book for you," she picked up my book and handed it tome.

"Do you want to check this one out, because if you do I would be glad to help you with it?"

"It's actually for Steve," I stated.

"So let me see if he wants it."

"I'll take it," said Steve, as his heavy hand came down on my shoulder, once again scaring the daylights out of me, and once again I dropped the book, and did my silent screaming disco dance. Megan and Steve both began to laugh uncontrollably at that point.

"I am sorry mate, I saw Megan and you talking and I just couldn't resist." Megan picked the book up once again, and whipped the tears of laughter from her eyes.

"Come on Steve I will check this book out for you," said Megan and the two of them walked off towards the check out counter.

That evening as I lay in bed, I couldn't stop thinking of Megan.

"Did she like me?" I thought to myself.

"Because if she did, the way I kept making a fool of myself around her was not helping things." Steve turned to me and said,

"Can we turn off the lights now mate, I'm getting tired?"

"Sure," I said. Steve unplugged the glowing pepper lights.

"What's on your mind mate? You seem a million miles away."

"I'm just thinking that I'm probably better off not getting involved with anyone right now, it only ends in heart ache."

"Are you thinking about Robyn?" Asked Steve.

"No," I said.

"I'm not thinking about anyone specifically, I am just making a statement."

"Oh I see," said Steve.

"You're thinking about Megan."

"I am not," I replied, even though I was.

"Well, you do whatever you want," stated Steve as he rolled over to face me.

"As for me, I like girls, and just because I may have one bad break up every now and then doesn't mean I am going to become a priest and take a vow of celibacy, like you seem to be doing."

"*What!*" I exclaimed.

"I have not taken a vow of celibacy, what is that suppose to mean?"

"It means you have girls talking to you all the time and you act like you don't even notice them, just because Mandy dumped you to go back to her old boyfriend, doesn't mean girls are evil and that you should just give up on them. It just means that she was not the girl for you and there is someone out there who is even better." Steve then rolled over and went to sleep.

Saturday evening came and I as I was getting ready to go I thought to myself,

"I will play things cool with Megan, she is a cute girl but I am not going to rush things."

I had decided that if I was looking for a romantic entanglement I could peruse Robyn, but I was not looking for love and so I resolved to keep things friends and friends only with Megan, besides I didn't even know if she liked me! For all I knew this was some sort of pity date, or maybe she was just being nice, or perhaps she was like me and just wanted a free dinner. I walked down to the main lobby and found Steve and Tom sitting in the overstuffed chairs chatting about how they thought midterms went.

"I will get "A" on everything," said Tom.

"And so will Steve," I exclaimed.

"Besides," I continued,

"This is an evening to forget all about midterms and enjoy ourselves, so let's get the girls and go."

Steve went over to the courtesy phone and a few moments later Robyn and Megan came out to the lobby. We all piled into Steve's yacht on wheels and headed to Slims private soirée. Upon entering Slims kitchen Megan ran over to Slim and put his arms around him,

"It looks just as good as it did last time Slim, what is on the menu for tonight?" I stood there feeling very confused while looking at Steve, who was now sitting on the leather sofa in the living room throwing green olives up in the air and catching them in his mouth. I went over and sat next to Steve to find out some information, I nudged him as he caught one of the olives in his mouth and he began to choke.

"*What?*" Asked Steve, as the olive it his throat became dislodged, sending it sailing into the dark hall adjacent to us.

"Did you notice how Megan gave Slim a hug and said something about dinner looking as good as it did last time?" I asked.

"So what?" Asked Steve.

"So," I replied.

"I thought Slim said he had one class with her last year and that was all."

"So what?" Asked Steve again.

"Never mind," I said, as I made my way back to the bar and sat next to Robyn. Robyn looked at me and asked,

"Do you know Megan, Jeremy?" I was confused even further.

"Yes, I invited her to dinner tonight."

"You did?" Asked Robyn with a confused look on her face.

"When?" She asked.

"A few days ago," I stated.

"Well that's strange because I invited her like two weeks ago," said Robyn.

"*What!*" I exclaimed.

"Yes, I invited her a while ago," Robyn, said as she picked up her glass of water and took a drink.

"Megan is my next door neighbor in the dorms, we spend a lot of evenings together," she paused for a moment and put her hand on my leg.

"At least the evenings I am not with you four loser's."

"*What!*" I exclaimed again.

"I'm sorry," said Robyn,

"You guys aren't total loser." Right as Robyn said that we were not losers, Tom tripped on the living room rug and fell behind the couch knocking over the lamp.

"Well not all of you are losers anyway," she said while shaking her head.

"You mean to tell me that you had already asked Megan to come to dinner with us, and you two are friends.

"Yes," said Robyn, she paused for a moment and then smiled while saying,

"Is that a problem, my pretend lover?"

"No, my fake sweetheart," I replied.

"That is not a problem; I'm just surprised that everyone but me knows Megan, that's all."

"Well let me introduce her to you," said Robyn as she motioned for Megan to come over to where we were seated.

"Megan," began Robyn.

"This is Jeremy, my pretend fiancé, hero, and he is the one who single handedly liberated me from my parents." I was so embarrassed that I could have died right then and there,

"You mean this is the guy you've been talking about?" Asked Megan.

"In the flesh," said Robyn.

"He is cuter than you described, but he does scare easily," Megan looked at me and ran her hand across my chest, winked, and headed towards the living room.

"Ok is everything good now?" inquired Robyn.

"Thank you," I exclaimed, and looked over at Slim who was busy preparing our evenings feasts.

"What's for dinner tonight Slim my man?" I asked.

"Tonight is all about the appetizers, I have chicken fingers, I have fireless jalapeno poppers, I have blue cheese dip with chips, I have gourmet nachos, I have spinach and cheese dip, I have buffalo wings, I have Italian sodas, and tonight is the John Wayne film festival on TV," he then looked at Tom, who did not like John Wayne,

"I don't care what anyone says I like 'The Duke' and we're in my house, well my dad's house anyway, and if you want to eat my food you will have to watch what I want."

"Cool, sounds good to me," I said.

"I like John Wayne and I like your cooking, you are the "Mr. Belvedere" I never had growing up."

"Very funny," said Slim.

"Hey Tom," I yelled across the room.

"If you aren't going to marry Slim I will, he can feed me and keep me barefoot and happy."

"What?" Asked Tom, with a confused look on his face.

"Slim is man, and I don't marry man, and why you no wear shoes if he is to marry you?"

"Never mind Tom," I said.

"Everyone find a place to sit because the appetizers are ready, and the Duke waits for no one," said Slim as we all headed towards the living room.

Megan sat next to Slim on the floor and Robyn sat next to me on the couch, Tom was sitting on the overstuffed loved seat,

"Tom buddy, I love you like a brother but you can't sit on my dads new $3,000 leather love seat, he just brought it back from Italy, so you can sit down here with me, until you finish eating," Slim said.

As we all sat watching the Duke in action, I found myself staring at Megan and feeling unusually jealous, because she was sitting next to Slim. I suppose I had been staring at Megan for some time, because after a while Steve looked at me and whispered,

"Hey father Jeremy, pass me the buffalo wings, and stop staring at Megan, she is a girl and you have taken a solemn vow, remember." I handed him the wings and mouthed the words ha, ha, ha, I then looked over at Robyn who was watching John Wayne very intently, with his chiseled face, and stunning features.

"Robyn," I whispered, with no response.

"*Robyn!*" I said louder as she jumped, and hit me on the arm.

"What do you want? You scared me."

"I'm sorry," I said.

"Do you mind if I rest my head in your lap for a few minutes, I have a bit of a headache?"

"Sure," said Robyn with an excited look on her face, so I put my head in her lap and kicked Steve to get his attention.

When he looked over at me I winked at him as if to say, "Who is the monk now!" Robyn started running her fingers slowly through my hair, and I began to sense that this might not have been the best idea, because I wanted to get Megan to notice me and this was not the way to do it, so I sat up.

"I think I better get some aspirin,"

When I got back from pretending to get some aspirin, Steve had his head in Robyn's lap and he was winking at me, but the funny part was Robyn, who had a look of disgust on her face, so I just winked back at Steve,

"You go, you animal," I whispered and I sat back down.

We finished our dinner and watched John Wayne early into the next morning, and as we all made our way tiredly down to Steve's car, Megan told me that she had a nice evening, and even though she was planning on coming anyway it was very nice of me to invite her. When we got home Robyn and Megan went back to there rooms to sleep, and Steve, Tom and I went to our rooms to do the same.

"Jeremy," Dan said, as I walked into work that next Monday morning.

"Come over here for a minute, I need to talk to you."

"Ok," I replied, and made my way out onto the dock, where Dan was smoking like a chimney.

"I have a bit of a problem on my hands, and I think you might be able to help me,"

"Ok Dan, what do you need?" I asked.

"Charlie, my assistant quit last Friday and when they asked me who I wanted to have as his replacement I told them you. I realize you have classes and so you come and go a bit, but when you are here I want you to help me deliver the cylinders of gas, what do you say, will you help me out?"

What could I say other than yes? Dan then told me to go into the dispatch office and let them know I would take the job, turn over my keys, and get Charlie's old gear to use until he could get me my own. I was not exactly thrilled about the job because I didn't really want to deliver huge cylinders of every kind of gas known to man all over campus. Dan delivered everything from oxygen to the hospital, to liquid nitrogen to the research labs, and acetylene to the metal shop on campus. It was a physically demanding job, and it would mean spending all day in a truck with Dan trying to breathe while he smoking his Marlboro Reds, however one advantage would be, no more paper deliveries, and Dan drove the brand new truck so I would not have to drive. I spent my first few days learning about the gasses and what they were used for, I also had to take a H.A.S.M.A.T. (hazardous materials) safety class, which consisted of Dan showing me a movie and giving me a test, that he had given me all of the answers to previously.

"I was deep in the jungle one day, sitting on the back of our cannon when all of a sudden the man sitting nest to me was hit, BAM, right in the face."

I must have jumped two feet when Dan hit the inside of the truck with his fist, I was facing the other direction when we he started telling me this particular story so when he made the "exploding" noise, I dropped the empty tank of chlorine that we had just picked up from the pool house, and it hit the ground with a thud, rolling to a stop at the front end of the truck's cargo area.

"I pulled out my gun and started shooting wildly into the bushes, bam, bam, bam," said Dan, while holding his scan gun like a weapon.

"But I don't think I hit anything, because I could still hear the little bastards running around," said Dan as he turned around and went back to work.

This was just one of the many stories I heard each and every day while working with Dan, sometimes they were amusing, and sometimes, like this story had been, they were a bit disturbing. It was just a few weeks before Christmas and there was snow on the ground, it was one of those cold days where your fingers ache and your nose is frozen. I had smashed the fingers on my right hand between two cylinders earlier that day when Dan told me the story of another buddy he had lost, while clapping his hands loudly, he shouted,

"*Bam*, his head blew clean off," scaring me that time too.

You would think I had gotten used to it by my third week out with him, but each day was a new adventure with Dan. Don't get me wrong, I really respected Dan for serving his country, and I looked up to him, but there were days I could have done without the stories. Sometimes I think he told them to me because everyone else had gotten tired of hearing them, or perhaps it was that I just listened, and did not try to judge, whatever the reason that will always be the thing I remember most about Dan, his Vietnam stories.

It had been a few weeks since I had seen Megan, and to be honest I was beginning to think that there was nothing between us, until one day after work when I was sitting down to watch some television when the phone rang.

"Hello," I said as I answered the phone.

"Is this Jeremy?" the voice on the other end said.

"Yes," I replied.

"Jeremy, hi this is Megan," she said.

"I know this may seem a bit odd, but I have a piano recital tonight, and I was wondering if you and Steve might want to come. Robyn already agreed to come and she suggested I invite you guys too."

"Sure," I said.

"What time and where is it?"

"It's at Gardner Hall, and it starts at seven, I am the first of two performers and my recital will be about an hour. When you get there just go to the ticket counter and there will be tickets for you in my name."

I really didn't think much of the invitation because Megan had invited all of us, and when Steve walked in a few minutes later I told him about the program and he said he would like to go.

Just before seven we all made our way to our seats, and within a few minutes the concert began. I had been envisioning in my mind, a concert like the ones you are forced to sit through in high school, where the band is horrible and you have no choice but to sit there and listen. This was nothing like a high school band concert; it was very impressive and very well attended by a lot of important people, including the governor of Utah. When the big red curtains came up, there sat Megan on the center of the stage in a black glittering formal dress, with black gloves up to her elbows, her hair was done up like a princess and she looked quite amazing. Megan began to play the piano and the music that filled the concert hall was like nothing I had ever heard before, she played a solo for a few minutes and then the entire orchestra began to play along with her. Robyn, was resting her head on my shoulder,

"You know she wrote all of the music she will be playing for this concert herself. This is basically her final test for her composition class, depending on how well she plays and how well it goes will be what her grade for this class is."

It was finals once again, and I had thought my finals were hard; I had no idea that this was Megan's final.

"She is here on a music scholarship, and last year her compositions won best of state between all of the colleges in the western United States." I was now, very impressed, and all of a sudden I found myself feeling very inept and miniscule compared to Megan.

"Oh by the way," whispered Robyn.

"I have my ballet final in two days, would you like to come, as my date for old time's sake?" Asked Robyn as she smiled at me.

"Don't worry, my parents won't be coming, they are allergic to the cold weather but I could see if Sarah's parents are coming if you would like."

"Who?" I asked.

"Sarah's parents," said Robyn.

"You know, you sat by them at my opening performance," I shook my head and rolled my eyes.

"Sarah was telling me a few days after the concert about some guy who told her parents she had a boyfriend, and they were so disappointed to find out that she didn't," Robyn smiled at me while patting my leg.

"I would love to go Robyn," I stated.

"For you anything." Robyn then took my hand and squeezed it tightly,

"Thank you," she said.

When the music director came on stage and announced a brief five-minute intermission, Robyn jumped up,

"I am going to go find Megan, and let her know we are here, I'll be right back." That is when Steve leaned over,

"I have some news for you,"

"What?" I asked.

"Megan likes you a lot, but she doesn't want anyone to know because she thinks you and Robyn are a thing."

"We are not a '*thing*,' I said in protest.

"Well it sure looks like you to are, the way she holds your hand and rests her head on your shoulder," said Steve, while he looked at me and shook his head.

"We are just friends, she is like a little sister to me, I am only watching out for her," I said.

"Ok don't get all jumpy on me, I am just saying that she likes you but is afraid to say anything because of Robyn," Steve paused for a moment and said,

"They are mates you know."

"How did you find this out?" I asked.

"Slim told me," replied Steve.

"What has Slim got to do with this? I mean why is Megan friends with him anyway?" I asked.

"I don't know, but Slim told me that she likes you, and she was asking him a whole bunch of questions about you the day after we had dinner at his dads place." Robyn soon made her way back to where she had been sitting.

"What have you two been talking about? You look like two little boys who have been caught steeling out of the neighbors garden."

"Nothing," I said, as Robyn sat back down and once again rested her head on my shoulder,

"See," said Steve.

When the curtains came back up I noticed that Megan had changed into a red formal dress but still had the long black gloves on. When the spotlight once again focused on Megan and she began to play I looked at her in a totally differently way; it's strange how you see someone differently when you know that they like you. After the last song, Megan's professor came out on stage and announced that she had written the music we had just heard, and that she was his top student, he also announced an upcoming benefit dinner in a few weeks, and stated that she would be performing for the president of the college, as part of the evenings entertainment. When the dean of music announced that the next performer would begin in five minutes, the three of us got up quietly and went out into the lobby. Megan was standing there in her stunning red formal, looking absolutely exhausted.

"You were amazing," said Robyn as she ran to Megan and threw her arms around her.

"Oh thank you," said Megan.

"Thank you for coming you guys," she said as she gave both Steve and I a hug.

"It means a lot to me, my parents, weren't able to come, so I had these extra tickets, and I wanted someone to be here for me, I was so nervous, I was shaking almost the entire time," said Megan.

That is when she made eye contact with me and for a brief moment the hairs on the back of my neck stood up, it felt like there was a small electric current running through my entire body. Megan looked so beautiful, standing there in her sleek formal gown with her long black gloves, and then she looked me in the eyes,

"Thank you for coming Jeremy, I was afraid you would be too busy with your finals to come." I was absolutely speechless. As I mentioned before, once you find out that someone likes you, everything changes. I found myself blundering like an idiot, tripping over my words.

"You look absolutely; I mean your music was, I think you did so good." So good, was that the best I could do, I felt like such a fool, and then Steve saved my pathetic butt.

"Megan that was amazing, I have never heard music sound so heavenly, it was absolutely breathtaking." My face had to be red, because I could feel it burning with embarrassment

"Thank you Steve," said Megan,

"That was very sweet" We could hear the next performance beginning to start.

"I have to get going; I need to be there for the next performance, but thanks again for coming guys." Said Megan.

As we made our way back to the dorms, Robyn said, "Jeremy would you be willing to take me to the airport this Saturday morning? I am flying home for Christmas and will be there for about two or three weeks."

"Sure," I said.

"I would be happy to."

"Thank you," replied Robyn.

"And would you be willing to pick me up when I get back?"

"Of course," I stated.

"Great," she said as we departed to our separate rooms.

Two days later I found myself sitting at Robyn's ballet recital, this one was a little more interesting than the first one because it was the students who were putting it on. It was a cross between ballet, and modern jazz, so at least the music was good! I sat there watching Robyn dance across the stage, but my mind was a world away. I was thinking about Megan, and I was thinking about my rather unique friendship with Robyn. Robyn and I had been friends, for almost three months now and in that three months we had done so much together, on top of the things we did with the whole gang, we still did our weekly grocery shopping, and we still went to dinner with the guys and without the guys. I really had grown to think of her as a little sister whom I was just watching out for. I really liked her company, her laugh was intoxicating, and she was always pleasant to be around, but was there something more to it? Was I just avoiding the big picture, or was I trying to push the "friends," thing too hard on every girl that I met? Then there was Megan, I had known her off and on for almost six months now, but it was only the last two or three months that I had even known her name. I was in an interesting position, I knew that she liked me, but no one knew how I felt about her, that however was the problem, I wasn't even sure how I felt about her. She was talented and beautiful, but so was Robyn, yet for some reason I just didn't see Robyn in the same light. The thunderous applause quickly pulled me back to reality, and I realized that the performance was over, I was expecting an intermission, I had prepared myself for a three-hour performance, but in less than one hour it was over.

"You were fabulous Robyn," I said as we met in the lobby.

"Thank you Jeremy, and thanks again for coming. Would you like to go to dinner, my treat?" She asked.

"I would like that very much, but it was your big night so it will be my treat."

We soon found ourselves sitting in the same little café where we had ended our evening after her last performance, watching the snow falling outside and listening to the Christmas music being piped through the cafes sound system.

"So are you done with your finals?" Asked Robyn as we began to eat.

"Yes," I said between bites.

"I had my last one yesterday, so I'm done."

"Are you going home for Christmas?" Asked Robyn. It was now only a few days before Christmas,

"Yes, I will go home for Christmas Eve and Christmas day and then I will come back."

"Why so soon?" Asked Robyn.

"Well, I guess, it's because this is my home now and you guys are my family, besides Tom and Steve are going to spend the day with Tom's aunt, and they will be coming back to the dorms Christmas evening." I looked at her and said jokingly,

"Who will watch over them if I don't? You really can't leave those two alone for very long, they are like two cats, they will just fight."

We finished up our dinner and then Robyn said, "Take me to see the lights downtown please, I have never been downtown in the winter time and I have always wanted to see the lights."

"Ok," I said, and we walked the three blocks to the Temple Square area, where millions of lights and the sounds of the Mormon Tabernacle Choir performing their Christmas concerts surrounded us. Robyn held my hand, as she did most of the time when we were in a crowd, and with her white furry coat, her hair all done up, and sparkly makeup on her face, she really did look heavenly that evening.

"Jeremy," Robyn said suddenly.

"We need to talk."

"Ok," I replied.

"What do we need to talk about?"

"Well, we need to talk about us, I mean our relationship, I mean our arrangement, what are we?

"Were friends aren't we," I stated without even thinking.

"Ok friends," said Robyn.

"But what exactly does that mean? Because people are starting to wonder about us."

"Who?" I asked.

"Just people," said Robyn.

"I think were friends too, and I am fine with friends but," she paused and look down at the ground, and then up at me, being too naive for the lack of a better word, I could not see what she was really trying to say.

"But what?" I asked. I could feel Robyn squeezing my hand a bit harder, and then she looked up to they sky and the snow flakes fell softy on her face and eye lashes.

"But nothing," she finally said.

"You have been the best friend I have had in a long time, and I will always be grateful for how you watch over me like the big brother I never had." She looked over at me and smiled then pulled my face down to hers and kissed me on the cheek.

"Let's go home, I am tired," she said.

CHAPTER 5

Difficult Decisions

I took Robyn to the airport the next morning, and for me Christmas came and Christmas went. My short visit home went quickly and in no time I was back at the dorms, sitting in the commons area with Tom and Steve, the three of us were just about the only three people on the entire campus. I didn't have to go back to work for a few days, and school would not be starting again for a few weeks. Tom, Steve and I were on our sixth hour of a Star Wars trilogy fest, the original, when we decided that we needed to get out of the dorm rooms and re-visit the real world. As we walked through the main lobby heading towards the parking lot, and Steve's car, I noticed Megan walking in the main doors.

"Hey I will be right back, why don't you pull around to the front and I will meet you in just a second," I told Steve and Tom.

I ran to catch up with Megan; she was just about to go into the girl's wing when I yelled out "*Megan.*" She stopped and turned around as I ran over to her.

"Why aren't you at home for the holidays?" I inquired.

"Well," she stated, with a disappointed look on her face,

"Let's just say I had a 'disagreement' with my mother, and I felt it would be best if I just came back to school early," she then paused for a moment and looked at me,

"Why are you here?"

"I couldn't leave Steve and Tom alone to fend for themselves, they would burn the place down," I said with a grin.

"It looks like they're waiting for you," she said.

I turned to see Tom and Steve with their faces pressed up against the big glass front doors, they were making faces and smashing there noses on the glass, and Steve was writing "let's go" across the frosty window pane with his finger.

"Well, I suppose that means I need to get going," I said.

"Why don't you join us, we're just going to get something to eat and hang out for a while."

"Thank you," said Megan, as she put her hand on mine.

"But I've had quite a day already, and I think I just want to lay down for a bit."

"All right, whatever you want," I replied as I turned and made my way towards the door.

"If you want to go get something to eat tomorrow night I'm free for dinner," yelled Megan, I stopped and turned back towards her,

"Ok," I said.

"Sounds good to me, I will see you tomorrow then."

As I walked up to the glass door where Steve and Tom were still making faces, I slammed my fist on the glass, and they both pulled back holding their noses, I turned and waved goodbye to Megan and Tom, Steve, and I made our way out to Steve's car.

"Have you ever wanted to bleach your hair, you know just lighten it up a couple of shades?" Asked Steve as we stood in the hair care product isle of the supermarket the next morning.

"No, not really," I said.

"Come on it'll be fun, I used to bleach my hair every summer," stated Steve, as he shook his head and ran his fingers through his hair and added,

"You know to get that sun bleached look, and let me tell you the girls love it."

So there we sat Steve, Tom, and me in our room watching TV with towels over our heads like old women at a hair salon.

"Don't you think forty five minutes is about long enough?" I asked Steve in-between handfuls of popcorn.

"Well the directions say to leave the bleach in your hair until it reaches the desired lightness, so let's give it ten more minutes."

"I thought you said that you did this every summer?" I asked.

"Yes," said Steve.

"But I always went to a salon to get it done, this is the first time I have tried it on my own."

At the end of the additional ten minutes, we all made our way into the bathroom, making it in all just short of an hour that the bleach had been in our hair.

"On the count of three," said Steve.

"We will do it together, one, two, three." We all stood looking in the mirror at the scene of horror, all three of us had white hair, not blonde, not the sun kissed surfer hair that Steve had promised, white hair, white as a baby's bottom, white as the pure driven snow, and we were all speechless for a moment or two when Steve said, "*cool.*"

"*Not cool Steve,*" I yelled back at him.

"Not cool at all, I have a date with Megan tonight and I look like a "Q-tip.""

"No you don't Jeremy, you look cool!" exclaimed Steve with a smile on his face. Tom just dropped his towel on the floor and without a word he turned and walked out of the bathroom.

"Steve, this has got to be the worst idea you have ever had, I look like an albino dog," I said in abhorrence.

I turned and walked out of the bathroom myself, absolutely disgusted that I had allowed Steve to not only talk me into bleaching my hair, but into letting us keep the bleach in for an hour. I walked into our room and grabbed the box containing the direction, and although it did say to keep the bleach in until you had reached the desired lightness, just below that it said; "Do not keep bleach in for more than thirty minutes, or you may encounter brittle hair."

"*Great,*" I yelled down the hall towards the bathroom where Steve was still admiring his new look.

"*We are going to go bald as well.*"

I turned to shut my door and I thought I could hear something electric running in Tom's room across the hall, so I wandered over to his room, and I opened the door just in time to see him with a pair of electric clippers in his hands, shaving off the last little bit of his hair. Tom had left about one half of an inch, but that was all, there was a pile of white hair on the floor around him, and I yelled,

"*No Tom,* you can color it again, you don't have to cut it all off."

But it was too late for poor Tom he had shaved it all off. Now we sat in front of the television two Q-Tips and a white q-ball, Tom, who had a very light completion to begin with, must have had a reaction to the bleach, because it bleached the skin on the top of his head and he looked absolutely hideous.

"I am going to dinner now," I said as I stood up and grabbed my University of Utah baseball cap, I pushed it down on my head as far down as it would go,

I then slammed the door behind me and made my way out to the lobby. I went over to the courtesy phone and dialed Megan's room.

"Be right down," she said.

I hung up the phone, and stood there looking at my reflection in the big glass doors trying to see if any of the white disaster was sticking out, but luckily my hat had covered it up pretty good. Megan came out into the lobby and we exchanged greetings and headed out towards my car.

"You know this is our first date," said Megan.

"I mean the first one where it has only been the two of us!" I had not really thought of that before, but she was right.

"So, tell me a little bit about yourself," she said.

"I really only know what Robyn, Steve, and Slim have told me but I want to know first hand who you are."

"Well," I said, as I began to give her the rundown on my family, and what I was studying in school, all of the basic stuff.

"What about you and Robyn?" Interrupted Megan.

"I mean she told me all about you pretending to be her boyfriend, and she tells me you two are just friends," Megan paused for a moment.

"I'm only asking because Robyn is my friend, and if there is something going on between the two of you, I wouldn't want to come between you, and I ruin my friendship with Robyn."

I sat there quietly looking at the menu in front of me, Megan was asking me to define something that I myself had not been able to put a definition to, and I was struggling to give her an answer.

"We are really, really good friends," I said after a rather uncomfortable silence.

"There has never been anything more to our relationship than that, we do things together, and we go places together, but there has never been any romantic involvement between the two of us, Robyn is like a sister to me, and I love her the same way I love my sisters."

I could hear myself saying the words, but I couldn't believe I was saying them, I suppose it was nothing more than a literal definition of what had been shared between Robyn and myself, but to hear myself say it was almost as if I was betraying our friendship. Somewhere deep down I had always thought that there might be something more between Robyn and myself, but quite truthfully nothing had ever really developed.

"Well ok," said Megan.

"That is exactly what Robyn told me, but I guess I just needed to hear it for myself before I," she paused for a moment,

"Before you what?" I asked in a playful tone.

"Nothing," Megan stated.

"Just before I, ah, before I ask you."

She was stalling and I could tell that she wanted to say more but had caught herself saying something she didn't want me to hear, at least not yet.

"Before you asked me to accompany you to the benefit concert that you are performing at in a couple of weeks," I said.

Megan was at a loss for words, I don't think she was aware that I even knew about the benefit concert, but it had been announced at her recital, and if nothing else it was a way out of the uncomfortable conversation we were having.

"Yes, yes, exactly," said Megan, and then she looked at me with a confused look.

"How did you know about the benefit dinner?" She asked.

"They announced it at your recital a few weeks ago," I said.

"Oh right, I had forgotten about that," she replied, while shaking her head.

"You forgot that I was there?" I asked.

"*No*, I forgot that they announced the dinner," she said in clarification.

"I would be happy to escort the lovely and talented Miss Megan to her dinner," was my response,

"Really, you would want to go with me?"

"Yes, I would," I responded with a smile.

We had a nice dinner just getting to know each other a bit better; we talked about our families, our goals, our ambitions in life, and as we finished up Megan said,

"You are a very interesting guy, and I hope we get the chance to know each other better."

The next few days were nice and relaxing for me, I didn't have to go to work, and I didn't have any classes, but the new quarter was looming ever closer.

"Can you believe we are heading into our third quarter already," said Steve as we sat discussing our up and coming classes.

Our class list had just arrived and we sat in dismay looking at the paper in front of us. Unlike traditional students who chose their classes each quarter our freshman year was laid out for us and we didn't have a choice in the classes we would be taking. However this quarter was our next to last in the freshman honors course, and we had earned more credits in the past two quarters than most of our fellow freshman would earn in a year.

"Global and Environmental Issues, Pre-Calculus, and Methods of Technical Research, just shoot me now," said Steve as we looked over the new class list. I had tried to be supportive up to this point, but I had to agree with Steve, this quarter looked like hell on earth.

"I don't even know what methods of technical research is," said Steve.

"What does that even mean? Who comes up with these classes? I want to take some architecture classes; you know the whole reason why I'm here!" Steve had a valid point, I was dying to start taking some classes that would feel relevant to my being in college, but I had to make an attempt at keeping a good attitude for the new quarter.

"One more quarter after this one," I said with a sigh,

"And then we are free to start taking whatever classes we want, we will be sophomores where as most people will still only be freshman."

"That doesn't make me feel good mate," said Steve in a frustrated tone.

"I don't care about other people, I only care about me, and how all this studying and test taking is killing me, I want a quarter where I have fun, and I don't care what kind of pep talk you try to give me, pre-calculus is not fun, or enjoyable in any way."

Once again Steve was right, but I had fought with him enough so I changed the subject.

"I have to go pick Robyn up at the airport tomorrow after work," I said.

"Do you want to go with me, and we can stop at the book store on the way home to get our text books?"

"No, I was going to get my books tomorrow morning, but I can pick yours up while I am at it," said Steve.

The next day I walked onto the dock with my hat pulled down as far as I could get it to go over my white hair, hoping no one would notice, but I had not taken two steps into the main office when I heard,

"*Good lord*, what happened to your hair, boy?" It was Dan's voice followed by a boisterous laugh.

"It looks like a huge pigeon took a crap on your head," Dan paused a moment and then yelled out,

"Don't tell me you did that on purpose." By then everyone in the office was staring at me, so I pulled my hat down to the point where I could hear stitches popping. I walked past everyone, without saying a word and went back to my locker. I shoved my stuff inside the locker, and put on my utility belt and steel toe boots, I slammed my locker shut and walked out to the dock to get my loading assignment from Dan, feeling embarrassed beyond words. I had actually forgotten that I had my disastrous hair, because Steve truly thought his looked cool, so I had just forgot that I even had the white disaster sitting on my head, until I got up for work that morning, and looked at myself in the mirror. The really sad part about it was, I had long dark sideburns but I had not even thought about trying to bleach them, so I had white hair on top and dark side burns, with a scruffy looking beard, I looked like a deranged cereal killer.

"You look like some kind of deranged cereal killer," said Dan as he grabbed my hat and tore it off my head."

"*Good god*," he yelled out.

"I don't want to be seen with you today," said Dan as he threw my hat back at me.

"It's a good thing most of the campus is empty, because your head would be blinding anyone who walked by."

This went on for eight hours, because when I was out of school for these longer quarter breaks, I was allowed to work a full eight hour day, and so this special self inflicted torture lasted all day long.

"I would take you to lunch today, but people would think you were my gay lover, looking like that," said Dan around lunchtime.

"Ok Dan I get the picture." I stated after the third or fourth hour of comments.

"My grandma's hair isn't even that white, and she is 92." Dan chuckled as he kept the insults coming.

"I can't get under shorts that white with a gallon of bleach, if you were in Nam' the enemy would have thought we were rising up the white flag."

"*I get the point*," I finally exploded after the end of our daily route.

"Clean the back of the truck out, lock it up, and you can go home, whitey," said Dan as he threw me the keys to the truck and walked into his office laughing the whole way.

"Flights 1237, and 1625 from New York and Michigan will be delayed, the white zone is for loading and unloading of vehicles only," said the slow monotone voice over and over again on the loud speaker in the Salt Lake International airport.

I sat in the nearly empty terminal waiting for the small prop engine plane that Robyn was supposed to have landed in some forty minutes earlier. I had already walked around to all of the phones and found a hand full of quarters left behind by hurrying passengers and with my treasure I had bought a drink and a candy bar. I kept telling myself,

"I should have eaten before I came," but it took me longer to finish up my delivery route that day then I had anticipated, and so I had to rush to get to the airport on time so that Robyn wouldn't be stuck in the large airport by herself.

Robyn's flight had been delayed due to the snowstorm we had experiencing in Salt Lake earlier that day. I kicked my feet up on to the table in front of me and started dosing off while watching the news on the monitors in the corner of the terminal. I was deep in thought about my upcoming classes, the new quarter started in a week and so my little Christmas/New Years break was almost at an end.

I thought about Megan and the dinner we had gone to together, I also thought about her upcoming benefit concert and how excited I was to see her again. I must have dosed off somewhere in my thought processes, because I didn't hear the small plane taxi down the runway, and I also didn't hear or notice the doors open and the twenty or so people on the small flight enter the airport. In fact it wasn't until I felt the ice-cold fingers going down the back of my shirt that I was jerked back into the land of reality.

"*Wholly crap*," I yelled.

"You have cold hands," I shot out of my chair and nearly fell on my face, forgetting that my feet were up on the table in front of me. I turned around and saw Robyn in her white furry coat and a big smile on her face.

"Did you miss me?" She asked in a playful tone, as she handed me her carry-on bag.

"Yes of course I missed you," I said.

"Well I missed you too," replied Robyn.

"But I didn't miss this cold weather one bit! That is the one thing about going home that I love. I can walk around in flip-flops, sit outside in the evenings, and go for walks with my dog. But not here, I always freeze to death here in the winter time." Robyn paused for a moment,

"I'm sorry my flight was delayed, I hope you didn't have to wait to long," she said with an apologetic look on her face.

"No," I lied.

"I haven't been here that long, and in fact it was a good thing your flight was late, because so was I."

"Well if you will help me get my bags we can get out of here, and get a bite to eat, I don't know about you but I am starving," said Robyn as we made our way out of the terminal.

We gathered Robyn's bags from the baggage claim and made our way out to my car, as we slowly headed towards the downtown area, and the university when Robyn laid her head on my shoulder just right and as she did my hat fell off my head, she looked up to say that she was sorry and she screamed.

"*What* happened to your hair?" Robyn put her hands over her mouth.

"Jeremy what did you do?" She asked. I sheepishly explained how Steve had this great idea and bought some hair bleach, and how we left it in a bit too long.

"*A bit too long*," said Robyn.

"How long did you leave it in, fifteen minutes," I pointed up wards.

"Twenty minutes," I kept pointing up.

"Don't tell me you left it in for thirty minutes, I kept pointing up.

"I leave you boys alone for two weeks and look at what you do to your-selves."

"Tom too," I added.

"Not Tom, Jeremy he is like a little kid, he doesn't know any better and he just goes along with what ever you and Steve say, so how long did you guys leave the bleach in for?" I sat there in silence for a few seconds and finally she said,

"Jeremy, how long," I sheepishly looked down and mumbled,

"Almost an hour,"

"I think you said almost an hour, but I can't believe that two college honor students could be that *stupid*, you're lucky your hair didn't fall out you big idiot."

"It was Steve's idea," I tried saying in my defense.

"So if Steve decided that you guys should tie rocks around your necks and dive into a swimming pool would you do it? Don't answer that just take me to the nearest supermarket," said Robyn in a tone of disgust. We pulled into the closest grocery store and Robyn grabbed my hand.

"Come on, you big idiot, let's see if we can fix this." We made our way to the hair product section and Robyn began looking at different hair colors,

"Take off your hat," stated Robyn, I looked around to make sure no one was watching and then I took it off,

"*What the hell!*" she yelled as I stood next to her holding my hat and looking at the ground. Robyn dropped the box of hair color onto the floor in shock.

"It didn't look that white in the car," she ran her fingers through my hair.

"Jeremy it looks terrible, you three stooges never cease to amaze me. I can't take you anywhere, can I?" Robyn picked out a color that was close to what my hair used to look like and then she picked out one for Steve and as she searched for Tom's,

"Ah, Robyn, don't bother with getting Tom any hair dye," she looked up slowly,

"Why shouldn't I bother with Tom's hair dye?" Even though Robyn stood a towering five-foot nothing, and could not have weighed more than 90 pounds on a good day, this compared to my five foot eight and 175 pounds, I felt like a little kid that had been caught by his mother doing something bad with his friends.

"You're not answering me Jeremy," she said impatiently, I leaned over to whisper the bad news into her ear, because I was afraid of how she would react.

"*No*, he did not, Jeremy," Robyn said while shaking her head.

I nodded yes.

"You and Steve should be ashamed of yourselves, he is a sweet little foreign exchange student, oh Jeremy," she just stood there shaking her head in disbelief. On our way back to the dorms I asked,

"Robyn I'm hungry, can we stop and get something to eat?"

"Absolutely not, I will not be seen in public with you looking like a freak, and if I would have known you looked like this I would have taken a taxi home, we are going home right now to fix this."

I opened the door to my room and Steve was sitting on the couch, eating potato chips and watching TV; Robyn walked over to him and punched him on the chest as hard as she could.

"*Ouch*," yelled Steve, chips falling out of his mouth.

"What was that for?" Robyn grabbed him by the hair of his head and gave it a hard yank, and then turned and pointed towards me.

"Are you responsible for this?" She asked, while shaking his head like a rag doll.

"Yeah but it looks cool," responded Steve.

"It does not look cool Steve, you two look like albino rats, and where's poor Tom?" Just as if it had been rehearsed Tom walked into the room, Robyn gasped and put her hands over her mouth,

"Tom what did you do?" She asked, Tom then turned and without a word walked right back out of the room.

"Get some old towels and take your shirts off boys, it's going to be a long night," barked Robyn.

"I don't want my hair colored," stated Steve, as he ran out of the room.

"Ok it is just you and me," said Robyn "I will get Steve later, but for now let's get this over with."

Steve refused to get his hair color changed back to normal until about a month later when his natural hair began to fill in, and he looked like a skunk, at that point he went to Robyn and asked her if she would please help him fix his hair.

The third week of February had rolled around and we were well under way with our winter quarter when Megan called me one evening to tell me that the benefit concert and dinner that I had agreed to escort her to was in two days. Megan explained that I would need to dress up, and that she would have to be there an hour earlier than the guests, so when I arrived I would just need to tell the person at the front door of the University of Utah Alumni house that I was her guest and they would let me in.

I set out on foot about twenty minutes before the concert and dinner was supposed to start and as I wandered down from the dorms towards the alumni house I recalled it being one of those cold nights where your breath hangs suspended in the air around you as you exhaled, and after being outside for a few minutes your ears and nose began to sting. As I got closer to the alumni house I cold see the warm glow of lights coming out of the windows and I could see the smoke coming up out of the chimney from the large wood burning fireplace, it all looked so inviting and warm. I go to the front of the building and could see the long line of people waiting to get into the building, so I quickly got into line and stood in the cold. When I got close enough to feel the warmth coming out of the building, I could hear the people at the front of the line being asked what their names were, and then the door man would check their name on the list and say,

"That will be $100.00 per person please." I thought to myself,

"Holy cow, no meal is worth a hundred dollars, even if it is for charity, I don't eat a hundred dollars worth of food in two months."

"What is your name sir?" Asked the man at the front desk. I gave him my name and he looked up and down the reservation list.

"I am sorry sir I do not see your name here,"

"Are you sure?" I asked.

"I am with Megan, the pianist, I am here as her guest." I said in desperation.

"I am sorry sir but if your name is not on the list, I can not let you in," said the man.

"Please just go ask, and Megan will tell you that I am with her," I said.

"There has to be some kind of mistake."

"Once again sir, if your name is not on the list I cannot let you in, however when all of the guests have arrived." He looked at the long line behind me and said,

"If there are any vacant chairs you may purchase a ticket for $100.00."

"I don't have that kind of money I am a student," I exclaimed.

"Once again sir, I cannot let you in if your name is not on the list." At this point I could see the people behind me looking a bit frustrated and getting impatient with the situation.

"Fine," I finally said, and stormed off.

I made my way around the building, peering through the windows, trying to open any other door that I could. As I made my way around the back of the building I saw one of the doors propped open just a little. I walked over to the door and opened it slowly. Peering in I could see the caterers preparing plates of food for the guests, and at that point I figured,

"What the hell, what's the worst thing that can happen? They will tell me I can't come in." I opened the door and walked in, unnoticed at first but as I made my way towards the banquet room one of the caterers asked if I needed some help.

"Oh I thought this was the way to the restrooms," I said as I stood crossing my fingers hoping he would buy it.

"You need to go down the hall and turn left," he said politely.

I thanked him and walked out of the room breathing a huge sigh of relief. As I entered the main hall there were people milling about drinking champagne, smoking big cigars, and eating finger sandwiches that were being served around the room by the caterers. As the tray came by me I grabbed three or four sandwiches. I put some of them in my coat pocket and shoved the others in my mouth. There was one big room filled with tables and chairs. A big accordion door that had been opened to allow maximum seating divided the center of the large room, however from where I was standing I could not see into the other part of the room where the piano was.

"Ladies and gentlemen," said the announcer causing the audience to quiet down.

"We would like to get started with this evening's entertainment, so if you could please find your seats I would like to introduce a lovely young lady who is studying music here at the University of Utah. She will be playing a few selected pieces for us. Megan has written and orchestrated all of the music you will be hearing tonight, and I believe many of you heard her last month at the fall quarter's final performance. Lady's and gentleman I present the lovely

Miss. Megan at the piano and a few select members of the Salt Lake Symphony providing her accompaniment. After she has played her selections we will hear from our guest speaker. We will now begin serving the dinner portion of the evening and afterwards we will be privileged to hear from the President of the University."

As he stepped away from the microphone, everyone applauded and I could here the piano begin to play along with the orchestra. As I mentioned where I was standing in the back corner of the adjacent room I could not see her, I could only hear the music. I slowly made my way around the outside of the room over to where the accordion door was and inched my way around the door into the other half of the room. I stayed back in the corner by a large potted tree, trying not to be seen by the door man who would not let me in. I was now in full view of Megan and the other performers, but I was also in full view of the doorman who was still checking names at the front door. I got my first glimpse of Megan and she looked like an angel. She was wearing a long white evening gown that glittered in the spotlight as it shined down on her. She also had white elbow length lace gloves that matched the lace trim on her dress and a tiara in her perfectly curled hair. I found myself starring at her, and I must have been staring for some time because an elderly woman sitting near where I was standing, pulled on my dress coat and whispered, "Young man why don't you come and sit here by me, where it won't be so obvious that you are gawking." I sat down feeling rather embarrassed for staring but even more embarrassed for being caught.

"She is a very lovely girl, isn't she!" stated the elderly lady.

"Um, yes, yes she is."

"Is she your girlfriend?" Asked the woman.

"Oh, no" I exclaimed,

"We're just friends."

"Just friends?" She asked.

"A beautiful thing that, and you two are only friends," she shook her head.

"My boy, a pretty little thing like that won't last long, some boy is going to come along and sweep her off of her feet, and if you're not careful she will no longer be around, to be "friends" with."

"Yes Miss," I said, we sat there enjoying the music and I suddenly felt a heavy hand come down on my shoulder.

"I thought I told you that you couldn't come in here without a reservation," it was the doorman and a security guard.

"Excuse me," said the elderly woman.

"This young man is with me, and I would invite you to take your hands off of him and go back to the door where you belong."

I looked over at her in amazement, why would she, a total stranger, tell the doorman that I was her guest; I didn't even know who she was.

"But Mrs. Giles, this boy doesn't have a ticket," said the doorman in protest, she then pulled out a $100.00 dollar bill and handed it to the doorman.

"He has one now," she said.

"So if you will please leave we would like to enjoy the rest of the performance." I sat there in awe, who was this woman who had so graciously given the doorman a $100.00 dollars on my behalf?

"Thank you Mrs. Giles I don't know what to say," I started to explain that I could not pay her back, when she interrupted me.

"Please I am trying to listen to the beautiful music, you just sit there and enjoy it, after all it is my treat."

I was beside myself with wonder, but at the same time I was very grateful. As Megan finished playing everyone stood up and began applauding. Megan stood up herself and took a bow and then pointed to the orchestra members who had accompanied her, she then stepped away from the piano and went and sat at a long table with all of the "important guests".

"That was wonderful, Megan," said the man who was announcing the events of the evening. "Let's give this talented young lady another round of applause."

After it had quieted down, he stood back up to the microphone and began to introduce the guest speaker. The guest speaker was a doctor in the area, who had donated thousands of hours and hundreds of thousands of dollars to the community and to various charities. He came from a very prominent family, and then they introduced Dr. Giles. As soon as they said his name I looked over at the elderly woman who had so kindly prevented my expulsion from the dinner.

"Is that your son?" I asked.

"Yes, doesn't he look so distinguished, and handsome," she said with a smile.

"Yes he does," I responded.

"My late husband and I have been coming to this charity event for over forty years now, we donated most of the money for this building, and when he passed away last year I couldn't bear the thought of coming to this event alone. I decided at the last minute that I had to come to support my son, and I had hoped to find someone else who was here alone to share the evening with."

I had to choke back my emotions when she told me her story. I was so touched by her obvious love for her late husband and for her son, and I was even more humbled that she had shown me such kindness and allowed me to be her date. We enjoyed our dinner and after all of the speakers had finished, she pulled a flower out of the exquisite center piece on the table and handed it to me,

"Go and give this to your little friend and remember what I said about her not being around forever. Don't take to long to decide whether or not you want to just be friends or someone else will make that choice for you."

I thanked her and made my way through all of the people who were headed toward the door, and up to where Megan was standing and talking with the guest speaker Dr. Giles. I stood patiently while people came up to her and to the Doctor telling them how nicely they had done, and when everyone had finished talking I walked up to Megan and handed her the flower.

"Oh thank you Jeremy, I didn't see you in the crowd, did you get in ok?"

"No problem just walked right in," which I had, only not exactly through the front door.

"You did a wonderful job, and you look very lovely tonight," I stated.

"Well thank you," she said with a smile.

"I am so glad you came, would you like to walk me home?" She asked.

"I would be honored," I replied as I put my arm out for her to take.

"Let me get my coat from the back room and I will be right back." I looked towards the front door as I waited for Megan to return, I saw Mrs. Giles and her son the doctor walking arm in arm, and I waved goodbye to them just as Megan returned.

"Who are you waving to?" Asked Megan as she took my arm.

"Oh just an old friend of mine," I said.

"You know Mrs. Giles?" Asked Megan with an astonished tone.

"Of course," I stated.

"She was my date tonight!"

Winter quarter has always seemed like the longest school quarter of the year to me. Perhaps it's because the days are cold and overcast and one spends most of the time in doors or maybe it's because it gets dark by 5:30 p.m. Perhaps it's because you have just had Thanksgiving, Christmas, and New Years, and then there is a post holiday let down. Whatever the reason, by midterm of winter quarter we were all feeling tense and uneasy so it started out one evening while we were watching a milk commercial on TV.

"I'll bet you $5.00 you can't drink an entire gallon of milk in one hour," Steve said to Slim.

"Oh whatever, I drink a gallon of milk a day," retorted Slim.

"Yes but you don't drink it all in one sitting, now do you?" Asked Steve derogatively.

"I can do it any time, any day," said Slim.

"You are both full of it," I said.

"Slim you can't drink a gallon of milk in one hour it's physically impossible, and Steve you don't have one dollar let alone five dollars to bet on whether Slim could do it anyway."

"Ok," said Slim,

"Meet me out on the balcony in one hour and I will prove it to you, I just have to go buy a gallon of milk, and you better put your money where you mouth is Steve."

"O" yeah, I'll buy the milk for you," said Steve as he grabbed his wallet and they both headed out the door.

"Why is it impossible to do?" Asked Robyn, as the two of us sat waiting for Steve and Slim to return.

"Because, I explained,

"The milk will begin to curdle in your stomach and even if you get it down, as it starts to churn it will turn into a curd that you won't be able to hold down."

One hour later we found ourselves sitting out on the cold balcony of the dorm room, Steve had a stopwatch in one hand, and his five dollars in the other, "Ok Slim let's see the color of your money mate," he said, as he pulled five dollars out of his pocket and they both handed there money to Robyn.

"Robyn will hold the money," said Steve, as he started his stopwatch and we all watched as Slim started guzzling the milk. He went quite fast at first but after a few big swallows he began to slow down. We all sat outside under big blankets in the cold night air and Robyn asked, "What does everyone want to be when they grow up?"

"I want to be an Architect and so does Jeremy," said Steve. I nodded my head in agreement. Then Slim piped up,

"I want to be a chef and open my own restaurant in New York City."

"What do you want to be?" I asked Robyn,

"You know I'm just not sure anymore, I thought I knew what I wanted out of life, but the older I get the less I think I know." We all nodded and Steve said,

"I want to get married some day, and have a few kids, I guess," he then looked over at Slim.

"Hey keep drinking, you only have 40 minutes left," and so Slim took another swallow of milk.

"I want to live in a nice house, and drive a car that is less than ten years old," I stated.

"Me too," added Steve. We looked over at Slim and noticed that he was starting to look a little bit green.

"Do you give up mate, because I could use your five dollars, and it doesn't really matter to me if I get it now, or in thirty minutes, it will be mine either way."

"I'm fine, just taking a little breather," said Slim as he chugged down another two or three swallows of milk.

"If you're really going to throw up, I'm leaving," said Robyn.

"I can't stand watching people vomit, it makes me feel like I am going to throw up myself."

"Don't worry," said Slim.

"I'm not going to be throwing up," as he swallowed another big mouthful of milk.

"I have always wanted to travel and see the world," said Robyn.

"Go on a cruse, and see all sorts of exotic places."

"Traveling is not what it's made out to be," replied Steve.

"We traveled on holiday when I was younger and it just wasn't as fun as people make it out to be."

"That's because you were with your family," said Robyn.

"You can't have fun traveling with your family."

"I don't know I have been to Jamaica, Spain, England, and France, and I didn't think any of those places were all that great," said Steve.

"Well I would like the chance to go and see for myself," said Robyn.

"What about you Slim, have you been anywhere cool?" Asked Robyn.

"Well I have been to," and right then and there, in mid sentence Slim let loose with the first wave of regurgitated milk, he opened his mouth to say the next word and instead of words milk came flowing out of his mouth and nose.

It came up like a fire hose was shooting milk from his stomach, it had such a huge amount of force behind it that it sprayed all over the sliding glass door, the floor, and Steve, who was unfortunately sitting right next to Slim.

"*Gross*," yelled Robyn as she buried her head in my lap. I was laughing so hard that I could barley breathe, while Steve was jumping up and down like he was doing some sort of dance.

"I have puke on me, you vomited right on me," Steve yelled at Slim.

"I am so sorry Steve I did not mean," and at that moment the second barrage, of curdled milk came launching up from his stomach and out of Slims mouth with such power that it went over the edge of the railing, and down onto the sidewalk below.

"Stop it, stop it, stop it," yelled Robyn.

"I'm going to be sick if you don't stop it."

"I think I am done," said Slim as he wiped his mouth with the back of his sleeve.

"That had to be the last of it," and then with a large belch one last spray came shooting out of Slims mouth, this time hitting and splashing off the wall of the dorm by the sliding glass door.

We all got up and ran into Steve's and my room, and as we all sat down the guys began to laugh, just a chuckle at first, but then we broke out into a hysterical laughter.

"I don't find this funny at all," said Robyn, and her making that statement made us laugh even harder.

"You guys are a bunch of sick pigs," she said.

"And look at you Steve you have Slims puke in your hair," Steve stopped laughing.

"Is there really puke in my hair," and with that Slim and I began to laugh so hard, tears were rolling down our faces.

"Robyn, give Steve the money, he won it fare and square," said Slim between gasps of air, Steve grabbed his money and his towel and stormed off towards the showers. The next morning as I was on my way out the door to class I could hear someone saying,

"What is this white stuff frozen to the sliding glass door all over the floor of the patio?"

As we neared the end of our winter quarter Megan and I had been seeing more and more of each other. We were still just in the "friends" stage, but the more time we spent together the more I could feel myself falling in love with her. For some reason though I found myself fighting back my feelings and trying to convince myself that it was not love, it was only a stupid schoolboy crush. One day when I was out doing deliveries with Dan, he announced that he needed to take care of some business in the engineering building, which was just down the street and behind the music building. So I asked Dan if I could take a twenty-minute break.

"Sure just be back in twenty minutes."

I wandered down to the music building just to see if I could find Megan. As I entered the main doors of the building I could hear the faint sound of a piano being played in a near by room. I wandered down the hall towards the sound of the familiar music, and as I approached one of the rooms I could see Megan through the glass door. She was sitting behind a piano playing three or four keys and then stopping to write on the paper in front of her. She looked so stunningly beautiful sitting there all alone in the room with the sun shining down on her through the large windows that surrounded the room. She had her hair pulled back and she looked so intent on what she was doing that I did not want to interrupt her. I turned to leave, but she must have looked up at the door while I was walking away because I did not get more than ten feet away from the room when I heard the door open and she stepped out.

"Jeremy, I thought it was you looking in at me."

"Oh I didn't want to disturb you." I said as I turned back around.

"You looked so serious sitting there that I didn't want to interrupt you."

"You're not interrupting," she said while motioning for me to come back.

"Come back in for a minute."

I turned and made my way back into the room and when we were inside she turned and asked,

"Aren't you supposed to be at work right now?"

"Yes," I said.

"I am at work." I paused for a moment and realized what I had said, so I tried to clarify my answer.

"I mean I'm working, I mean I'm taking a short break, but yes I am supposed to be working right now."

"Ok," said Megan.

"Then I won't keep you long, I've just been thinking of you a lot lately, I mean I have been thinking of us, and well we've had some nice times, haven't we?" Asked Megan,

"Yes," I replied.

"We have had some nice times."

"Have you ever thought of maybe, being together, I mean have you ever thought that perhaps a guy like you might," she was struggling to tell me something and I was pretty sure I knew what it was, but for some reason I felt an odd sort of panic come over me.

"I am not sure what you are trying to say but if you are asking if a guy like me would ask a girl like you out for some ice-cream tonight, you are absolutely right." I stood up and quickly made my way towards the door.

"That's not quite what I was going to say, but that would be nice," she said with a tone of disappointment.

"Great," I said I will see you at seven," and I quickly made my way out the door.

"What was I doing?" I thought to myself as I made my way back up to where the truck was parked, she is a really pretty girl, she is talented, and she likes me. I couldn't explain the sudden panic that had come over me but as the day went on; I contemplated it deeply and finally, for reasons I cannot explain I asked Dan.

"Hey Dan," I said, getting his attention.

"I have this friend who knows this girl that really likes him, and he thinks he likes her, but he has been hurt before so he's not really sure what to do about the situation. I have tried to give him some advice but he's really being stupid about the whole thing, so what do you think I should tell him?" Dan took one look at me, took the cigarette out of his mouth and said,

"You like that girl who plays the piano don't you?"

"*No,*" I said defensively.

"I don't like her," then I paused to rethink about my response.

"I mean it's my friend, we're talking about not me."

"Right," said Dan.

"Your friend, whatever! Well I guess the first thing I would ask your "*friend*," is this; was it last summer that his girl dumped him, on a trip to Jackson Hole."

"Well I know he got dumped but he didn't give me those kinds of specific details," I said looking straight ahead so I wouldn't make eye contact with Dan.

"Right," he said again.

"No details, well any way I guess I would ask your "*friend,*" if he was gay, because I may not know much but I do know that if a pretty little thing like that liked me, I would not hesitate to make her mine." Dan looked at me.

"You're not gay are you?"

"*No!*" I retorted.

"I'm not gay,"

"Then what the hell is your problem boy? Your girl dumped you over nine months ago and you're playing this dumb, "let's just be friends game," with every girl that comes along, you have that little ballerina girl who follows you around like a love sick puppy dog, and now, god only knows why, you have this little piano player girl who likes you and you are asking me what you should do, what's your problem? Do you need three or four girls before you can make a decision, or are you practicing up to be one of those polygamists?" I was very embarrassed at this point, but I suppose I had it coming. Dan had a good point, even if he was a bit harsh in his delivery, his message had sunk in and hit home.

"You're right Dan I have been an idiot."

"You mean an ass," stated Dan.

"Ok an ass, fine." I said.

"I suppose I have, I really like Megan and maybe it's time I told her, I suppose if you never take a chance you will never know if you will win or fail."

"That's the spirit, now what did all of this have to do with your friend?" Asked Dan as he began to laugh.

That evening I picked Megan up and we walked down to the student union building to get an ice-cream cone, and as we sat down to.

"Would you like to take a walk?" I asked.

She agreed, and so we made our way out into the pleasant April evening, it was still a little bit chilly but spring was in the air, as we walked you could smell the fresh spring grass, and the new spring flowers filling the air with their wonderful fresh aroma.

"You were trying to tell me something earlier today, but I was in kind of a hurry to get back to work, so I think I cut you off before you were done," I said.

"No, I was just rambling on, I had been sitting in front of that piano for way too long, and you just happened to come by as I started talking to myself out of desperation," said Megan.

"No I really think you were trying to tell me something," I said while biting the last of my cone.

"I interrupted you and that was very rude of me."

"No really Jeremy it was nothing," she said again. We made our way down to the waterfall behind the library and as we sat watching the sun go down, and listening to the sound of the water splashing pleasantly behind us, I moved closer to Megan.

"I know that I can be sort of, I don't know slow, I guess, when it comes to things. I mean; you know I had that thing last summer with that girl, and it didn't turn out so well, and for some reason I have let it get in the way of my feelings, because I have been so paranoid about getting hurt again. I also know that I can be sort of dumb about things, and I don't always take hints very well, because I guess I am a guy and it's sort of a guy-thing,"

I could feel my heart beating so hard that it was shaking my whole body with each beat. I was also sure that Megan could hear my heart thumping. I could not see quite straight, and my ears were ringing from the pressure of my rapidly beating heart. I was stalling and all I could think about was Dan asking me if I was gay earlier that day.

"So what I guess I am trying to say is yes, I think a guy like me and a girl like you could like each other, and maybe even fall in love."

I stood up and gently pulled her close to me. I took her arms and put them on my shoulders, and then I gently put my hands on her face. I was so nervous that I could see my hands shaking as I lifted them up. I very slowly and very gently pulled her in towards me and as our lips touched I could feel the hair on the back of my neck standing up. As I pulled back after our first kiss, Megan pushed the hair off my forehead.

"I was beginning to think you were never going to do that, in fact I was starting to think that maybe you didn't like me."

"I'm sorry," I said.

"It has just taken me a while to come around I guess."

We stood there for a while longer holding each other and reveling in the acceptance of our new love. I thought to myself, "nothing could be better, my life was perfect," and perhaps for that wonderful but brief moment in time it was.

I walked with Megan hand in hand as we made our way back to the dorms talking about everything and nothing all at the same time. I was feeling so good about life that my good mood and happiness carried over into the next day.

"What are you smiling about like a deranged clown?" Asked Dan in a joking tone.

"Did all that bleach you put in your hair a few months ago finally soak through your skull and give you brain damage?"

"No," I said with a smile.

"I'm just having a good day."

"Well we'll just have to put an end to that now won't we, go get the delivery orders for today and load the truck," said Dan as he threw me the keys to the truck.

I loaded the truck and as we went out into the world to make all of our deliveries I was still on cloud nine. It wasn't until I got home and saw Robyn leaving the dorms crying that my mood changed.

"Robyn," I yelled, rushing to catch up with her.

"What's wrong?" I asked as I got close enough to talk.

"Nothing," said Robyn, as she wiped the tears from her eyes and looked away from me so I could not see that she had been crying.

"What?" I responded.

"I can see that you've been crying, what's wrong?" Robyn looked up at me and smiled through her tears.

"Nothing's wrong, I really need to go, I'm late for," and she paused for a moment,

"Something and she turned and took a few steps away from me and then started to run and began to cry again.

"Do you have any idea what's wrong with Robyn?" I asked Steve as I walked into our room.

"Don't you know?" Asked Steve.

"Would I be asking you if I knew?" I asked with a tone of sarcasm.

"She was coming out of the library last night and she saw you and Megan, well you know, so she talked to Megan last night after you walked her home, and Megan told her that you two were seeing each other exclusively now." I stood there a bit confused for a moment.

"Why would that make her cry?" I asked, talking more to myself than I was to Steve.

"Because, stupid," said Steve as he wadded up a piece of paper from off the floor and threw it at me.

"She's in love with you, and you have been too dumb to see it." I continued to stand there trying to process what Steve had just said.

"No she isn't," I replied.

"We pretended to be dating when her parents were here, and then we decided to just be friends," I said to Steve in my defense.

"Were you just pretending, because I don't think she was," said Steve as he grabbed his book bag and left me standing alone in the room.

I picked up the phone and called Robyn's room but there was no answer so I left her a message,

"Robyn this is Jeremy, hey give me a call when you get this message, I would really like to talk to you."

I hung up the phone and sat down on the couch. I had never intended to hurt Robyn. The fact was I had chosen not to see what was there for so long now that I started to believe my own lie, that there was nothing between us. Just then I heard a knock at my door, I got up and walked over to the door and when I opened it I found Robyn standing with Steve,

"I found this in the parking lot," he said as he gently pushed her into the room.

"I think you two need to talk," and he gently closed the door and walked away.

"I am sorry," I began to say, as Robyn walked up to me and slapped me across the face.

"What was that for?" I asked in shock.

"For being such a stupid boy," said Robyn.

"But I thought we were just friends," I stated.

"We were, I mean we are, I guess," said Robyn.

"I still want to be friends, but now that you have a "girlfriend," she said in childish way,

"You will spend all of your time with her and we will never see each other anymore."

"That is not true," I replied.

"We will still do stuff together, we're friends, and my seeing Megan won't change anything."

"Oh yes it will," said Robyn.

"If you spend as much time with me as you have in the past she will get jealous, and break up with you, and then she will hate me, and I don't want that because I'm her friend just as much as I am your friend, the only difference is."

Robyn paused for a second, and then she looked up into my eyes while the tears began to flow again, "I fell in love with my friend," she reached up and kissed me, then turned and walked out the door, and for the third and last time in my life I just stood there and let her walk away.

Later that evening as I was sitting in my room with Steve feeling dazed and confused, watching re-runs of Cheers on television, I heard a knock on the door, and I looked over at Steve, who shrugged his shoulders and then got up and walked over to the door.

"Come on in love," he said, and I looked up to see Megan with a big smile on her face.

"How is everyone doing?" She asked in a bubbly tone.

"Good," said Steve as he walked out of the room.

"You don't have to leave Steve," said Megan, as the door closed behind him.

"What was that all about?" She asked. I motioned for her to sit down and I recapped what had taken place earlier that evening with Robyn.

"I had no idea Jeremy I'm sorry, if I would have known that she was," Megan paused for a moment,

"I would never have," and she looked at me for a moment.

"Do you feel the same way about her?" She asked with a concerned tone.

"No, it's not like that at all Megan, I just feel bad that she thinks we can't be friends anymore."

"That's silly," said Megan.

"I'm not going to come between your friendship, I know you two have been friends for longer than I have even known you, and I wouldn't dream of coming between you." Megan then turned around and said,

"I am going to go talk to her right now," and as I stood up to protest she darted out the door, a few moments later Steve came back in the room.

"Wow, you ran off two girls in one evening, pretty impressive, mate."

"I didn't run anyone off; she said she wanted to go talk to Robyn."

I sat there trying to imagine how bad this could really be, if the two of them started to fight or worse yet, if they both decided they didn't like me, and then I would lose both of them. About an hour later we heard another knock at the door and Steve didn't even look up,

"It's for you," he said. I walked over to the door and expecting the worse I opened it up to see Robyn and Megan laughing and standing in the doorway arm in arm.

"He did not," said Megan.

"You have got to be joking."

"No he did, and I was just as shocked as you," replied Robyn, and as soon as they realized I was standing there with the door and my jaw dropped wide opened they looked up at me and Megan said.

"Well are you going to make us stand out here all night?"

"No, come in," I said a bit bewildered at the seemingly pleasant turn of events.

"We have talked things over, and this was all just a misunderstanding, Jeremy you and Robyn are more than welcome to remain friends," stated Megan.

"And if you two want to date, you have my blessing," said Robyn.

"Now the two of us are going back to our dorm rooms to have a girls night, so if you will please excuse us, we'll see you boys later," and with that they turned and made their way back to the girls wing of the dorms.

A few days later I asked Megan what they had talked about.

"Sweetie, girls just need a little reassurance from time to time, and the problem with boys is they just don't know how to do that."

"What are you talking about? I can be reassuring," I said.

"Ah, no, you can't dear, but don't worry about it, most boys can't so that makes you normal."

I stood peering through the glass doorway of the music room where Megan was concentrating on what she was doing. She was so intent on her music that she didn't even notice me looking in at her. She looked so cute with her glasses pushed back in her hair, and her pencil behind her ear. She would play a few notes on the piano and then write something down, and then play it again, and erase something and write something else. I was so in love with her, and I was so happy that we were together. Megan had filled the void left behind by Mandy, she was so talented and I felt so honored to be her boyfriend.

"Go on, do it," said Steve as he pushed me into the door with a thud.

We were trying to do something nice for Slim, and needed some help from Megan. I had come to ask for her help, and I really didn't want Steve or Tom to come along. But despite my insistence they followed me anyway to make sure I didn't chicken out.

"Don't push me Steve, I'm going, I'm going," I paused for a moment.

"But what if she says no? Or what if she thinks we're stupid for even asking?"

"Just go," said Tom in his broken English.

"Alright, alright I'm going, I'm going," I said as I slowly opened the door and, with another big push from Steve I stumbled my way into the room. Megan paused a moment and then looked up.

"Hey, what's up," she said as she went back to writing on the piece of paper in front of her. I walked over and stood behind her and while putting my arms around her and asked,

"How's it going?" I asked.

"I'm a bit frustrated with how this piece is turning out, but I can work through it," said Megan as she turned to look at me.

"Is this visit for business, or pleasure?" She asked. I looked over towards the door and saw Steve and Tom mouthing the words, "*ask her*," over and over, while pointing towards us.

"What do they want?" Asked Megan, as she turned to see what I was looking at, when they realized Megan had seen them, Steve disappeared around the corner and as Tom continued to mouth the words, "ask her," I could see Steve grab Toms arm and jerk him violently away from the door.

"Who?" I asked innocently.

"Steve and Tom," said Megan.

"They were just standing outside the door yelling "ask her, ask her.""

"What?" I asked.

"I didn't see anything," Megan then turned around on the bench seat and stood up.

"What do they want you to ask me, dear?" she said as she put her arms around me.

"Well, Slim is sort of catering a big dinner thing for his dad, and some of his big New York business clients, who just so happen to own a restaurant in New York, and if this goes well it might help Slim get an internship at one of these restaurants." I gave Megan a cheesy smile, and she asked,

"So, what does that have to do with me?" I paused for a second and then continued,

"We told Slim that we would help him out by serving, and after we agreed to help him, Steve, Tom and I thought it might be nice to have some live music for this dinner, because we think that it would help make his dinner even better. I didn't want to volunteer your services without asking first, so I told the guys that we would have to check with you, I told them that just because we were dating didn't mean that I would volunteer you without,"

"Sure," said Megan, interrupting my rambling, but I must not have heard her because I continued talking.

"And so I thought I would ask you, but if you don't feel comfortable doing it," Megan put her hand over my mouth.

"I said yes honey," and she gave me a small kiss.

"Tell Slim that I would be happy to help," and at that moment I could hear Tom and Steve cheering in the hall. Megan shook her head and said,

"I don't know about you honor student boys, I thought the boys in band were strange, but they don't hold a candle to you guys," I gave Megan another quick kiss.

"Thank you honey, I owe you one, I'll see you later."

I ran out into the hall to join Steve and Tom and we headed off to tell Slim the good news.

"Slim, we have a special treat for you," Steve said as we burst into his room scaring him half to death.

"Megan agreed to play the piano for your dad's little dinner party."

"What?" Asked Slim.

"You guys are pulling my chain, right?"

"No," I answered back.

"I asked Megan and she said that she would be happy to play at your dinner."

"You guys are the best, I owe you one," said Slim as he jumped to his feet and grabbed his jacket.

"Where are you going?" Asked Steve.

"Shopping," replied Slim.

"I have a lot to do to get ready for this dinner."

It was good to see Slim so excited, he had been studying business at the University of Utah to get a good start on the business end of running a restaurant, but his true love was cooking, and if this little dinner party could get him into one of the big New York Restaurants it would be the chance he was dreaming of.

It was the last week of the winter quarter and we were all buried under our finals. Steve, Tom and I had been studying like mad to pass the next to last quarter in the Freshman Honors course. Robyn had her final recital and I really did feel bad about missing it but I couldn't get work off because her recital was in the middle of the day. Steve and Tom went to support Robyn and take her flowers while I went to work and slaved under the drudgery of delivering gas tanks. Although the job was convenient and they worked with my school schedule I was looking forward to the day when I could finally quit.

Megan's recital was that evening after work, and I managed to sneak into her dressing room beforehand and leave her some flowers with a note, telling her how proud I was of her, and that I would be in the audience with, Steve, Tom and Robyn cheering her on. Once again we found ourselves seated in nearly the same place as before when the curtain went up and the lights when down. Robyn looked at me and whispered in my ear, "Can I lay my head on your shoulder just for old time's sake?"

"Sure, just for old time's sake." I replied.

I was glad that Megan and Robyn had come to an understanding with each other. I was glad that everyone was still friends, because Robyn was like a little sister to me, and I enjoy having her around. Megan made her way onto the stage looking as radiant as ever. She was wearing a red evening gown with the traditional long black gloves, her hair was done up, and she looked like an angel as she took a small bow and sat down at the piano. The dean once again came to the microphone and introduced to the audience who would be playing that evening. He introduced Megan, and then the lights went down.

This recital was a bit different than the previous one I had been to because instead of an entire orchestra playing along with Megan, it was just her and one violinist. The sound of the piano and the violin playing together was so forceful and strong, yet so sad at times. They played four or five songs together, and then the violinist sat down as Megan played her final solo piece on the piano. I was very impressed with Megan's last concert, but this time it meant even more to be in the audience because this time I had a better understanding of how much time and effort went into composing a piece of music. I had seen first hand the frustration and joy that went into her music, and somehow I felt more connected to it.

As Megan finished up her final piece she looked into the audience. I was not sure if she could see me over the bright spotlights but she had a warm smile that I could feel, and I could tell that she was both excited and relieved to be finished for another quarter. After the performance we all made our way out to the lobby and stood in line with the other people to congratulate Megan on a job well done. After standing and waiting for what seemed like hours Steve said,

"Jeremy tell Megan "good job," for us, but we need to go shopping for Slims big dinner party tomorrow evening." I said I would and Robyn, Steve, Slim, and Tom all left to get things ready for the following evening.

I finally made eye contact with Megan, and motioned to her that I would meet her in her dressing room when she was finished. Megan was so very talented, I had never known anyone who could play music, let alone write music like she could. I could not even read music. I remember when I was younger I tried playing the trumpet, and by the time I had finally mastered Mary had a little lamb I was so frustrated that I quit.

The dressing rooms behind the stage where for whoever was performing at any given time. The room Megan was assigned to had her name written in magic marker on a piece of paper that was taped to the door. I thought it was pretty cool that she had her own dressing room, even if it was only for that evening. I sat on the overstuffed couch in Megan's dressing room waiting for her to return. When Megan finally made her way into the room she looked absolutely exhausted, she came over to where I was sitting and fell into the couch and into my arms, "Just hold me for a minute," she said, as she grabbed my arms and pulled them tightly around her.

"Didn't the rest of the gang come with you?" Asked Megan.

"Oh, yes they did but they needed to go shopping for Slim's dinner thing tomorrow night." I said.

"Oh yeah I had forgotten about that, I am glad you said something, I have been so stressed about tonight's performance that I almost forgot. So how did it sound?" Asked Megan while she scrunched her nose up.

"I thought it needed some more work, but I just ran out of time," she said.

"I thought it was wonderful." I replied.

"You're just saying that because you have to," she said in a playful tone.

"*No* I'm not." I replied.

"It was good, and I'll bet that all of those people in the hall who mobbed you after the performance would agree." Megan looked up at me and with a smile on her face she said,

"You're sweet, and I think I'll keep you around for a while."

"Oh," I responded,

"You will keep me around."

"Yes," she said.

"I will tell all the other boys who want to date me that they will have to wait until I have grown tired of my pool boy."

"*Pool boy,*" I said loudly,

"Is that what I am to you, a pool boy?"

"Yes," she said with a big smile on her face.

"It has always been a little fantasy of mine, to have a wild affair with the pool boy."

"Ok," I said.

"Remind me to never get a pool then." We both laughed and sat enjoying the moment, until Megan finally said,

"Ok Mr. Get out of here, so I can change."

"Do I have to?" I asked playfully.

"*Yes,*" she said with a smile.

"Go wait outside like a good boy and I will be out in a few minutes."

I stood outside watching the stagehands running back and forth getting the place cleaned up, until finally Megan came out and took my hand.

"Ok, we can go now," she stated.

"I've been meaning to ask you." I said as we made our way up the big hill toward the dorms.

"Do you own all of those dresses that you wear to your concerts?"

"Heavens no," said Megan.

"They belong to the theatre department and they loan them out to us for concerts and other events, why do you ask?"

"Oh, I guess it's just because I never see you in them other than when you perform, that's all, and what about your hair and makeup, do you do it your-self?"

"No, just an illusion," said Megan.

"There is a theater makeup and hair class that comes in and does our hair and makeup before the performances too."

"Why?" She asked.

"Are you disappointed, that I don't look like this all the time?"

"No," I said.

"I was just wondering, I think you look beautiful all the time, but you look heavenly when you perform."

The evening of Slims big dinner soirée had arrived and Slim was an absolute basket case, Megan sat at the piano warming up while Tom, Steve, and I cleaned every inch of the already immaculate apartment.

"What happened to your mom?" I asked between dusting the ceiling fan and the entertainment center.

"What do you mean?" Asked Slim as he stood slicing onions in the kitchen.

"Well I see pictures of her, but I have never met her, does she live here?"

"No," said Slim.

"Her and my dad has a sort of working relationship, she works in Manhattan, and Paris, and he works here in Utah and in parts of New York and Chicago, and as long as they are working they are happy."

"Are they divorced or separated?" I asked.

"No," said Slim, as he moved on to cutting mushrooms.

"They just live separate lives and once or twice a year they get together and we pretend like were a normal family, as you may have noticed my dad is only here once or twice a month, and even then he is usually with clients like the ones he will have over here tonight."

"What does your dad do?" Asked Steve.

"He is a food import agent for a company that imports high end and exotic foods for really expensive restaurants," Slim stopped chopping for a moment.

"My dad knows all of the famous chefs in New York and has a standing table at all of their restaurants; my mom is a fashion consultant for some magazine in Paris that I cannot even pronounce."

"Is that why you want to be a chef?" Asked Robyn.

"Because of your dad, I mean?"

"Well," began Slim.

"Once when I was about twelve, my dad had this chef over to our house and I was just mesmerized watching him prepare a meal for us, I guess that is what started it all." Slim stopped chopping again.

"My parents have only ever paid attention to important people, so I figure that if I become an important enough chef my dad will actually want to spend some time with me, and he might even want to be my friend." Robyn came over to me and whispered in my ear,

"That's really sad, I mean I don't get along with my parents all that well, but they have never ignored me," she then said in a joking way.

"I wish they would from time to time, but not like that."

"Ok guys," said Slim as we all stood at attention moments before his dad and the guests were supposed to arrive.

"Just serve the plates on the right hand, don't talk to anyone, and come back into the kitchen when you have served them, Robyn dear you look lovely, please serve the appetizers when I give you the signal," Slim then pointed at Steve and I.

"When I give you two the signal you can go get the dishes between courses."

"What are you going to be doing?" Asked Steve.

"I will be overseeing, and giving the guests a run down on the meal."

"What do you need me to do?" Asked Tom.

"Tom you will be washing dishes, and helping me get the plates ready for Jeremy and Steve to serve to the guests." Slim stepped back and took a deep breath.

"Alright guys, once again thank you all, and remember above everything else, no talking." With his orders being given we all took our places and Megan began playing the piano softy, as Robyn opened the door to let the guests into the apartment.

"I have never seen important people before," said Steve.

"They look pretty plain to me."

"Me too," I replied.

"But remember we are doing this for Slim."

The evening was going absolutely perfect, the food was superb, or at least that's what the guests kept saying. They commented on Megan and her lovely music and how it added just the right touch, and it really wasn't until Steve tripped going into the dining room dropping a flaming plate full of Crème Brule on his dads $2,000 dollar rug that the evening got even remotely interesting for us bus boys. Lucky for Steve, no one saw it but Megan and myself. Megan had to try her hardest not to burst into laughter as she sat playing at the piano in the living room.

"I am no critic, but I think this evening was a huge success," said Slims dad after his guests had left for their hotels. Slim walked into the room.

"Thank you dad for giving me a chance to show them what I could do,"

"You did great son," Slims dad stated while gathering his things together.

"I would love to stay and chat but I have a midnight plane to catch so I have to get going, but you did great." I could see the look of disappointment in Slims eyes.

"Do you have to go tonight dad, we can clean this place up later, I mean let's go and see a show, or we can just hang out here and talk."

"Oh yes," said Megan.

"It's getting late and we are all on our way out."

"No." Said Slims dad.

"Your friends don't need to go, I wish I could stay son but I have a meeting at 7:30 in the morning in Chicago and I can't miss it, you understand, right," Slim nodded his head.

"Sure dad, I understand." As Slims dad slipped out the door we all stood there looking at Slim, and looking at each other,

"We can stay tonight if you would like," said Robyn.

"Yes, we can stay," we added.

"No, it's fine, after twenty years I am used to it, don't worry about me guys, really I'll be fine, I'm just glad that you guys were willing to help me out, I couldn't have pulled off alone."

We helped Slim clean the dishes and when we were done, he showed us to the door and reassured us one last time that he would be fine. We all piled into Steve's yacht on wheels and were half way home, when he jerked the car around.

"I can't leave him alone, not like this," Steve looked at all of us and said.

"We need to go back." We stopped at the video store and rented a hand full of John Wayne movies, and then we stopped at a gas station and got some junk food. Ding, dong, went the doorbell. Slim opened the door.

"What are you guys doing here? I told you I would be fine."

"That's nice," said Steve as he pushed his way into the apartment.

"We will just be fine with you mate," and we all piled back into the apartment.

"You guys really don't need to do this," said Slim.

"We know," said Robyn as she sat down beside him and put her legs in his lap.

"I need a foot message Slim, and no one else can do it quite like you!"

"I have never given you a foot message before," said Slim with a confused look on his face.

"Well it's time that you did then." Robyn wiggled her toes while smiling at Slim. Megan and I sat on the floor and we all spent the evening at Slims house watching movies and enjoying one another's company, although he never said it, I think Slim was glad that we had come back that evening, to help cheer him up.

CHAPTER 6

Then There Were Four

Spring break was upon us, and our final quarter of the freshman honors course was just around the corner when Tom came in to the room one evening, and made an announcement that set all of us back a bit.

"I have cousin from Poland that is going to school and so I will move in with him in one week." We were all shocked that he was going to be leavening us; Slim was probably the most shocked of all.

"What do you mean you're moving out with your cousin? What am I suppose to do?" Asked Slim as he stood up from the couch and looked right at Tom.

"I don't want another roommate, I like having you as a roommate, and besides what about them?" Asked Slim as he pointed towards the rest of us.

"Leave him alone," said Steve.

"If he wants to move in with his cousin, then let him," Steve stood up and walked over to Tom.

"In fact if you need any help, you just let me know mate."

"I'll help you too," I said.

"Thank you," said Tom as he turned around and went back to his room.

"What are you guys doing? Don't encouraging him, I don't want another roommate, this is bad, this is really bad," said Slim, as he left the room to talk with Tom.

It would be strange without Tom; after all he was part of the original group he was one of the three amigos, the three musketeers, he and Steve were the first friends I made when I moved in, and we had spent nearly every day together since.

"We need to do something for him," I said turning to Steve.

"Like a going away party or something."

"Ok," replied Steve.

"I'll talk to Slim and see if he will let us have a party at his dads place, and I'll ask him if he will cook something up for it."

"No, way, no how am I going to cook anything for that traitor," was Slims response when Steve and I asked him a few days later if he would host a little party for Tom.

"Come on Slim, he's been your roommate for almost six months, you can't be mad at him for wanting to move out with his cousin." I said.

"Oh that's where you're wrong," said Slim, pointing at me as he continued ranting,

"Because I can be mad at him, and I am mad at him, and furthermore I will not give him a party, do you guys understand what this means? I could have a roommate next quarter that is some sort of cereal killer, or some stalker, or even worse he could listen to Barry Manilow and I'm not prepared to share that kind of hell with anyone. I'm sorry guys, but I can't be happy for Tom, or help out a guy who would abandon me like this."

"He's not abandoning you Slim, he wants to be with his cousin," said Steve as Slim slammed the door in his face.

"Well," I said.

"I had hoped it wouldn't have to come to this, but I suppose it's time to bring in the heavy hitters!"

"What heavy hitters?" Inquired Steve?

"Megan," I said as I went back to our room, picked up the phone and dialed her number.

I knew that Slim had always had a thing for Megan, and although I was a bit jealous at first, now that Megan and I were dating, I didn't feel that way anymore. "Hello," said Megan as she picked up the phone,

"Hi sweetie," I said.

"Will you please come to my room I need to have a little chat with you about our good friend Mr. Slim body?"

"Sure, I'll be right over," said Megan. When Megan entered the room she asked,

"What's this all about?" I filled her in on Tom's decision to move out with his cousin.

"So I figured if anyone could help convince Slim to give Tom a little going away party it would be you. Steve and I have already tried talking to Slim without any luck," I said with a smile.

"But since he has a crush on you, and to my knowledge Slim doesn't have a crush on either of us, I figured you could get him to do this, if not for Tom then for you."

"Besides," stated Steve with a smile,

"Who could say no to a hot little tomato like you?"

"I would do it," I continued.

"But, I just don't have the same kind of persuasion over Slim that you do, and besides I have other things to do tonight, like wash my hair." I said jokingly.

"Ok, I will do it for Tom, but you two owe me big time," said Megan as she made her way across the hall and knocked on Slims door.

He opened the door a crack, and talked with Megan for a moment and then he opened the door all the way and she went inside. Steve and I looked at each other, then dashed across the hall to Slims door and pressed our ears up to it, trying to hear what was being said.

"I can't hear anything, do you think they're making out," said Steve, I looked at him and slapped the top of his head, which was just below mine.

"That's not funny," I replied.

"Well you did send Megan over to convince Slim to throw Tom a party, and you do know that Slim likes her, so I was just saying," Whap, went the side of Steve's head as I slapped it again.

"Well just don't say anything!" I said.

"It's not funny." We both pressed our ears tightly to the door once again trying to hear the conversation on the other side of the door, but it was difficult to make anything out. We could hear mumbling and a little bit of laughter and then the door was quickly jerked open by Slim; Steve and I fell into Slims room, and jumped up quickly to our feet.

"So how are things going?" I asked in a guilty tone.

"Great," said Megan, as she stood on her tiptoes and kissed my forehead on her way out of the room.

"The party will be this Friday night at seven," she said as she walked away, I stood there looking at Slim and then at Steve, and then down the hall to where Megan had gone, and then back at Slim.

"You changed your mind, that's great mate," said Steve as he gave Slim a big hug.

"Don't touch me," said Slim as he pushed Steve away.

"I'm doing it for Megan, not you two geeks, or for that back stabber Tom," and with that he slammed the door in our faces again.

"So how did you get Slim to agree to do the party?" I asked Megan later that evening as I sat in her room, watching her paint her toenails.

"I told Slim that you and Steve would pay for everything, and that you would help both of them move out.

"Both of them?" I asked in a confused tone.

"Yes," said Megan in a very mater-of-fact tone.

"Slim has decided that he would rather move back in to his dad's apartment then take the chance of getting a roommate who he doesn't like."

"That is ridiculous," I said.

"No it's not, he doesn't want to get some crazy new roommate, he would rather live with his dad, who is never there anyway," said Megan in Slims defense.

"No," I said.

"It's ridiculous that you told Slim that Steve and I would pay for the whole thing, do you know how expensive it is when Slim cooks?"

That Friday afternoon, I found myself standing in front of the meat counter in the grocery store with Megan standing behind me, Steve wandering down the bread isle, and a grocery list five miles long in my hand. I leaned over the large glass counter and pointed to one of the items on my,

"What the hell kind of Italian meet is this suppose to be?" I asked the man behind the deli counter. Slim had written something down that I could not pronounce or read, and he wrote next to it, Italian meet. Before the man behind the counter could answer me, Megan reached over and grabbed the list out of my hand while punching me in the arm.

"*Ouch,*" I exclaimed as I rubbed my arm.

"Please excuse my boyfriend, he is an honors student in college, so that means he's in a special class, and sometimes the special kids need a little extra help." The man behind the counter began to laugh, and I realized that I had been a bit rude.

"I am sorry," I said.

"Why don't you try to find Steve and the two of you can get some of the other things on the list and I will take care of the meats and cheeses," said Megan as she tore the list in half giving me the non-deli items to look for.

I walked down the fruit isle frustrated with the list Slim had sent me and Steve out with, I was sure that he was doing it to protest the whole going away party, and I was sure that he would not need half of the items on his list.

"Don't be so moody," said Megan as she found me trying to figure out what the difference between canned muscles and canned oysters really were.

"After all you and Steve were the ones who wanted to have the party for Tom."

"I know," I said.

"Don't you want to do something for him too?" I asked Megan.

"Of course I do," she said.

"I will miss Tom as much as you guys will, but he's not going away forever, he's just moving off campus that's all."

Even though Megan was right, Tom was just moving a mile or so off campus, it would change everything. I knew that in time all of us would move on, but it just seemed so strange to be loosing Tom. I knew that he would visit from time to time, but I also knew that after the next quarter he would not be in any more classes with us and it would just be a matter of time before he went his own way in life. It was hard to explain, because Megan was my girlfriend, and she was part of the group by association, but she was not a part of the "Fab-Five" that Slim, Steve, Tom, Robyn, and I had become, and in fact she was relatively new to the group herself. I suppose it was more the actuality that if he left, it meant that things were changing, and I had grown so close to my little group of friends that I had somehow thought, or at least hoped that it would last forever.

We found ourselves eating, listening to loud music, and enjoying ourselves that evening, Tom looked a bit sad to be leaving us, and Slim who had not spoken to Tom much the last week or so, finally opened up a bit and actually wished Tom good luck.

"Don't move out," I said to Slim, as we sat out on the balcony just off the kitchen watching the stars dance in the sky.

"Give it a little while and if your new roommate doesn't work out you can stay with Steve and I for a bit," I said pleading with Slim.

"It's hard enough having Tom move out but don't you move out too, things just wouldn't be the same."

"Why?" Asked Slim in a sarcastic tone.

"You guys would have to cook for yourselves for a change."

"That's not the only reason," I said with a chuckle.

"We all want you to stay," said Robyn as she walked out onto the balcony to join our conversation.

"Please don't move in here, I mean it has to be the coolest apartment I have ever seen, and you would have every luxury known to man, but we need you in the dorms, you are one of us and things just wouldn't be the same."

We continued talking for a while and Slim still insisted that if Tom was leaving, so was he and so it was on a bit of a sad note that we all said our good nights, wished Tom the best and went home for the evening.

"Advanced Technical Writing, you have got to be kidding me," said Steve as he looked at the class schedule for our final quarter of the freshman honors program.

"I thought we already took all the writing classes we would have to take, and would you look at this "Philosophic Anthropology" please, I know I say this every quarter but just shoot me now."

"Come on Steve," I said while shaking his arms as hard as I could.

"This is the last one, the last quarter and then next quarter we can take what ever classes we want," I said trying once again to encourage my Aussie roommate.

"Hell no, Physics, I can't do physics, Jeremy I cannot do physics," stated Steve as he continued reading the class list.

"Come on buddy, breath, put your head between your knees and breath, we can do this, just tell yourself; "I'm good enough, I'm smart enough, and I can do this!"

The honest truth was I had no desire to take the classes that were set before us either, but I had gone this far, and out of sheer willpower, or perhaps it was stupidity I was not going to give up. That first week was horrible, and I would like to say that it got better but the truth was, not only did it not get better it just got worse. I don't think I have ever struggled so hard in school as I did that quarter, even my final quarter of my senior year, didn't seem as difficult as that last quarter in the honors program.

It was sort of funny, for the lack of a better word, but we had started the program with somewhere in the neighborhood of 150 students and we would end that quarter with about 20 of us still standing. I suppose you can't make an honors program on a collegiate level easy, or everyone would take it, but they could have eased up just a little bit on us poor freshman. It didn't help that it was spring and the weather was nice, and it was staying lighter later and my concentration level was next to nothing. I was so burned out and longed for a class that I could just sit back and enjoy, but I had no one to blame but myself, no one made me sign up for the program and at the same time I was determined to finish.

Slim had decided at the last minute to wait for one more quarter and see what his roommate turned out to be like before he moved back into his dads place. I think in the end, Slim was glad that he did wait to move out, because of all the dumb luck Tom had forgotten, or perhaps he didn't know that he was requited to tell the front office that he was moving out, so they didn't assign anyone to replace Tom in the room assignments. Slim figured as long as they didn't know, he wasn't going to say anything, and all that would happen to Tom is they would eventually evict him from the dorms, but since he was already gone, it didn't really matter.

It was early in the evening, sometime in the first few weeks of the spring quarter when Steve, Slim, Megan and I, found our selves at our favorite little pizza place "The Pie." The band had just finished up; we were enjoying our pizza, and writing on the wall when Steve leaned over the table,

"You two make such a cute little couple you should get married!" I spit the cola out of my mouth and began to choke.

"What did you say?" I asked.

"I said you should ask Megan to marry you," said Steve.

"That is what I thought you said, and I think you are crazy." Megan then turned to me and pinched my arm.

"*Ouch,*" I yelled.

"What do you mean Steve is crazy, don't you think I would make a good wife?" Inquired Megan.

"I didn't mean it like that." I said.

"I just meant that."

"I know what you meant," replied Megan, not letting me finish my sentence.

"And I think I would make a good wife."

"You would make a great wife, love," said Steve.

"And if this loser doesn't think so, I might just ask you myself," he winked at Megan and smiled at me.

"Ha, ha," I said. And then out of the blue sky, Steve got this look in his eyes.

"Let's go to Vegas," he said, as we all laughed out loud.

"No, I am serious," he said.

"Tomorrow is Friday, we could leave right after you get off work," he looked at me and at this point I still didn't think he was serious.

"Ok," I said jokingly,

"And if we don't like Vegas we can go right on to San Francisco." I looked over at Steve and realized that he wasn't joking.

"Wait a minute, my little kangaroo boxing buddy, do you have any idea how far away Vegas is from here? It's like five hours."

"Seven and a half to eight hours," said Slim,

"I've been there a number of times."

"Ok, eight hours," I said.

"If we leave at 4:30 when I get off of work, it will be midnight or later when we get there."

"That's fine," said Steve,

"I like the night life, and they say that the best time to be in Vegas is at night." I looked around the table.

"You guys aren't really thinking of going to Vegas with Steve tomorrow night are you?"

"No," said Megan,

"There is no way I an going to Vegas with you guys, Jeremy your car is too old, and Steve your car is, well there is no way I am going in it for eight hours, if you boys want to go that's fine with me, but count me out."

I stood on the dock at work looking at the huge wall clock in the warehouse thinking to myself, "There is no way they are seriously going to go to Vegas tonight," and that is when Dan came up to me.

"Hey there are two goofy looking guys in my grandpa's old Cadillac sitting out in the parking lot honking the horn; do you know who they are?" I looked over to the far side of the parking lot and there was Steve and Slim jumping up and down waving me over to the car,

"No," I said to Dan,

"I have no idea who they are," Dan looked at me and looked back at them, and then back at me.

"They're yelling your name," I ran into the main office punched out on the time clock and ran out to the parking lot.

"What are you guys doing here?" I asked as I jumped into the back seat of Steve's car.

"Going to Vegas baby," said Steve as we pulled out of the parking lot onto the main road.

"I didn't think you guys were serious," I said while rolling my eyes,

"Besides I need a change of clothes, I don't want to go to Vegas in my dirty work clothes." Slim grabbed a bag from off the floor next to him and tossed it back to me.

"We had Megan pick some clothes out for you, go ahead and change back there we won't look," I sighed and sat back in the large plush seat feeling a bit frustrated about the trip, but we were already getting onto the freeway by then.

"Just enjoy it," stated Slim,

"You need a break as much as we do, and besides who knows if this will be the last big thing we do for a while."

Slim had a point, I did need a break, and it had been a while since we had done anything as just the guys, so after about an hour or two I figured I was in it for the long haul and I might as well just enjoy myself. It was almost one o' clock in the morning when we pulled onto the Vegas strip, "sin city, the city of lights" and Steve and I were in awe. "Have you ever seen anything so beautiful in your life?" Asked Steve as we slowly made our way down the strip, the flashing lights and dancing water was so mesmerizing.

"Not to be a downer guys, but where are we going to stay?" I asked. Slim turned around,

"I called my dad this afternoon and he booked a room at the "Golden Nugget" for us." We made our way to the casino and as we walked in Steve and I saw for the first times in our lives the barrage of sights and sounds that were foreign and strange to both Steve and me.

"You two hang out here for a minute while I go and check us in," said Slim as he disappeared into the depths of the casino.

Steve and I were absolutely memorized by the sound of change being dropped into the slot machines, and the sounds of music over the intercom, mixed with the laughter and all the lights and noise of the casino. We must have stood there gazing into the crowd for some time because we were snapped out of our trance by the sound of Slim yelling, "*Hey, you two, Hey,* come on, this way to our room."

We made our way past roulette tables, poker games, bingo tables, and thousands of slot machines to a stair case that lead to an elevator that took us up to our room.

"Ok, you three look like under aged college boys," said the lady who had been assigned to take us to our room.

"So you might want to stick together and not wander to far from the strip." She walked us to our door.

"Watch yourselves boys, and have fun in Vegas," she took the cigarette out of her mouth, opened the door, handed us the keys,

"Good night gentlemen." She said, as she disappeared back down the hall. Steve immediate turned around.

"I'm out of here to find something to eat, who's with me?" We all turned in unison and went back the way we had come, and as we sat in a booth at one of the many restaurants in the casino a rather scantily clad young lady came up to us and asked if she could take our order.

"You boys here to gamble?" She asked, while writing down or orders. Slim and I said no, but Steve said "yes."

"Well, here are some complimentary tokens for you then," she said as she handed Steve the brightly colored tokens.

"What are you going to do with those?" Asked Slim.

"I am going to use them," said Steve as he stood up to go into the casino.

"Hold on big fellow," said Slim,

"I don't know how old you have to be in Australia to gamble but here in the good old U.S.of A. you have to be 21 to even walk into the casino." Slim said while pointing to the big sign above the casino door that read,

"No one under 21 admitted into the casino, *no* exceptions!"

"Sorry buddy but you're only 20, and that is off limits to you," said Slim.

"Well," retorted Steve,

"They don't know I'm not 21, and I'm willing to take my chances," and off he went.

"So," said Slim turning back and looking at me,

"How are thing going between you and Megan?"

"Good," I said.

"That's good," said Slim.

"You know she's a really nice girl, and I am envious of you," he said as he picked up his sandwich that the waitress had just set in front of him.

"Why is that?" I asked.

"Because Megan likes you, and she is such a nice girl," he took a bite of his sandwich.

"She's very talented, and she is pretty hot too." I felt myself blushing just a bit.

"Well I agree with you, and I am very happy being with her." Slim went on to explain that he had been dating one of Megan's friends about a year ago, and that is how he had met Megan in the first place.

"I can tell that she really likes you," said Slim.

"Because she just seems much happier with you than she did with that other guy, he was an idiot for letting her go, but I guess that's good for you."

"So what happened with the girl you were dating?" I asked trying to change the subject, because it was getting a little weird.

"Oh, well we were getting a bit on the serious side, you know, talking about marriage, but then out of no where she hit me with the old; if you really love me you would have asked me to marry you by now. When I tried to tell her I wasn't ready she decided it would be in our "best interest," if we started seeing other people. So long story short she met some guy who worked at Jiffy Lube, of all places, and the next thing you know I am getting an invitation to her wedding reception. We dated for over a year, and she dumps me, meets this guy, and like three months later she is engaged, and then like two months after that she is married to this guy, can you believe that?" I was really not sure what I should say and so I just shrugged my shoulders.

"Wow man that's tough."

"Yeah," said Slim.

"So anyway I'm sure you know that I have always kind of liked Megan but after this girl dumped me, I didn't want anything to do with girls, and by the time I woke up and got with it, you two had already started dating, not to say that she would have gone out with me, but I'm just saying, if I had a chance I let it slip away."

Once again, I was left not knowing what to say, or how to respond, so I did what any guy does in an uncomfortable situation with another guy, I stood up and said,

"Boy I am tired, I think I'm going to head off to the room and get some sleep."

As I laid there in my uncomfortable casino bed, I found myself thinking about Megan, and how much I had fallen in love with her, I though about how beautiful she looked up on the stage at her recitals, and how excited I got just thinking about seeing her every day. I must have drifted off to sleep because when the hotel phone started ringing it scared me out of a deep sleep. I stumbled over to the phone, picked it up, and the voice at the other end said,

"I am sorry to disturb you sir, but do you know a tall Australian kid, who claims to have come here with some of his college friends?" I looked around the room and the morning light was already beginning to permeate into the room, I saw Slim laying on the other bed, snoring like a chain saw, but Steve wasn't anywhere to be seen.

"Yes, he's our Australian," I said to the man on the other end of the phone,

"What has he done this time?"

It was about ten or eleven o clock when the casino kicked Steve out for not only gambling under age, because you wouldn't have known Steve was under- age unless you checked his I.D., but also for winning one of the jackpots in the quarter slot machine. He probably would have gotten away with it to, but when the quarters starting flowing out of the machine he started jumping up and down and screaming,

"I told them I wouldn't get caught." So after taking his winnings away from him and giving him a warning they escorted him onto the street.

"What happened to the beautiful city we came into last night?" inquired Steve as we pulled out of Vegas and onto the freeway, he was right the streets were lined with garbage, there was graffiti all over the freeway pillars, and there were homeless people living in tents along the side of road.

"It's all an illusion," stated Slim.

"Vegas is nothing more than a lie, here to take your money, suck you dry and spit you back out."

It was about nine o'clock when we pulled into the dorm parking lots, and when we opened the door to our room Megan and Robyn jumped up.

"Hi guys," they said as Megan ran over to me, put her arms around my neck and gave me a kiss.

"Well how was Vegas boys?" She asked.

"It was all a lie, a big fat lie," said Steve and with each step he made towards his bed he pulled off his shoes, and then his shirt, and then he climbed into his bed.

"Don't wake me up until Monday."

"What was that all about?" Asked Megan.

"You don't want to know." I said as I fell onto the couch.

"Well I am going to go home," said Robyn as she walked towards the door.

"Call me tomorrow and we'll go shopping," she said to Megan as the door closed behind her.

"You two look exhausted." Megan said, as Steve started to snore.

"I am."

"Do you want me to go? Because I will?" asked Megan.

"No, you can stay if you like." I said. Megan walked over to my drawer, pulled out a pair of flannel pants and a t-shirt and threw them at me.

"I am going to go back to my room and change, why don't you put on something comfortable and I will be right back." She walked out of the room while I changed, and then I laid back down on the couch. I don't remember Megan coming back, but she obviously did because when I opened my eyes some time later she was rubbing my feet, and watching something on TV.

"Go back to sleep, honey I'm fine watching my show." I sat up and put my arms around her, kissed her, and whispered,

"I love you," and then I laid back down on the couch. I am not sure if it was extreme sleep deprivation, or the fact that I was not really awake, but Megan grabbed my hand.

"Did you just say what I think you said?" We had been dating for about three or four months by then, but neither of us had used the "L" word before, I thought about it for a moment and then said,

"What do you think I just said?" I asked.

"You know what you said, but why did you say it?" I was not quite sure at that moment if I was in trouble, had I said the "L" word too soon in our relationship, was my saying it putting things in jeopardy, or was she glad I said it, so I froze and stared at her for a minute waiting to see what she was going to do.

"Did you say it because you meant it, or did you say it because you're tired, and I am rubbing your feet for you?" Asked Megan.

Once again I did not know how to respond, and in fact I was not sure why I had said it. At that moment I was in love with her, and I did feel like I meant what I had said, but I didn't want to jeopardize our relationship by saying it, so there I sat once again, "deer in the headlights" look on my face, not knowing whether to jump out of the way, or keep staring until the car hit me. Finally I could hear myself saying the words, but I could hardly believe it was coming out of my mouth.

"Yes, I love you Megan." She looked at me for a moment and then tears started rolling down her cheeks.

"Damn," I thought to myself, I should have jumped out of the way and not let the car hit me. Then Megan leaned over and while laying her head on my chest she whispered,

"Jeremy, I love you too."

Life went on as we struggled through our final quarter, but as all things, both good and bad must eventually come to an end Steve, Tom, and I found ourselves standing outside of the English building hugging each other and jumping up and down for joy. We had just finished the last of our freshman honors course finals and just like three convicts who were being set free at the end of a prison sentence; we stood there breathing in the fresh air of freedom. It was now summer time and in order to keep our places at the dorms we had to enroll in at least one class, so Steve and I had opted to take a basic camping class, and although I loved college and I loved learning it was the nicest reprieve I had encountered in a long time.

Classes were twice a week for one hour each time we met and we had to go camping as a class for three days the end of the summer quarter, it felt almost wrong to be getting credit for camping, but if the college wanted to give it to me, I would gladly talk it. It was the end of June and late one warm afternoon, the sun was just starting to go down, and the air was finally beginning to cool off when Megan and I found ourselves at the Utah arts festival, and as we wandered around looking at the various artists' booths, and stopping to listen to the live music, I realized that it had been a year since I had been here with Mandy, it seemed like a life time ago that I was dating her, and it defiantly seemed like a life time ago when I pulled up in front of the dorms for the first time.

"You should come home with me and meet my parents one of these days," said Megan as we sat sipping our sodas by one of the many sidewalk café attractions at the festival.

I sat there thinking about what she had just asked, and I could feel my fingers getting tingly and the hair on the back of my neck standing up. That was a big step, you only meet the parents when things are getting serious, and all though Megan and I had spent nearly every day together since that evening last spring when we ate ice-cream together and went for our memorable walk, I was still not sure if I was ready to meet her parents.

"I thought you didn't get along with your parents," I finally said trying to avert her question.

"Well, we get along alright I guess, I mean we defiantly get along better since I live an hour and a half away from them, but that's not the point," she said as she put her drink down and looked at me with a serious face.

"The point is I would really like them to meet you. I have been talking about you to my mom and she keeps telling me to bring you home with me, next time I go."

"But you haven't been home since Christmas." I said.

"I know and that's why they want me to come home," she said.

"They don't even come to your recitals," I said once again trying to convince her that she doesn't even want to go home, so why would I want to go with her.

"Ok, I get the hint, never mind," she said as she pulled her sunglasses down over her eyes and looked the other way.

"No," I said as I took her hand in mine.

"That is not what I meant; I guess I have just always thought of meeting the parents as a really big deal, and I'm just not sure if I am ready to take that step yet." Megan looked at me.

"I understand, and I'm not trying to rush anything so you just think about it and when you think you might like to see my house and meet my family you let me know."

Although Megan didn't bring the subject up again I could tell that she was a bit hurt that I was not ready to take that all important step, but at the same time she respected my feelings and didn't push the subject any further.

It was a few short days after the festival when Megan came into my room and made an announcement that would eventually change our relationship forever.

"I have known for a while but I didn't want to say anything until it was confirmed," my mind was racing, trying to think of what she could possible be talking about, and after a moment of silence I said,

"Well, go on."

"I have been invited along with a few other members of the music department to perform at the Atlanta Georgia Summer Olympic Games, I will be in Atlanta from July 21 to the 28th, and I will be performing in the plaza at the Olympic park," said Megan with a huge grin on her face.

"That's awesome," I said as I jumped up and gave her a hug.

"Why didn't you tell me earlier?" I inquired.

"Because, I wasn't sure if I could go, and I wasn't sure who they were going to invite from the music department, but the dean called me in today and asked me if I would be willing to go, and I told him yes."

I was once again amazed by Megan's abilities and talents, to be hand picked to perform at the Olympic Games was an honor so special that I could barley comprehend it. I found myself feeling both excited and sad at the same time, Megan and I had spent so much time together, and this would be the first time we had really been apart since we started dating. I suppose I was also a bit jealous because she was going to be part of the Olympics and I would be here watching it on TV. Megan became very pre-occupied in the days leading up to her departure, she spent most evenings in the music department practicing, alone as well as with the others who were going with her. It was finally the night before she was supposed to leave for Atlanta when I wandered down to Gardner Hall after work and found Megan sitting at the piano, with her head resting in her folded arms on top of the piano. I quietly opened the door and called out to her,

"Megan," nothing,

"Megan," still nothing,

"*Megan*," I shouted and she jumped, sitting up while banging the keys of the piano.

"What, what, I'm in here practicing you can't use the piano till I am done." I walked over to her. "I don't want to use the piano I just wanted to see how you were doing, and persuade you to take a break and go get something to eat with me." She looked over at me and put her glasses on the top of her head.

"I can't stop right now honey I need to go home and pack, and I still have so much to do before tomorrow." I pulled her up to her feet.

"If you aren't ready by now, you will never be, come on let's go get something to eat, then you need to get some rest, you have a big week ahead of you." She reluctantly agreed but we soon found ourselves sitting at a small café down town.

"You are going to be great," I stated as we sat eating french fries, and discussing her trip.

"What are you going to do while I am gone?" Asked Megan.

"Well Steve and I will probably hold up a bank, and then drive our car off a cliff after a three hour long police chase through the canyon," she looked at me and raised one eyebrow slightly,

"Do I need to have Robyn keep an eye on the two of you, because I don't want to come home to find the two of you with shaved heads, or tattoos?"

"We'll be fine," I said.

"We have our class, I have work, and we will watch the Olympics in the evening to see if we can catch a glimpse of you on TV."

The morning Megan was to fly out of Salt Lake to Georgia, we found ourselves sitting in the airport terminal holding hands and talking about how exciting it was for Megan to be part of something so big.

"I wish I could put you in my suit case and take you with me," she said just before she disappeared down the long hall to enter the airplane.

I stood at the large terminal windows and watched the plane slowly taxi out to the runway, it slowly started down the runway and with a huge burst of speed it shot down the last few hundred feet of the tarmac and then it lifted off the ground and quickly disappeared into the clouds. I slowly made my way back to the parking terrace, jumped in my car and headed home. Steve and I had been watching some of the Olympics on TV but after the first few days we realized that they were not going to show anything that was going on in the plaza, so we would watch a little here and a little there but we had other things to do and were really not all that interested in watching. The morning of July

28th Steve and I found our selves sitting at the student union building, eating breakfast and discussing the upcoming week.

"What time are you supposed to pick Megan up from the airport?" Asked Steve.

"Not until this evening some time," I said while looking at my watch.

"I think around 6:00, she was going to call when her plane landed."

"Well what do you think about," Steve began to say, when I noticed the television in the corner of the room showing scenes of chaos, and what looked like an explosion.

"Just a minute Steve." I said as I waved at him to be quite, I stood up and walked closer to the television so that I could hear what was being said.

"For those of you just joining us, we regret to announce that late last night a bomb exploded in the Olympic Park Plaza, injuring at least 100 people and possibly killing ten or more but those numbers have not yet been confirmed," at that point I went numb, and I fell back into the seat nearest the television.

I sat there starring at the newscast while scenes of the explosion, and then the panicked people running were played over and over again. In the background I could see part of a stage where people had been performing just prior to the blast, every nightmare that I had ever experienced came rushing into my head, my hands began to shake and I could feel my eyes welling up with tears. I felt helpless, all I could do was sit starring at the screen, the commentator was talking, people were eating all around me but I heard nothing, and I could not look away from the horrible scene being repeated over and over again. As the numbness wore off, it gave way to worry and then a feeling of panic,

"I hope she's ok," said Steve as he put his hand on my shoulder.

"Me too." I replied.

We made our way back to the dorms where Steve got on the phone and tried to get a hold of someone from the music department to see if they had any news, but we couldn't get any information, we then checked on her flight but it was still scheduled for that evening, there was nothing we could do but wait. As I slowly went through one of the longest, most tense days I had ever experienced I kept thinking of Megan, and how much I loved her. I thought about the arts festival and how she wanted me to meet her parents but I didn't want to so I kept changing the subject, and now she may be hurt, or even worse, and I may not have the chance to meet her family even if I wanted to. I thought of her recitals and how lovely she looked when she was playing, I though of the good times we had experienced, and how there may not be any more of them. I soon found myself feeling angry, angry with myself for taking so long to get to know her, and angry with the bomber who had done this, and how the selfish act of someone Megan and I had never even met, may have taken away something so dear to me.

"You have got to relax," said Steve repeatedly as I paced up and down the hallway in the airport terminal, we had arrived nearly an hour before Megan's planes was scheduled to land and it was now 6:45, almost an hour after it was scheduled to land, and still no plane.

I was an absolute wreck when the voice over the loud speaker announced that her flight would be landing in ten minutes, I could feel a sick feeling come over me when the passengers finally started to make their way off the plane. With each passenger that walked by it felt like a million people had passed me, and when there was a break in the flow of passengers walking off the plane, my heart began to sink and I could feel a cold sweat breaking out over my whole body, then the door opened again and passengers continued to fill the terminal, finally the door opened and Megan came walking out into the crowd of people, I could not hold back my emotions any longer and as I rushed over to where she was I threw my arms around her while spinning her two or three times,

"Hello," she said as I put her back down and kissed her like it was our first time.

"What was that for?" She asked as Steve made his way to where we were standing and threw his arms around both of us.

"Are you ok love?" Asked Steve.

"We thought you were there, and we have been trying to get a hold of you all day."

"I love you Megan," I interrupted.

"And I'm sorry about being so slow to commit to things, and I know that sometimes I can be a bit overbearing but I have been thinking a lot about things and if you are willing to keep trying I am willing to change and be a better person."

I was spewing out all of the thoughts that had been in my head all day and that was when Megan stepped back a little bit and said,

"What are you two so hysterical about? I knew I should have asked Robyn to keep an eye on you, have you two been sniffing glue or something?" Then she paused for a moment.

"Oh, it's that bomb thing, you two thought that I was," and she paused for a moment as it all caught up to her, and she started laughing.

"I am sorry that you guys have been so worried, that happened on the other end of the park, and besides we were at our hotel more than five miles away when it happened, to be honest I didn't even know about it until we were in the Houston airport this morning and I saw it on the news."

I was so glad that Megan was ok, that I didn't care how much Steve and I had overreacted, as we headed home Megan told us about her wonderful 7-day trip to the Olympics. She told us about the athletes she had meet, and how her performance was met with a standing ovation, and how the people there were so friendly and the atmosphere was absolutely electrifying, and how if she ever had the chance she would love to go back to Atlanta and visit.

CHAPTER 7

All Hallows Eve

It was the beginning of October, when I finally agreed to meet Megan's parents for the first time, we had taken the hour and a half drive to a remote little town in northern Utah where her family lived, and upon entering the neighborhood I could sense that Megan was getting tense.

"What's the matter?" I asked.

"Nothing," stated Megan.

"I just don't get along with my family all that well, so coming home just gives me knots in my stomach, and makes me feel uneasy."

"I suppose I can respect that," I said.

"But I'm the one meeting your folks for the first time, so if you think you're nervous, just imagine how I feel."

"I'm sorry honey," she said as she gave my hand a reassuring squeeze.

"Things will be fine, I'm sure that I am just over-reacting."

We pulled into the driveway late that evening, and as we walked into the house I was expecting the worse, but I was very pleasantly surprised, as Megan introduced me to her sister and brother, and then disappeared to other parts of the house.

"*Mom, I'm home, Mom are you here,*" yelled Megan.

"I'm in the kitchen," answered her mother. We walked into the kitchen to find Megan's mother hard at work preparing dinner.

"Mom this is Jeremy, Jeremy this is my mother Karen," Megan looked around for a moment.

"Mom where is dad?" She inquired.

"Oh your father is still at work, he would sleep there if they gave him a bed." Karen turned to me and said,

"So Jeremy, have a seat," she then turned to Megan.

"Megan go and take his stuff down to the spare bedroom in the basement and make sure there are clean sheets on the bed."

"Yes mother," said Megan, and as she turned around to go down the stairs Megan leaned over and whispered to me,

"Don't let her intimidate you."

"What?" I whispered back, but Megan had already left the room.

Karen then gave me a stern look and with the big kitchen knife she had in her hand she pointed it straight at me.

"What are your intentions with my daughter young man?" I was taken off guard by her question and I stammered.

"Uh well I guess that would depend on what her intentions are with me; I mean we haven't really discussed the future all that much." I was lying through my teeth, and since I'm not a good liar my face was turning red and I couldn't really look Karen in the eye.

"My Megan is a musical genius," continued Karen.

"She has been writing, not just playing, but writing music since she was thirteen years old. I would assume that you were aware of that." Karen went back to preparing dinner as she talked to me.

"Megan is a very passionate person and with that kind of geniuses there is always a trade off. I mean she is like Mozart at the piano but she has the temper and the extreme moodiness that goes along with the genius. It's no secret that we don't get along, in fact Megan has never really gotten along with any member of this family," Karen leaned over the counter and said in a quiet tone,

"Megan has a gift that puts her on such a higher level than the rest of us, and it frustrates her to be around us "simpletons.""

I was mortified at this point, I had never seen any signs of this person whom Karen was talking about, I knew Megan the talented, kind hearted girl whom I had fallen madly in love with, but she was describing a person I had never met, a Jekyl and Hyde.

"The only reason why I am telling you this," said Karen.

"Is because if you love, or think you love my daughter, it's going to take a strong man to tame her wild heart and an even stronger man to love her for who she is and what she can become. Megan has all the talent in the world and could easily become a world class composer, but she has all the passion in the world to burn out to quickly." I had no idea what Megan's mom was talking about and it would be years before I would.

"If you love my daughter and want to marry her you have my blessing, but you had better be sure this is what you really want."

Megan's father came home soon after our little talk and we all conversed around the dinner table until late in the evening when I announced that I was tired and ready for bed.

"Come on then, I will show you where your room is," said Megan as she took me by the hand and led me down to the guest room.

"So," began Megan when we got to the bottom of the stairs.

"What did you and my mom talk about when she so conveniently sent me away?"

"I have to level with you," I said as we walked into the room.

"She scared the hell out of me, but I suppose she did give me her blessing."

"You didn't tell her that we've talked about getting married did you?"

"No," I responded.

"She was just talking about Mozart and Jekyl and Hyde, and I think I may have wet myself just a little bit."

"Jeremy, be serious," said Megan as she hit my arm.

"I know my mom is a bit crazy, but in her own way she means well." We talked for a few more minutes and then Megan gave me a little kiss on the forehead and said,

"Good night, I love you and I will see you in the morning."

I must have laid there half the night thinking about what her mom had told me, what if she was right and Megan has some side of her that I had never seen, or what if Karen was just trying to scare me away? At any rate I couldn't sleep that night, and the drive home the next day kept me wondering and hoping that Karen was wrong.

Halloween was almost upon us, my two favorite celebrations take place in October, first, my birthday on the 29th and All Hollows Eve. Because I was born so close to Halloween, my child hood birthday parties always had a Halloween theme surrounding them, so consequently I loved Halloween. I know there are many people who think that Halloween is the "devils" holiday, and refuse to celebrate it, but I always thought of it as an extension of my birthday where everyone celebrated and gave me candy. I had gone through the entire day not knowing if anyone was going to remember my birthday. I had given subtle hints to everyone for the past few weeks, so I was not sure if they had forgotten or were just planning on doing something at the Halloween party Slim was hosting on Halloween night. Celebrating my birthday on Halloween was not uncommon, so as I was finishing up my work day and getting ready to go home I noticed a small envelope with my name on it taped to my work locker, I pulled the note off my locker door and proceeded to open it. Inside was a card that read.

"Roses are red, violets are blue, today is your birthday and we know it, so we have planned a little something for you, don't come home before 6:00 or you will spoil the surprise, love Megan, Steve, Robyn, and Slim."

It had a big red lipstick kiss on the bottom, and Megan must have sprayed it with her perfume because it smelled just like her. I wandered around the campus book store, and the student union building until it was just about six and then I made my way up the hill to my dorm room. When I opened the door and turned on the lights there was no one there, just another note that red.

"Roses are red violets are blue, today is your birthday so go to the basement of the Gardner Hall, through the south east side entrance, and meet us there, love Megan, Steve, Robyn, and Slim."

Gardner Hall was where Megan had her recitals, so I knew the building well; the only problem was it was on the other end of campus. I made my way down the winding sidewalks, past the library, and into president's circle, where Gardner Hall was located; I then made my way to the east entrance and down to the basement. As I entered the hallway, where the music rooms were located I could see lights coming out of one of the rooms towards the end of the hall, and I could here laughter and music blaring from the room, as I got a little closer I could hear Steve yell,

"Here he comes everyone," the lights went out and the music and laughter stopped instantly.

I walked into the room and everyone yelled surprise and jumped out of their hiding places, even thought it was not exactly a surprise it was nice to see my friends, and their friends, and guys from the honors society, and people that I didn't even know, and some kid who appeared to have passed out in the corner of the room there to celebrate my birthday. The music started right back up and people began to laugh and talk again, I noticed a black cake on one of the tables in the far corner, and it was painted with frosting shaped bats and ghosts, there were black and orange streamers hung around the room, and almost everyone was dressed up in costumes.

"We're just practicing for Slims Halloween party on Thursday night," said Megan as she came up to me in her black gothic looking, low-cut dress, with fishnet stockings, tattered angle wings, and a black cocktail mask that covered her eyes. She put her arms around my neck and said,

"Happy birthday baby," and she kissed me, then took me by the hand and said,

"Ok everyone let's sing happy birthday." They all sang a very off key and very loud rendition of happy birthday and when they finished everyone clapped, I then turned to see Slim in his full Roof Top Restaurant chef attire wheeling in a big cart full of food.

"Appetizers are here, and I will be bringing in the sandwiches and deserts in a few minutes."

"*Who spiked the punch?*" yelled Steve.

"That's so not funny," he stated as he looked around the room in disgust. It was one of those little things in life that just make you glad to be alive, and happy to be thought of in such a nice way by the people around you.

"I have a little surprise for you," Megan said, and she motioned for the music to be turned off, as she made her way to the piano.

Megan sat down and began to play happy birthday for me on the piano and after finishing, she paused, and in came a small orchestra consisting of Megan's friends, some of whom I recognized from her recitals, and some of them I had never seen before. They began to play something for me that was so beautiful and so filled with passion that words could not describe it. Robyn walked softly over to me and whispered in my ear,

"Megan wrote this for you, as a birthday gift, she has been working on it for weeks."

I could feel the tears filling up in my eyes, this was without a doubt the most unique and personal gift anyone had ever given me, and as I looked around the room everyone had fallen silent as they watched and listened to the music in almost a trance like state. When the music finally stopped everyone was silent for a moment, and then Megan stood up,

"This song is a gift from me to you, on your birthday," she paused for a moment.

"I hope you liked it."

I began to clap, as did everyone that was not passed out from our spiked punch, I ran over to Megan and put my hands around her waist and lifted her up in the air and spun her around, while whispering in her ear,

"Thank you, that was absolutely breathtaking."

The rest of the evening was sort of a blur, we ate and danced and enjoyed each other's company. I remember thinking to myself as we all walked home that night, how lucky I was to have the friends I did. I also came to the realization that although Megan and I had talked about marriage, in sort of a "what if," kind of way, but never anything serious, I knew for the first time in the nearly a year and a half that I had known her, that I really did loved her and I decided that evening that I wanted to marry her, and make her mine forever.

Steve and I were finally in the architecture classes that we had longed to be in for some time now, and it was absolutely fascinating, I really enjoyed those first few classes, Introduction to Architecture, Basic Design Principles, and Architectural Fundamentals. It was now that I could take the classes I wanted to take without worrying about my general educations credits that I was glad I had taken the honors course. I remember soaking up every lecture, and every time a guest architect came to speak I was on the front row asking questions and taking notes. I knew this is what I wanted to do and I knew for the first time in college that I was really there for a reason. It was a Monday night in November, just a week or two before the Thanksgiving holiday when Slim called all of us together at his dads place for an important announcement,

"Remember that dinner we had for my dad and some of his clients last spring?" He asked.

"Yes."

"Well one of them called me last night and offered me a position as a junior chef in his restaurant."

"That is wonderful news." We all said and began to congratulate him.

"When do you leave?" Asked Steve.

"I will fly out to New York in two days for a one week trial visit, and if I think it's something that I want to pursue full time, I will come back long enough to get my things out of the dorm and I will be gone."

We all congratulated him once again, and enjoyed the dinner he had prepared for us for his celebration, it was rather quiet however because we were all a bit sad to see him go. Tom had moved out, and we saw him quite a bit at first, but as the weeks went on and school continued we saw less and less of him, it had actually been almost two months since anyone had heard from or seen Tom, and we just didn't want to lose another friend.

That evening after we made our way back to the dorms I was sitting on the edge of Megan's bed as she read through one of her class's textbooks.

"Then there were three," I said without realizing what I had said.

"What was that?" Asked Megan as she put her book down for a moment and looked up at me.

"Nothing," I said.

"No you said, "then there were three," what does that mean?"

"Well I guess it means that if," I paused for a moment.

"Who are we kidding, when Slim takes this new job he will be gone, just like Tom and it will be down to Steve, me and Robyn."

"What about me?" Asked Megan.

"Don't I count?"

"Of course you do, I just mean of the original five, there would only be three of us left." Megan looked at me for a moment and then said,

"I think you mean two."

"No, I mean three," I said a bit confused.

"Ok three," Megan said as she pulled her book back up in front of her face. I reached over and gently pulled the book away from her face.

"What aren't you telling me?"

"Nothing," she said, and pulled the book back up.

I didn't push the issue but found it rather odd, that Megan was acting this way, what did she know that I didn't, and why wasn't she telling me? It was not long before I had the answer to my question. A day or two after Slim had left for New York there was a knock on my door and when I answered it Robyn was standing in the doorway wearing the same formal gown that she was wearing the night we went to dinner with her parents,

"I talked to Megan and she has given me permission to take you out to dinner, so get changed, I will be in the lobby waiting for you," she then turned around and walked away, I turned to Steve and he looked back down at his books quickly.

"Steve, what is going on?" I asked as I began to change into my Sunday best.

"What?" Steve asked as he looked up pretending like he didn't hear me.

"I said, what is going on Steve, do you and Megan know that I don't?"

"Nothing," said Steve, rather unconvincingly.

"I mean I don't know what you are talking about, I mean what?" I looked over at him and pointed.

"You know something, and I know you know something," he looked up again and in a bit of a melancholy tone said,

"Have a good time tonight," and then he went back to his book.

I met Robyn in the hall, and she took me by the hand,

"I'll drive," she said. We went out to her car and sped off into the night.

"What's going on?" I asked, as we turned into the dance theatre parking lot.

"I just wanted to show you something before we go to dinner," said Robyn as she grabbed my hand and we walked into the main lobby, where I instantly noticed a larger than life poster of a ballerina, and as we got closer I realized that it was her.

"Wow," I said.

"What's it like to finally be over five feet tall?" Robyn gave me a playful push.

"Go up to the poster and read it," she said as we got to the wall where it was hanging.

"The New York School of Performing arts would like to congratulate its newest member on a stellar performance at the University of Utah."

I stopped at that point because there was no need to read on, I was apprehensive when Tom left, I was a bit sad when Slim left, but I could feel the tears filling up in my eyes with the thought of Robyn leaving. Even though she was like a sister to me, and even though I was preparing to ask Megan to marry me. I suppose there was still a little something inside of me that would miss Robyn more than any of the others. I tried my very best to act excited as I turned around and threw my arms around her.

"Congratulations Robyn, I'm so excited for you, when do you leave?" I asked.

"I am leaving for New York after Christmas, so I will finish out the last week of this quarter and then when I go home for Thanksgiving that will be the end of my time here." Robyn stood there looking deep into my eyes, she was searching for something but I didn't know what that something was.

"Jeremy, I know we have been good friends for a while now," Robyn stepped closer and took my hand.

"I know that you love Megan very much, and I know that she loves you too," Robyn stepped back and looked down at the ground.

"I wish the two of you the very best," she said.

We both stood looking into each other's eyes and finally Robyn took my hand once again and we walked out of the lobby and went back to her car. We went to the same little café where we had escaped from her parents all those months ago and as we finished eating and started for the car, Robyn asked,

"Can we go for a little walk before we go home, please?"

"Sure," I said, and she took my hand as we walked out into the chilly November air. Neither one of us talked for some time, I think we both knew what the other was thinking but we didn't dare put words to it. Finally Robyn stopped and turned so that she was standing right in front of me. The bright moon light was shining down on her and she looked so lovely, the stars seemed to dance around her as she looked deeply into my eyes once again, and I noticed the tears starting to flow down her soft cheeks.

"Jeremy I have always loved you, but I know you don't love me in the same way," Robyn was trying to fighting back the tears as her voice began to shake.

"I have come to grips with that a long time ago but I cannot walk out of your life forever without telling you how I feel. You did something for me that no one else has ever done, you gave me freedom, that night when you stood up to my parents, it changes my life forever and I can never thank you enough for that. I want you to know that going to New York was my decision and it had nothing to do with my mom." I started to say something and she put her finger to my lips.

"Please don't stop me because if you do I won't have the courage to continue, I will never forget you, and I will never forget what you have done for me." By this time the tears were rolling down both of her cheeks and I reached into my pocket, pulled out a handkerchief and gently wiped the tears from her eyes.

"Thank you," she said.

"Please don't be angry with me, I do not want to leave you, and the rest of our friends behind but I need to do what is best for me, please don't be angry with me for this." She then pulled herself tightly into my arms and while standing up on her tip toes she gently pushed her lips to mine, after a moment she began to press her lips tighter and tighter, and as she did I could feel her shake as she continued to cry.

"I love you Jeremy, and there will always be a place in my heart for you."

Robyn left just before thanksgiving and I never saw her again.

It was about one week before Christmas as I stood nervously in front of the ring counter at the jewelry store, I held the delicate ring in my fingers and, as I sat counting out more money then had ever run through my hands in my lifetime the woman behind the counter asked me if I wanted it gift wrapped. I went home that evening, carefully opened the box, and took the ring out to show Steve.

"I'm so excited for the two of you," Steve said.

"When and where are you going to ask her?"

"I'm not sure yet, but I have a big favor to ask of you."

"What's that?" Inquired Steve.

"I want you to be my best man." Steve looked at me and a big grin came over his face from ear to ear.

"I would be honored to mate!" said Steve.

I had called in one last favor of Slim, he had gone to New York and worked his trial week, and at no surprise to any of us he accepted the position. Steve and I helped him move his stuff out of the dorms and during the move I had explained to Slim that I was going to ask Megan to marry me, and I asked if he would be willing to do one last favor for his friend.

It was gently snowing as I opened the passenger door of my car to let Megan in, Steve, Slim and I had been preparing for this evening for days now, and if all went well Megan would have no idea what was about to happen. I had asked Megan to dress up in one of her concert gowns, and she did not disappoint me! Megan had worked out a deal with the costume department and they had allowed her to take one of her concert dresses for the evening, and she looked like an angel. Megan was wearing the white gown she had worn to the benefit concert I had attended a year ago, and she had talked the hair and markup girls into getting her all dolled up as well!

"Where are we going?" She asked as we turned into the parking garage of Slims place.

"This is Slims place, but isn't he in New York?" Asked Megan as we made our way up the elevator to his apartment.

"Good evening," said Steve as he opened the door and let us in.

"May I take your coats?" He said. Steve was wearing his driver's uniform from work so he looked very regal as he led us into the dining room.

"May I suggest the chef's specialty tonight? Chicken cordon blue." And he disappeared into the kitchen.

"What are you boys up to?" Asked Megan. Steve came back out and clapped his hands twice.

"May I introduce the chef," out stepped Slim in his black chefs uniform complete with his name embroiders on the front right hand side and the name of the restaurant on the other, he looked very professional, and he had a big grin on his face.

"*Slim*," giggled Megan as she jumped up and gave him a hug.

"My, my, my, don't you look sharp," said Megan as she stood back and eyed him over.

"Please, if madam will be seated we will continue with the meal," said Slim as he clapped his hands signaling for Steve to begin bringing our plates out. Slim walked over to the candles on the table and lit them with his lighter and then he dimmed the lights in the dinning room.

"I think there is something you two should see," said Slim, he looked over at Steve, and snapped his fingers, then Steve ran over to the sliding glass door leading to the balcony and knocked on the glass, as soon as he did music began to play, but not just any music. Megan sat there for a moment, and look at me, and then at Steve, and then back at me, her lips began to quiver just a little, and her eyes began to glisten.

"That's the song I wrote you for your birthday isn't it?"

I nodded my head, and signaled to Steve to open the blinds, and as he did Megan's small group of friends who had performed the song for me a couple of months ago were all bundled up in their coats playing our song on the balcony. Megan wiped the tears from her eyes and then the piano behind her in the living room began to play along with the small orchestra on the balcony. Megan turned around to see one of her friends whom had performed with her from time to time playing the piano piece that went along with the orchestration. Megan leaned over and with tears streaming down her cheek she kissed me.

"Jeremy what have you gone to all of this trouble for?" I paused for a moment and looked at the bright moon and the stars in the background. The snow was still falling lightly like large sugar crystals falling from the sky. I took a deep breath and thought to myself,

"There will never be a better moment than this."

I pulled the small ring box out of my jacket pocket and got down on one knee right in front of Megan, she immediately began to shake and she put her shaking hands to her mouth, and gasped out loud.

"Megan, I have assembled all of these people here tonight because I wanted the evening to be perfect. I know that I have taken things a bit slower than you may have liked, but I just wanted to be sure that you were the one for me, and I wanted to be sure that you thought I was the one for you."

With the song Megan had written for me playing in the background, my best friends by my side, and the snow gently falling in the bright moonlit sky, I asked her the biggest question of my life.

"Megan I love you, and I want you to be my wife, and if you will have me I want to be your husband."

By this time Megan was crying and all her makeup was running down her face, she took my hands in hers and motioned for me to stand up, and as soon as I was standing she put her arms around me tightly and whispered in my ear,

"Yes, I will marry you."

Steve and Slim began to clap their hands and jump up and down, Steve ran over and pulled Megan away from me and while picking her he gave her a huge bear hug and spun her around,

"I love you guys, and you are going to make the nicest couple," said Steve as he put her down.

"I agree," said Slim as he too gave Megan a big hug and shook my hand. I put the ring on her delicate finger, and as we stood holding each other, I thought to myself,

"Life cannot get any better than this moment right here, right now." It had truly been one of the happiest evenings of my life, and I was so glad that I had spent it with Steve, and Slim.

Consequently Slim left the next morning for New York, and we received a wedding card from him, and an open invitation to come to the restaurant where he worked any time we were in New York, for all the times we spent together, all the laughs, the good times and the bad Slim was a good friend but I never saw him again.

I have always considered myself a rational person, capable of making decisions, and capable of thinking and acting for myself, I had also thought Megan was a rational person, likewise intelligent and capable of making decisions, but a funny thing happens when you become engaged and start planning a wedding reception, you somehow lose those abilities. I know in her own way Megan was just trying to include me in the planning and preparation of our big day, but like most guys I truly didn't care one way or the other what our announcements looked like, I had no preference in what flavor the cake should be, and to be honest, chicken, fish, or steak really was not a big deal for me, but for some reason these issues had become so important that I found myself loosing my temper over what color napkins should be on the table. When I had said to Megan,

"What ever you want to do is fine with me."

I really had meant it, and I really would have been fine just showing up on our wedding day, and enjoying the festivities. We had picked a date in the latter part of March and since the first part of January this brief five or six hour period of time had become all encompassing, and it had engulfed ever minute of my not so free time.

I remember slamming the truck door and looking straight ahead. I was too frustrated to explain to Dan why I had just slammed the door hard enough to rock the truck back and forth. I couldn't even explain why I had put our stack of delivery tickets on the clip-board upside down and backwards, but I think Dan could tell that I had been having "one of those days." I had been as patient as I possibly could, but when it came to picking out socks to go with my tuxedo, I figured that a pair of dark socks was a pair of dark socks and all you needed to do was choose a pair that fit. I had found out during my lunch break that this was not the case. I had run over to a local men's clothing store during lunch to pick out a pair of socks with Megan. Once again, one of those items that I had figured I was intelligent enough to do myself, but when Megan insisted on going with me I decided not to fight it, and let her come along.

"Ok," I said grabbing the first pair of socks I came to.

"Let's pay for these and get out of here."

"You cannot be serious?" Asked Megan with a look of disgust on her face.

"Those socks are navy blue, and you are not wearing navy blue socks with your tuxedo, on my wedding day."

I didn't think they were navy blue, but for arguments sake I grabbed the ones next to them.

"Ok let's get these, and be on our way," I got the exact same look from Megan.

"Ok, which ones do you want me to get?" I figured I had better just ask her and forget about trying to pick out my own socks.

"We will need to get an attendant to help us," she stated as she started looking around for someone to help us.

"An attendant?" I asked quizzically.

"Are we buying socks, or are we buying a suit here?" Megan looked at me and smiled politely.

"Let me get someone," as she disappeared down one of the isled of suits. I was standing looking at the clock on the wall thinking of how soon I needed to get back to work, when a rather feminine looking man with a bad hair piece came walking up the isle with Megan.

"So what are your colors, what time of year is your wedding, what color suit will he be wearing, and what color shoes will he be wearing?" were the questions he was asking.

I stood in disbelief, we were buying socks, not deep sea diving equipment, what on earth did this strange little man need to know all of those things for? While Megan was off looking for help in the form of Mr. Humphries, I had taken the liberty of picking out three or four additional pairs of socks, and upon their return, I said,

"I think I may have found something here" The odd little man took the socks out of my hands.

"Why don't you be a dear, and sit over there while we work this out." I gently pulled on Megan's arm and with a fake smile on my face said,

"Can I see you for a moment, over there by the door, in private," she looked at me as if to say no, and so I pulled her over by the door.

"Was I just shot down by Sergeant Fancy Pants, or am I misreading this situation, because I think I was just shot down by some clown with a dead rat on his head." Megan looked at me in a state of shock.

"Jeremy," she said in a tone that I had heard my mother use when I was a child.

"Don't talk like that, he is a professional, and he's going to help us pick out the right pair of socks."

"I have never needed help picking out socks before," I said in an irritated tone.

"I know dear, and look at your socks." I looked down and pulled up the edge of my pants.

"What's wrong with my socks?" I asked not really wanting an answer.

"Sit down and take off your work boots," I looked at her in a confused way.

"Just do it," she said.

I sat down, took off my boots and pulled the white tube socks I was wearing up to where they belonged.

"Ok, so what's wrong with my socks?" Megan pointed to the heel, which was half way up my calf.

"They're too big, and so are all of your other socks."

"They have to be, in order to keep my work boots from rubbing on the back of my legs," I said in my defense.

"I understand that dear, but all of you socks are like that, even your dress socks."

I figured at this point, it was futile to continue arguing so I just sat for the twenty five minutes it took to decide which pair of socks would be appropriate, and I almost died when the bill came to $20.00, I had not paid that much for a pair of pants, let alone one pair of socks.

I was of course late returning to work and when I pulled into the parking lot I could see Dan standing on the dock smoking and looking at his watch, I punched in as fast as I could and on my way to the truck I accidentally dropped our afternoon delivery forms, which is why they were all messed up when I clipped them to the clip board.

"I don't want to talk about it," I said as Dan started to ask why I was late, he just laughed at me.

"Save yourself the trouble man, just tell her whatever she wants to hear, and agree to whatever she says, because you will end up doing this thing her way, whether you like it or not."

I did learn a valuable lesson after my little sock incidence and that was to just let Megan do her thing, and be there when she asked me too, and stay away from the whole planning thing as much as I possibly could. After changing my view, things did go smoother for the most part. I was involved when she needed me to be, and beyond that I just let her make all the decisions. I quickly came to realize that when she was asking for my opinion she was not asking it because she wanted my input, she was asking it because she wanted validation from me for the choices she had made.

The difference between boys and girls when it comes to weddings is that a boy thinks about the wedding as soon as he asks the girl to marry him, while the girl has been thinking about her wedding since the time she was six years old. Most girls have their entire wedding planned out before their fourteenth birthday, and all they really need from the groom, is the ring, and for him to show up at the right time and the right place on the day of the wedding. I think if it were up to most guys, the wedding would be held in the lobby of the honeymoon hotel, and there would be a room for people to leave the gifts in, a table would be set up with a small buffet of sandwiches and mints, so that the people would at least feel a bit justified in coming. A cardboard cutout of the happy couple would be set up in the lobby just outside of the gift room, with a mechanical arm on the bride that waved back and forth greeting the guests. I suppose you could get fancy and have a pre-recorded message that would play phrases like,

"Thank you for coming." And,

"Thank you for the gift." But really you wouldn't need much more than that.

I had placed our names on the married housing waiting list, the week after we picked a wedding date, and it was now three weeks until the wedding and I had not heard anything back from them. I was on my way out the door to go and talk with the housing people when Steve came down the hall towards me.

"We have to talk mate," said Steve with a rather concerned look on his face.

"I'm on my way out right now, but we can talk when I get back," I said as I continued walking towards the door.

"No," said Steve you don't understand, we need to talk right now." He paused for a moment and then said,

"I am going home on Thursday," I turned back around.

"It's Monday Steve, and we still have two weeks until the end of the quarter, what do you mean you're going home?" I asked.

"Let's go get something to eat and I will fill you in," said Steve.

I was quite surprised because Steve had not said anything about going home in between the quarter break. For that matter he had not said anything about going home ever. Steve had not gone back to Australia since he had arrived in the U.S. almost two years ago, and now he was saying he needed to go home in three days.

We sat down with our chili dogs and fries that we had bought at the student union center when Steve started to explain that his aunt, who had been very close to the family had just passed away from cancer, and so he needed to go home to be with his family.

"I have already worked things out with all of my professors, and since we are so close to the end they will let me take my finals tomorrow, I will leave after the last one on Thursday," Steve stopped eating, and he got a bit choked up.

"I am sorry, Jeremy, but I won't be back in time to be your best man, and I feel really bad and wish that things were not like this, but I hope you and Megan will understand."

I could not believe what Steve was telling me, this was very hard to swallow on a multiplicity of levels. Steve had been the very first person I met on my very first day of school. He had been my friend and roommate for almost two years now. We had talked about finishing school and starting our own architectural firm together, and he was suppose to be the best man at my wedding, which was only three weeks away. I could not be mad at him, this was something that was out of his hands, but I sat there in disbelief.

"Couldn't you go home for the funeral and then come back?" I asked, trying somehow to come up with a solution.

"No, I can't," said Steve.

"And to be honest with you I don't think I will be coming back at all."

"*What*?" I asked.

"Why not?"

"Because it was my aunt who has been helping to pay for my college tuition."

"So get a second job," I said without missing a beat.

"I'm paying for my tuition, it isn't easy, but it can be done." I said not fully understanding his situation.

"You don't get it," he said while shaking his head.

"I'm not a resident so I pay out of state tuition, it's like three times what you are paying mate, and I can't afford to make that kind of payment."

I sat in disbelief, how could I have not realized that, and what could I do to help my friend out, as we sat and talked, I threw out every option that I could think of until Steve finally said,

"Look I have thought about all of those things, and believe me if I could stay I would. But it just isn't going to happen, you have been a good friend, and I will miss you. I am sorry I won't be here for your wedding but I know you two will make a great couple."

The next few days were very hard on me, and I am sure they were hard on Steve too. He sold his car, and the personal items that he didn't want to take with him he either gave to me or put in the lost and found pile in the laundry room. It was a sad and melancholy day when we helped each other dismantle the scaffolding and all of the junk in our room. As the two of us got the room cleaned out nearly two years of memories were shuffled, dismantled, boxed, or thrown away.

I had talked with the married student housing people and after a little discussion and a twenty-dollar bill; I was able to get things worked out so that I could move into our apartment the week before the wedding, so it only made since to have Steve help me dismantle everything. I had intended on leaving the room and most of its contents for Steve but with the sudden and unexpected turn in events we decided to just get the room cleaned out.

Megan and I stood in the airport with Steve a few moments before they announced the boarding of his flight, and after making all the typical "guy," small talk Megan walked up to Steve and gave him a big hug.

"We will really miss you Steve, you have been a good friend to Jeremy, and a good friend to me, please come and visit us if you can." Megan then turned to me and nudged me as she walked by whispering,

"Give it to him, and tell him how you feel." She turned back to Steve and said,

"I will give you guys a few minutes." She made her way to the other end of the terminal, and looked back motioning to me to give him the gift that we had picked out for him. I pulled the small wrapped package out of my front jacket pocket, and handed it to Steve.

"This was supposed to be your best man gift, it isn't much, but Megan and I still wanted you to have it." Megan and I had gotten him a nice pen and pencil set with his name engraved on it along with the words "architectural genius."

"I can't take it mate," said Steve as he stood blushing.

"I'm leaving you without a best man just before your wedding, if anything you should be mad at me for walking out on you, and I should be giving you a gift."

"Just take it," I said, as I shoved it into his hands, and as he took it I could see his eyes starting to get a bit glossy.

"Thank you," he said as he put his arms around me and gave me a big hug.

"I will never forget you guys," he said, just as they announced his plane would now be boarding.

"Take care of yourself Steve, and please come and visit if you can, you have been a good friend and I will miss you," Steve and I hugged one more time and he turned to where Megan was standing and motioned for her to come back over to where we were, as she came back over Steve said,

"I won't get the chance to do this at the wedding, so with your permission?" He asked as he looked at me, and I nodded to him. Steve gave Megan one last hug and a small kiss on the cheek, and with tears starting to run down his face he turned and walked down the long runway to board his plane.

Steve had a long 16-hour flight to Sydney in front of him, and as Megan and I stood in front of the window waiting for the plane to take off, we were very sad to see him go. We watched the plane speed down the runway, take off, and disappear into the clouds, and as it did I could feel myself getting choked up, it was so strange to think that on Monday Steve and I were best friends and would be forever, now here it was three days later on a rainy Thursday evening and Steve was gone forever. I wish I could say that Steve came back a few months later, and everything went back to the way it was before, but life is not like that, and just like my other close friends from college, I never saw Steve again.

CHAPTER 8

New Beginnings and Tragic Endings

It was a beautiful spring morning in March when I stood holding Megan's, hand saying, "I do," to the love of my life. It was such a surreal experience, here stood the woman I had been dating for almost a year and a half, whom I had spent so many good times with, and now she was no longer just my girl friend, she was my wife. I stood there remembering the first time we met, I recalled how Steve told Megan that my girlfriend had died, and that I was in counseling, I could have killed Steve at the time, but if I had known what meeting Megan would lead to, I would have thanked him. I could remember our first date, all of her recitals, the benefit dinner, and so many more remarkable times we had spent together.

She looked absolutely stunning in her long white wedding dress, I had thought she looked like an angel many times before, but that day, I truly felt like I was marring an angel from heaven. As I stood, hand in hand with Megan, at the top of the grand winding staircase in the reception center greeting guests, some of whom were friends and family members, and some of whom I had never met before, I could not help but to feel a little bit sad for my good friends whom I had laughed, cried, and loved with, but were not there.

Steve had gone back to Australia only a few weeks previous and consequently was not able to be at our wedding, or be my best man. Slim was not able to get away from the restaurant in New York. However he sent us a letter stating how much he liked living and working in New York, he also went on to explain that he was doing great with his apprenticeship, and he wanted to be at the wedding but would not be able to get away. Robyn, who had also gone to New York, was in the middle of a ballet production and although she sent a nice card, and a letter wishing us the best, it was not the same as it would have been if she were there. I really wished all of my friends could have been there, but life has a funny way of directing people in an unexpected way.

With the joy of the wedding festivities in full swing, I found that my brief moment of sadness for the loss of my friends was quickly replaced by the love and warmth of the people who surrounded me that day. It had indeed been a long road to get to where I was in life, but the joy that filled my soul on that day made all of the pain worth it.

As the evening began to wind down I found myself on the dance floor holding Megan, my new wife, tightly in my arms. It seemed so unreal to think that we were married, when only a few days before we were finishing up our winter classes and taking our final exams and now here we were husband and wife.

"Do you recognize this song?" Asked Megan, whispering quietly into my ear.

"This is the song I wrote you for your birthday, last year." Most of our wedding guests probably didn't know it, but the music playing over the sound system in the large ballroom, had been written, performed, and recorded by Megan with the help of her music professor, and the University of Utah orchestra.

"Yes, I do recognize this song," I whispered back into her ear as I pulled her even closer.

"I love you more today than I did yesterday, and I will love you more and more each day for the rest of your life." Megan whispered back into my ear, as we danced long into the evening.

Megan and I spent the next week in Park City, Utah, site seeing, and enjoying being newlyweds, but as all good things must come to an end, we soon found ourselves back in our small, one bedroom cinderblock apartment in the married housing complex at the University.

During the week between the end of the quarter, and the wedding, while Megan was busy with last minute details, I had moved all of our humble belongings over to the new apartment. Together we had very little, but we were so happy to be together and in love, that it didn't matter.

Our first year of marriage was wonderful, it was full of new challenges, new joys, and it flew by very quickly. Megan finished out the school year and we decided that it was just too expensive for both of us to be going to school at the same time, so the plan was; I would work part time while I finished school, and Megan would work full time to help support us. When I got close to finishing up my education, we would then look into having Megan go back to finish her degree in music composition, it was against the dean of music's wishes that she withdrew from the University, and I know that Megan was sad to be leaving, but we knew it would only be temporary.

After we had been married for almost a year we decided that the time had come for me to find employment off campus, and in my field of study, partially because I had worked on campus longer than I had ever planned, and I was only making $6.75 an hour. I started the long process of applying, interviewing, and being turned down by almost every architectural firm in the Salt Lake Valley, and It wasn't until I had almost given up hope of finding work in my field, that a ray of sunshine shown through the dark clouds, and I was given a job as a junior apprentice architect in a small architectural firm specializing in renovating old churches. The job was not nearly as glamorous as I would have hoped it would be, but at least I was finally getting my foot in the door. I had been going to school for almost three years, and I had been taking architectural classes for more than two of those years, so I was happy to finally be getting a job in architecture.

I had quickly worked my way up the latter in the architectural department at school, due in large to the fact that I had taken the honors program and earned my general's so quickly, but also because I was so fascinated by my studies that putting in extra time on my assignments was a joy. I had my own desk in the architectural design studio, an honor bestowed only upon students who had achieved the junior level in college, so I was beginning to feel like I could see the light at the end of the tunnel.

Leaving the warehouse was a bittersweet experience, I knew that I would not miss the work, but I would miss working with Dan. I had spent almost three years working side by side with Dan, through thick and thin, hot and cold, and we had grown to be good friends. Dan was not one for goodbyes, so on my last day of work he left a note tapped to my locker door, and all it said was, "thank you," he didn't show up for work that day because he didn't want to say good bye.

I came home from work one afternoon, soon after starting my new job to find a letter in the mail addressed to me from the University, and upon opening it I found a memo inside that read something like this:

"We are pleased, as a school to announce that in six months time we will be converting all of our classes and curriculum from a quarter based system to the semester system, this will save the school money and in return will save you the student money. We understand that this change may affect some of our students and so we request that you make an appointment with your guidance counselor to discuss how this change may affect you."

I was a bit confused by what the phrase, "this may affect some of our students," meant, so I picked up the phone right then and made an appointment with my counselor. Early the next morning I found myself sitting in a long line waiting to get into the counseling center, after waiting for what seemed like hours I was finally able to meet with one of the general education counselors, and she explained to me that the curriculum would be changed in each department, so in order to get my specific questions answered I would need to meet with one of the counselors in the architectural department. I was feeling very frustrated for having already wasted so much of my time, so needless to say, I was not in a good mood as I made my way over to the architectural building and sat in yet another long line waiting to see the architectural departments counselor.

"So," said the counselor, when I finally got in to see him.

"We are taking most of our sequential classes such as architecture 203, 204, and 205 and making them one class." It took a few moments for the real horror of what he was telling me to set in, perhaps it was denial more than the fact that I didn't understand what he was saying, but I couldn't help asking more questions to clarify the answer.

"So what about the sequential courses that I have not completed?" I asked in a frustrated tone.

"For example," I said to the counselor,

"I have taken architecture 203, and 204, but I have not been able to get into 205 yet, because it is offered to seniors before the juniors have a chance to sign up for it?" I asked the counselor my question knowing in the back of my mind what the answer would be, but I didn't want to hear it.

"You will not lose any credit for the classes you have taken," said the counselor in a not so reassuring tone.

"But if you have not completed one of the sequential classes, you will need to re-take that particular course, but on a positive note if you are a senior with graduating status we will be willing to work with you to convert your credits so that you will not have to retake anything."

I sat in my chair across from the counselor, staring at him, the wheels were turning in my head, and I could hear what was being said, but I refused to believe it.

"So what you are telling me, just so I am clear about it, is this," I said pointing at the counselor.

"Due to the fact that most all of the courses in the architectural program are currently sequential, I will need to retake nearly all of the classes I have taken in the last two years, just to catch back up to where I am today." I sat for a moment, mentally counting up the classes I had taken in my head.

"You realize," I said in a frustrated and angry tone,

"That will mean half, to three quarters of the classes I have already completed, I will have to retake because they are only part of a sequential course."

"I know it sounds a bit harsh," stated the counselor.

"But you are not the only one being effected by this."

"I am sure I'm not," I said as my voice and my temper began to rise.

"But quiet frankly, I am the only one "*I*" care about, and I am two and a half quarters away from starting my senior year."

I stood up and said, "So what you are telling me is that I don't qualify to have my credits converted so I will virtually have to start all over in this program." I could feel myself loosing my temper, with each word I said I got a little bit louder, and I could feel my face getting red hot.

"I am sorry, I wish I could help you," said the counselor.

"But as I stated before you are not the only one being affected by this change, it will be affecting thousands of students, but we have to draw the line somewhere."

I was so angry that I couldn't even speak, I stood up while the counselor continued talking to me, I opened the door and slammed it hard enough to feel the wall shake behind me, I looked at the twenty or thirty people waiting to get in to see the counselor and I shook my head as I walked out of the architectural building.

My head was spinning as I made my way back home, and I must have looked as angry as I felt because when I walked in the door Megan jumped up.

"What's wrong?" She asked. I explained what had just transpired, between the counselor and me.

"What are we going to do?" She asked, with a look of concern on her face.

"I'm not sure," I said as I sank into the couch and stared up at the ceiling.

"But I will think of something." I was so angry that I couldn't even think straight.

"How could they do this to me?" I asked Megan as she started preparing dinner.

"What about the thousands of other students who have been going to school for two and three years now?" Inquired Megan.

"Won't they have to start over as well?"

"I guess so." I said without taking my eyes off the ceiling.

"But I don't really care about what the other students are going to do, this is huge, this is a big deal." I said.

"This is going to set me back almost two years." Megan looked over at me and said,

"What about me? Don't you think this is going to affect my education as well?" Megan was right, I was being selfish, and so after we finished eating dinner, I announced that I needed to go for a walk because I knew that I would do or say something I would regret, I was mad at the school, not at Megan and it was not fair to take it out on her. So there I sat in the student union building, fuming over what had happened when one of the guys I had seen in some of my architectural classes came and sat down across from me.

"So what are you going to do?" He asked. I just shook my head.

"I have no idea."

"Well," he said.

"Some of us are looking into transferring to a technical college, just to salvage our credits, I mean it's not really what any of us want to do, but at the same time none of us want to start over either."

I made my way back home to find Megan sitting on the couch drinking tea, and reading a book.

"So, do you feel any better?" She asked me as I sat down next to her. I put my head in my hands and sighed out loud.

"Some of the guys are taking about transferring to a technical college to save their credits." Megan began to rub my back as she asked me,

"What do you want to do?"

"I don't know," I said.

"I always dreamed of graduating from the University of Utah, and I'm not too excited about transferring to some second rate technical college." Megan walked into the kitchen and poured me a cup of tea, she walked back into the room and handed it me.

"You know that I love you and will support you in anything that you do, I won't think any less of you for graduating from a technical college, then I would if you graduated from Harvard," she said as she took my hand.

"The thing you need to consider is this, will you really have to start over if you stay here, and if you do have to start over will you be able to swallow your pride and retake all of those classes?" She pulled the hair back off my forehead as she continued saying,

"Can we afford for you to go to school for another three years or more or will that max out your student loans?" Megan took my hand.

"The most important thing to consider would be this, if you don't graduate from the "U," will you still be able to work in the field of architecture, or will you have to give up your dream?"

The truth was I didn't know! I had been doing what I thought I needed to do in order to achieve my goal of becoming an architect, but fate has a way of making your plans explode in your face, forcing you to make changes.

After thinking seriously for a few weeks about what would be the best thing for me, as well as for our little family, Megan and I made the painful decision to drop out of the University of Utah Architectural program, and transfer my credits to a technical school. By so doing, I would have my bachelor's degree in just over a year, which was better than loosing everything and having to start over, and it was just not practical for us to be paying so much money for schooling when I could get the same end results from a technical school.

So, it was with a sad and heavy heart that I made my way over to the architectural design studio to clean out my desk, and turn in my final design project. I had decided to go late one evening when all of the other students had gone home, or at least I thought they had gone home, but as I made my way out of the building that evening I noticed a couple of the other guys whom I knew from the program, cleaning out their desks as well. I walked away from the architecture program and the University of Utah that evening, never to return again.

Time marches on, and as we neared our second wedding anniversary a number of monumental changes had or were about to take place in our lives, such as, after a year and a half with the architectural firm that I had worked so hard to join, Megan and I came to a difficult resolve that I would need to quit my day job and find something in the evenings. I had reached a point were I needed to have a job that both paid more money and would better accommodate my class schedule.

We had found out a few months earlier that a new member of our little family would be joining us sometime in the fall; I just had to make more money in order to support my family. The meager apprentice wages I was making would not support our new arrival, and my class schedule had gotten so intense as I headed into my senior year, that I needed to go to school during the day and work in the late afternoons and evenings, so I was forced once again to take a job that I really did not want, but had to take in order to accommodate our needs. The only job I could find that would pay more and be flexible with my schedule was in an outdoor power equipment shop, where I was made the inventory manager.

I was very unhappy to be leaving the architectural firm that I had worked so hard to get into, I loved working in the firm, and I loved rubbing shoulders with architects and engineers. On Fridays I would go out in the field and do site inspections with Ben, one of the project architects, who had taken me under his wing and had taught me a lot about how to inspect a building, how to read as well as produce architectural drawings, and how to make field work an exiting adventure.

There was one particular instance that stands out in my mind; our firm was getting ready to remodel an old church parking lot, however it would not drain properly and when it rained the parking lot turned into a pond. We needed to identify the problem and come up with a solution before we could move forward with the design work, so Ben and I were sent out to access the situation and come up with the best solution to the problem. When we arrived on site, it had been raining the previous evening, so the parking lot looked like a small lake, "what are we looking for?" I asked Ben as we put on our rubber boots and wadded out into the parking lot.

"We need to open the man hole cover next to the storm drain and see if we can figure out what's going on," said Ben with a smile on his face. We wadded out to where the blueprints indicated the manhole should be and then Ben took the shovel he was holding and began to feel around with it.

"I think I have it," said Ben after about five minutes of searching.

"Get the other shovel out of the back of the truck and give me a hand."

We each began to lift on either side of the manhole cover with our shovels, and after a minute or two there was a huge sucking sound, with a big "pop" the manholes cover came off and in an instant all of the water from the parking lot rushed into the concrete manhole box. With a bewildered look on his face Ben said,

"I didn't think that would happen," we both stood looking into the now full manhole box, Ben then looked at me.

"According to the drawings the drain manifold should be accessible underneath this manhole box." I looked at Ben.

"What is that suppose to mean?"

"It looks like they stacked two manhole boxes on top of each other." He said.

Each manhole box was made of concrete, and it was about six feet deep by about six feet wide, it had metal stairs mounted on the inside wall closest to the lid so that when opened you could climb down inside.

"How are we supposed to get to the lower one, when this one is full of water?" I asked while plunging my shovel into the manhole box to see how deep it was.

"Watch and learn my young apprentice, watch and learn," said Ben, as he headed back towards the truck.

After a few minutes, Ben returned with a hand operated water pump and a couple of long garden hoses. "Take this end of the hose over to the far side of the parking lot where the other storm drain is located, and stick it down into the pipe, and then come back."

I returned a few minutes later to find that Ben had connected all of the pumps parts together, he shoved one of the two garden hoses into the flooded manhole and then he connected the other end of the same hose to the pump. Ben and I began the slow process of pumping water out of the flooded manhole and sending it down the long hose to the other end of the parking lot where I had put the other end of the hose directly into the storm drain. We took turns pumping the water out of the manhole, and after about two and a half hours the water was shallow enough that we could get down into the box to open the next manhole lid. We used the same method as before, and on three we pushed down on our shovels lifting the next manhole lid with the same results, a huge sucking noise and all of the remaining water drained down into the lower box. Ben climbed down into the second manhole box, flashlight in hand, and a few minutes later he called up to me.

"Here's the problem," he shouted.

The main storm drain pipe, which was accessible in the storm drain box next to us, was completely full of concrete, it appeared that someone had been pouring concrete in the neighboring area and when they had finished, they dumped the remaining concrete down the storm drain thinking it would be washed away, but it had set up before it was washed away and now the entire system would have to be tore out and replaced. In retrospect, the thing that really stands out the most in my mind was not going down into the underworld to see how storm drains worked but it was the fact that Ben had done all of this in dress pants and a tie. Ben always had a way of making our site work an adventure, so it was with a heavy heart that I went to my boss and explained to him that I needed to leave the firm in order to finish school, and with a new baby on the way I needed to make more money.

After explaining my situation to my boss, he was sad to see me go, but understood my reasoning. My new boss in the outdoor power equipment shop was a nice man, he knew I was going to school, as well as having a new baby, so he was very accommodating and willing to work with my schedule.

Later that fall shortly, after our baby Julia was born, things started to change between Megan and me. Some people said it was the "baby blues," and that things would get better with time, but I don't know, it seemed to be something more than that. I tried desperately to help Megan find her way out of the state of depression that she had fallen into, but the more I tired to help the more she seemed to resent me. I could feel the tension mounting between us, and whenever I would try to suggest that perhaps if she were to start writing music again, or perhaps take on a few piano students, she might start feeling like herself again.

When we were first married, after a few months of scrimping and saving we put some money down on a small upright piano for Megan. Although we knew we would not have enough money to get the piano out of layaway for some time, we wanted to start paying for one, so that one day it would be ours. When my mother heard about what we were trying to do she stepped in and helped us out by paying the remainder of the balance on the piano, telling us that we could pay her back as soon as we had the money. It took us three or four months to get situated and then Megan began teaching piano lessons in our apartment to help pay for the piano and make ends meet. With Megan teaching piano lessons, we were able to pay my mother back in a relativity short amount of time, and we also started paying back some of Megan's student loans. Having her own piano made Megan so happy, she had played her mother's piano all her life, and she had used the pianos in college, but to have her very own piano was a dream come true. Megan would sit and play the music she had written in college for hours and hours, she also played the music she had written for me, and when Julia was born she wrote a song for her as well.

It was not long after Julia's birth however, that for some unknown reason, Megan stopped teaching, stopped writing, and almost stopped playing music all together. Megan would claim that she was too tired to play and when I would try to ask her why, she would tell me,

"You try being a mother and see how you feel at the end of the day." I could tell that something was wrong, but I could not get Megan to open up and tell me what it was. Megan's mother had suggested anti-depressants, but the idea only made Megan more upset,

"I am not depressed," she would say.

"I am just at a point in my life where I need to find myself again." We tried marriage counseling, but after one session Megan refused to go, we tried yoga, acupuncture, herbal therapy, and physical therapy but nothing seemed to make a difference. I was getting very worried about Megan, I wanted to be there for her, and I wanted to help her, but she told me there was nothing wrong, and my trying to "help" only seemed to make things worse.

I was entering the last half of my senior year of school, and for the first time since Julia was born Megan began to talk about going back to school, I was of course very happy and supportive of the idea and tried to encourage Megan to keep preparing because I would be done in a matter of months.

Megan started going to her mothers house for days, and then weeks at a time, claiming that the city was beginning to close in on her, and that she didn't want the baby to grow up in a crowded, and crime ridden city, so it was not uncommon for me to come home from school and find a note left on the door, or on the kitchen table stating that she had gone to her moms for a few days and that she would call me.

I had been putting in long hours at school, with all of my senior research, thesis papers, and projects taking up so much of my time, and I had been spending as much time at work as I could in order to make ends meet. I would get up at six most days, and not get home until eleven most evenings, so I admit I was gone a lot but in my mind I was doing it for the three of us. Megan began to complain about how much I was gone, and how she felt like she was raising the baby alone, I was gone all day and most Saturdays, and she needed me around the house. I tried to explain that I was just about there, I was almost done with school, it had been almost six years now and I could finally see the end in site.

My decision to transfer to a technical school, and be done in a year, seemed like a good idea at the time, but I ended up needing to take more classes than I had anticipated, and so my one-year had quickly turned into two. I was feeling so burned out, and I knew if I was to stop to take a quarter off like Megan kept asking me to do, I would not have the will power to go back. So it was with a feeling of desperation that I ended up staying in school year round in order to make myself cross the finish line. Megan would go to birthday parties and family events with Julia, while I sat in class, or studied at the library, there were many holidays that I missed all together, due to a paper that needed to be finish, or a project that I could not put down until it was done.

I knew that it was hard on Megan, but I always thought she understood how important finishing college was to me, and I figured if she could hold on for just a little while longer, I would be done and we could move closer to her parents or anywhere else she wanted to go. I could get a job in an architectural firm and we could start all over, having the life we had always dreamed of, but life has many twists and turns and as I was about to find out, fate had other plans for us.

It was late on a Friday evening, just one month before my 25th birthday when I returned home from school to find a note on the kitchen counter from Megan stating that she had taken Julia and gone to her mom's house for the weekend, and that she would call me around 10:30 p.m. that evening. I had only been home for a few minutes when the phone rang and I anxiously picked it up and said, "Hello."

Megan answered the phone and sounded very distant as we exchanged our hellos. I started asking Megan how the drive was, and when she thought she would be coming back,

"Don't talk for a minute please, just listen to what I have to say and don't interrupt me,"

"Ok I said," in a surprised tone.

"Is everything alright?"

"Please just listen," she stated.

"I have been giving this a lot of thought, and I have really felt strongly about this for quite some time, I just haven't had the courage to do it until now," she paused for a moment and took a deep breath.

"Jeremy, I think the time has finally come for us to go our separate ways." Megan paused again, waiting for my reaction, but I was too stunned to speak.

"I'm leaving you Jeremy, I have already been to a lawyer, and I have already started the divorce paperwork."

At that moment Megan and everything around me went quiet, absolutely dead quiet, my vision started to blur, I felt dizzy. Everything, including time itself seemed to slow down and almost come to a complete stop, I felt as though I had fallen out of a boat into a bottomless abyss, and was running out of air as I struggling to get back to the surface. I could feel myself being pulled down by an imaginary force, it was as if I was going down towards the bottom of the ocean and the water was surrounding me, as it crushed my chest, I could hear people talking and I could see their silhouettes in the water next to me, but I could not understand what was being said. Then, as if an enormous sledge hammer hit me in the chest, and brought me back to reality I herd

Megan say, "Please don't call me back, I have made my decision and nothing you say will change my mind,"

She hung up, and I stood there holding the phone until I could hear the beeping sound indicating that our conversation had ended, beep, beep, beep, beep. I hung up the phone, and felt as though I was absolutely drunk with panic, I could not see straight, I could not hear, and as I staggered towards the couch I could feel myself dropping down into the cushions like I weighed a thousand pounds. I could feel my heart pounding in my chest so hard that I thought I was going to have a heart attack, and my head began to throb as I sat contemplating what had just happened. Each breath I took was getting harder and harder to take in. I thought I was suffocating, but in fact I had begun to hyperventilate, and as I consciously felt my breathing getting heavier and heavier, it felt like the walls were closing in around me.

I felt like I was being buried alive. I could see the last glimpse of light, as the coffin was nailed tightly closed for the final time. I could almost feel and hear the ropes strain as I was lowered into the cold earth. I could hear myself screaming and kicking inside the coffin as dirt was being thrown onto the casket until the hole was completely filled in, all the while no one hearing my cries for help. I stood up and the light from the street lamp in the parking lot pierced my eyes like the light on the front of a freight train coming towards me at 100 miles an hour, I could feel my soul being hit by this train and I could almost see my body being thrown hundreds of feet into the air and landing with a thud next to the tracks. I could feel my stomach tightening as I began to sweat profusely. I stood up and while gasping for air I made my way towards the kitchen. I opened one of the cupboards and grabbed a glass to get a drink of water, hoping that a cold drink might help calm me down. As I turned on the faucet to let the water fill up in my cup I could feel myself squeezing the glass so hard that it shattered in my hands, sending shards of glass flying towards me, and a large piece of glass wedged itself deep into my hand. I began to shake and I felt weak as I saw the blood spiraling down the drain with the current of water. I could feel myself beginning to vomit and I threw up once, twice, three times and each time was more violent than the last. I turned and slid slowly down the cabinet door onto the cold tile floor. I looked at my hand and could see blood and glass clinging to the skin, I was shaking violently and it was at that moment I began to sob uncontrollably. I grabbed my face with my hands and began to cry like I had never cried before or since.

I was crying for everything that had ever been bad or wrong in my life. I was crying for my failed marriage, I was crying for the loss of my daughter, I was crying for the loss and pain of every failed relationship I had ever had, every failure in my life, and everyone that had ever hurt me in any way, shape, or form. I screamed at the top of my lungs and looked up towards heaven as I yelled,

"*Why, God, why*, what have I ever done to you? And what did I ever do to deserve this?"

I could feel the tears, which had been bottled up inside of me for so long flowing down my cheeks without end landing on my arms and soaking my sleeves. I could feel the warm blood from my hand running down my face, and arm, as I held my head in my hands, it was dripping on my shirt, and pooling on the floor around me. I had never felt such deep anguish in all my life as I did that night, lying on the floor of the kitchen in our apartment. It was a pain that can never be described in a million words, by a million poets. It was the kind of pain that I suppose many people in this world experience, but few ever live to talk about because it is so consuming, and so dark that the thought of dying to make it stop becomes more real than anyone can ever imagine. I laid there for quite some time bleeding and sobbing, wishing somehow to bleed to death and die, but the truth was it was not that kind of cut, in fact had I not been crying, and hyperventilating it probably wouldn't have bled for more that a minute or two. I could feel my strength slowly being drained from my body, and I could feel my soul groaning in anguish under the extreme pressure; it was a feeling that I hope no one ever has to experience, it is one of the worst feelings this life has to offer, one of the blackest darkest cups in life and I found myself drinking from it. It was a pain that ran so deep and created such an unfathomable void in my soul that it shook me to the very core, and it changed my life forever, part of me died that night.

I often wish that I could get that innocence back, I wish to god that I could be the person I was before that night, but I know, at least in this life, that I will never be that innocent boy who was now lying all alone on a cold kitchen floor sobbing uncontrollably.

With out a doubt that was the darkest and loneliest hour I had ever encountered in my life, and nothing to this day has ever been so devastating to my soul as those feelings that raced like demons through me that night. I had nightmares for years to come about that horrible event, and until now I haven't been able to tell anyone what happened that evening or how I felt. After a while I was somehow able to pull myself together and I decided that I needed to clean myself up a bit, I was feeling so horrible that I did not trust myself to be alone the rest of the evening, so I called the only person I could think of who would come and see me at that late hour, and that was my father.

"Dad, I'm sorry to be calling so late," I said when he answered the phone.

"I didn't mean to wake you up, but I need to talk to you, so could you please come over to my place?"

I didn't give him any details at that time, I only explained that I needed him to come over and it was a bit of an emergency, he agreed and twenty later there was a knock at the door.

"Thanks for coming over dad," I said as I let him into our little apartment. My father stood in the doorway looking around, and I am sure he could tell something was wrong,

"Where is Megan?" He asked as he sat down on the couch. I tried to hold myself together as I briefly explained the phone conversation to him, and her decision to leave.

"Why would she want to leave?" Asked my father.

"I don't know," I replied as my voice began to quiver.

"She has not been herself lately, ever since Julia was born, she has been talking about needing to find herself again, she keeps saying that we were married to young, and that she needs space to grow. I don't know dad, I thought she wanted to move closer to her mom, or at least out of the city, but I never thought she meant that she wanted to do it alone, I always assumed she was talking about us."

"Let's go for a ride," said my father.

"You need to get out of here."

We jumped into his Chevy blazer and drove off into the night talking about what happened, and as we talked I came to the realization that I did not know why she was leaving me, there were some things that I could have done differently, and of course there were things I could have done better, but I would be graduating in two months and then everything would change.

My father told me that I was welcome to move back home until I could get things figured out, and so that very night I gathered up a few things and followed my dad back to the home I had left nearly six years earlier. I was grateful that my parents allowed me to move back in, but it was one of the most humiliating, and self-defeating actions I had ever experienced. I had worked so hard to be independent, and I had done everything I could to get out of their home in the first place, but like a war torn veteran, whose country lost the war, I was forced to go home and face my dishonor and shame. My family was very supportive, they treated me with kindness and love, and none of them were ever judgmental or unkind, but the battle that raged within my soul would prove to leave harsh and long lasting scars.

I sat across from Megan in the lawyer's office a few days later as the lawyer read the divorce decree to me, and when she got to the part about child support for our two children I sat up and stopped her.

"We only have one child," I said in a confused tone.

"I am sorry," said the lawyer as she stopped reading and looked at me, and then looked at Megan.

"Didn't my client tell you that she is two and a half months pregnant with your second child?" She asked.

I could not believe what I was hearing, the first thought to run through my mind was; "is this my child, or is this why I am sitting here watching my life fall apart?"

"No," I exclaimed in a tone of surprise.

"She didn't tell me that she was pregnant with our second child." As I looked across the table at Megan she looked down at the table.

"I have wanted to tell you, but I thought you would be angry with me, so I kept it a secret."

Once again I sat in total disbelief, not only was my wife of three years, the woman whom I adored and thought was my soul mate divorcing me, but she was also pregnant, and had not said a word. At this point the lawyer said the only thing that made any sense to me during this entire process; she looked at Megan and with a puzzled look on her face said,

"Most women will stay married to a man, even if he is abusive, while they are pregnant, I find this very strange that you are filing for a divorce at this time, are you sure there is nothing you need to tell us?"

Megan shook her head no, and the proceedings continued. The entire rest of the day I could not stop thinking about the fact that she was pregnant, and divorcing me, Megan had filed for divorce under the grounds of "irreconcilable differences." I did not understand what that was suppose to mean, and to this day I do not agree with that statement. As I drove home from the lawyers office, only two weeks after the phone call that had change my life forever I still could not fit the pieces together, I could not understand why I was now divorced, and I still did not have a concrete answer as to why she had left me. Megan claimed that there was not another man, and truthfully I had not suspected that there was, I suppose however if there really was another man involved I will never know.

As I sat alone in my room that evening the only thing I could think of was her mothers warning years before, of how Megan was a genius, but with this intelligence comes a trade off, and she could be very unstable, and very irrational. I recalled her mother telling me of times when Megan would lock herself in her room for days and days, without coming out, refusing to go to school, and refusing to see friends. I had dismissed it as adolescent immaturity because I had never seen that side of her. I also recall her mother telling me that Megan had a history of being irrational, and would do things that made no sense to anyone, like the time she had spent months and months writing some of her first musical pieces, at age 13 and when she had completed it she took the manuscripts out to the back yard, put them in a small tin box and burned them. Once again I had dismissed this, as I had dismissed all of her mothers warnings, because I thought she was telling me those things to scare me off, I knew very well that Megan did not get along with her mother, or the rest of her family and so I did not believe what was being told to me.

There were many times over the coarse of our marriage that our visits to her parents home were cut short. Megan would get into fights with her parents, there was one time that we had only been there for about an hour. I was downstairs studying for a test when Megan came into the room with tears running down her face, and she said "take me home, I don't want to be here any more."

We packed up our things and made the hour and a half trip back to our apartment. I knew now, when it was too late, that Megan's mom had been trying to warn me for years that her daughter, and my wife, was very special, but very unpredictable.

Life for me, after the divorce was difficult, I became very depressed, I had tried in vane to work things out with Megan, despite the fact that we were now divorced I still loved her, and I missed her. I missed not having her around, and I missed listening to her play the piano in the evenings, I missed Julia, and I felt like my love had been betrayed. I sat thinking back on my life, of the other girls I had dated, and whom I had allowed to slip through my fingers like sand on a beach, and for the first time I really questioned if I had done the right thing in letting them go, would I be divorced, depressed, and lonely if I had married Robyn, or Misty, or would I be happy right now?

I finally came to the conclusion that I could not turn back the clock, and thinking about what might have been, was only making things worse for me. I got up, I went to work, I went to school, and I came home, that was it that was my life until one day when a happenstance meeting would once again turn my life around forever.

CHAPTER 9

Light at the end of the Tunnel

I had finished up with school a bit early that evening; due to the fact that it was Halloween and my professor had about as much of a desire to be in class as the rest of us. I pulled up to the house and noticed an unusual amount of cars parked in front and in the driveway, so I drove past the house and parked my truck a few homes down. I went in through the garage like I usually did, and when I looked into the living room to see why there were so many people at our house, I saw people, some who were dressed in costumes, and some who were not, but all of them were laughing, and eating at what appeared to be a Halloween party. I went into the kitchen to put my lunch box away and I asked my mother what was going on in the front room, she informed me that my sister Gina was having a party with some of her friends and that I was welcome to join them if I so desired. I told my mother that I was in no mood to join anyone for a party and so I made my way towards the stairs, and headed down to the basement to escape the noise and crowd that had gathered in the living room.

I had to walk past the group in order to go down to the basement and in so doing I noticed a girl sitting in the corner of the room and for a brief moment our eyes made contact, and when they did I froze on the stairs. She was a very stunningly beautiful girl with long auburn hair and deep brown eyes. I quickly broke our gaze and headed down the stairs to the basement thinking to myself as I entered the family room.

"Wow, who was that?"

She looked familiar, like someone I had met before, but at the same time I was sure I didn't know who she was. I sat in front of the television watching who knows what, as my mind was racing, trying to locate somewhere in the deep recesses of my mind a picture of the girl I had just seen, but I could only draw a blank. I then came to the realization that I had just experienced an instant attraction to whoever that girl with the long red hair sitting upstairs was, and that had only happened once before in my life; I began to shake my head as I said to myself;

"What are you doing? I have no desire to get involved with any one ever again, women are evil, evil people and I don't want anything to do with them."

A few hours later Gina came downstairs to make the announcement that her party was over and I no longer had to hide in the basement.

"I'm not hiding," I said.

"I just didn't feel like socializing this evening!" I looked up at Gina as she was turning to go back upstairs.

"Who was the girl with red hair?" I asked.

"That was Heather, she is my friend, she is very nice, you went to high school with her and she lives just around the corner," Gina said. When Gina said that we had gone to school together I started thinking of everyone I had gone to school with, but I was still drawing a blank.

"By the way," stated Gina with a smile on her face.

"You can marry Heather if you like she is pretty, nice, available, and unlike some people she would never leave you," and with that Gina turned around and headed back upstairs.

"Marry her," I thought to myself.

"What's that suppose to mean?" I yelled up the stairs to Gina who had already disappeared and who apparently did not hear me or was choosing to ignore me.

I was going through a devastating divorce, the woman who I had given my whole heart and soul too was in the process of taking me to the cleaners, why on earth would I be thinking of getting married again, let alone date. I went to bed that night thinking of Heather and how beautiful she was, I wanted to get to know her but not now, not with my life in such terrible turmoil, besides what did I have to offer?

"Hello I am Jeremy, my wife of three years has left me for no apparent reason, and has taken my child. Yes I have a child, and another one on the way, which I just found out about in the divorce lawyers office. I am living in my parents basement and I work for an outdoor power equipment store. I am about to graduate in Industrial Design although I want to be an Architect, but after giving three years of my life, and thousands of dollars to The University of Utah they told me I would have to start all over again, so I transferred to a Technical school."

What girl would pass that invitation up? I truly wanted to die at that point in my life, I felt as thought there was nothing left to live for! All of my hopes and dreams, everything I had fought so hard for was gone. I felt like a hopeless loser, I hated myself and I hated where my life had gone, how anyone else could love me when I could not even look at myself in the mirror, I did not know. I have had my ups and downs in life, but the past two months had proven to be the lowest I had ever been in my entire life. I thought to myself as I lay in my bed that evening,

"Why don't I just end it all?" I would be better off, my kids would get a huge insurance claim and everyone would be happy."

I felt a dark blackness, almost like a blanket slowly wrapping around me, it felt like a noose was beginning to tighten around my neck and I was struggling to breath.

I pretty much avoided everyone and everything for the next few months. Other than one last meeting with the lawyer I didn't have any contact with Megan, and I had given up asking her why she was divorcing me. I went to work, I went to school, I came home and went to bed; that was it, day in day out I was like a zombie. If I had not been in my last few weeks of school, if I had not been so close to graduation, I know I would have dropped out. The only thing that kept me going was the thought that five, almost six years of school was almost at an end and I could at least say that I did it. I would not have the degree that I set out to obtain, but I would have a degree nonetheless.

My nights were spent in front of the television, not really watching anything but staring into the dancing lights feeling myself slip deeper and deeper into the abyss of depression and self loathing. I was not eating, I did not sleep, I had lost a lot of weight, and I was spending more and more time at school. School was the only thing I had to hang onto, I was so burned out I could hardly stand going but at the same time it was the only thing left in my life that was familiar, and the only thing I had any control over. It was the first or second week of December when Gina came down to my dungeon.

"Look you have got to do something with yourself. Get out and interact with people, go to a movie, do something with your friends, shower! You are rotting away down here and even though life may seem horrible for you right now, things will get better." I looked over at her,

"Go to hell, and leave me alone."

I had never talked to any member of my family like that before and I suppose that was the point where I realized what a distasteful person I had allowed myself to become. I had been so wrapped up in myself that I had given up on those around me, but Gina being the person that she is, walked over to where I was sitting and hit me in the chest as hard as she could, just about knocking me off the couch.

"No," she said, as she put her hands on her hips.

"You can go to hell, and I hope you do. All you do is sit around here feeling sorry for yourself being an ass to everyone who tries to help you. You may think you are the only one who is being affected by this whole thing, but you're not! Julia is my niece and I miss not seeing her as much as anyone else! Megan treated you bad the whole time you were married and no one in this family said anything. We just smiled and pretended to like her for your sake. Now you can either get off your ass, and take control of your life or you can rot in your parent's basement, but don't come crying to me or anyone else in this family when you are forty years old and still lying here all alone. I don't know what or who you are waiting for to make this all better, but the only one who can change this situation is you, and the only one not trying to get over this or make your circumstances better is you."

She then turned and went back up stairs. I sat there for a while not really affected by what she had said, but the more I thought about it the more I thought she was right about one thing, the only one who could change this situation was me, and the only one not trying was me. I got up and went into the bathroom, looked at myself in the mirror and decided that I could start making some changes by shaving, for the first time in weeks. I gathered up my clothes and put them into the washing machine. I made my bed and spent a few hours cleaning my room. I had been so involved in my own problems that I had not even looked around the room for weeks, and it was disgusting. Not since my early days in college had I allowed my surroundings to get so out of control, and gross. After spending the better part of a day cleaning my room, and getting myself back into a presentable state I did something I had not done in some time, I went upstairs to be part of the family.

Over the coarse of the days following my re-birth into life and society, Gina told me that some of her friends were getting together to tie quilts to donate to children in need of Christmas gifts, and invited me to go with her. As I thought about the "oh so enticing" invitation that day at work, I was dead set against it.

"There is no way I was going to tie quilts with Gina and her friends." I said to myself all day.

I was trying to re-build my self-esteem not tear it down by participate in an activity typically reserved for old women in rest homes. I went on with my day absolutely sure that I was not going to attend such a ridiculous activity, after all I had my dignity to defend, even though I did not have much of it left, I would defend what I had. I went to school that evening and after finishing my classes early I headed home.

I was about to turn into the neighborhood where I lived, when I saw the house where Gina told me her and her friends would be meeting, and for some reason that I cannot explain, I stopped in front of the house and turned the truck lights off. I got out of the truck and made my way up the icy driveway to the front door and before I could stop myself from making a huge mistake I found myself ringing the doorbell.

"What am I doing?" I thought to myself, after waiting for about three seconds I decided there was no one home, even though every light in the house was on, and I could hear loud music and laughter emanating from within.

I turned and took the first step away from the door as I heard the door swing open and the sounds of music and laughter got much louder.

"Can I help you?" I heard the person holding open the door ask me, while I turned around very slowly, I was half tempted to just run and not look back but for some reason I didn't.

"I'm Jeremy, Gina's my sister and she told me to meet her here tonight to help with your activity." The girl behind the door gave me an awkward look, I am sure it was due to the fact that I was still wearing my work clothes which consisted of a t-shirt and jeans, an old greasy ball cap and steel toe cowboy boots.

"Oh," she said, after a moment of thought.

"Gina has not arrived yet but you are welcome to come in and help us, if you want to."

I felt my face and ears burning with embarrassment as I walked into the doorway, the crowed fell silent and all eyes were on me as I awkwardly entered the room.

"This is Jeremy, Gina's brother he came to help us," said the girl who had let me in. I walked over to the nearest chair and slumped down into it trying to hide myself from the staring eyes.

I awkwardly smiled and waved my hand as if to say please stop staring at me and go back to whatever it was you were doing, and it must have worked because the music and laughter started back up as if I were not even there. The room had a huge quilt frame in the center of it and there were girls all around the quilt sewing and tying knots, chatting with each other, and eating snacks.

"I am going to kill Gina, I will tear her arms off and beat her to death with them, I came over here to help her out and she didn't even show up." I thought to myself as I looked around the room for a way out.

Those were the thoughts running through my head when I looked over to the other side of the room and I noticed Heather, the pretty red headed girl I had seen at my sister's party a few months earlier, she was talking with the person next to her, and every so often she would look over at me and smile in a very tender way. I sat there for quite some time observing everyone's conversations, but not really listening to what anyone was saying, and then Heather got up from where she was sitting and made her way over to where I was still slumped down in my chair.

"Would you like some help?" She asked, as she sat down next to me. I had no intentions of working on this quilt, every fiber of my being was screaming out,

"*No* don't do it!" But once again I found myself doing something that not even I can explain.

"Sure," I said.

"That would be great."

I sat there dumbfounded as to why I had told her that I wanted help tying a quilt, all I really wanted to do was get up and leave this most uncomfortable situation, however as I looked up and saw Heather's striking features, and soft brown eyes I found myself letting her show me how to tie a quilt.

"You see it's very easy," explained Heather, as she moved closer to me to show me how to tie the knot.

"Down, around, up and through, now you try it," said Heather. To be honest I was staring at her and had not seen a thing she was showing me.

"Over down through, what?" I asked.

"Here let me show you again," she said, as she moved just a little bit closer.

Heather's perfume was heavenly, and I could feel little lightning bolts running through my body as she took my hand and guided me through another knot. I made many more attempts to get it right that evening but quite frankly I didn't care if I was doing it right or not, I was happy to be sitting next to Heather. Towards the end of the evening Heather looked at me,

"I am having a few work friends over tomorrow night for dinner and then we are going to play pool, if you think you might be interested there is room for one more person."

"Yes," I said.

"That would be nice."

I was shocked to hear Heather inviting me to a social activity with her and some friends, and I jumped at the opportunity.

"I would love to come with you if it is not too much trouble."

"It's no trouble," exclaimed Heather, as she smiled at me, making me feel like a sixteen year old with a schoolboy crush.

"Your sister has my number and she knows where I live so ask her to give you the information," and then Heather got up and walked out the door.

I quickly got up myself seeing that the quilt tying was over, and having no desire to stay any longer, especially if Heather was gone, I made my way quickly out the door and to my truck. I didn't go straight home that evening, instead I drove around for a while trying to make sense of what exactly it was that I was feeling. I had been hurt so many times before in my life and I was not looking to get back into a relationship, but something about her filled me with an over-whelming feeling of peace. She was so beautiful, but this was only the second time I had ever seen her. I wondered if she knew about my dismal past, had Gina told her everything, had Gina told her anything? It had been nearly five years since I had been on a date with anyone besides Megan, what would I say, what would I do? I had become so bitter over that last few months that I was afraid my bitterness would come shining through and I would be seen as someone that I was not, or someone that I did not want to be.

"This is not a date." I kept telling myself, it was Heather and a group of work friends getting together for dinner and a round of pool, I was worrying about nothing!

For all I knew she felt sorry for me and had asked me to come along out of pity, and I was blowing this thing way out of proportion. I made my way home to find all of the lights out and everyone in bed, so I made my way to my room and went to bed myself. I recall lying there most of the night tossing and turn-ing, worrying about what would transpire the next day. It was about six o clock in the evening as I stood in front of Heather's house wanting to ring the door bell but feeling very uneasy about doing it, I could see the other guests sitting in the living room chatting with one another about I could only guess what.

"What would I say to these people, how was I suppose to act around total strangers, and what would they think of me?" I thought to myself, as I tried to get up the courage to ring the bell.

I felt like I was back in junior high all over again, worried about my hair and worried about my clothes, getting all worked up thinking about what people would think of me.

"Just ring the bell and act like an adult." I told myself as I finally reached out to ring the bell. I had almost pushed the button when the door opened and there stood Heather, looking absolutely magnificent, there was defiantly something about her that took my breath away and made me feel warm all over.

"I am glad you could make it," said Heather as she pulled the heavy glass door open to let me in.

"This is Jeremy," she said to her friends as I walked into the room.

"The guy I was telling you about, he is Gina's brother," she then looked at me while explaining,

"Gina is one of my friends that I do things with outside of work," and when she said that everyone laughed. Heather then introduced me to all of her friends and showed me to a chair.

"I am almost done with the dinner preparations, so everyone just hold tight for a few more minutes and then we can eat." As soon as Heather left the room, I could feel all eyes slowly turning towards me as if I were a Democrat sitting in the middle of a Republican dinner party.

"So Jeremy why don't you tell us a little bit about yourself," said one of Heather's friends.

"Heather has told us a few things about you, but we were just wondering what you did for a living, and who you are?" I could feel my face going pale, and the sweat was beginning to run down my face, my hands began to quiver and I could feel my throat getting tight.

"Well," I said to the "Spanish Inquisitionist".

"I am currently a student, finishing up my degree in Industrial Design; I plan on being an Architect when I am done with school, but in the mean time I am working at an outdoor power equipment shop to pay the bills."

I sat there looking into the faces of Heather's co-workers waiting for a response, or a snicker, or any thing, but there was nothing, not a smile, not a nod of the head, nothing so I continued.

"I just met Heather really quite recently," I said.

"But it's kind of funny that she lives so close to me, in fact I think I may have gone to high school with her but to be honest I don't remember her at all."

Still nothing, I could hear my voice cracking with each sentence I delivered, I felt like I was on trial for murder and the jury was not buying my story in the least bit.

"Well you know," started one of the ladies sitting on the couch across from me.

"Heather is a very special girl and she just got out of a bad relationship so we are not about to let her get hurt again, if your intentions are not gentlemanly we suggest that you go home right now." With that everyone in the room nodded their heads and I could hear the whispering begin.

"Heather is almost 26 years old and she has never been married, she has only had one serious relationship and it failed miserably just a few months ago. Heather is in no mood to play games with anyone and we will see to it that if she gets her heart broken again, that man will pay."

How does one respond to that? On one hand it was really great that her friends were so protective and supportive of Heather but on the other hand I was waiting for one of them to pull a gun on me.

"Well I assure you that my intentions are good, and that I am only interested in being friends," I said hoping to calm the crowd back down.

"She has friends, we are her friends, if she invited you to dinner tonight it is for her *friends* to see what they think of you, and so far."

Just then I was saved by the announcement that dinner was ready and we all make our way into the dinning room. Dinner was heavenly, Heather had made Chicken Parmesan and it absolutely melted in your mouth.

"Heather is an excellent cook," said one of the girls who sat across the table from me.

"Don't you think so Jeremy?" She asked.

"Yes, absolutely," I said between bites.

"This is a wonderful dinner." It really was good, but even if it had been dog food I would have praised it in front of that tough crowd. The mood of the inquisitive dinner guests slowly shifted, and soon they were back to laughing and telling stories about other members of the office who were not present. I sat in my chair quietly trying to make sense of the evening, not wanting to say a word to anyone about anything, when the announcement was made.

"Let's head over to the pool hall and play a few rounds of pool."

Everyone made their way towards the door and upon entering the cold December night air they all began piling into their cars and driving away.

"You can come with me if you like," stated Heather.

"I have two other people coming with me but you are welcome to sit in the back seat if you want to."

"I would like that very much," I exclaimed as I walked over to her Isuzu Rodeo and got into the back seat.

"Is this yours?" I asked a bit timidly because it was brand new and looked very expensive.

"Yes," replied Heather,

"Don't you like it?"

"Oh yes, I like it a lot, it is very nice," I said.

"I guess I just didn't picture you as an SUV kind of girl."

"Well I am," stated Heather as we pulled out of the driveway. I sat there feeling dumb for making such an unintelligent comment about her car,

"Heather was 26 and had no other finical obligations, why shouldn't she own such a nice vehicle," I thought to myself.

We made our way to the billiards hall, and claimed two tables while splitting up into teams, I did not say much the rest of the evening, I felt I had already made a fool of myself, and I didn't think any of Heather's friends liked me, so I figured why open my mouth and give anyone more reasons to think I was inadequate for Heather. Later that evening, as I got out of Heather's SUV in front of her house and quickly found my keys while heading towards my own truck, I and was about to open my door when Heather called out to me,

"Jeremy I had a good time tonight, I'm going out of town this weekend to visit some family but I would like to call you some time if you don't mind."

I didn't know what to say, I had figured that the evening was a bust, and that I had struck out for sure. I had not spoken ten words to Heather and after being roasted alive by her friends, I figured that it was all over before it even got started, but if she wanted to call me by all means I would not pass up the opportunity.

"Sure you can call me any time you want," I replied. Heather waved goodbye and went into her house, I turned the keys to my ignition and made my way down the street, back to my house.

"So how did it go?" inquired Gina as I walked in the door.

"I have no idea," I replied.

"That was one of the weirdest dates, outings, or whatever you want to call it, that I have ever been on.

"Well, did you talk to Heather?" Asked Gina.

"Did you ask her out on another date?"

"No," was my reply.

"But she asked me if she could call me some time!"

"Well there you go," said Gina.

"Way to get back out there and keep fighting, see this is much better than sitting in the basement all evening and feeling sorry for yourself."

I went down to my room and turned on the television, my life had turned a full 180 degrees in the past few months and I was very confused about what I should do next. I missed Julia my little girl, and I still missed Megan, but she had completely shut the door on me and wanted nothing to do with me, so I felt very alone. I was not sure if I wanted to pursue anything further with Heather, but as I sat there staring off into space I remembered something that someone had once told me, "You might have true love sitting right in front of you, but you are too comfortable with your current situation to see it," although I was not comfortable with my current situation, I was still unsure if I had true love sitting right in front of me.

The following day was Saturday, and my boss had asked me to come in to help get caught up with some of the odd and end projects that had been looming around the shop. As I stood at the honing wheel sharpening chain saw blades for the fourth hour in a row I started to feel like I was going insane with boredom. Nearly six years of college, nearly $50,000 in student loans and what I am doing with myself, I then said out loud,

"Jeremy look at yourself, standing in the middle of a dirty small engine repair shop sharpening chain saw blades for a living, it's time to make a change."

Even though the guys I worked with were nice, and they had been very supportive during this horrific time in my life, this was about the farthest thing from what I wanted to be doing with my life as I could get. I would be graduating from college in just two weeks, and I had settled for this crummy job for over a year now, I could feel myself sinking into a routine that was not pleasant, but because I had become comfortable with it, I was afraid to change. I remembered my grandpa Gates telling me when I was younger, that he had the same "damn job for 40 years," and he hated every day and every minute of it, but in those days you took a job for life. He worked as a machinist for nearly his entire adult life, doing the same thing day in and day out, and when he retired they gave him a plaque with his name engraved on it and a gold watch that to this day still sits in the original case, unopened and collecting dust. I didn't want to get comfortable doing something I hated, and I didn't want to hate my job every day of my life for the next 40 years.

I finished up with my work and went into my boss's office and asked him if he had a moment to talk.

"Sure Jeremy what is on your mind?" was his response.

"I really appreciate all the kindness you have shown me. I mean you gave me a job when I was really in need of one and I am very grateful for that. But I just think it's time for me to branch out and move on. I will be graduating from college in a few weeks and I think it's time to go out and find a job in my chosen field before I become too comfortable doing something I was not meant to do."

"Well you have been the best inventory manager I have ever had," he said as he motioned for me to sit down.

"I really hate to see you go, but to be honest I am surprised you lasted as long as you have. You have done an excellent job but you really don't fit in here, in the last 30 years I have had a lot of employees come through those doors but you have been by far the brightest and most ambitious one I have ever seen. The day I hired you I knew you were not meant for this business. This business has been good to me, and this is what I always wanted to do, so I can't imagine doing anything else, but at the same time I can just imagine how miserable I would be doing something I didn't want to do. So go, and find a job doing what you want, it isn't going to hurt my feelings, in fact take all the time you need, my shop doors are always open."

I thanked him for being so understanding, then I told him that I would work for two more weeks and then call it quits, because I knew that if I didn't make a clean break I would hold on to the job forever, it had become so comfortable, like an old pair of tennis shoes that look pretty torn up but you keep them around because they are so comfortable.

I got home that evening happy with the decision I had made, but a bit apprehensive about finding a job in architecture, with only the year and a half experience behind me it was not going to be easy, most potential employers want someone with five years or more experience, but all I could do was try, I did almost have my bachelor's degree completed, which I hoped would count for something. I was sitting down for dinner when the telephone rang and upon answering it my mother informed me that the phone was for me; apprehensive that it may be the lawyer's office again, I half heartedly answered the phone but to my surprise it was Heather. "I hope I'm not interrupting anything," said Heather.

"No, not at all," was my reply.

"I'm here in Nephi with my aunts and my grandma and we are working on some quilts, but I was kind of missing you so I thought I would give you a call," said Heather.

"I had fun last night playing pool," she hesitated for a minute.

"I wish I could have talked to you a little bit more last night, my friends got to talk to you a lot more than I did, but I would like a chance to get to know you better."

I was absolutely floored that Heather wanted to get to know me better, of course in the back of my mind loomed the inevitable conversation about my recent divorce and the fact that I had kids; not that I was ashamed of my kids, but having children is not the most successful pick up line a guy could have.

"Well great," I responded.

"When are you going to be back from your grandmother's house?"

"I will be back Sunday night," responded Heather.

"Would you like to go out to dinner Monday evening then?" I asked.

"That would be nice," said Heather.

"Great I will pick you up at seven if that will be alright with you?"

"It sounds like a date," said Heather, we talked for a few more minutes, and then said our goodbyes. I turned around to see my mom and Gina staring at me.

"Was that Heather?" Asked Gina.

"Yes," I responded.

"It was."

"Are you going out on a date with her?"

"Yes I am, on Monday." Gina clapped her hands and exclaimed

"They are going to get married, I just know it!"

The rest of the weekend went painfully slow, like the day before Christmas does for a small child. I was very excited that Heather wanted to see me again, and very nervous about the conversation that I knew she would want to have in order to begin any sort of relationship.

I had cornered Gina during the weekend and made her tell me everything she had told Heather and anything that Heather may have heard from other people about me.

"She knows about your situation, I didn't get into any real details," explained Gina.

"But she knows that you have just gone through an ugly separation, and that you have a little girl." Gina looked and me and shook her head.

"Obviously Heather is fine with it because she called you didn't she, and she wants to see you again, so don't worry about it, just be yourself and tell her the truth, if she still wants to see you after she knows the truth, then you have nothing to worry about. If she doesn't want to see you after you tell her the truth, then she is obviously not right for you or Julia."

I knew what Gina was saying was true, but it is awfully hard to tell someone the truth about yourself when you are trying to win them over. The funny thing was, I was not looking for love, I was not looking to date, I was defiantly not looking to get married again, but here was this beautiful girl who was obviously interested in me, and who I was instantly in love with. I had apprehensions and the logical side of me was saying,

"What are you doing? It is way too soon to be seeing people." Not that there is a pre-determined amount of time after a divorce to start dating again, but it had only been a couple of months and I was still leery. I was torn and feeling unsure of myself, I couldn't help but to ask questions, was this just a rebound thing for me, was I just trying to fill the huge void that had been created in my life, or was I really feeling love. At any rate the weekend came and went and I found myself once again standing at Heather's front door ringing the bell and waiting for the door to open.

Heather opened the door and we said our hellos as I escorted her to my truck. I asked her how her weekend had gone and how the drive to Nephi and back went, and then I figured I might as well get it over with. I started out by asking her what she already knew about me, and what she wanted to know. Heather told me the few things that she had heard,

"I want to know everything, why did you get divorced, and what are your plans for the future?"

I began by telling Heather about the divorce in general, I did not go into any of the depressing details, I told her that I didn't understand why it had happened, and although I realized it takes two to make a mistake. I had tried to resolve things but Megan was the one who pushed the divorce and would not look at any other avenue. I then told Heather all about Julia and I explained how much I missed not seeing her for more than a day or two every few weeks. I talked about how I learned while in the lawyer's office that we were expecting another baby in the spring, and although I knew it would be hard, I would love my new child the best I could. I told Heather that if we were to purse this relationship further that I would introduce her to Julia, but I didn't want to expose Julia to anyone that I was not serious about. I explained to Heather that I would not blame her if what I had told her was enough to scare her off and if she didn't want to see me any more I would respect her wishes, but I did tell her that I felt a connection to her that I could not explain and I wanted to get to know her better.

After telling Heather this information and answering a few miscellaneous questions that she had, I sat back and prepared myself for the worst. Heather looked over at me.

"I really like you and I think there is something between us that I would like to explore further," she said.

"I would really like to meet Julia when you think the time is right, and hearing you tell me what happened makes me feel better than hearing bits and pieces from other people." I sighed with relief and felt so very blessed that she was not scared away by my past.

We found ourselves later that evening sitting at a restaurant, and after ordering our food I looked across the table at Heather and noticed how lovely she looked. I had not had a chance to sit across from her and look at her closely, but seeing her now she looked more beautiful than ever, with her long red hair, thick eyelashes, and lovely brown eyes. I had only known one red headed girl who had ever rivaled Heather's beauty and that was Misty, my roommate's sister from college, however sitting there with Heather that evening I would not have traded that for Misty or any other girl.

I could feel myself getting nervous. Up to this point I had been so worried about telling my story that I had not even thought about what I would do if she decided to continue seeing me. I leaned across the table and said,

"I thought you wouldn't want to see me after I told you about my past, but I am very glad that you still want to peruse a relationship. I would also like to say that when I saw you for the first time at Gina's party a few months ago I really wanted to ask you out but the timing was just not right for me." Heather looked back at me and said,

"I felt the same way when I saw you. In fact after the party I hung around a little bit longer than everyone else to talk to Gina, and I had hoped that you would come back upstairs but you didn't. I asked Gina who you were and to tell me a little bit about you," said Heather as our food arrived and we began to eat.

"I was very surprised to hear that you went to the same High School that I did," said Heather.

"But since you were one grade level lower than I was, I'm afraid I didn't remember you. I asked my brother Michael, who was in the same grade as you if he knew you and he said he did but only as a brief acquaintance."

Until that moment it had not dawned on me that Heather was older than I was, but she was in fact seven months older than I was. We kept talking that evening and learned that we had gone to the same High School, I had known her brother Michael, she had known my older sister Amy, and my younger sister Gina and Heather's younger sister Heidi had been friends with one of my younger sisters, Holly. We were also able to establish the fact that our parents even know each other, but with all of that we didn't know each other even existed.

"Isn't it amazing how two people can be so close for so long and never even know that the other one exists until the timing is just right?"

Heather then began to ask me who some of my friends in high school were and when I began to tell her abut Mark and Jason, and some of the other people I was friends with, she commented on how that was the intellectually cool crowd and she knew who they were but didn't ever really associate with them. Heather told me about some of the people that she was friends with, but I very apologetically told her that I knew very few if any of the people she was talking about.

By the end of the evening I was feeling much better about myself and I had gained quite a bit of confidence, I was really beginning to connect with Heather and I was even having a nice time. Just before we left the restaurant to go home Heather took the paper wrapper that went around her silverware and wrote her home phone number and her work number on it,

"I would be very happy if you called me some time, either at work or home or both if you like."

"I would like that very much," was my reply. I took Heather home and asked if I could call her the next day, she said yes, and then I asked her what her plans were for the following evening.

"I don't know yet, what are your plans for tomorrow evening?" She asked. I told her I needed to do some grocery shopping and some Christmas shopping, but that was all. Heather then looked at me and said,

"I will be grocery shopping and Christmas shopping tomorrow with you."

As I made my way back home after dropping Heather off my heart was on cloud nine. I could not believe that the evening had gone so well, she was nice, beautiful and she liked me.

The next evening we ran errands, went to dinner, and started talking about other topics like what kinds of things each of us liked and did not like, we talked about work and what each other did. I told Heather that I would be quitting my job in a week's time but that I was confident that I would find something in the field of architecture, Heather looked at me and said,

"Oh, I didn't know that's what you were going to school for, my dad is a residential designer and he owns his own company." I just about fell over.

"*You have got to be kidding,*" I shouted.

"No that is what he does, you should meet my dad, and I think the two of you would get a long really well."

"Where does your father live?" I asked.

"He lives in St.George, Utah most of the time, but they come up here to Salt Lake every so often when he needs to meet with his clients or when they have other reasons to come up."

"So whose house are you living in, I thought it was your house?" I asked.

"The house belongs to my parents; they have two houses, one in Southern Utah and this one, my brothers and sister and I all live in and take care of this house."

"That must be a nice arrangement for you guys, no rent and you get to live in a nice house without your parents." I said.

"It has been nice and it has worked out well for all of us, my dad has an office and my parents still have a bedroom in this house, so when he and my mom come up they have a place to stay, and he has an office to work out of. They should be coming up soon for Christmas, so if you would like to meet my parents I can arrange it."

I was a bit apprehensive about meeting the parents after only a few dates, but I agreed anyway because I suppose this would be round two of the acceptance issues. Later that evening as we walked around the down town Salt Lake area looking at the Christmas lights holding hands I could not believe how fast and yet how wonderful things were going. There was just a deep connection between Heather and myself that no one could explain but both of us felt it with out a doubt.

Over the next few weeks Heather and I were absolutely inseparable, we spent every evening together, and I would take her flowers to work and meet her for lunch. We were growing so close and even though we had only been dating for a few weeks it felt as though I had known her for a lifetime. Heather called me from work one day to tell me that she had just found out that her parents would be there for the weekend and would like to meet me.

"I am not so sure about it Heather." I stated.

"What are they going to think about me? I am sure once they know about my past they won't want us to see each other any more."

"Jeremy I am 25 years old and way past the point where my parents can tell me who I can and cannot date, besides even if they don't like you we only see them for a few days every couple of months," Heather paused for a moment.

"I'm kidding; they are going to love you."

"Joking like that doesn't really help," I added.

"I'm kidding, I have already told them about you and they are excited to meet you, Dad was really excited to know that you have worked in an architectural firm, and that you are interested in designing homes, maybe he can get you a job?"

I was actually quite excited about the prospects of working with or for Heather's dad, so if not for any other reason, I agreed to meet them and give things a try. I recall being very nervous when I arrived at Heather's house the evening I meet her parents for the first time, what would they think of me, what would they think of me dating there daughter so soon after being divorced, what would they think of me being unemployed as of that day, and what would I do if they didn't approve of me, Heather kept telling me not to worry, but believe me I was worried, this is what was running through my head when Heather's mom opened the door.

"Good evening you must be Jeremy, I am Diane and this is Larry," she said as she motioned for me to come in.

"Nice to meet you both," I said, in as polite a voice as I could.

"Have a seat and tell us a little bit about yourself," said Heather's father, as he waved me down into the couch next to Heather.

When I had been sitting down for just a moment or two, I began to notice that it had to be at least 80 degrees in the house and since I was wearing a long sleeved shirt and a sweater, I began to sweat almost instantly. I leaned over to Heather and whispered,

"Is it really hot in here or am I that nervous?" Heather said.

"They don't like the cold that is why they live in Southern Utah, so when they come here they crank the thermostat way up to keep warm."

"Great," I said to myself.

"This is all I need to add to my already red and blushing face, an 80 degree house."

As we began to talk I told Heather's parents a number of things about myself, how I had moved around as a kid, where I was going to school, the fact that I wanted to design homes, and that was when Heather's father perked up a little, but Heather's mom piped in,

"Are you feeling alright you look awfully red in the face?" I told her how I was just not accustom to having the house so warm.

"I think you might have a thyroid problem," was Diane's response, I sat up and did everything I could to keep from laughing out loud.

"I think it's really quite comfortable in here," Diane commented.

"And I have known of people who think it's hot but they really have a thyroid problem."

"Mom it really is warm in here," said Heather in my defense.

"You do keep it warmer than what most people would consider comfortable."

"Well I am just saying that he may want to get his thyroids checked, because I think it's quite comfortable right now."

I could not believe that the very first conversation I was having with Heather's parents was not about me or my divorce or the fact that I was dating their daughter; it was about my thyroids,

"At least we were not discussing any of the hard subjects," I thought to myself.

"I would like to see some samples of your work," said Larry.

"I am always on the lookout for someone to help me when I get busy."

"I would be pleased to show you my portfolio, and I would be grateful if you ever had any need of my help if you would call on me for assistance." I said energetically.

"Dinner is ready," said Diane

"You two can talk about work later, right now let's eat."

We had a nice dinner and after we finished eating I found out something about Heather's parents that would haunt me for the rest of my life.

"Do you like to play card games Jeremy?" Asked Larry.

"Because in this family we love to play card games."

The truth was I absolutely hate playing card games, I hated it as a child and I have always hated it as an adult. Playing strategic board games like chess, or Risk like I use to do when I was in college was fun to me, but not card games. I suppose to some people a relaxing evening consists of, playing card games that build upon themselves round after torturous round, with at least one person at the table becoming so competitive that you almost have to perform an intervention to get them away from the table. That person, as I was about to find out was Heather's father, he won every card game we ever played, annihilating everyone at the table and since I could absolutely care less about any card games I did not try to win, nor did I care, making me the easy target for every-one at the table.

I had finished school and was just waiting for graduation day, which had quickly come upon me. Tiffany, Daryl and my parents came to support me at the graduation ceremony, I had not invited Heather for two reasons, first of all I had not told any one of my friends from school that I had been divorced, and second I knew that I would be an absolute mess, and I didn't want her to see me like that.

As I sat there listening to the speakers go on about the college graduates of 2000 and how they will make all the difference in the world, and how we need to reach for the stars and so on and so forth, I could not help but to feel sad and think back upon the last six years of my life. I remembered that first day I arrived at the University of Utah so young, and so excited, I remembered all the countless hours of studying and all the classes I had taken, I remembered all the crummy jobs I had worked at to get me to this point. As the speaker went on the talk about or futures, I remembered talking with Megan just a few months earlier, about how I was almost done with school and when I finished I would be able to spend more time with her and Julia, and we could move and go anywhere we wanted to go. Why couldn't she hold on for just a few more months, I was so close, why couldn't Megan see how important it was for me to finish my education.

I wondered if my pursuit of education had been the reason for her leaving me in the first place, had my pursuit of this damn bachelors degree become so encompassing that I had allowed my marriage of three years to fall to pieces. I had been gone so much the last year with my senior projects and research papers that there had been weeks at a time that I would not really see Megan or Julia other than to help change the occasional midnight diaper, but she knew from the time we met how important school was to me, and how important my degree was. Megan had never really complained about dropping out of school herself to support me, but I guess it really was more of an issue than I thought.

Whatever the reasoning, and whatever had happened in the past there I sat graduating with high honors and a perfect attendance record, relieved that I was finally done with it, happy for all the people I had met and all the wonder-ful experiences I had had, and absolutely miserable to watch everyone else go up and get their diplomas with their spouses and children cheering them on. I remember breaking down on the way home. I was so happy to have Heather in my life now but I was still heart broken, and I missed not having my little baby to hold and play with. I was so sad that I would not get to see her grow up like I wanted to, one weekend every two or three weeks was not what I had ever wanted when I thought about being a father, but what could I do at this point it was out of my hands and not up for debate.

It was soon after graduation that I had arranged to get Julia for the weekend and I figured that since things had been going so well between Heather and I that the time was right for them to finally meet. It was a few weeks after Christmas but since I did not have Julia for Christmas my family and I decided that we would have a little party for her, and so I invited Heather to come and meet Julia. It was about 5:30 p.m. when Heather arrived and as she walked into the living room she handed me a gift and said, "I got this for Julia, it's just a little something to add to her Christmas presents." I was very impressed that she had taken the initiative to bring a gift, because I had not even mentioned to her that we were having a party.

Julia was sitting with her Aunt Gina when we walked into the back room, Heather made her way over to where they were sitting and said,

"Hi Julia, I'm Heather will you come sit with me?" and sure enough Julia; who was barely one year old at the time, went and sat with Heather, the two of them played together and hit it off immediately. I was so happy to see that Heather and Julia had accepted each other almost instantly because I could not bear the thought of the two of them not getting along.

After we were able to get past all of the formalities, Heather and I began to spend a lot of time together, I think we both knew early on in our relationship that there was magic between us, but because I had been through so much it was harder for me to see it, however Heather was very patient and understanding with me. One evening after Heather had gotten home from work she called me up,

"So how was your day?" She asked, when I answered the phone.

"It was good, I guess," was my response.

"Did you have any luck finding a job today," she inquired.

"Nope," I stated.

"Well I think I may have found something for you, it is not in architecture, but it could be a good paying job."

I perked up a bit, because I was beginning to feel a little bit desperate, and I figured that I could at least listen to what she had to say.

"I work with a girl whose husband is the foreman for one of the biggest dairy bottling and shipping companies in Utah, and she said that if you go in tonight and talk to Randy, her husband he may be able to get you a job as a shop foreman."

I could tell that Heather was excited, and even though the sound of it was not at all appealing to me.

"Ok," I said.

"Well let me get changed into my suit and we can go out there right now."

With an excited look on her face, Heather was in my front driveway about five minutes later. I went out to the truck and climbed in.

"You look very nice," said Heather.

"I know you will make a great impression."

I tried to sound as enthusiastic as I could as we made our way out to industrial part of town where the large processing plant was located. I could remember taking a tour of the facility when I was in junior high, and I distinctly remember the comments my fellow classmates made about how they would never in a million years work in a place like this. I remember joining the revelry of my classmates and now here I was ten years later trying to get a job at the same place.

"Ok sweetie, go in there and impress them," said Heather as she gave me a quick kiss on the cheek.

I got out of the truck, in my suit with a resume in hand and made my way into the large processing plant. The first thing I noticed was the pungent aroma of the dairy air; it pierced my nose and made my eyes water. As I wandered around I could tell in an instant that I was way over dressed for the occasion, if I would have worn jeans and a sleeveless t-shirt, I still would have been over-dressed. After about five minutes of aimless wandering, someone finally came up to me and asked me what I was doing; they probably thought I was a health inspector dressed like I was,

"I am looking for Randy, the plant manager," I said in desperation.

"Down the hall and to the right, you can't miss it," said the man looking at me like I was crazy for coming into the dirty, and hot processing plant dressed like some sort of accountant.

I knocked on the door of Randy's office, and after a moment or two he hung up the phone and opened the door.

"What do you want?" Asked Randy, as he stood glaring at the person who was obviously interrupting something important, Randy's arms were covered in tattoos, and he had a huge bulge of chewing tobacco in his lower lip, the smell of something I could only describe as years of musty body odor, and cigar smoke came oozing out of his office. I stood in disbelief for a moment or two and then I took a deep breath of pungent air and handed him my resume.

"I am Jeremy, and my girlfriend works with your wife, your wife told my girlfriend to have me come down here and talk to you about a job." Randy looked at me for a moment and then looked at the resume in his hand.

"Come in," he said as he pushed the door open for me.

I entered the small and rancid office and he pointed to a chair in the corner of the room that looked like it had been there for twenty or more years, it was covered in black gunk, and the leather had huge cracks running from the back of the seat cushion to the front. I moved slowly towards the chair, and when I got to where it was, I turned and sat down, hoping that my suit would not be ruined by the twenty years of grease, or torn by the jagged metal edges of the arm wrest, and legs. I tried to pull the chair closer to Randy's desk when I noticed it was bolted to the floor, so I gave up trying to move it, and I sat as forward as I could without looking anxious.

The chair was far enough away from the desk that I felt uncomfortable, not that the whole situation wasn't extremely uncomfortable, but this just added to the experience.

"This looks like you want to be some sort of an architect, are you sure you came to the right place?" Asked Randy as he spat a huge black wad of spit into the coffee mug on his desk.

"I haven't been successful in finding work in my field." I stated.

"So I am looking to broaden my horizons and find work elsewhere." I said as I watched the black goop that missed his coffee mug and hit the edge of the desk run down the side, I was glad at that moment that the chair was bolted to the floor and that I was not sitting any closer to him.

"What kind of job do you want?" Asked Randy in almost disgusted tone, as if to say why you are wasting my time.

"Well, my girlfriend said that your wife told her you were looking for shift managers, or a foreman, or something like that." I said, knowing that this conversation was not going well.

"*Foreman*," said Randy as he spat another wad into the mug.

"I have guys that have worked here for fifteen years, and have still not made foreman, I have a position for shop cleaner, or I have truck driving positions and that's it." I quickly stood up.

"I'm sorry to waste your time, have a nice day." I said.

I ran out as fast as I could. As I re-entered the parking lot I could see Heather reading a book and looking excited as she waited for me to return, I opened the door and got back into the truck.

"Well, how did it go?" Asked Heather in an excited tone.

"They are just not hiring right now," I said trying to be supportive of Heather's well meaning actions.

"Are you sure you talked to Randy?" She inquired.

"Oh yes," I replied.

"I talked to Randy, and they are not hiring right now."

"Well that is odd," said Heather.

"I will have to talk to my friend tomorrow and see what went wrong," I held back the urge to yell out "*No*," and instead I calmly said,

"I am just not sure if this is the job for me, so let's just keep looking." I was grateful for Heather's concern and willingness to help, but I decided that I would not be going to anymore of her so called "job leads."

With every day that went by I found myself falling more and more in love with Heather, she had such a pleasant and positive attitude that I could not help but to feel happy when I was around her. It was sometime in late February when we found ourselves walking hand in hand out of a crowded movie theatre, and Heather said,

"Let's go to dinner, there are some things I want to talk to you about."

We sat down in one of the restaurants booths and I looked over at Heather, as she reached across the table and took my hand,

"I just want you to know that I don't have any problems with you being divorced," began Heather.

"I know it has not been easy on you, and I know it must be hard to trust people after what happened to you, but I am not like other people, I have really enjoyed our time together the last few months and I just wanted you to know that."

I could sense that she was feeling my apprehension towards our relationship. I was finding myself falling in love with her but just as I had done in times past, I found myself fighting my own feelings and trying to make things slow down. It was not that I didn't want to be with Heather, I think if anything the problems was I had been instantly attracted to her, and because of what I was trying to recover from in my life it was hard to acknowledge the fact that I was sitting across from someone that I could very easily see myself spending the rest of my life with.

It was nice to hear Heather's reassuring words that she supported me, and that she would stand by me despite my past. As I lay in bed that evening pondering everything that had happened, a strange calm came over me and I began to realize for perhaps the first time that I really did love Heather, and there was an unexplainable connection between us. It was like we were meant to be together all along, but for some reason fate would not allow us to meet until after I had gone through all of the experiences I had gone through first. One thing that did strike me as ironic was when we had Julia with us, people thought Heather was her mother, because they both have brown eyes, and although Heather has red hair, Julia's light brown hair has red highlights in it, so they do look quite a bit alike.

Tiffany and I were talking a few days after my graduation, and she pointed out, that I would be very hard pressed to find someone who would accept me and my little girl with such open arms as Heather had, Tiffany also said,

"I think you need to think very hard about what you do in the next few months, because someone like Heather only comes around once, and you don't want to risk loosing her by being indecisive and uncommitted. I know you have been through a lot, but you have a wonderful girl who accepts you and loves you for who you are, with no strings attached."

Gina was also telling me constantly how much she likes Heather, and how well we fit together. But I didn't want to move forward in my relationship just because my family thought it was for the best, I needed to be sure for myself that this was the right thing.

My father had just finished getting some work done on his Chevy Blazer when he asked if I would be willing to drive it up to get Julia for the weekend, it would get some good freeway and canyon travel, so he figured it would be a good test for the truck. He told me that he would fill it with gas if I would test drive it for him, and seeing as how I was out of work, I agreed.

It was a cloudy Friday morning as I set out for my hour and half journey to pick up Julia, the truck ran alright until I got into the canyon, when it slowed down to a snails pace of about 25 miles an hour. Once I was out of the canyon it picked back up again and so I didn't think much of it. I picked Julia up and headed back for Salt Lake, but this time I did not even make it 10 miles from Megan's mother's house, where she and Julia were living, when it started to sputter and choke, I pulled over and turned off the engine letting the engine sit and cool down for a few moments and then I started it back up again and continued on my way.

This went on for about three hours, the running fine for ten miles or so and then sputtering out and dying. I was getting so frustrated with the truck that I finally pulled off at a gas station and tried calling my dad, but he didn't answer, I tried calling home, but there was no answer there either, so I continued on my way. After a few more frustrating hours of driving for a few miles and then pulling over because the truck had died, I was getting really upset; Julia had thankfully slept up to this point but when I began to beat on the steering wheel in frustration after what felt like the one hundredth time of pulling over she began to cry, she was hungry, needed her diaper changed and was starting to call out, "mommy".

The weather was not helping, a thick fog had rolled in and I had been driving on the freeway shoulder for the last hour, but as the big trucks screamed by some honking their horns in anger, and others just splashing water all over the windshield I began to get worried for our safety. I finally pulled off the freeway, deciding that it was getting too dangerous to be on the road any longer, we were only about thirty miles from home and the sun was beginning to set behind the low foggy clouds. I pulled into a parking lot and got Julia out of her car seat and held her for a few minutes until she stopped crying, I then changed her diaper, and gave her one of the bottles that Megan had sent me home with. When Julia had once again settled down, I went over to a nearby pay phone and tried calling my dad once again, and then my house and when there was no answer on either line, I began to feel the rush of panic coming over me, if I had been alone I would not have been so worried, but because I had Julia I did not want to be stranded in some parking lot for the night. I got back into the truck with Julia, and after a few minutes I had a thought come to me, one that I am not sure why I didn't think of sooner, I got out of the truck and went back to the pay phone and dialed Heather's work number, I held my breath as I waited for her to answer and after a few rings she picked up,

"This is Heather, how may I help you?"

"Heather," I yelled out in desperation.

"I know you're at work and I am sorry to bother you, but Julia and I are stranded somewhere in the Bountiful area," The city of Bountiful is only a few minutes drive from Salt Lake, but due to the weather I could not tell exactly where I was. After explaining my situation, and giving her the best directions I could Heather said,

"Jeremy, I can't believe you didn't call me sooner, I'll be right there."

I went back to the truck and within twenty minutes or so Heather pulled up in her Rodeo, she immediately picked up Julia.

"Jeremy, I was so worried, after you hung up the phone I raced here as fast as I could, are you ok?" I told her that I was fine, and besides being in the car for too long Julia was fine as well. Heather got Julia calmed down while I put our things into Heather's SUV, and after I had loaded everything we put Julia in her car seat and headed for home.

As we drove back, I think it hit me for the first time that Heather really meant what she had been telling me all along, she loved me and Julia, and would do anything for us, I think it was that day that I realized I could trust Heather, and all of my doubts went away. As we pulled into the driveway of my house I looked over at Heather,

"Thank you very much, I really appreciate what you did for me today," Heather looked back at me.

"I would do it every day if you needed me too."

When she said that something inside me opened up and I knew what everyone had been telling me was true, she really was the one, and she really did love me, it was me who needed to wake up and realize that it was foolish not to trust people just because I had been hurt. I leaned over and put my hands softly on Heather's cheeks and pulled her close to me.

"I love you Heather," I said for the first time, even though I had felt it for a while; I finally had the courage to say it.

"I don't know how things are in your family," said Heather's mother in a rather intimidating tone.

"But in this family divorce is not an option." These were some of the first words I heard from my prospective in laws.

"We don't run away from our problems, we believe in working things out and sticking together whatever this life might bring. We have been married for 28 years and if you think it has been easy, then you have another thing coming," said Heather's Father.

"We love Heather very much and are not about to let her make a mistake, we are not saying that you are necessarily a mistake, but we watch out for each other in this family."

"Blah, blah, blah, her parents went on like this for hours, and with each passing minute I could feel my face getting redder, and redder with embarrassment, I could feel myself slumping deeper and deeper into my chair, and I just wanted to go home. Since we had announced our engagement a few weeks previous, Heather's parents had already written me a scathing letter warning me of how serious a matter marriage was, and since I was "obviously" incapable of abiding by the laws of marriage, I had better watch myself this time around, they also stated that if I had any second thoughts about marriage now was the time to be a man and graciously step out of the way.

I had tried to explain to them what had happened; the hard part is that I myself was not really sure what had happened. It was difficult to explain to people that my previous wife had left me and now refused to talk to me, but had never given me a real reason as to why she had left. Regardless of the reasons there I sat in what would prove to be the first of many of these "Spanish Inquisitions" sentenced upon me by certain members of Heather's family.

I realize now that my self-image was not very good at the time, and so even though Heather's family was only trying to watch out for her, it really came across as harsh, and sometimes even mean to me, I am sure they had not intended to hurt my feelings, but I felt at times that I would be better off just walking away from the situation and telling Heather that things would not work out between us, the only problem was, I loved Heather too much to let her family get in the way. It would literally be years before Heather's parents would trust me, or really except me into the family.

"Well son," said Heather's father, as the inquisition continued.

"If you really think this is what you want to do we will support you, but remember what we have said about the importance of responsibility." Just as I thought we were finished Heather's mother said,

"There is one more thing I would like to bring up, and that is the small matter of your current employment situation, or the lack there of." It was like they were tag teaming me as Heather's father spoke up.

"I have provided for my family all of my married life and Heather has become accustom to certain things that I will expect you to continue providing for her, like a home, and an income." They both looked at me as Heather's mom took over.

"Heather has a good job and makes good money, but I don't want you to go into this marriage thinking that you will just be sitting at home all day while Heather works to support you and make your child support payments for you."

"No, that is not what I intend to do," I said in my defense.

"I am looking every day for work, I have been turned down by all of the top architect firms in the valley." I then looked at Heather's farther.

"You of all people know how hard it is to find work as an architect when you only have a little bit of experience."

"That is why I am self employed," he said.

"But I haven't always been. When I was your age, just starting out I took jobs just to put food on the table, just because you have a bachelors degree doesn't mean that work will be handed to you on a silver platter."

With this sudden turn in the conversation I politely said, "Dinner was great, it was nice to see the two of you again but it's getting late and I must be going." I stood up quickly and made my way towards the door, not wanting to look back, I just wanted to get out of there.

"Just a minute, we are not finished," said Heather's father as I slowly turned back around thinking to myself,

"What more could you possibly want to talk to me about this evening?"

"Let's play some card games," said her parents. It's true I had played card games with Heather and her family over Christmas but it was only to be polite and not to offend anyone more than I already had by being a lousy choice for their daughter, what else could I do? I mean what a better way to end this horrific evening from hell than to spend the next three hours play card games, at least my evening could not have gotten any worse.

Despite her families well meaning interrogations, and letters of condemnation regarding my past, I was still very much in love with Heather, and she was in love with me.

"Don't worry about my family," she would tell me.

"They don't understand the situation, but I do, and I am the one that matters not them."

My family on the other hand loved Heather, and was very glad to see me happy again. One evening just as I returned from picking up Julia for the weekend, Heather called me up and said,

"I would really like to have Julia stay with me for the evening; I think having her sleep here would be a good chance for the two of us to get to know each other better."

At first I was a bit apprehensive, but after thinking about it for a few minutes I agreed, and soon found myself setting up the portable crib in Heather's room, Julia was about 17 months old and a very social little girl.

"Thank you," said Heather as she ushered me to the door and gave me a kiss.

"We will be just fine, don't worry, I will call you in the morning." When Heather called me the next morning she told me that everything had gone just fine, Julia took her bottle and went right to sleep and didn't wake up once all night.

I found myself going on five months of unemployment, and I was beginning to feel desperate, for the first couple of months I had applied to architectural firms all over the Salt Lake Valley, and for the first couple of months I had been interviewed and rejected by some of the top firms in Utah.

As the wedding date got closer and closer, the letters from Heather's parents and then her grandparents kept coming and kept getting more and more critical, accusing me of being lazy and telling me that if I didn't find work soon they would absolutely protest my marriage to Heather. I knew that Heather's family was not pleased with her choice to "settle" with me, because they all knew she could do better; however despite the opposition, I really did want to show them that I was a good person who had just gone through a misfortunate turn of events in my life.

I was not happy that I had been unemployed for so long, I wanted desperately go back to work, there is nothing more detrimental to a person than being out of work, and here I was a college graduate with a bachelor's degree, nearly six years of education behind me and I couldn't find work.

Just two months before the wedding I received a call from Megan, she was at the hospital and had given birth to our second child Maia, the news was met with mixed emotions and later that evening when I told Heather of the news, she was very excited.

"We need to go up to the hospital to see your new daughter," was Heather's immediate response.

"Don't worry," she said, when she saw the look on my face.

"I will go with you," she clapped her hands in excitement.

"I am so excited to see her and we need to be there to support the baby."

As we made the long hour and half drive up to the hospital, we talked about having children ourselves, "I really want to have children, I have always wanted to be a mother," said Heather.

"I realize that you already have two kids, but I hope that won't change your mind about having more," she said in a concerned tone. It was not that I didn't want to have more children, because I was not apposed to the idea. I was just sad that I had two children but could only be a part time dad.

"You should tell Megan that if she ever gets to a point where she can't or doesn't want to keep the children that we will be very willing to take them," said Heather as we pulled into the hospital parking lot.

We made our way to the maternity ward, and up to the room where Megan and her mom were sitting, and chatting. It was so strange to be sitting in the

same room as my x-wife, my x-mother in law, and my fiancé, although everyone else seemed calm and all right with the situation, I was a wreck.

"It is soon nice to see you again," said Karen as we entered the room.

"And this must be Heather, we have heard so much about you," said
Megan's mom, as they shook hands.

"Where is Maia?" I asked.

"I would really like to hold her," I said as we took a seat.

"She is in the nursery, I needed a bit of a break but I will have the nurse
bring her in for you," said Megan.

My heart was so heavy that day as I sat with my new born baby held tightly
in my arms, thoughts rushed through my head of how she would grow up not
knowing her dad like I wanted her too. I had to fight back the tears as I held her
tiny little sleeping frame in my arms, I wanted so much to have my children
back, I missed Julia, and one look at this little angle was almost enough to
crush my soul completely.

If Heather had not been there I don't know what I would have done, Maia
was so small and she looked so peaceful. I had not gotten married in the first
place to get divorced and I thought of my now two children growing up without me in their life, and it almost made me sick. Everyone was cordial and very
fake with one another, I handed Maia to Heather who was patiently waiting to
hold the newborn baby, and as she did I could see her eyes light up,

"Oh she is so beautiful," she said looking at me, and then at Megan.

"I just want to hold her forever."

I could see the love in Heather's eyes as she sat with Maia in her arms, and
although I was sad, I was happy to see that I was marring such a loving and
kind woman. She had done what most people are incapable of doing; first of all
she was marring a divorcee, second of all she truly loved my children as her
own, and third she was willing to go to the hospital with me, to see my x-wife,
and my new born child. I could barely hold it together and here sat Heather,
with a big smile on her face holding Maia, and talking cordially with Megan,
she was truly a remarkable girl. As we made our way back home Heather said.

"If we ever get the chance to take the girls full time, I would jump at it, and
adopt them." She put her hand gently in mine.

"Jeremy I know that going to the hospital was difficult for you, I know not
having your girls has been and will continue to be difficult, I know seeing
Megan brings back a lot of mixed emotions, and I realize that you loved her
very much at one time, but I want you to know that I love you as much or
more than Megan ever could. I love your children as if they were my own, and

I want you to know that I will never leave you, I will stay by your side for the rest of your life. I know that you are carrying a lot of pain inside and I hope that over time you can let go of these feelings and replace them with the love I have for you."

I do not know why Heather couldn't have come into my life earlier, but for what ever reason fate didn't allow us to come together until that point in our lives. I leaned over and pulled Heather's face close to mine.

"I love you too Heather, and I know you love the girls which means a lot to me, I wish things were better, I wish we had met five years ago, and I could have bypassed all of this, but I am grateful that you are here now."

I leaned over and kissed her, she truly was my soul mate, and even though I had taken a lot of twists and turns in life, I was so glad that I had finally found her.

Three or four weeks before the wedding I finally swallowed my pride and took a job in a warehouse, as a shift manager overseeing the pulling and packaging of orders, it was not what I wanted to do, but it was a job. I had spent most of my life in a warehouse, I had gone to school so that I would not have to do that sort of thing for a living, and here I was in a warehouse yet again. I was more than qualified to be a manager in a warehouse; with my degree I had more education than nearly everyone I worked with, including my boss, and even his boss. I was not very happy with my job, but at least it kept the angry letters at bay and helped appease the minds of Heather's family.

It was a warm summer day late in July when Heather walked out of her house and onto the back lawn, she looked absolutely stunning in her wedding dress, it was a long flowing white dress, which shimmered in the sunlight. As she made her way arm in arm with her father to were I was standing, time felt as though it was almost standing still, with every step she took I could feel my heart beating faster and faster, she looked like a beautiful renaissance painting that an artist had spent weeks and weeks perfecting, with some of her long beautiful locks of flowing red hair curled to perfection and draped over her shoulder and the reminder placed perfectly on top of her head around the crown of her veil, every brush stroke was made with passion, every tone, and every color was radiant and flawless.

She looked like a princess right out of a fairy tale book, and I felt so undeserving of her greatness, as she made her way to where I stood, her father handed her to me and I could feel her delicate hand shaking. I looked into her eyes and I could see love, compassion, and honesty looking back at me, she was breathtakingly beautiful and I stood in a state of near disbelief as the words,

"I now pronounce you husband and wife," were said, and we kissed for the first time as husband and wife

CHAPTER 10

A Twist of Fate

It was Saturday evening, the 13th of December 2003, Heather had picked the girls up the afternoon before, and after meeting with Megan in the lobby of a downtown hotel to get them, Heather commented to me how pale Megan had looked and how odd she was acting. Heather said that Megan was saying good-bye to Julia and Maia as if she would never see them again.

"It was just creepy!" Heather mentioned to me as we ate dinner.

Heather had put Julia and Maia to bed about an hour or two before we sat watching television; she had just finished getting ready for bed herself when the phone began to ring. Heather and I looked at each other and commented on who would be calling at 10:30 in the evening? I jumped up and ran into the kitchen to grab the phone.

"Hello," I said, and all I could hear on the other end of the phone was sobbing.

"Jeremy this is Karen, Megan's mom, I just got done talking to the police, and Megan is dead." Everything in the room went silent, and my vision became blurred as I stood there trying to comprehend what she had just said to me, I shook off the double vision and asked,

"What did you say?" I asked just to make sure I was not hearing things.

"Megan's boyfriend found her dead in his bedroom about three hours ago," said Karen between sobs.

"He told the police that he had gotten up and gone work this morning and when he got home this evening she was still in bed where he had left her, but she was dead." I could still not believe what she was telling me, Heather had come over by me to see why I had such a perplexed look on my face, and she whispered to me

"Who is it," I waved her off and whispered

"I will tell you in a minute."

Karen went on to say that Megan had been complaining of a migraine the morning before she brought the girls down to Salt Lake, and she had said if it got worse she would be going to the emergency room to get something for it. Megan's boyfriend had said that she went to the hospital after meeting Heather and dropping off the girls, and they gave her some sort of time release migraine patch that would slowly release medication for up to twelve hours or so.

"She must have had a reaction to the medication and that is what killed her." After a few minutes of brief conversation, Karen said she would give us more information as soon as she knew anything else and with that we hung up the phone.

I could not help to think that not so many years ago I had caught Megan mixing her medications, and not telling one doctor about the prescriptions she had received from another doctor. I could not help wondering to myself if this was the same thing? Was she taking some other medications and didn't tell the doctor in the ER, thinking it wouldn't matter, like she had done so many times before? Was it an accident or did she know what she was doing? Why did she look so pale and tell the girls goodbye like she would never see them again? Did she know something yesterday morning that she didn't want anyone else to know, was it a pre-meditated suicide or was it a total accident? All of these questions were flooding my mind as I turned to look at Heather; I stared at the ground for a minute still trying to gather my thoughts.

"Megan is dead, she passed away sometime today and they found her body a few hours ago at her boyfriend's house." Heather gasped and grabbed her mouth; huge tears immediately started flowing down her cheeks, and she began to shake.

"What happened? How did she die? Are you ok?" She asked.

Words cannot explain how I felt at that moment, I was sad, but at the same time I was relieved that my little family could now be complete, Julia and Maia could now live with us permanently and our new baby that Heather was carrying, who was due in about three months would be borne never knowing anything different than her sisters always being there. Julia had just turned four years old and Maia was only two, so in just a short time they would adapt and we could be a complete family. Heather looked at me and said,

"Aren't you going to cry or something, I am bawling like a baby, and I didn't even know Megan all that well."

"I cried for her, and made my peace with her being gone when she left me almost four years ago." I said to Heather.

I was not trying to be cruel, and I was not without some remorse for the loss of a once great friend, but it was true that part of me, the part that had deep feelings for her had died long ago, and so as sad as it may sound I found no tears in my heart for her passing, I was sad for her mother, and her family and I was very torn thinking about how I would break the news to the girls, but I just couldn't find it in myself to cry for her.

After talking briefly to Heather about what we needed to do next, and how we would break the news to the girls, I picked up the phone to call Tiffany and tell her what had happened.

"It's a bit late to be calling people don't you think?" Asked Heather, as I dialed the number.

"It will be fine." I replied.

"I need to talk to Tiffany about this."

"Hello," said Daryl as he answered the phone.

"Daryl," I said apologetically.

"I'm so sorry to be calling this late but I really need to talk to Tiffany, it's quite urgent." I could hear Daryl make his way to whatever room Tiffany was in, and then some whispering about who it was.

"What's wrong Jeremy?" Tiffany asked in a concerned tone.

"We just got off the phone with Megan's mom and I still can hardly believe it's true, but Megan is dead."

"*What*!" exclaimed Tiffany?

"What happened, are the girls ok?" She asked, somewhat frantically.

"The girls are fine," I said.

"We just so happened to have them this weekend so they are sleeping in their beds, and don't even know what's happened yet, Heather and I will talk to them in the morning."

"Are you and Heather ok?" Asked Tiffany.

"Yes were fine, just beside ourselves, and not quite sure what to do next."

Tiffany and I talked for about ten or twenty minutes and then we hung up. Heather and I went to bed that evening but we lay awake talking for a number of hours about what we were going to do. It was only a couple of weeks before Christmas and we did not plan on having them this year, we also talked about what we would do with the girls during the day because Heather was working full time, we did not plan on needing a sitter until the baby was at least two months old. We talked about adoption for Heather, and we talked about how grateful we were that we had gotten into our new home just three weeks earlier, and how it was a miracle that everything had worked out the way it had. Not even knowing that this was going to happen, things still worked out as if god new it was going to happen and he was helping to prepare us.

That next morning I called my dad and told him what had happened, he told me not to worry, that he would contact the rest of the family. Heather and I woke the girls up and got them some breakfast, we each took one of them into the front room to give them the news that they had just lost their mother.

How do you tell a four and a two year old that their mommy will not be coming to get them ever again? How do you help them feel safe, and how do you assure them that you are not going away? They had always known me as dad, but Julia was not even one-year-old when she left, and Maia had never lived with anyone else but her mother. I had stayed awake most of the night trying to decide how to approach the topic in a way that was both sympathetic to their needs, and would not be to traumatizing to their little souls.

"Your mommy has been feeling kind of sick for the past while," I started to say.

"And sometimes when people get really sick they have to go to heaven and live with the angels."

I looked at them both, waiting for a reaction, but Maia, only being two years old did not stop playing with the doll she had in her hands, Julia on the other hand who was four was watching me very intently, I could tell that she was understanding some of what I was saying, so I continued.

"Your mommy has gone to heaven, and so we would like it very much if would come and live with us from now on." At that point Julia began to cry,

"I want to go home with mommy." It broke my heart to see the pain in her eyes; I picked her up and cuddled her a while.

"I know you do honey, it's ok to be sad, but your mommy still loves you and she will be watching you from Heaven from now on." Maia began to cry at this point, mainly because Julia was crying, and so Heather picked Maia up and held her, and then Heather began to cry as well. We sat together for a few minutes holding each other as a family, and then I tried to help cheer Julia and Maia up by saying,

"Guess what, you get to live here from now on, and we will get all of your toys and clothes and bring them here, and we will get to have all the fun we have on the weekend every single day!"

This cheered them up for a few minutes and Heather took them into their room to help them get dressed, we spent the rest of the day trying to take in all of the new changes, and figure out what we were going to do.

I had been working once again in the field of architecture for almost a year when Hannah was born. Soon after we were married I started doing architectural work for my father in law, small remodeling jobs at first, but they were a good way to get my design skills back up to where they had been previously, and a good way to learn basic client-designer relationships.

After working as the shift manager in the warehouse for almost two torturous years I decided that enough was enough and it was time to re-enter the field that I had fought so hard to get into. To my surprise I was able to find employment after only three months of searching. I found a job in the architectural department of one Utah's leading home builders, doing red-lines and some design work, even though it was not entirely what I wanted to be doing I was happy to be back in my field of expertise.

The few jobs I had done for Larry were just enough to give me my confidence back and remind me that designing homes was what I had always wanted to do. I had finally, after nearly six years of school, and warehouse job after warehouse been able to start my career in architecture, and I have been working in the field of architecture ever since.

I had arranged to take the week off in order to be with Heather and our new baby, so the afternoon after Hannah was born, Heather's mom, who had been watching the girls brought them up to the hospital to see their new baby sister, Maia and Julia's little eyes peered over the edge of Heather's hospital bed as they stood gazing at their new baby sister,

"Can we hold her mommy?" Asked Julia in a tone of wonderment. One at a time we carefully helped the girls wash their hands and then as they sat in the large rocking chair in the corner of the room, we brought their new baby sister over to see them for the first time. I helped Julia, and then Mia hold their new baby sister for a few minutes each; they were both very calm and gentle with her, and my heart was filled with joy to see my family complete. It was a beautiful sight to have my two little girls living with us permanently so that Hannah would grow up with them, not ever knowing anything different then her sisters, who would be there all the time now. Seeing Heather and Hannah together was such a beautiful sight, I had to hold back the tears as I watched Heather care so lovingly for our new baby, holding her and singing little lullaby's to her.

We spent four days in the hospital while Heather recovered and then after the fourth day, we brought Hannah home. Julia and Maia were so excited to have a little sister, we had set up one of the bedrooms as the baby's room, Heather and I had let the girls help us decorate and paint the room, so that they could feel like they had helped prepare for their little sisters arrival. Julia and Maia, being so young were of coarse sad to lose their mother, but were quick to embrace Heather as their new mother, and within a very short time they started calling her mom.

Two weeks after Hannah was born we found ourselves sitting in the private chambers of the judge who was about to grant our petition of adoption. We had started the paperwork to have Heather adopt the girls a week or two after the news of Megan's passing, and although we could have had the proceeding earlier, we chose to wait until after the baby was born, because Hannah's birth was taking all of our time and attention.

I remember feeling nervous for some unknown reason, I suppose it may have been because the last time I sat in a judge's chamber it was for a very unpleasant reason, and it left a negative impression of lawyers and judges in my mind. After about ten minutes of rather basic questions the judge looked at Heather and asked her if she understood the responsibilities that would befall her by adopting these girls, and Heather responded with a heart felt,

"Yes," he then looked at me and explained that Heather would be the legal mother of my children, and that their birth certificates would be changed making Heather their mother. He asked if I was supportive of this action, I answered,

"Yes." The judge who looked like a kind grandfather then took his pen and signed the paperwork, handing it to our lawyer who in turn signed it and then handed it to us to sign.

"Congratulations folks," said the judge.

"You are now the legal and binding mother of these two beautiful children," he said as looked at Heather. He shook our hands on the way out, and I picked up the car seat containing our peacefully sleeping baby, while Heather took Julia in one hand and Maia in the other and we walked out of the court building as a complete family. Words cannot explain my joy that day, I had my family back and for the first time in four years I had my girls back, and this time it would be forever

CHAPTER 11

Full Circle

It was a beautiful evening early in the month of June when Heather and I sat out on our back porch talking about life, and how things can change so suddenly. Heather commented on how it seems like you think you know what you want out of life, and you think you know where you're going, but fate has a way of changing all of that. I have heard it said that "life is 75% chance and 25% decisions that we make based on the paths that chance throws in front of us."

Heather and I were talking about the good times in our past, my college life, and her single life, we discussed some of the influential people who had crossed our paths and made a mark in our lives. We reminisced about how we had met and how funny it seemed now that her parents were so paranoid about me, and the two of us getting married. We talked about how lucky we were to have Maia and Julia permanently added to our little family, and how Hannah would not ever know anything else but her two older sisters. Our three little girls had grown to be inseparable; they played together, ate together, and did everything together. We talked about how much our lives had changed in the four years we had been married and how blessed we were to be together.

After telling Heather some of the more humors stories of when I was in college, I suggested the we go up to the University of Utah and I would show her and the kids where I had gone to school, where I had worked, and the big fountain by the library where I had so many pleasant memories from the past. Heather agreed and the next day we got the kids up and dressed and headed up to the University's campus. I couldn't help but to noticing as we got to the bottom of campus, that so much had changed since I had gone to school; it seemed like only yesterday I was driving my blue Mercury Topaz with everything I owned in the back seat and trunk up to the University, and now it had been 10 years since that time. I could hardly believe it was that long ago since Steve and I had been inseparably best friend.

As we drove around campus, the place that I had called home for almost three years, I pointed out the place where I worked, and it still looked exactly as I had remembered it. I showed Heather where I dumped the pallet of paper, and I showed her the dorm rooms where I had lived for nearly two and a half years. As we pulled into the parking lot of the old dilapidated dorms it was sort of sad and heartbreaking to see the place so run down.

When the 2002 Olympics came to Salt Lake City they had built the athletes village on campus, and now that was where the students lived; as far as I could tell the old dorms were being used as offices and storage space.

We parked in the parking lot where I had parked my car, and where Steve's boat had been docked all those year's ago. Heather and I got the kids out of the van and put Hannah, who was now one and a half years old into her stroller. We let Julia and Maia run around the parking lot stretching their legs for a few minutes, and then I took my little family for a stroll down my old memory lane. It was funny, I thought to myself as we walked along the winding sidewalks, but I had not been back to the University of Utah since I left some seven years earlier.

"This is the room that Steve and I had," I said to Heather as we tried to peer into the dark room that had been abandoned long ago.

"That's the main lobby that connected the different wings of the dorms together, and there is the old main office," I said as we looked in through the big glass doors.

We then wandered over to what used to be the volleyball pit. It had been torn down and the grass had grown in where the sand used to be and the only thing left of the old pit was the two metal posts poking up out of the ground where the poles had been long, long, ago. We sat in the grass, Heather and I holding hands, while the girls ran around picking dandelions, and enjoying the day.

"This is where we used to have barbeques, and that was where Steve hit Tom in the face with a Frisbee," I said while laughing at the thought of Tom standing next to me covered in his dinner.

"It all seems so far away and so long ago," I said to Heather as we sat in the warm sunshine.

"It's like a dream; it feels like it was nothing more than a surreal dream." I felt sad looking at the empty dorms, and the empty field where so many of my memories where still being living out in my mind.

I could almost see myself playing *"Risk"* with Tom, Steve, and Slim in the lobby. As I looked deeper into my memories, I could see Robyn sitting in the large overstuffed chair waiting for me to get home from work. I remembered meeting Steve for the first time as he stood behind the front desk, and I smiled when I thought about having dinner at Slims place. I was happy to be with Heather and my girls, I couldn't imagine and didn't want to live my life without them, but part of me wished I could go back and re-live some of those college days. I wish I could see some of those people and find out how they were doing, and what their lives were like now.

After some reminiscing, and personal mediation we made our way over to the General Store warehouse. I showed Heather the large delivery trucks that I used to drive. Even though the actual truck was long gone, it had been replaced by the exact same make and model of truck, only newer.

We made our way down to the art department, and the architectural building where I had spent countless hours studying with Steve and other members of my class. It was all so sad and yet so happy to see the places where I had spent so much of my time and lived out so much of my life. I felt myself getting chocked up as we made our way down the winding sidewalks of campus to the big fountain on the back side of the library, I thought to myself as it came into view,

"Of all the things that have changed on campus, thank god that the fountain had not changed one bit." It was exactly as I remembered it. The fountain stood majestically looking over the bottom half of the campus, with the water cascading down over its edges, it sounded just like it had in all of my dreams since I left the school so many years ago. As we walked up to the giant waterfall Julia and Maia immediately took off their shoes and ran over to stand in the cool water, they giggled and splashed while Heather and I helped Hannah out of her stroller. We helped little Hannah take off her shoes and socks and soon we were all standing in the wake of the crashing waterfall letting the cool mists of water gently land on our faces. We stood right in front of the sign that read, *"No standing, or playing on, in, or around the waterfall,"* and it made me laugh inside. We played in the fountain as a family and it gave me such a feeling of joy to watch all of my girls enjoying them selves in the water; all four of them, and for that brief moment in time I felt so calm and peaceful like everything was right with the world, and life could not get any better.

As the sun was beginning to set behind us, Heather and I got the girls out of the water so that we could make our way back up the hill towards the car. Heather took my hand and pointed towards a young couple sitting on the opposite side of the fountain with their feet in the cool water. The girl had her arm wrapped tightly around the young mans arm and as they held hands she rested her head on his shoulder. Heather smiled at me, as we looked at our beautiful children, and I could not help but to feel peaceful and calm inside. I thought to myself, "everything is right with the world, and I could not be happier than I am at this moment."

I recall the words of Annie Besant, the British social reformer and Theosophist whom I studied in college. "Never forget that life can only be nobly inspired and rightly lived if you take it bravely and gallantly, as a splendid adventure in which you are setting out into an unknown country, to meet many a joy, to find many a comrade, to win and lose many a battle."

THE END

978-0-595-84124-0
0-595-84124-4

Printed in the United States
78276LV00008B/28